Jezebel's Tomb

David Hilzenrath

For Maralee, who showed the way in Jerusalem, with thanks and admiration. David

Washingtonpost.Newsweek Interactive

Published by Washingtonpost.Newsweek Interactive
Arlington, Virginia

ISBN 978-0-615-13550-2

Cover layout and lettering by Cathi Stevenson
Cover concept by David Hilzenrath

www.jezebelstomb.com

For Julie,

Forever

"You must not leave a soul alive."

Deuteronomy 20:16

"I have not come to bring peace, but a sword."

Matthew 10:34

"Surely we have prepared for the unbelievers chains and shackles and a burning fire."

The Holy Qur'an, 76:4

Prologue

Jerusalem, 70 C.E.

He hurried through deserted streets, past darkened houses. He could picture families huddled in fear, in the false security of their cellars, and he could almost hear their prayers. Over his shoulder, flames licked at the night sky, and smoke drifted down from the Temple Mount. Cries of desperation carried on the wind, along with the smell of smoldering cedar.

He was a leader of the resistance, and he bore the wounds of the long struggle against Roman occupation. His body had wasted from hunger, and his strength had ebbed, but his eyes still burned with intensity. A stabbing pain pierced his side—an enemy sword had split the thin covering of flesh and cracked ribs—but he forced himself to keep moving.

He had made his decision, and he vowed to see it through. Some would consider it a betrayal, but Aaron ben Matthias intended it as an act of faith.

If it's not too late.

Months of siege had come to this. The Roman army had broken through the Temple's outer walls and set fire to the gates, the building's last line of defense. Inside the sanctuary, Jewish defenders—his brethren—prepared for a final stand, while the Romans held back, waiting for the dawn.

In a few hours, maybe less, he estimated, the Romans would invade the Temple and overrun Jerusalem.

Already, beyond the city walls, hundreds of Jews hung from crosses. The Romans had caught them scavenging for food. Now birds pecked at their rotting flesh.

Driven by hunger, hundreds more had fled the embattled city, hoping to gain freedom at the enemy lines. At first, the Romans allowed them to pass. Then reports swept through the ranks that a refugee had smuggled gold—in his belly. Mercy gave way to greed and madness. The exodus ended in slaughter.

Aaron had watched the refugees straggle across the valley into a spoiled land. The surrounding hills were covered with stumps; the Romans had turned the olive trees into war machines. His wife had looked back, once, searching the ramparts, and their eyes had met. He had persuaded her to leave with their infant son. He had pleaded with her to save the baby. "I'll see you again," he promised. "I'll find you."

She didn't understand why he refused to go—he never fully explained—and it was obvious that she didn't believe his promise. But she wanted the baby to live.

He could still see the look in her eyes, a blade between his ribs.

Despite Aaron's pleas, his mother had stayed behind—only to succumb to the famine. She, too, lay unburied, piled with countless others. The dying city was an open grave.

He wondered: Had God abandoned Jerusalem?

Had Jerusalem abandoned God?

Somewhere inside the Temple, Aaron's father waited for the attack. Old Matthias was more than just a fellow priest—he was a learned scribe, part of the inner circle. He denounced any man who would plan for an hour like this, and Aaron was such a man. Bitterly, Aaron had argued with his father. He had even appealed to the high priest, but the high priest had sent him away.

Aaron reached the front of his house. He opened the door. Motes of dust hung in the air, illuminated by a shaft of moonlight. The place was silent. He could see the dim outline of a table and chairs and large ceramic jugs that were once filled with oil. He lit a lamp and cupped it with his hand.

For five generations, his family had lived there in harmony. Now, Aaron stripped the mezuzah from the doorframe. The carved wooden ornament, no longer than his index finger, was a symbol of the family's religious devotion, installed by the patriarch of their distinguished line. Aaron set it on the table. With a sharp knife, he scraped gently at one end, exposing a narrow cylindrical hollow. Slowly, delicately, he teased out the miniature parchment rolled inside. It was inscribed with the watchword of the Jewish faith, the affirmation that pitted Jerusalem against the most powerful empire on earth.

Shema Yisraeil: Adonai Eloheinu, Adonai Echad.

Hear, O Israel: the Lord is our God, the Lord is One.

Aaron read it aloud. After all these years, the ink was as sharp as ever.

He knelt beside the table and pried a stone from the floor. A fragment of lamb's bone lay embedded in the dirt—an antique table scrap, or so it seemed. A light tap dislodged its secret: The marrow concealed a tiny, tightly coiled scroll of fine gold foil. It was Yehoshua the goldsmith's final commission, and he had done an admirable job.

Carefully, Aaron slid the gold foil into the mezuzah. He plugged the open end with a chip of wood and whittled it flush. Then he tucked the relic in his cloak. He realized he was being optimistic. In search of gold, the Romans had disemboweled refugees. Still, religious objects were seldom confiscated.

He studied the parchment he had removed from the mezuzah, wondering what to do with it. *The Lord is One,* it proclaimed. He couldn't just throw it away. With no particular purpose, he inserted it in the lamb's shank and buried it beneath the stone in the floor. He extinguished the lamp.

He took one last look at his home, and stepped into the street.

He looked across the housetops, toward the east. The Temple loomed over the city from the high ground, centered on a broad stone plaza, surrounded by massive walls. A beacon of hope through the months of siege. He could see it with his eyes closed: towering columns and colonnades, massive blocks, marble dressed in gold. In daylight, it mirrored the sun.

Its treasury overflowed with the faith and prosperity of the Promised Land.

For the people of Jerusalem—starving, weakened, encircled by the enemy and unwilling to yield—the gilded fortress had symbolized God's power. Now, save for burning cedar and a shroud of smoke, the Temple lay exposed.

It was too late to save Jerusalem, too late for the Temple. But the future—that was another matter. While others prayed for deliverance, Aaron plotted his route in.

In the underground recesses of the Temple Mount, the Jewish guards were slow to grasp the threat. With four priests as accomplices, Aaron bloodlessly overpowered them. As he tied their wrists, one of the guards reared his head and spat. The nearest of Aaron's men raised a sword.

"No," Aaron commanded, wiping his eye. "Never our own."

With a turn of the key, the heavy doors opened. The conspirators set to work. They knew what they were looking for.

Or so they thought.

Inside the storeroom, crates were overturned, their lids cast aside. Many more remained stuffed with objects of copper and bronze—pots, pans and other vessels, which the priests used to prepare the burnt offerings.

"Hurry," Aaron said in a hoarse whisper.

Farther in the shadows, gold and silver gleamed in the torchlight. The floor was littered with ritual treasures—candelabras, wine cups, plates, and platters—gifts of foreign kings, offered in diplomatic tribute, and private riches deposited for safekeeping.

Aaron led his men past stacks of gold ingots, piled like bricks, and rows of cauldrons brimming with coins. Dozens of cauldrons lay empty, and circles in the dust marked vacant spots where others had been removed. Barrels overflowed with the tiny dull coins the poor used to pay the Temple tax.

Aaron ignored it all.

In the rear of the storeroom, he came to another door, which refused to open. One of his men attacked it with an axe, and the dry planks splintered. The dark space beyond was hardly larger than a closet. In the center of the floor stood his objective, a wooden chest, repository for some of his people's most precious writings—holy texts, histories, the chronicles of Jerusalem's high priests, among them his grandfather Caiaphas.

Aaron pried it open and distributed the contents.

Outside, flaming timbers crashed to the ground. Roman soldiers poured through the breach, and thousands more scaled the walls. The fighting spilled into the Temple courtyard. Where throngs ordinarily assembled to sacrifice lambs and doves, the blood of priests spattered the altar.

Aaron and his men raced through a winding passage, bent by the weight of their cargo. The passage widened into a cavernous chamber hewn from the bedrock. In the center, the floor gave way to a narrow well, scarcely as wide as a man's shoulders. A faint draft rose from somewhere far below, a cool hint of rushing water. Aaron held a torch over the opening, and the flickering light drowned in blackness.

They lowered their cargo by rope. Then, one by one, they descended into the well. The leader went last. As he reached for his torch, footfalls scraped against the rock. Then a voice. His name, echoing: "Aaron?"

The voice was surprised, uncertain. Aaron tensed. Slowly, fearfully, he looked up. His father merely stared, uncomprehending. He clutched a ram's horn at his side.

"Come with us, father. Help us. I beg you."

The old man looked wounded, betrayed. He looked frightened.

"Aaron, my son, you don't understand. You don't know the danger."

Aaron reached into the folds of his cloak. There were noises in the passageway, muffled shouts of desperate men. Were they fleeing the Romans . . . or trying to stop him? The din drew closer.

Matthias raised his horn.

"Don't," Aaron pleaded.

Matthias pressed the horn to his lips. He emptied his lungs, and the room reverberated with a blast of sound.

Aaron threw the blade.

The old man's eyes widened. He tried to speak, but the only thing that crossed his lips was a trickle of blood. The hilt of the knife protruded from his chest. Matthias fell to the floor.

Aaron said a prayer for his father, and another for himself. Then he disappeared down the shaft.

Part I

Chapter 1

Northern Lebanon—October 2007

The stark beauty of the land was almost enough to make Benjamin Jordan forget the purpose of his journey. Twisted cedars clung to barren hills. Now and again, he sensed their fragrance in the morning air, or maybe he just imagined that he did. His was the only car on the road, and he was grateful for the solitude. All was still save for sunlight and shadow, which slowly moved across the slopes and escarpments.

His eyes wandered the terrain, observant and introspective, clear as ever despite his lack of sleep. Part of him was impatient to reach his destination, to claim the story as his own and tell it to the world. Another part of him hoped that it wasn't true, that all of this would amount to nothing. Which impulse was stronger, Jordan couldn't say. But as the road carried him farther into the hills, his foot grew progressively lighter on the pedal.

The tip had reached the reporter by email. The source, a militant Islamic group, had been blamed for the latest terrorist outrage, the destruction of a Jerusalem museum.

Within hours of the explosion, Israel had retaliated. A pair of warplanes had bombed a compound in Lebanon's Bekaa Valley.

Israel's Defense Ministry said the compound was a training camp for terrorists.

Jordan's source said it was an orphanage.

From the militarized zone along the border, Jordan had hitched a ride to Beirut with a team of U.N. workers and borrowed an old friend's car on less than an hour's sleep. The friend, a Lebanese writer, had eyed him with concern. "Be careful," the writer had said. "You may be a journalist, but you're an Israeli in Lebanon."

The borrowed old Mercedes groaned as he downshifted through a hilltop pass.

He could probably pass as an American, but that wouldn't win him any points, either. Not in this neighborhood.

A flock of scraggly sheep crossed the road, slowing him to a stop. He drummed his fingers on the steering wheel.

If everything came together, he would soon have his own weekly news broadcast and an international audience. The network had recruited him, dangling a large paycheck and the authority to set his own agenda.

No more editors sanitizing his copy, stripping away uncomfortable facts.

The network's market research predicted he would attract viewers in the coveted 18-to-36 female demographic. "Rugged, natural, dangerously charismatic," the focus groups had said.

What a crock.

Regardless, he had earned the job. And he had paid for it. In broken relationships and battles with editors, in canceled scuba vacations and forfeited tickets to the summer Olympics, and in hate mail received from across the political spectrum, proving that he gave equal offense.

The TV contract wasn't a done deal—Jordan hadn't even told anyone about it—but he was looking forward to telling his boss. He was looking forward to telling the manipulative, self-serving bastard exactly where to go.

One more big story might make it happen.

The last of the sheep scampered up the slope, followed by a young boy in a *keffiyeh,* his face hidden behind the checked cloth. Jordan put the car in gear.

The road descended into a bleak, arid flatland that shimmered in the noonday sun. A village loomed into view. If he was reading the map correctly, this was the place, the village of el-Adir.

On the outskirts of the town, what appeared to have been several large cinder-block buildings lay in ruin. Part of a two-story wall remained standing, the only hint of what had been. Orphanage? Barracks? From a distance it was impossible to say. Women veiled in black sifted through the wreckage.

With a sense of foreboding, he got out of the car. He walked slowly toward the ruins, stopping every few paces to frame a wide-angle photo.

He was glad he never visited this long-suffering country as a soldier, glad he never contributed to its pain.

He approached the nearest woman and summoned his limited Arabic.

"I'm a newspaper reporter," he said, exaggerating each syllable with an unmistakable accent. "My name is Benjamin. Please, tell me what happened."

"Israeli," the woman spat. He thought it was the beginning of an answer, then he realized it was a curse. In a torrent of rage, she spilled out her story, too fast for him to write down. She pointed at the sky, and at the ruins, and jabbed a finger in his face. The bombs had fallen without warning, just before sunset. She was shrieking now. One of the planes made a low pass, just to mock them. None of the children got out alive.

The woman stooped to pick up a fistful of dust. He noted the poignancy of the gesture. Then she threw it in his face.

Stung, Jordan rubbed his eyes. Before he could open them, the woman struck him again. Pebbles this time.

Jordan shielded himself with his palms.

"I'm a reporter," he protested, his voice rising. "I'm here to write about it."

Blinking, he saw other women running toward them. Something hard struck him in the forehead, dazing him. *A rock.* Then another, in the chest, and a third, in the knee.

They were stoning him.

He shouted for them to stop, his exasperation tinged with alarm.

A chant went up. First one voice, then a chorus. He strained to interpret the words.

"Kill the Jew! Kill the Jew!"

Didn't they understand? He was here to tell their story.

With blood dripping in his eyes, Jordan backtracked awkwardly, then turned and tried to run.

Gotta reach the car, unlock the door —

Stinging pain in his left elbow.

Faster! Run faster! Run —

A sharp blow behind the ear.

Disoriented, he stumbled and fell.

"Kill the Jew! Kill the Jew!"

They were screaming it now. He could hear stones striking his body, and little chunks of concrete. The barrage prevented him from getting up.

Through crimson ooze, he saw two women shuffling toward him, sideways. Stooped, as if sharing a heavy burden. Struggling not to drop it.

Struggling to raise it higher.

He looked up at a block of concrete, twice as big a man's head.

Blocking out the sun.

"Kill the Jew! Kill the Jew! KILL THE — "

The crack of a rifle silenced the chant. Several shots followed in quick succession.

Jordan could sense the women backing away. He felt the pounding thud of concrete against ground, the unburdening of the executioners. He opened his eyes and wiped at the blood.

Four Arab men were getting out of a car. Two of them pointed AK-47s at the sky. One of them scolded the women angrily, and they retreated further.

Jordan rolled over, shaking. The cut over his eyebrow began to throb. He was a mass of cuts and bruises. The largest of the men looked down at him.

"You look like shit."

Jordan squinted into the sun, and the Arab offered a hand to help him to his feet. Jordan took it.

"Who are you?" the Arab asked.

"I'm a reporter for *The Shofar*. I came to write about the bombing."

"An Israeli," the Arab said, still sizing him up.

"Yes, an Israeli," Jordan rasped.

The Arab nodded gravely, and Jordan nodded back.

The Arab looked Jordan in the eye and swiftly raised his rifle butt, smashing Jordan in the groin. As Jordan doubled over, a boot rushed up to meet him. He felt a thunderclap to the back of the head and everything went black.

He opened his eyes in time to be blindfolded. He tried to resist, but his hands and feet were already tied. They gagged him with an oily rag. He felt them lifting him, dumping him into the trunk of his car. They slammed the lid and gunned the engine.

His bruises amplified every bump in the road. He was choking in a swelter of exhaust. *Now I'm going to suffocate,* he thought, before losing consciousness.

Chapter 2

When Jordan came around, he was sure his back was burning. Every nerve seared in screaming agony. His chest constricted and his lungs gasped in shock, as if he had plunged into icy water.

Jordan willed himself to get a grip. His eyes focused. He was on his side, bare from the waist up. A young man with olive skin and a thick, dark beard was leaning over him, observing his reaction. The man nodded approvingly.

Torture. I'm being tortured.

"Relax, Benjamin. It's only iodine. For your wounds."

The stranger spoke in Hebrew, with an Arab accent.

Jordan tried to formulate a question, but the soft-spoken Arab spared him the effort.

"I'm a doctor. They asked me to clean you up. You're not very pretty, but you're not dead either."

"Where are we?"

"I'm not permitted to say. They were very clear about that."

"They?"

The doctor dodged the question.

"You know, for an Israeli, you're awfully thick-skinned. The face should heal well enough. Fortunately for you, I had some very fine sutures."

Jordan felt the bandage on the back of his head.

The doctor frowned. "Unfortunately, I have no MRI."

He handed Jordan a pair of Tylenols and lowered his voice. "I'd offer you something stronger, but it's best you keep your wits about you."

Then, with a knowing look, he zipped his bag and left the room.

Jordan sat up carefully and studied his surroundings. He was resting on a military cot made up with clean white sheets. A bare lightbulb hung from the ceiling. The room was windowless, scarcely larger than a prison cell. Yellow watermarks stained the ceiling and walls, which had once been white. At knee level, one of the plaster walls bore four parallel gouges caked with something dry and rusty. Blood.

Jordan examined his fingertips. The tracks belonged to someone else.

But the doctor appeared to have taken blood or given him an injection. A small square of gauze was taped inside his right elbow.

He popped the chalky tablets in his mouth and swallowed, grimacing. He tried to stand, but the rippling of his muscles seemed to tear at his flesh. Three lines of neatly tailored stitches crossed his abdomen, binding his wounds. Jordan found them a comforting sight. They wouldn't spend this much effort on a condemned man.

Or would they?

The executives at the network had said they admired his daring. They didn't say anything about stupidity.

You dumb son of a bitch—now you're assured of a spot on the network. On every network.

Whimpering and pleading and groveling for mercy, until—

An Arab in military fatigues entered the room, armed with a pistol. The Arab tossed him a khaki tunic and told him to put it on. Then he gestured with the pistol, leading Jordan into a narrow hallway.

Until some ninja with a knife cuts your throat and enshrines you in cyberspace.

Inside, Jordan was quaking, but he tried not to show his fear.

If it's the last video you ever record, make it count.

Turn the tables.

They climbed a flight of stairs, leaving what Jordan took to be a basement. A door opened into the anteroom of a vaulted chamber.

Jordan looked around. The walls were made of drab concrete, and the pillars were similarly plain. The space was unlit and unfurnished. The guard restrained Jordan with an outstretched arm.

Across the mosque, his back to Jordan, a barefoot man knelt on a rectangular rug, his posture so humble he could kiss the floor. Jordan listened as he finished his prayers.

"Allahumma barik ala Muhammadin wa ala ahli Muhammadin, kama barakta ala Ibrahima, wa ala ahli Ibrahima . . . ."

"Allah, bless Mohamed and the people of Mohamed, just as you have blessed Abraham and his nation . . . ."

The Muslim rose from his worship and turned around. The first things Jordan noticed were the lines of his face—deep shadowy rifts and valleys crossing his forehead, descending from the sides of his nose, cleaving his chin—like traces of long ago rains on a desert landscape. He couldn't be much past middle age, judging from his welterweight build and slightly graying hair, but life had engraved him with hardship.

The Arab smiled at Jordan, and the landscape came to life.

"Mr. Jordan, I'm honored by your visit. It's not often we have such distinguished company."

Jordan was puzzled, clearly at a disadvantage.

"My name is Farouk. Khalid Farouk. Perhaps it's familiar to you."

Jordan answered with a steady, emotionless gaze. "I know your work."

The corners of Farouk's eyes betrayed his amusement.

"Please, accept my hospitality."

Jordan thought it an odd request. So this was the infamous Farouk, a man who planted bombs in playgrounds and incited devout young Muslims to suicide. Such was the depth of his hatred. Farouk had long ago declared war on peacemakers and compromisers.

Within the last 48 hours, the Israeli government had linked him to the bombing of a museum that housed one of the country's most important archaeological institutes, and it claimed to have retaliated against a base he was using in the village of el-Adir.

As far as Jordan knew, Farouk's picture had never been published. Strange, he didn't look evil.

Farouk strode to the anteroom and clapped his hands. An armed guard produced a pair of cushions, which he set on the stone floor. Farouk beckoned Jordan to sit. Somehow, it didn't seem optional. Yet obedience had its price: The doctor's meticulous stitches exacted their punishment.

No cameras? No knives?

Before emotion could get in the way, a reporter's instincts took over. Who was Khalid Farouk? What clues lay hidden in the rifts and valleys? Jordan reached for the notebook he kept in his back pocket, but the pocket was empty.

A guard presented a pair of tiny cups and filled them with thick black coffee.

"L'chaim," Farouk said, in Hebrew.

"To life," Jordan answered, in Arabic, suppressing his discomfort.

The drink went down bitterly.

"I apologize for your reception. Apparently, you arrived unannounced."

Jordan flashed an accusatory glare.

"I thought I was invited."

He searched for a hint, but the desert crags kept their secrets.

"All the same, it was good of you to come. What happened in el-Adir was criminal, a tragedy. The world must know. And it's well that you should be the messenger. You command a great deal of respect, Mr. Jordan. We admire your fairness, your search for the truth."

Jordan squirmed. This was how he saw himself—a seeker of truth—but being flattered by Khalid Farouk was almost nauseating. He locked Farouk in an unblinking stare.

"What happened in el-Adir—was it a crime, Mr. Farouk, or was it punishment?"

Farouk looked offended.

"It was a tragedy. Another brutal example of Israel's contempt for Arab life. Seventeen orphans, murdered without warning in the middle of the afternoon prayers."

"Can you prove it?"

Farouk's eyes turned cold with indignation.

"I can show you the bodies, Mr. Jordan. At least what was recovered. Is that proof enough?"

Farouk poured more coffee. "You know, I knew many of the victims personally. I visited their home from time to time, contributed food and religious books. I was even there in the hours before the attack. I wanted to help them fulfill, to fulfill . . . their potential."

Jordan cringed at the implication.

"Then who was responsible for the bombing of the museum?"

"Ask your government," Farouk said, enigmatically.

"My government seems to have given its answer, quite forcefully."

"Ask again."

Jordan had little patience for games. Then again, he was hardly in control of the situation.

"It wasn't us, Mr. Jordan. As you've observed, I take credit for my work. What's more, the museum is just as important to us as it is to you. It's our land, our history."

"That's what I would say—if I were trying to disavow a catastrophic mistake."

"A mistake?"

"The unintended slaughter of 23 Palestinian schoolchildren touring the museum when the bomb went off."

Anger rose in the rifts and valleys, as dangerously as a flash flood follows a storm.

"Do you abuse my hospitality, Mr. Jordan?"

Jordan matched Farouk's stare, refusing to be intimidated. He could almost hear the blood pounding in the terrorist's neck. It was the Arab who broke the silence.

"You came for a story, and you shall have one. But I doubt it's the story you expected." Farouk paused for effect. "When the bomb went off, the International Council on Cultural Antiquities was at the museum for a highly unusual Sunday meeting."

Jordan waved a hand dismissively. "That's been widely reported."

Farouk leaned forward and lowered his voice.

"And has it also been reported that the man who convened the meeting, the chairman of the Council, the venerable Rabbi Meyer Elazar, was himself absent at the time?"

Jordan stared blankly.

"Would your readers find that fact significant, Mr. Jordan?"

Jordan could picture Elazar, a barrel-chested man in his 70s, his voice an angry rumble, the wrinkles around his eyes multiplying like cracks through the ice of a frozen pond as he thumped a lectern, exhorting Israelis to reclaim the West Bank.

Theoretically, Elazar was first among equals on the Council, which oversaw excavations and coordinated access to artifacts. By Israeli invitation, the Council included members from a dozen nations. But no one accused Elazar of deferring to his colleagues.

The Orthodox rabbi and ardent Zionist was more than just a powerful figure in the world of archaeology. He was a political lightning rod, a polarizing figure for Jews and an antagonist to Arabs. In other words, a target.

But an absent target?

Tempted by the bait, yet wary of the hook, Jordan studied Farouk's face.

"My readers aren't interested in rhetorical questions," Jordan said.

"Quite right," Farouk said. "These are the facts: In the moments before the blast, Rabbi Elazar phoned the Institute. He spoke directly to one of his colleagues in the conference room. The purpose of the call was plain."

Jordan rewarded him with an inquiring look.

"The purpose was to verify the presence, in the building, of the other Council members."

"You were listening?"

"One of our people was monitoring the traffic. He phoned me from the West Bank, within minutes of the explosion."

Jordan's surprise showed.

"Yes, Mr. Jordan, we cast a wide net."

"You expect me to take it on faith?"

"No, I don't."

Farouk glanced at the first guard, who handed him an ordinary microcassette recorder.

"The first voice you'll hear is Martin Stanley, a Council member from Britain. He's dead now. The second voice is Meyer Elazar, on a cellular phone." Farouk set the recorder between them and pressed the play button.

The cheap recorder and the overlay of static made the voices seem all the more disembodied.

> "Meyer, I can barely hear you. Are you in the car?"
> " . . . me now?"

> "Where are you? The meeting was scheduled for eleven."
> "I know that. Listen, tell everyone —
> "Hold on . . . . Sorry, someone was talking to me —"
> "Is everyone there?"
> "Yes."
> "Yes?"
> "I mean, no — "
> "No?"
> "We haven't seen Altieri — Where the hell are you? — or Ramsi for that matter. Other than that we're all — "

A high-pitched electronic screech, more static, and then the recording went silent.

"That was the explosion, severing the connection."

"Altieri and Ramsi?"

"A Catholic and a Palestinian, both close allies of Elazar."

"How can I confirm the recording's authenticity?"

"I'm not sure you can."

"Where was Elazar? What does it mean?"

"My friend, we have great confidence in your investigative skill. We trust *you* to provide the answer."

Jordan hid his excitement behind a poker face.

"I'll check it out," he said.

Chapter 3

The Arab in military fatigues guided Jordan back to the basement cell and locked the door. The room was stuffy and confining. Jordan sat on the edge of the cot, gripping the metal frame. He got up and paced.

How seriously should he take Farouk's story? And, what, exactly, was Farouk insinuating? That Rabbi Meyer Elazar, one of the more outspoken members of Israel's right wing, was somehow complicit in a plot to wipe out the international archaeological council, along with the contents of the museum? It was a lot to swallow. And Farouk hadn't even speculated as to the motive.

Then again, the modern history of the State of Israel was a series of improbable stories.

Jordan could remember a time when his patriotism was simple and pure, when Israel held the high ground in a struggle between darkness and light. He had grown up with the heroics of the Six Day War and the Yom Kippur War, stirring victories against hopeless odds. He was inspired by the daring of Entebbe, when Israeli commandos flew thousands of miles to rescue a planeload of hostages—from a building purportedly wired to explode.

After all these years, the tragedy of Munich haunted him still. Occasionally, in restless dreams, he saw Israel's doomed Olympians and the hooded terrorist who sealed their fate, bogeyman of his youth.

Then came the massacre at Sabra and Shatila, where the victims were Palestinian, and the story became more confusing.

An Israeli prime minister had been cut down at a peace rally—*by a Jew.*

The assassin shared Elazar's uncompromising brand of Zionism, ceding no ground to the Palestinians.

The possibility that the Israeli military had bombed an orphanage stirred Jordan on a deeper level, because Jordan had no parents. Terrorism had made him an orphan before his first birthday.

The random, endless suicide bombings, the killing of innocents, filled him with fury. More than most, he understood the pain of the survivors. With each explosion, he felt an instinctive lust for vengeance as indiscriminate as the terror itself.

And yet, even the hardest of the hard-liners had to wonder what inspired such madness. What combination of hatred and desperation and emptiness and resolve drives people to walk into a crowded supermarket, where mothers are filling baskets with milk and honey and sugarcoated breakfast cereal, and blow themselves up?

At least Jordan wondered.

Maybe that helped explain why he became a journalist. He thought Israelis and Palestinians alike should face the truth, however painful it might be. In Israel's right-wing circles, even within certain quarters of the paper, there was always an undercurrent of criticism, more dependable than the cheers: *"Whose side are you on?"*

Whose side was he on? Jordan dismissed the question. As a journalist, he didn't have to take sides.

The door opened, and a pair of guards appeared. They blindfolded Jordan and tied his wrists. Grabbing his arms, they led him up the stairs, through the chapel, outside into the hot, dry air. They bundled him into the backseat of a car, pushing his head down to avoid banging it on the doorframe. Someone was sitting beside him, rolling up his sleeve, rubbing his bicep with alcohol.

"This may sting a little," the young physician said in a soothing voice as he stabbed Jordan with a needle.

All the anxieties faded away.

After a long dreamless sleep, Jordan awoke with a dry mouth and a stiff neck, slumped behind the wheel of the borrowed Mercedes. He was back in the village of el-Adir, near the rubble of the Lebanese orphanage. Several women veiled in black were sifting through the debris.

Chapter 4

Tel Aviv

"Go, go, go!" Itzhak Goren shouted from the sidelines, spilling lukewarm coffee as he pumped his fist with enthusiasm.

At the far end of the field, one of the kids tripped over the ball, got back on his feet, and dribbled toward the goal, past a daydreaming defender.

It was a cloudless afternoon, and the commander of the Israel Defense Forces was coaching a soccer team of seven-year-olds, among them his grandson. With his rumpled uniform and expansive waist, Goren projected a genial air. His drooping eyelids and jowls reminded strangers of a sad and loyal hound. But his fighting instincts were never far from the surface.

An aide handed him an envelope, and he grumbled with irritation, tempted to brush it aside. Instead, he opened it, and the joyful exuberance drained from his body. The goalie deflected the kick, but the general was beyond noticing. He deputized his son, a lean and sinewy captain in the special forces, and briskly left the field.

The envelope contained a printout from the website of *The Shofar*, another banner story by that menace Benjamin Jordan. Goren crumpled the pages and climbed into a waiting car.

Ten minutes later, surrounded by his staff in his Defense Ministry office, Goren cursed and fumed with all the sudden, heart-stopping force of a coronary.

"How the hell could this happen? How the hell?"

"It seems there was an intelligence failure," an aide replied.

"An intelligence failure? It was a triumph of stupidity. Tell Mossad I want a full accounting."

Disgusted, the general flattened the printout on his desk. The story carried a large, boldfaced headline over a picture of a child's shrouded corpse.

> *The bombs struck their target with surgical precision, delivering instantaneous death. But they missed their intended victim Khalid Farouk by several hours and untold kilometers, a point he noted over coffee Monday after reciting his evening prayers . . . .*

The old familiar pain was coming back. It began as a dull ache and slowly tightened its grip, until Itzhak Goren felt as if someone had his heart in a fist. Some wounds were like barometers, warning of a coming storm. Goren's early warning system was much less practical: It gave reminders after the fact.

Cursing, he popped an antacid and washed it down with the dregs of his coffee.

"General, you should be aware that this puts us in violation of two U.N. resolutions," another aide said.

"Colonel, diplomacy is the least of my concerns."

The general vented his emotion on his subordinates, but the truth was, Itzhak Goren was angriest with himself. He had directed the retaliatory strike on the compound in Lebanon.

The newspaper provided a wrenching post mortem. Several of the dead children had been orphaned by the Israeli invasion of 2006. Their religious home had a sinister patron, a terrorist who saw them as future recruits. In hushed conversations with the story's author, villagers related that one boy left el-Adir with Khalid Farouk months ago. Some time later, word filtered back that the child found paradise—by way of a Jerusalem commuter bus and a kilo of plastic explosives.

The reporter couldn't say where he had met Farouk. They had drugged him before returning him to the scene of the air strike, and, according to the odometer in his borrowed car, the journey had covered quite a distance. Toward the end of the article, Jordan speculated that the meeting wasn't in Lebanon at all, but rather in neighboring Syria.

The room rattled from the vibration of a distant jackhammer, like a drill to Goren's molars. Deep beneath the ministry, crews were upgrading the bunker that housed the IDF's war-room.

The general's thoughts turned to the pilots who delivered the bombs, living victims of a fatal error. "Get me a meeting with the airmen," he said. "We can't allow this to weigh on them."

Like many who survived the Holocaust or came of age in its shadow, Goren lived an oath: *Never again.* Never again could the world be allowed to close its eyes. And never again would Jews march to the slaughter, blinded by lies and false hope.

At 61, Goren had spent most of a lifetime defending his nation. His biography was in many ways the story of the Jewish state. He had fought in the Sinai, and in the Golan Heights. He was born in Europe after the War, in a camp for displaced persons. He arrived in Israel before it was Israel, as a child and a refugee. His mother had survived Auschwitz, but first she had survived the Warsaw Ghetto, where the rest of her family died amid famine and epidemic or in the final doomed uprising of 1943. Goren had seen footage of the Jews' overcrowded, walled-in neighborhood. He had seen German artillery reduce it to rubble.

For those who waged war on civilians, Itzhak Goren had nothing but contempt.

The general waved his aides out of the office. An intelligence failure, they said. How could it be explained?

According to Mossad, a known Tears of God operative named Saeed had phoned Farouk at the compound in Lebanon two hours after the explosion at the museum. The operative had briefed Farouk, and Farouk had offered his congratulations.

Goren looked again at the partial transcript of the call, translated from the Arabic. According to the intelligence analysts, the briefing Farouk received from the operative clearly indicated that one of the terrorists' associates—not yet identified—gave the signal to trigger the explosion.

SAEED: "He was on the phone to the Institute as it happened, monitoring the situation. A direct line to the Council."

FAROUK: "What did he say?"

SAEED: "He confirmed that the members of the Council, that they were at the Institute. They were in the building when the bomb exploded."

FAROUK: "That's brilliant. Brilliant! Well done."

The conversation must have been longer, but that was all intelligence had managed to intercept. Even now, the brazen horror of it chilled and infuriated the general. He had been all too glad to hit back.

He had visited the museum with his son, when Yaron was a boy, and he had returned with his grandson. The Institute for Cultural Antiquities was a symbol of Israel's history, of Jewish claims to the land stretching back to biblical times. Located on the outskirts of Jerusalem, it was a storehouse and showcase for some of archaeology's most remarkable finds, including several of the fragmentary texts recovered from caves near the Dead Sea in the late 1940s. It was also the headquarters of the International Council on Cultural Antiquities, which was assembled in the boardroom at the time of the blast.

And the Council members weren't the only casualties. A group of elementary school children, half of them Palestinian, had been mid-way through the ground floor exhibit when the bomb went off.

Had the geniuses from intelligence read too much into the intercepted phone call? If so, was it simply carelessness? Or was there unusual pressure to declare the museum avenged?

Whatever the case, the enemy had escaped to strike again.

Goren stared at the photo of the child's corpse, and his stomach began to churn.

Chapter 5

In a brightly lit conference room just off the paper's news floor, a television interviewer leaned in intimately for the question everyone was asking.

"So tell me, Ben, how did it feel to sit face to face with the notorious terrorist?"

Jordan blinked.

"You know, I did my best to put personal feelings aside and learn what I could while I had the chance," he said.

The rest of the media was hungry for the story behind the story, Jordan's personal drama. He was doing his best to oblige.

The editor of *The Shofar*, Shaul Meltzer, had also been granting interviews. It was good for the paper, Meltzer explained, as the producer clipped a microphone to his lapel.

In his mind, Jordan replayed the terrorist's tape of Rabbi Elazar, analyzing the implications. Jordan had not mentioned it in his story on the bombing raid. There was no way of knowing whether it was real, or when it was made. As far as Jordan knew, the rabbi's call to the museum boardroom could have been recorded weeks ago, or months ago, as the Council assembled for an earlier meeting. For the moment, Jordan kept it to himself.

But Farouk's tip had gotten under his skin, into his bloodstream. If it held up to scrutiny, it would produce more than just shock waves. It might seal the T.V. deal—unless Jordan's account of the air raid gone awry had already put him over the top. And it might expose a monstrous crime.

"We're all very proud of Ben's courageous reporting," Meltzer told the camera. "I had a hunch we were onto something when I sent him to Lebanon."

Sent him?

Jordan hadn't even asked. He was afraid of what Meltzer might say.

A diminutive man with a pigeon face and a mercurial manner, Meltzer was too loyal to his own cause. That made him a dangerous man to cross. He was also extremely well-connected—maybe too well-connected. Inexplicably, he had gutted some of Jordan's best stories.

All of which guaranteed that Shaul Meltzer would never be a guest on the Benjamin Jordan News Hour.

When the interview was over, Jordan left the newspaper's conference room and returned to his desk, where the display on his telephone told him he had 12 messages. He lifted the receiver to his ear and punched in his code. On the recording, the network's executive vice president sounded distinctly upbeat.

"Outstanding work, Ben. We'll be counting on you for more of the same, as soon as the chief signs off. We need to get the two of you together fast, before he heads back to New York. Say, tomorrow at eleven? See you then."

The network had been stung by charges of bias in its coverage of the Arab-Israeli conflict, and the executives considered Jordan a credible, independent voice. Apparently, they needed him, or someone like him. It didn't hurt that he'd spent a few years reporting from Washington.

He advanced to the next message and felt a hand on his shoulder. It was Leah Lefkowitz, and she was looking at his bandages with a mixture of concern and admiration. He lowered the phone.

"I hear some women roughed you up," she said.

"No comment."

Leah laughed.

"I can make you talk. How about dinner?"

He hesitated.

"I'd like that, but I can't."

"Next week then," she said. "I'll hold you to it."

From the day she arrived in the newsroom, he was drawn by the softness of her curves, the warmth of her eyes, the haphazard cascade of her dark brown hair. He felt her compassion. She wrote with eloquence, and empathy for life's victims. But woe to the hypocrites. Her profiles in the pages of *The Shofar* unerringly laid bare their secrets and foibles.

"How was Europe?" he asked.

"Too short. But the flight from Frankfurt took forever, worrying about you. Damn it, Ben, if you don't stop taking these chances, you're going to end up dead, and I swear, I'll make you regret it."

"I'm afraid to ask how."

"Simple—I'll write your obituary."

She was joking, of course, but the threat had an edge.

"I'll be sure to stick around," he said.

To friends and colleagues, their long-simmering mutual attraction had been obvious, and their sudden cooling was puzzling. Now she was dating one of Israel's leading philanthropists, the chairman of the Jerusalem Symphony. Her friends assumed Jordan was too independent, too driven, too devoted to the next story. Or too irreligious for her deeply observant family. If he ventured into a synagogue, it was only once or twice a year, for the high holidays, and even then, it was out of a sense of obligation rather than any genuine belief.

The truth was, she had broken through his formidable defenses—and left him with a sense of emptiness.

She was studying his expression now, evidently troubled by what she saw. She raised a hand to touch his wounded face, and stopped herself before walking away.

He watched her retreat to her desk. He could admit it to himself: She had the power to bolster his confidence—or to weaken it.

Forget about her, he told himself. *Don't get drawn back in.*

The wider acclaim was a rush, too, but it was never that simple for him. There was always something in the background, a weight that never lifted.

An awareness of his parents.

He was driven to make something of his life, to make up for their truncated lives. But nothing he did could lift that weight.

And the story everyone was so excited about sank into insignificance compared with the story he had yet to write, the tip he had yet to run down about Meyer Elazar.

Chapter 6

He left the office early, blaming his injuries. He needed to clear his head. Not that home was much more conducive. The building on Jabotinsky Street dated to the 1930s, when Tel Aviv architects housed the body without regard for the soul. Small windows, overbearing concrete, modest spaces. He opened the door to his second-story apartment and turned on the lights.

Mail was piling up on the dining table, mostly unopened bills. He pushed the pile aside and took a seat, absorbed in the enigma of Meyer Elazar.

Elazar apparently summoned the International Council on Cultural Antiquities to its final meeting. Was the rabbi a victim—or a perpetrator?

At Jordan's request, the newspaper's library had gathered a sheaf of stories on Elazar. The oldest were clippings of yellowed, brittle newsprint going back more than 50 years. The newest were crisp computer printouts culled from the Web and commercial databases.

Inkstained footprints of a life's journey, trailing off in an electronic ether.

He set the folder of stories on the table and stared at its blank exterior.

What did he know about Elazar?

He had seen Elazar up close on several occasions, most recently a demonstration in the West Bank, where the rabbi had faced down Israeli soldiers sent to dismantle a Jewish settlement. "We follow God's law," Elazar had shouted through a bullhorn.

That's the same thing your enemies say, Jordan had thought.

Elazar was an extremist, and extremists tested Jordan's objectivity.

Though Elazar's political party occupied the fringe, it wielded disproportionate power in the Knesset, where governments were often formed by fractious coalitions. The election of 2003 had produced no clear parliamentary majority, leaving the fringe in a position to tip the balance. So it was that Rabbi Elazar had played kingmaker, and so it was that he claimed the Council as his reward.

Strange—why settle for the Council when he could have demanded so much more?

Elazar's appointment rankled many people, not just Jordan, but even the man's enemies had to give him his due. The rabbi was fluent in multiple languages—and an acknowledged authority on Hebrew antiquity.

Jordan picked up a cordless phone. A call to the Jerusalem coroner confirmed that he was still in business: The rabbi's body had not been recovered from the museum's wreckage. Efforts were continuing slowly, at an archaeological pace.

In fact, when the lone feeble heartbeat faded beneath the rubble, when the bloodhounds and the infrared sensors and all the delicate acoustic probes detected no remaining sign of life, the authorities held back the bulldozers and brought in a team of archaeologists. They hoped to rescue what they could of the Institute's cultural treasures, down to the last charred fragment. The morning papers had described a gruesome scene: forensic experts sifting for clues, pathologists and rabbis placing human remains in zip-loc bags, scholars in surgical masks tweezing scraps of antiquity from the debris.

It was too awful to contemplate.

Jordan opened his folder on Elazar.

A scrap of newsprint from the early Fifties showed a skinny teenager planting trees in the desert, trees purchased with donations from American Jews. The young Meyer beamed for the camera.

A decade later—the date wasn't entirely legible—Elazar appeared in a group photo at Masada, the ancient mountaintop fortress where a community of Zealots chose death at their own hands over Roman slavery. The text said that Elazar, a promising young archaeologist with a doctorate from Tel Aviv, was assisting on a dig. Wearing black horn-rimmed glasses and a white short-sleeve dress shirt, Elazar practically hummed with earnestness.

August 1966 — Now in charge of his own project, a more mature and robust Elazar poses in scuba gear at the stern of a small motorboat. He is supervising a survey of Caesarea, the Herodian port city partly submerged beneath the Mediterranean. In an accompanying photo, his wife and collaborator Mishka bobs in the surf, grinning beneath a face-mask.

June 1967 — A rising star of the academic establishment, Elazar proudly displays cases of Dead Sea Scrolls captured from Jordan when Israel took East Jerusalem in the Six Day War.

May 1969 — In a magazine profile, Elazar discusses his most daunting challenge: the terrible twos. A snapshot captures him negotiating with his toddler for the release of a Sumerian pottery shard.

April 1970 — A desolate Meyer Elazar walks in a funeral procession for his wife and three-year-old daughter, killed in a cross-border raid on their northern kibbutz.

March 1975 — An unsmiling Elazar graduates from yeshiva to answer a new calling, that of Orthodox rabbi.

September 1985 — Addressing a New York audience in "strident tones," Elazar seeks political contributions for a fledgling religious party.

February 1989 — Elazar is sworn in as a member of the Knesset.

December 1992 — His sleeves rolled up, his yarmulke pinned to his graying hair, a bearded Elazar helps Jewish settlers build houses on the Israeli-occupied West Bank, defying Palestinians who claim the land as their own and Jews who would use it as a bargaining chip.

May 1994 — At a Tel Aviv news conference, Elazar introduces a bill that would invalidate religious conversions performed by Reform and Conservative rabbis. "The only true Jews — the only true converts," he says, correcting himself, "are those initiated by Orthodox rabbis."

October 1995 — Following the assassination of Prime Minister Rabin, a warrior turned peacemaker, Elazar tells reporters he "can understand the killer's motivation," a comment he later complains "was taken out of context."

February 1996 — Elazar officiates at the opening of an archaeological tunnel in Jerusalem beside one of Islam's holiest shrines. Protesters denounce it as a deliberate provocation.

October 2000 — To "prove a point," Elazar accompanies the leader of the Likud Party and a phalanx of Israeli police to ground zero in the Arab-Israeli conflict, the Temple Mount. The visit triggers the worst fighting in more than a decade.

March 2003 — A grim-faced Prime Minister congratulates Elazar on his appointment as chairman of the International Council on Cultural Antiquities.

Somewhere outside Jordan's apartment, a siren blared, breaking the haphazard biography's spell.

Jordan bit his lip. Could it be true? Was it conceivable that this scholar turned rabbi turned nationalist politician had committed mass murder? And, assuming just for argument's sake that it was plausible, what on earth would have inspired it?

Jordan closed the folder.

Where to begin?

The official investigators answered his phone calls quickly enough; maybe celebrity had its advantages. But as far as they were concerned, Elazar was buried beneath the concrete. The rabbi had called the meeting, and they were working on the assumption that the rabbi was presiding when the bomb exploded.

Jordan went down a mental checklist. Elazar's political associates would be a logical starting point, but they would spread gossip, tipping off the competition. Ordinarily, relatives were a natural, but Elazar had no surviving family. Co-workers might know the most, but they would have perished in the blast.

Elazar had summoned the Council on short notice, and the timing was unusual. Normally, the offices at the Institute were empty on Sundays in deference to the Christian members. Jordan closed his eyes and pictured the Sunday scene: children bounding out of school buses, Council members arriving more casually than usual, desks vacant as secretaries and other staffers enjoyed the day off . . . .

A quick call to the headquarters of Elazar's political party yielded the name and address of his personal secretary at the Institute, Miriam Wiesman. She lived in Maale Telulah, in the hard-baked hills east of Jerusalem. Jordan began to dial but stopped on the third digit.

Better to do this in person.

Chapter 7

Maale Telulah

Grafted onto a barren brown and white slope, the settlement's modern suburban townhouses seemed lonely and isolated, a fragile presence. It looked as if a heavy rain might wash them away—assuming it ever rained.

She answered the door apprehensively, not knowing who or what to expect. He could tell from the ember of her cigarette that she was trembling. She crossed her arms as if to hold herself together and squinted through a thin gray halo.

Yes, it would be okay if he came in, she decided, opening the door the rest of the way.

She was alone in the apartment. It was dusk, and she had yet to turn on the lights. As he adjusted to the dimness, he could see she was distraught. He estimated she was in her fifties, a slender, attractive woman whose looks were obscured though not altogether hidden by a nondescript wardrobe, plain hairstyle and obvious exhaustion. A glint of sunset caught his eye, a reflection in a picture frame. It was a portrait of Meyer Elazar. Jordan looked around. It was the only photo in the room.

"I'm sorry to say I never met the rabbi," he said, softly. "Maybe you can tell me about him, how you'll remember him."

Miriam Wiesman stared at a blank wall. She answered slowly, in a monotone. "He was a loving father and a faithful husband."

Jordan wondered if he had missed a chapter.

"Did the rabbi remarry?" he asked.

"No," she said, looking away. "The rabbi never remarried."

Jordan nodded gently. "You must have been as close to him as anyone. You worked with him for—what was it?—twelve, thirteen years?"

Wiesman buried her face in her hands. "Oh God," she sobbed. "He didn't have to be there. He shouldn't have been there . . . . I tried. I told him, I told him he should take a holiday.

" I thought . . . I thought it was something he should have done a long time ago. It was as if he had forgotten how, he just needed someone to . . . ." Her face was streaked with emotion. "There were so many times when I almost, I wanted to . . . I thought . . . and he never . . . All those years . . . . Finally, I just, I did it. I planned everything, I thought I'd surprise him.

"I said, 'Let's go to Eilat.'"

The secretary pulled on her cigarette.

"I thought he would be happy. Can you believe it? And he just looked at me. He looked at me from the God-awful depths of his bottomless God-forsaken well and said, 'Mishka loved Eilat.'

"*'Mishka loved Eilat.'* That's what he said. That was all . . . . And that was the last we spoke of it."

Miriam ground out her cigarette.

"I'm sorry," Jordan whispered.

He remembered the photo of Elazar's wife bobbing in the waves, grinning beneath a face mask, before the violence claimed her.

Miriam nodded, embarrassed by her outpouring.

"May I offer you some coffee, Mr. Jordan?"

The truth was, Jordan disliked coffee, but it seemed like a good idea. "Yes, thank you very much."

Jordan studied the framed photo of Elazar, the tight-lipped expression frozen under glass. He pictured the secretary casting a stone into a well, waiting for a splash, an echo, and hearing . . . nothing.

Miriam returned with a pair of mugs, looking slightly more composed.

"Your conversation about Eilat, that was the last time you saw him?" Jordan inquired.

"No, that was Monday. As I told the police, the last time I saw Meyer was Friday, middle of the afternoon. He arrived at the office late and left in a hurry . . . You know, I can't even remember if . . . if I wished him good shabbas. What I remember—what I can't forget—is feeling angry. As if I had a right."

Jordan's eyes mirrored her heartbreak.

"I'm sorry," she added, self-consciously. "I can't imagine that interests you. All I know is, he pulled a file from the cabinet and said he was going to the Ministry of Cultural Affairs, for a meeting with the minister. He was worried about getting there and finishing his business by sundown. He told me to schedule a Council meeting for Sunday, to let the others know. And then he was gone."

"Do you know what it was about? What was going on?"

She sighed and shook her head.

"I wish I knew, Mr. Jordan. But I didn't ask and he didn't volunteer. Usually, I would know. But I hadn't been in the office for three days—I just couldn't."

"Any idea what was in the file?"

"There was a name on the file, an American name."

She searched her memory, but it was blank. She shook her head in frustration.

"I'm sorry, Mr. Jordan."

Jordan nodded sympathetically. "Maybe it'll come to you." He took a sip of coffee. "You've been more than patient, Ms. Wiesman. I don't mean to impose on your kindness. There's one more point you might help me with . . . ."

"Yes?"

"Can you tell me anything about Altieri and Ramsi?"

According to Khalid Farouk's tape recording, the Council members representing the Vatican and the Palestinian Authority had been absent from the fateful meeting.

Miriam's eyes lit up, startled. "I had completely forgotten. How stupid of me."

"You've been under a lot of stress."

"Ehud mentioned it when I returned to work Friday morning. He had been working late the night before. He said Meyer had been huddled with Ismail Ramsi and Monsignor Altieri past midnight. They were still in Meyer's office when Ehud left for the night."

"Ehud?"

"The custodian. A wonderful man."

"Do you know where I can find him?"

"He was saving money to visit his grandchildren in America . . . ." Miriam fought back a tear. "He was working nights and Sundays."

Chapter 8

Altieri and Ramsi.

Jordan pulled away from the curb, lost in thought.

If the Italian and the Palestinian were somehow complicit, approaching their friends and relatives in ignorance could be tricky. He had so little to go on. But that was the problem.

With one hand on the steering wheel, he reached for the addresses the grieving secretary had scribbled.

A pair of headlights glared at him from the rearview mirror. He adjusted the angle and stole a glance at the piece of paper. Ramsi lived in the West Bank town of Ramallah, a place to which Jordan was loath to return. Altieri rented a flat in Jerusalem. The priest no doubt lived alone, which meant he was surrounded by fewer potential sources. Jordan took the turn toward Ramallah.

So did the headlights.

Jordan made a mental note.

His car, a 20-year-old Alfa Romeo Spider convertible, tackled an incline with authority. He had purchased it badly used and restored it to something approaching peak performance.

On the fringe of urban sprawl, he passed a Bedouin tent, draped like a bat-wing against the stars. Sheep huddled in its embrace, and the blue light of a television escaped into the night.

At a security checkpoint, soldiers studied Jordan with curiosity. The scrutiny made him uneasy, just as passing through customs or being pulled over by a traffic cop gave the innocent a sense of guilt. It was like entering a foreign country, which in a way it was.

The checkpoint soon receded in the rearview mirror. Before the unhurried soldiers could wave the next car through, Jordan had turned off the main road.

Blocks he once patrolled bore the scars of conflict—houses bulldozed and blown up and cut away like dollhouses, revealing floors and walls and wrecked interiors. The Israeli military had destroyed them in the hunt for terrorists, or to punish families that nurtured suicide bombers. There were stirrings of recovery, too—a regal home under construction, a foundation being dug. Where buildings belonged, wide open swaths of sky.

The smell of lamb roasting in garlic wafted through the neighborhood, surprising Jordan's senses. The first time he was here, tear gas filled the air.

He was just a teenager at the time, a soldier on foot patrol during the first *intifada*. In those days, he willfully avoided the faces of the

Palestinians. Their eyes burned with hatred and resentment; he feared they might one day see the same in his.

In the heat of a Ramallah afternoon, an Arab boy of no more than seven or eight began pelting the patrol with stones. As such incidents went, it seemed harmless enough. In the few seconds it took Jordan to wonder how David became Goliath, the boy turned and fled.

Much to Jordan's surprise, Private Menachem Goldstein, a tall, gangly yeshiva boy, took up the chase. Goldstein was a rarity; most of the ultra-Orthodox avoided compulsory military service, claiming their religious studies were more important. Jordan hung back, content to let Goldstein make an impression. He watched his fellow soldier disappear into an alley in breathless pursuit.

Moments later, the afternoon exploded with automatic weapons fire. Civilians scrambled for cover. Jordan gauged the direction of the shooting and bolted after his comrade.

At the far end of the alley, a crowded open-air market had become a war zone of screaming, bleeding, dying people, some running to get away, others cowering beneath overturned push-carts, still others sprawled amid a mess of scattered fruits and vegetables. In the midst of it all, Menachem Goldstein stood in attack posture, firing bursts from his assault rifle at anything that moved.

For an instant, the shock stopped Jordan. The deranged Israeli chose another target—a fat man pounding frantically on a locked door—and pulled the trigger.

Then Jordan sprang forward. He extended from a sprint into a flying tackle, into Goldstein's peripheral vision. Goldstein spun toward him with a sweeping arc of bullets.

In an adrenaline-enhanced freeze-frame, Jordan noticed something dripping from the soldier's uniform. *Eggshells? Was that how it started?*

He caught Goldstein beneath the rib cage, knocking him to the ground, deflecting the Uzi. Bullets ricocheted off the pavement. Goldstein tried to club Jordan in the head or grab his throat, but Jordan had the advantage. He pinned the shooter with his knees and shook him violently, screaming through a blur of tears: "Why? Why?"

Goldstein grinned, and Jordan reacted by impulse. With three remorseless punches, he splintered Goldstein's front teeth and crushed his nose, releasing a gusher.

The next thing Jordan knew, several Israeli soldiers were pulling him loose, restraining Goldstein, training their weapons on the marketplace. Slowly, numbly, Arab survivors emerged from the chaos.

Jordan remembered a bent old woman reaching for his hand, kissing it. He remembered a blood-soaked merchant pressing an orange into his other hand, wordlessly. And he remembered his comrades dragging him away as the friends and relatives of the dead wailed in grief.

Somehow, a BBC crew captured most of it on tape. For the better part of a week, television news replayed it regularly, beginning with the whirl of sky and ground that marked the cameraman's initial reaction. Most of the commentators spoke of Jordan's courage and selflessness—a few right-wing extremists called him a traitor—but their words were little more than background noise. What struck Jordan was his initial moment of hesitation—and the satisfaction he had taken in breaking Goldstein's face.

The episode had won Jordan a measure of trust in the Palestinian community. After all these years, it continued to open doors.

Thirty-two Nasser Street was a well-kept two-story house, with curtains flowing in the night breeze. An old woman answered the door.

Jordan introduced himself, apologizing for the hour. "I'm looking for the family of Dr. Ismail Ramsi," he said. "I was hoping you might help me."

The old woman scowled. "No one here can help. We've been through enough."

Inside, a baby cried.

"I promise, I wouldn't be here if I didn't think it was important."

The woman was unmoved.

Jordan handed her his business card. "Maybe at a better time," he said, optimistically.

He heard a younger woman's voice: "Who's there, Mama?"

Mama shut the door.

Disappointed, Jordan looked up and down the block. He thought of waiting until morning, but realized that many of the neighbors would be at work. He saw the glow of a television through a window across the street and strode toward it.

The door to the Ramsi residence opened again and a younger woman ran after him.

"Mr. Jordan, wait."

She was roughly Jordan's age, a small woman with large brown eyes and distracting cleavage. She untied her apron as she caught up with him.

"Forgive my mother-in-law, she's very upset," the woman said. "The government people questioned her mercilessly, but she wouldn't cooperate. She distrusts all Israelis."

"You must be Mrs. Ramsi."

"Raya," she said, shaking his hand.

"Ben."

"It's an honor to meet you. I'd invite you in, but it's probably better if we walk."

Jordan followed Raya's lead.

"So you're a mother?"

She almost smiled. "He has his father's curiosity. I don't know what he enjoys more, hiding his toys or looking for them. Lately, though, he's been looking for his father."

She wiped away a tear with one hand and took Jordan's arm with the other, squeezing tightly. "Please, tell me, what have you learned?"

Jordan searched for something comforting, something honest, wishing she hadn't put him on the spot. "I'm afraid I'm still in the dark," he said, hesitating. "Even as to your husband's fate."

Raya looked shocked. "What are you saying?"

Jordan was on shaky ground, trying to find his footing.

"I don't know. I don't mean to upset you—or raise your hopes."

She ran a hand through her hair and pulled at it, unconsciously. "The waiting, not being able to say goodbye, not being able to bury him, it's been awful. I try not to think, but — "

Her voice trailed off.

Jordan looked deep into her eyes. "Raya, I need your help. I need to know what was going on at the Institute."

They walked in silence. She looked at the night sky, wavering.

"The discovery had created an atmosphere of suspicion, Ben. No one trusted anyone. All the submerged jealousies and hostilities and conflicting agendas rose to the surface."

Jordan held his breath. *What discovery?*

Raya stopped walking.

"You didn't know?"

Jordan shook his head.

Raya grasped for words. "I don't know the details," she said. "Only this: The Institute had made an important archaeological discovery. The precise nature was a closely held secret. My husband wouldn't discuss it. But, whatever it was, it threatened to turn colleagues into rivals. Ismail was losing sleep over it."

A car rolled past them, slowly, and disappeared around a corner.

"Did he tell you anything else? Anything at all?"

"Ismail and Monsignor Altieri, from the Vatican, met with Rabbi Elazar a few nights before the bombing. They were trying to hold things together. Ismail and Monsignor Altieri believed the only solution was to make it all public. The rabbi wanted to keep it secret. Apparently, they had a heated argument."

"Why the three of them?"

"Ismail and Monsignor Altieri were Meyer's closest advisers. I know it sounds strange, but they were friends—maybe Meyer's only real friends on the council. I got the sense that they knew more than the rest."

"What did they decide?"

"I don't think they decided anything. When Ismail came home, he was all torn up. The way he was acting, it frightened me. He mumbled that he might have to take matters into his own hands."

"Is that what he did?"

She looked anxious.

"Monsignor Altieri was supposed to come to the house Friday night, to talk things over. But he never showed up, and he didn't call. Ismail tried him by phone, no answer. Ismail was impatient at first, then he started to worry. He told himself there was probably a delay on the road, that the Israelis might be blocking traffic into the West Bank. Saturday morning passed, and still no word from Altieri. So Ismail got in the car. He said he was going to Amman."

Amman.

Jordan knew what that meant. Ramsi's patron in the Jordanian capital took an enlightened and scholarly interest in all matters archaeological.

"Can you be sure he was in the building Sunday?" Jordan asked.

"He didn't come home the night before the bombing. He warned me that he might not, but he didn't call, and he didn't answer his phone."

Chapter 9

As Raya waved from an upstairs window and pulled the shade, Jordan revved the Alfa's engine and let out the clutch.

What did Elazar and his colleagues discover that sowed such distrust?

Ismail Ramsi had taken the answer to Amman. Jordan would leave in the morning and be there by mid-day.

He turned left at the end of Nasser Street and headed out of Ramallah. The night was brisk, but Jordan preferred driving with the top down. It put him in closer touch with his surroundings.

On a street corner, three Arab men stopped conversing and stared as he drove by.

Lights glared in the Alfa's rear view mirror. Jordan squinted.

He was supposed to meet with the network executives in the morning. Taking an eye off the road, he dialed and left an apologetic message, asking to reschedule.

If Ramsi had made it to Amman, Jordan's most authoritative source could be uniquely helpful. Unless the source had a reason to be unhelpful, which was also a possibility.

The side streets led him back to the main road. Ahead lay the Qalandia refugee camp, an overcrowded warren of tin shacks and squalid misery. Terror's incubator. The darkness blotted it out, but he knew it was there, one of the area's enduring features. Nearby, the Israeli military maintained a checkpoint, controlling the movement of people and vehicles.

The traffic signal ahead turned yellow. Jordan accelerated through the intersection.

The vehicle behind him ran the light.

He looked at it more closely. Was it the same car that had followed him into Ramallah? He wasn't sure. He looked back again, by way of the driver's side mirror, but he couldn't see inside the other car, couldn't see through the brights.

He shifted into higher gear. On an open stretch of road, the car behind him fell back.

He glanced in the rear-view mirror. A pinpoint of red light floated in the glare of the brights. It floated across the mirror, like a spot in his eye, and disappeared.

What the—

He swerved to the left as the mirror imploded with an audible *chink.*

He pressed the pedal to the floor. The bouncing dot traced a fever line across the windshield. Toward his head.

He swerved sharply to the right. The second shot punctured the windshield.

He veered between lanes, around a bend, and sped over a pothole with a jarring crunch.

Concrete barriers lined the road, leaving little room to maneuver. He gripped the steering wheel as the white lights bore down on him.

Wind and dust in his eyes. Teeth gritted in terror.

The red dot reappeared in the windshield. He swung suddenly to the left and overcompensated to the right.

Holy—

The passenger-side mirror clipped the concrete, screeching sparks.

Ahead, from a sandbagged checkpoint, Israeli soldiers raised their weapons.

Covering him?

Aiming at him.

Jordan slammed the brakes and spun the steering wheel. With a squeal of rubber, the Alfa fishtailed, hurtling sideways toward the roadblock.

He opened his door and rolled out of the car, hitting the pavement with his left shoulderblade, rolling hard.

He felt the shockwave before he heard the sound. The concussion filled his ears. Fragments of glass and twisted metal tore through the air. Far away, it seemed, there were shouting voices, and a roar of flames.

He looked toward the checkpoint. A short distance from it, mashed against the concrete, the convertible was a mangled, burning hulk.

The soldiers had unloaded on the Alfa.

He could tell from the spreading stains that he was bleeding, but he felt no pain. Soldiers were running toward him.

He looked back at the road from Ramallah, looking for the vehicle that had chased him.

Chapter 10

Tel Aviv

On television, there were pictures of the mangled convertible, soldiers diverting traffic, investigators studiously inspecting the scene. The news cut back to the anchor.

"The same journalist who survived a recent brush with death in Lebanon—the same reporter who brought us that interview with the notorious Khalid Farouk—nearly plowed into a military roadblock tonight outside Ramallah. Benjamin Jordan dove from his car as soldiers opened fire with rifles and a rocket-propelled grenade." Jordan's picture flashed on the screen. "Was it all a bizarre accident? The authorities won't say whether they'll bring charges against Jordan, and the reporter's whereabouts are unknown. He disappeared from the Jerusalem hospital where he was treated for minor injuries."

The video cut to a talking head, a man identified as a captain in the IDF.

"We found no trace of explosives in the car, no indication that Jordan was intoxicated. And no evidence to support his contention that he was chased by would-be assassins."

In the obscurity of a hotel room, registered under a fake name, Jordan clicked off the television. The chase car had vanished, and the newscast made him sound like a nut.

Was it a random attack, or was it personal?

He mourned his Alfa.

He wanted to think of it as a coincidence. The West Bank could be a dangerous place. But what were the odds?

Cautiously, Jordan peered out the hotel window and closed the drapes.

Whatever its ambiguities, the attack sent him into hiding. But it didn't deter him. If anything, it deepened his determination to get to the bottom of the story.

Who had destroyed the Institute? And what had they hoped to accomplish?

His gut told him to gamble.

He was fortunate to have met several times with Ismail Ramsi's sponsor in Amman. In the past, they had discussed the on-again, off-again Mid-East peace negotiations, the rise of Islamic fundamentalism, and the war in Iraq. In each interview, the King of Jordan had gone off the record to impart his own take on events—and to part the curtain just enough to show Jordan how much he didn't know, how much the reporter could never know.

The King impressed the journalist as a man of courage. Of course, Jordan held no illusions: The ruler of the Hashemite Kingdom was a survivor, and that more than proved his agility in matters of principle and allegiance.

The King had given Jordan a number to call if he ever needed to speak directly. For the first time, Jordan used it. The King's valet promised to get back to Jordan within the hour.

In the meantime, Jordan checked his email. His Blackberry was cracked, but it still worked. He spotted a message from "A Reader in Lebanon" and clicked.

> Once again, I'd say someone was forging our signature for his own devious ends. As I told you, I take credit for my work. Trust me when I say it wasn't us.

Jordan turned pale. He closed Farouk's message. The next arrival in his mailbox was captioned "A Prayer for Benjamin." Flattered, Jordan opened it.

> *Yitgadal veyitkadash shemei raba* . . . .

It was the Mourner's Kaddish, the Jewish prayer for the dead, sent from a random address at yahoo.com. At the bottom, a warning:

> Be careful where you dig. The grave could be your own.

Jordan felt a touch of light-headedness. The shrapnel wound in his buttock began to throb. He downed a couple of aspirins and chased them with an antibiotic. The doctor in the emergency room had provided serious painkillers, too, but Jordan favored the advice of his Arab physician: Best to keep his wits.

He paced the room. It beat sitting down.

Was the email a serious threat, or merely a crank?

He went into the bathroom and splashed cold water on his face. Standing in front of the mirror, he saw Khalid Farouk staring back at him. If their places had been reversed, would he have become Farouk? Would his face be etched with the same hardships, his heart poisoned with the same venom?

He noticed the crows' feet at the corners of his eyes, and a few gray whiskers in his otherwise dark stubble. In his mind, he was still young, but his youth was vanishing. Every year, on his birthday, he tried to run a

10K as fast as he did in his commando days. A few weeks ago, he had hit the mark again—but only with a grueling final kick.

Jordan wondered: If he died today, would anyone say Kaddish for him? A disturbing sense of vulnerability and isolation crept over him. Being an orphan had instilled self-reliance and independence of spirit. But long before he was wise enough to understand the many ways it shaped him, he understood the feeling of being disconnected. He remembered an afternoon when he was no more than five or six, a holiday when school let out and the other boys and girls ran from the classroom to hug their waiting mothers and fathers. No one was waiting for him.

There was a time when he knew so little of his parents that he felt he had been set afloat in a basket, or given up for adoption. He had only the vaguest memory of a family, a melody his mother sang to comfort him. There wasn't even a grave for him to visit.

As a child, he wondered what tragic circumstances had driven his parents to give him up, or why he was so unwanted. He was nine when he went in search of answers. The adults of the kibbutz tried to comfort him, but they gave only empty reassurances.

He turned at last to one of the elders of the kibbutz, a man whose grim demeanor made him unapproachable to some of the adults, never mind to a young child. Avram Bromberg had emigrated from Chicago in his youth to help create the Jewish state. He was a hero in battle and in the malarial swamps of the Northern Galilee, where he had helped carve out a thriving agricultural community. The children of the kibbutz were raised on stories of his pioneering spirit. Avram walked with an air of sadness and determination, as if he worried that the rock he had taken such pains to push up the hill was destined to come crashing back down.

He had looked at Benjamin with warmth and kindness that made the boy wonder, *Is this what it's like to have a father?*

"Your family is the kibbutz," Avram had said. "You should never doubt that. As for what came before, the past is eternal. Six million of our people perished in the Shoah. But some lived to build this kibbutz. The Jewish people survives."

And that's probably where the old man would have left it, but Avram must have seen the deepening sadness in Benjamin's eyes. Seeming to go against his better judgment, Avram let the boy in on a secret.

"Your parents were patriots, Benjamin. They died risking their lives for a cause they believed in, for you and future generations."

His eyes widened with excitement. At last he had something to hold onto, a source of pride and inspiration. He wanted to know more.

"There are battles fought in daylight, and battles fought in shadows. And some must stay in shadows," Avram had said.

Days later, Avram's wife Ellie pulled Benjamin aside and gave him a photograph. It was a snapshot of a young man and woman on a beach. The man was tall and muscular, the woman slender and beautiful. She had her arms around his neck, and he was leaning over to kiss her. A penciled inscription on the back said "June 1965, Haifa." Ellie told Benjamin he could keep the picture if he promised not to show it to anyone—and not to mention it to her husband.

It was a big burden for a little boy, but in time Jordan came to understand. He accepted that his parents were bound up in Israel's life and death struggle, killed on a mission that remained somehow unfinished. The secret was something to draw upon when other children could look to the sidelines and see their parents cheering, or consoling them in defeat.

But it also entered his dreams unbidden, a faceless enemy pulling the trigger, taking them away.

Jordan looked out at the lights of Tel Aviv and the black, endless sea. It was 3:43 a.m., almost seven hours since he left Ramallah. He thought of the laser gunsight and the bullet in the rear view mirror, inches from his head.

Others might call it fate, destiny, the hand of God. Jordan shuddered at life's randomness.

The phone rang, twice, jangling his nerves.

"Your friend regrets that he cannot speak with you personally," the King's valet said. "But he suggests it might be fruitful for you to visit with one of his associates."

Jordan scribbled the instructions.

Chapter 11

He caught the first flight the next day to Eilat, at Israel's southern tip, and hailed a taxi at the airport. He watched closely to see if he was being followed but noticed nothing unusual. As the car merged with the traffic, he wondered if he was being paranoid. The relief more than compensated for the embarrassment.

Settling into the backseat, Jordan relaxed enough to appreciate the scenery. Beneath a pale, clear sky, the Red Sea beckoned, deep and blue. Rose-hued mountains ringed the coast, as arid and desolate as the desert beyond. And in between, there was Eilat, an oasis of white hotels and unshaded shoreline.

Jordan remembered Mishka, Rabbi Elazar's young wife. Mishka, bobbing happily in the surf in a picture taken long ago. Mishka, who loved Eilat.

Maybe she loved the yachts and the powerboats and the bright white sails, in the age before jet skis.

Maybe she loved to swim with the dolphins and dive the coral reef.

Or maybe she was drawn by the carefree spirit of the place. The mountain ridges provided more than a dramatic backdrop: They formed a psychological enclosure.

They also bound Israel to an Arab neighbor. To the east, the Jordanian port of Akkaba straddled the same waters. Only the name was different. What Israel called the Gulf of Eilat, Jordanians knew to be the Gulf of Akkaba.

Though his directions ended at the water's edge, Jordan guessed Akkaba was his ultimate destination.

He told the driver to stop at the boardwalk and ducked into a souvenir shop. He picked out a pair of sunglasses and an American-style baseball cap emblazoned with "Eilat." It was protection from a blistering sun—and, incidentally, a bit of tourist camouflage. He walked the rest of the way to the marina, limping slightly from his injury.

He had expected a speedboat, or a modest cabin cruiser, but the Queen of Sheba was a full-fledged yacht with a gleaming white hull and smoked black windows. The skipper, a thickset man wearing white clothes and impenetrable shades, met him at the dock.

"Where are the others?" the skipper asked.

"They took a glass-bottomed boat," Jordan replied, as he had been instructed. "To see the fish."

In the water below, beneath a film of motor oil, schools of tropical fish hovered and darted.

Jordan walked up the plank. The skipper led him aboard. On the foredeck, three women in bikinis lay face down in the sun, their dark bodies slathered in suntan oil. Part of the cover, Jordan surmised. The skipper showed Jordan to an enclosed lounge and offered him a seat as the crew cast off.

They passed the first minutes of the trip in virtual silence. Something about the skipper's manner discouraged conversation.

Jordan looked out the windows toward Eilat, receding in the distance. He reflected on the fact that no one knew his whereabouts—except his hosts. Beneath him, he felt the vibration of the motors accelerate. They were heading south.

"I thought we were going to Akkaba," Jordan said.

"You were mistaken," the captain answered.

The door to the lower deck swung open and a muscular, dark-skinned man stepped into the cabin. He gestured toward the stairs.

"Down," he said.

Jordan looked to the skipper but learned nothing from his impassive expression. He did as he was told. At the bottom of the stairs, another big man pressed Jordan against a wall, painfully, and searched him for weapons. Finding none, he nodded an okay. They walked the length of a narrow carpeted passageway, toward a closed door at the bow. The second man knocked on the door.

"Come in, Benjamin," a voice called out heartily.

The door opened into a spacious stateroom.

Samir Salam greeted Jordan like a long-lost friend, though as far as Jordan could recall, they had met only twice. The first time was in East Jerusalem. When Jordan's interview with the King was over, the King had invited Jordan to accompany him to a mosque, and Samir had been part of the entourage. The last time, at the palace in Amman, Samir was wearing the uniform of a colonel in the Jordanian army. He had comported himself with military formality as he briefed the reporter on the state of the Syrian leader's domestic opposition. Now, Samir was dressed in tan linen pants and a yellow silk shirt, open at the neck. He looked at home amid the yacht's polished teak and off-white leather. His rigid bearing had given way to a relaxed, confident manner—part of the day's pose, Jordan guessed, or perhaps a reflection of the staff officer's elevated status.

Long known as a royal confidant, Samir had entered the inner circle in title as well as fact. On his 50th birthday, the King had named him chief of security. The word among Middle Eastern diplomats was that, increasingly, the King was entrusting Samir with sensitive political missions—tasks that stretched his job description.

Like the one at hand.

"Benjamin, how good to see you," Samir said, kissing each cheek. "How are you feeling?"

"I'd feel much better if I knew what was going on."

"Maybe, and maybe not."

The Jordanian used English, meeting the Israeli on common ground. His accent bespoke years in an exchange program at Sandhurst, the British military academy. It was the sort of accent that could ease a Westerner's suspicion of Arabs, breaking through the cultural bias.

"Please, be comfortable," Samir said, pointing to a pair of sleek leather chairs. As Jordan sat, Samir set out a plate of hummos and pita and a bowl of figs. Through a porthole, sunlight glinted off the water.

"Someone took a shot at me last night as I was leaving Ramallah," Jordan said.

Samir dipped into the hummos.

"It wouldn't surprise me. But we have no hard information on that."

"Who?"

"The more important question is why."

"You have my undivided attention."

"It would seem someone wants you to desist from your reporting."

"But why?"

Samir looked at him gravely.

"You really have no idea?"

"Suppose I did. What could you confirm?"

"For the record, nothing."

"Confidentially?"

"My friend, you must understand. These matters are difficult to discuss."

"I appreciate the difficulty, Samir. But I'm sure we can agree: You didn't go to all this trouble for the pleasure of my company."

Samir's eyes smiled.

"If you use anything I say, Benjamin, you must protect us. You cannot reveal your source."

"Agreed."

"Then tell me, Benjamin, what do you know about the Copper Scroll?"

Jordan thought for a moment. "It's a famous artifact," he said. "One of the ancient scrolls found in caves near the Dead Sea, some time in the 1940s."

"Nineteen-fifty-two, to be precise. A truly extraordinary relic. Alone among the Dead Sea Scrolls, this one was etched in copper. As if the author was determined to ensure its survival."

"With good reason, as I recall."

"Yes, for a very unusual reason. The other scrolls addressed biblical and religious themes. This one dealt with something tangible. It was an inventory of treasure on a staggering scale—gold bars, silver coins, precious religious relics. All hidden.

"Amazingly, the so-called experts dismissed it at first. A fantasy, a fable, the product of some scribe's fevered imagination, they said. But the so-called experts' account sinks under the weight of its absurdity. After all, what could possess someone to invent such a thing?

"The truth was, by the time it was translated, the Copper Scroll threatened to discredit years of scholarly research. The professors who controlled the Dead Sea texts had long since decided they were left by a community of ascetic monks known as the Essenes, Jews so pious they denounced the decadence and materialism of Jerusalem. In other words, you see, not quite the sort who hoard gold."

Jordan pondered.

"Maybe your pious religious sect was hoarding gold secretly," he said. "After all, some modern-day cults amass fortunes. They persuade their converts to sign over their bank accounts, their inheritances —"

"True, quite true. And for centuries, the churches and monasteries of Europe got rich by holding their priests to a vow of celibacy. Fewer heirs meant more for the Church. Unfortunately, that won't solve our puzzle. For one thing, the quantities involved in the Copper Scroll are too immense—wildly out of proportion to the size of the Essene community. For another, unlike the Church of Rome, this community on the edge of the Dead Sea was thoroughly nonmaterialistic. Their writings—and those of others—make that clear."

Jordan was forming an answer, but Samir cut him off with a wry smile.

"I know what you are thinking, my friend, but as best we can tell, the Essenes of Qumran had no limousine leaders, no Rolls Royce rabbis indulging at their followers' expense. No, Benjamin, I believe in a simpler explanation."

The Jordanian lowered his voice and leaned toward his guest.

"I believe that these were the treasures of the Jerusalem Temple, spirited out before the city fell to the Romans in 70 A.D."

Jordan felt the boat rock beneath him.

"There are less glamorous theories, but none as plausible," Samir said. "The evidence is right there in the text, inscribed in the copper. The catalogue of treasures includes 'offering vessels,' which would have been used in ceremonial rites or in payment of the Temple tax; 'guilt offerings,' which were given in atonement for sins; and 'sacred tithes.' There is even a reference to precious vests of the type worn by the high priests. But the scholars who once controlled the Copper Scroll didn't want people to focus on any of these facts. They didn't want people to dig."

"The scroll described the hiding places, didn't it?"

"It listed 64 caches of hidden treasure and identified each location by a cryptic clue—a natural landmark, a historical reference, or something man-made, such as 'the salt pit under the steps' or 'the rock pile beside the river crossing.'"

"And they've never been found?"

"Deciphering the clues is difficult enough. In all but a few cases, linking them to something recognizable today is hopeless guesswork. For decades, archaeologists and fortune-seekers have searched in vain. The King's father sponsored an expedition in '59 and '60—and was embarrassed to see it fail completely. The scholarly consensus is, if the treasure ever existed, the Romans found it. And the limited historical record tends to support that view."

Samir pulled out a bookmarked copy of *The Wars of the Jews,* the eyewitness account of the 1st Century historian Flavius Josephus.

"Josephus writes that when the city fell, the Romans possessed such vast quantities of plunder that in Syria gold sold for half its former price. What's more, when the conquering hero Titus returned to Rome, his triumphal parade displayed golden 'ornaments of the Temple'—trophies of war, lifted high for all to see."

Samir flipped to another page.

"What's especially interesting is that some of the Jewish priests turned over sacred objects to save their necks. 'The son of Thebuthus, whose name was Jesus'—a different Jesus—gave up the golden candlesticks, and the treasurer of the Temple, whose name was Phineas, surrendered the purple and scarlet garments of the priests, along with 'many other treasures.'

"The Romans were adept at eliciting secrets, and the custodians of those secrets were only human. So you see, Benjamin, it seemed sensible to assume that the treasures of the Copper Scroll didn't stay hidden for long. Indeed, that was probably the most logical conclusion." Samir closed the book. "Until now."

Jordan was stunned. "You mean they found the treasure? Elazar and his Council actually found the treasure?"

Samir laughed. "Not quite."

"What, then?"

"Imagine, if you will, that the riches recovered by the Romans were merely a portion of the whole—a token to sate their appetite, or throw them off the trail."

"I'm not following you."

"In the days before the blast, Benjamin, the International Council on Cultural Antiquities discovered a second scroll. It was a silver scroll. And it superseded the first. Mind you, we haven't seen it. But the King received first-hand reports. According to our intelligence, the scroll explained that, in the days following the siege, Romans tortured captured Zealots into revealing some of the original hiding places. In a panic, members of the Jewish resistance dug up much of the hidden treasure and reburied it elsewhere, presumably keeping it from the Romans. The Silver Scroll described 24 *new* hiding places and their contents. At the very least, it helps explain why the Copper Scroll has led us nowhere."

Jordan was speechless.

"I didn't realize the Council had any active digs," he said.

"We know for a fact they had been excavating in the Negev south of Sede Barak. There's no reason to believe they were looking for the scroll—one assumes they simply stumbled upon it. And the Council was coming apart at the seams over the discovery."

"So Ramsi made it to Amman," Jordan whispered.

"Excuse me?" Samir said, taken aback.

"The source of your intelligence. Ismail Ramsi."

Samir's astonishment showed. "That was confidential."

"Where is he now?"

The Jordanian paused. "As best we can tell, he was taken by the Israelis. Soldiers were seen pulling him from his car near a roadblock in the West Bank. I can't tell you how, Benjamin, but we have been given to understand that Ismail Ramsi died in Israeli custody."

"Why would they kill him?"

"Maybe it's the thought of Muslims and Christians putting their hands on the Jewish patrimony. Or maybe someone within the government just wants it all. From what Ramsi told us, the finger of suspicion points first to Meyer Elazar—and, by extension, his powerful allies."

Jordan wasn't buying it.

"Are there witnesses to the arrest?"

"I doubt they'd speak to you, considering the danger."

"Try."

Samir looked noncommittal.

"And the attack on me?" Jordan asked. "It took place in the West Bank. It damn near took out some soldiers in the process."

"What better way to deflect suspicion?"

"You think the *Israelis* did it?"

"Do you have a more logical explanation?"

"What about the Catholic, Altieri?"

Samir nodded, pensively.

"He's dead, Benjamin. An apparent suicide. One bullet to the temporal lobe."

Jordan grimaced. "When?"

"Before the bombing. As a courtesy to the Vatican, the Israelis have refrained from disclosing it."

"I don't understand."

"The Israelis claimed to have turned up some particularly unpleasant evidence at the priest's flat, where the body was found. Photos of children, if you know what I mean." Samir shook his head in disgust. "I find it hard to believe."

"Why are you telling me this?"

"The King holds you in highest esteem, Benjamin. He trusts you. And he thinks you should know what you're up against."

"That's very gracious of the King. But really, Samir, why are you telling me this?"

Samir frowned. "Ever the cynic, aren't you?"

"It's my only virtue."

Samir rose from his chair.

"Men like Meyer Elazar are the single greatest obstacle to peace in our time," the Jordanian said, flush with anger. "It's an affront to God that they control the balance of power in Israel. We think people should see them for what they are."

"Even at the risk of inflaming the situation?"

"It's a calculated risk."

Chapter 12

Jordan found a pay phone near the marina and dialed Meltzer. Turning his back to the vacationers strolling along the boardwalk, he summarized the loose strands of his reporting, beginning with the excavation in the desert and ending with the dead priest.

The editor was arbitrarily insistent: Jordan had two days to pull it all together.

"Two days?" Jordan protested.

"You don't want to get beaten, do you?" Meltzer asked.

"At this point, I'm not sure what the story would say."

"How about *Plot to Conceal Sensitive Archaeological Discovery; Trail of Death Points to Elazar*?"

"There's no confirmation yet for any of that."

"That's why I'm giving you two days. But if you don't think you can nail it down, I'm sure a few of your colleagues would be happy to team up with you, or take it from here."

And put their bylines on my exclusive?

"Let's see where we are the day after tomorrow," Jordan said.

"Fine. But if you don't deliver, I'm deploying additional forces."

Meltzer hung up.

Jordan gazed across the Red Sea at the coast of Akkaba.

There was no way he was going to share the story. And there was no way he was going to fumble it. If all the pieces fell into place, he would emerge wreathed in professional glory—and rid of Shaul Meltzer.

At least Meltzer believed in the story.

Holed up in an Eilat hotel, Jordan worked the phones through the following day and night. He tried the wives of the Council members killed in the bombing. Most were completely in the dark. Finally, the mistress of the French representative provided corroboration: There had been a discovery at the Institute, a hint of buried treasure. But that was all she knew. It was a boast, whispered in the night, and Guillaume had sworn her to secrecy.

By email, Jordan received the names of two Palestinians and the address of a West Bank pharmacy, their place of employment. Jordan guessed the anonymous message was from Samir and these were the witnesses to Ramsi's arrest. He placed several calls to Ramsi's widow to see what she had heard, but no one answered.

A police inspector Jordan knew from an earlier story was able to shed some light on the Altieri matter. The investigators initially theorized that the priest's death was somehow related to the sordid pictures found in a drawer by his bed. Then they noticed something odd about the photographs: None of them bore any fingerprints.

Strictly off the record, the papal nuncio in Jerusalem confirmed the death of Monsignor Altieri, the Vatican's man on the Council, and the fact that the Israelis had declared it a suicide. But he vehemently denied that Altieri was a pedophile.

"Why won't you go on record?" Jordan asked.

"Who would believe me?"

The excavation that turned up the silver scroll was harder to penetrate. Two of the Institute's senior archaeologists died in the bombing, and a third was in critical condition. One member of the research staff didn't return calls, and another proved impossible to locate. Several lower-level staffers pleaded ignorance.

As the sun rose over the seaside resort, Jordan eased himself into the driver's seat of a rented car and headed north, past the red sandstone pillars of Timna, into the open desert, toward the dig Samir had talked about. His discomfort kept him from daydreaming as the kilometers blurred past. Bleached and lifeless and vast, the Negev conjured a vision of the apocalypse, or a time before creation.

Hours passed. From the floor of the great geological depression Makhtesh Ramon, a crater as wide and deep as an inland sea, the ascending road traversed a cliff to the wind-whipped outpost Mizpe Ramon, a town perched on the edge. Even there, in the heart of Israel, as far as you could get from hostile borders, the barbed wire bespoke fear and anxiety. And then the town was behind him, and the road went on.

The solitude was complete, the desolation unnerving. He drove on, in an emotional twilight. Stone monoliths rose from the plain, objects of primitive worship. Distant foothills, eerily eroded, faded into mountains of limestone, clay and flint. Against the horizon, notched peaks tore at the faintest of clouds.

Along the side of the road, a grassy tangle engulfed a cactus, sapping its precious juice.

It was late afternoon when Jordan arrived at the kibbutz Sede Barak, the outpost closest to the excavation. He found his way to a cluster of cube-shaped houses. His eyes were drawn to telephone wires strung against a vacant sky. The poles leaned at odd angles, and the lines seemed to connect the place by a slender thread.

Residents of the kibbutz knew how the dig began, but little else. The president of the kibbutz took Jordan to the spot, a bumpy ten-minute drive from the communal dining room. Shielding his eyes from the setting sun, the slightly built scientist pointed as he explained.

"The army started it all. They use the wilderness for training exercises, including live mortar fire. When they pulled out, some of the kids from the kibbutz moved in, staging a different kind of war game."

Jordan scribbled while the kibbutznik talked. At the bottom of an artillery crater, just over the crest of a low hill, one would-be warrior had found a protrusion of stone, newly exposed. It was a cluster of acanthus leaves, carved in marble, peeking through untold centuries of sand. The children dug farther, revealing the capitol of a Corinthian column. Beneath that, part of the marble shaft, seemingly intact and vertical.

The find was entirely unexpected. Whatever lay buried in the hill had been lost to memory. And columns didn't stand in isolation; there had to be more. The Institute dispatched a team.

As the exploratory work proceeded, the archaeologists were uncharacteristically reluctant to discuss the results.

"They could have hired some of our people to assist," the kibbutznik said. "Instead, they shut us out."

By now, much of the hilltop was shrouded in black tarpaulins. But the dig was dormant. The crew had withdrawn before the bombing of the Institute.

Jordan trudged to the top of the hill. The loose ground shifted beneath his feet. The kibbutznik watched without commenting as Jordan removed a few of the rocks that held down a tarp. A hot breeze filled the plastic sheet, and it flapped noisily.

Jordan peered into the dig.

He saw the tops of three marble columns, excavated to a depth of just over a meter. The tallest featured a magnificent Corinthian capitol. The others had been decapitated—whether by war or natural forces, Jordan could only guess. The entire excavation was about five meters long and about a meter and a half wide. To his untrained eye, it was not especially revealing.

Jordan replaced the stones and walked to another patch of tarps lower on the slope. The kibbutznik helped him remove the covering. This second trench was cut into the hillside perpendicular to the first. Jordan recognized that it was merely meant to test the site, the archaeological equivalent of a biopsy. The archaeologists were probably trying to find out if the hill concealed a layered record of human habitation—whether one set of ruins was buried beneath another and another going back through the ages.

Jordan felt the vicarious thrill of discovery. The shallow exploratory cut appeared to have hit pay dirt. The trench exposed a series of three rough walls or foundations.

Plus whatever else the archaeologists had taken away.

Standing on the desert hillside, Jordan felt a powerful connection with the distant past—with the faceless individual who walked there ages ago and left a silver engraving, never imagining how it would resurface.

In a text message, Meltzer ordered Jordan to come back and write what he knew, but Jordan wasn't finished. He accepted an invitation to supper at the kibbutz and interviewed residents late into the evening, adding little to his knowledge. He slept a few hours in a Spartan guest room. Then he drove through the dawn.

He arrived at the West Bank pharmacy before it opened, hoping to find the witnesses to Ramsi's arrest. He peered through the window. A skinny teen with a wisp of a beard was unpacking bottles of shampoo and stacking them on dusty shelves. Jordan rapped on the glass, and the boy unlocked the door.

Jordan followed him into the store.

"Are you Mohamed Abboudi?" he asked.

The boy looked at him warily. Jordan introduced himself and offered his hand. The boy's suspicion seemed to ease, as if he had been expecting Jordan.

"Mohamed's my brother," he said, hesitantly. "But I saw it, too."

The boy's name was Hamdi. His voice gathered speed as he described Ramsi arguing with the Israeli soldiers at the roadblock, insisting on his rights, demanding to know what they wanted with him. The boy didn't actually hear the words, but he could read the body language. He saw a soldier punch Ramsi in the gut before they dragged him to a waiting vehicle and shoved him in the back.

Jordan could feel the boy's anger, the sense of powerlessness.

"How can you be sure it was Ismail Ramsi?" Jordan asked.

The boy looked over Jordan's shoulder at his brother, newly arrived.

"It was Dr. Ramsi," the elder brother said bluntly.

"Couldn't you be mistaken?"

"He's a regular customer," Mohamed said. "He comes in to pick up his prescription. And, last time, medicine for his baby."

"May I see his records?" Jordan asked.

Mohamed looked at Hamdi, and nodded.

A dog-eared file showed that Ismail Ramsi suffered from hypertension.

"You'll stand behind what you've told me?" Jordan asked.

"Yes," Mohamed said.

"Yes," his brother echoed. "All the way."

Chapter 13

Tel Aviv

Jordan's sudden reappearance sent a buzz through the Tel Aviv newsroom. What could he be working on, colleagues wondered, as he made a final round of calls.

Eventually, Jordan tracked down an archaeologist in Cairo, an authority on the Nabataean people whose trade route traversed the Negev in the late 1st Century. Yes, he had been consulted. He even visited the site. No, if any engravings turned up, no one bothered to tell him.

The archaeologist gave Jordan the names of his contacts at the Institute. Both appeared on the list of bomb casualties.

The reporter's net yielded one last detail: A member of the Knesset remembered a passing conversation with the Minister of Culture the Friday before the blast. The Minister had been expecting a visit from Rabbi Elazar—just as his secretary Miriam had said.

The Minister himself wouldn't speak to Jordan, and official spokesmen for several government departments were scrupulously unenlightening. It would be improper to comment as long as the bombing remained under investigation, they said.

Asked about the arrest of Ismail Ramsi, the government gave Jordan a single sentence: "We have no such prisoner." Jordan pointed out that the denial was couched in the present tense, but officials refused to elaborate.

Inside Meltzer's glass office, Jordan outlined his findings.

"It's all circumstantial, but however you look at it, it's a deeply disturbing picture," Jordan said. "There's no way the conspiracy ends with Meyer Elazar. He would have needed extensive and sophisticated support."

"It's the opening curtain, not the last word," Meltzer said. "We'll publish what we know, before anybody else can take credit for breaking the story."

"With luck, our report will shake loose more information," Jordan said.

"Right. So what are you waiting for?"

The story filled Jordan's computer screen in staccato bursts of keyboard-clacking.

> Before a bomb destroyed the Institute for Cultural Antiquities last week, killing members of its governing council, officials at the Institute had

unearthed and fought over a relic that appeared to describe the locations of an ancient hidden treasure.

By one account, the scroll, etched in silver, pointed the way to ceremonial objects and vast quantities of silver and gold buried during the 1st Century.

The chairman of the Institute's governing council, Meyer Elazar, had been trying to keep the discovery a tightly held secret, according to sources close to the council.

One colleague who clashed with Elazar disappeared into Israeli custody at a West Bank roadblock the day before the blast, according to witnesses in Ramallah.

Another council member who argued for public disclosure died of a gunshot wound to the head in an incident the Israeli government has yet to disclose. Privately, Israeli authorities have told the Vatican that its representative to the international council, Monsignor Nicolo Altieri, appears to have committed suicide shortly before the blast. Altieri's body was found in his flat with a trove of child pornography, leading the authorities to suggest he was driven to suicide by a troubled conscience or fear of exposure.

But a source involved in the inquest said police have found a problem with the official explanation: The photos bore no fingerprints.

When the bomb went off, members of the council were assembled at the museum for a meeting Elazar scheduled just two days earlier. It has been generally assumed that Elazar died with his colleagues in the museum boardroom. But Elazar's remains have not been recovered.

Elazar's longtime secretary Miriam Wiesman said she last saw the Orthodox rabbi and former Knesset member the Friday before the explosion, when he directed her to notify council members about the Sunday meeting. As he issued those instructions, Elazar was rushing to see the Minister of Culture, Wiesman said. The ministry declined to comment.

The scroll was unearthed at an excavation in the Negev a short distance from the Sede Barak kibbutz. Today, the site lies dormant, the archaeologists' trenches covered with tarps.

The Israeli government has blamed the museum bombing on the Palestinian terrorist Khalid Farouk, and the IDF has retaliated by striking a compound in Lebanon. In a recent interview, Farouk, who has claimed responsibility for 12 other deadly attacks over the past four years, denied that he had anything to do with the bombing of the museum.

However, Farouk would have good reason to disavow this latest bombing: The casualties included a group of Palestinian children visiting the museum on an elementary school field trip.

Speaking on condition of anonymity, a foreign intelligence source said the government of Jordan suspects the deaths of the council members were part of an Israeli plot to control the treasure . . . .

When Jordan finished typing, he pushed back from his desk. He felt the icy rush that came from handling high explosives, or lighting a fuse and waiting for the result. Then the ice melted in a flare of anger at the cruel injustice of the plot.

It was an important story. And it was Jordan's exclusive. For once in his life, he savored his achievement.

Constrained by time, he had relied heavily on his main source, the Jordanian Samir Salam. But he had also exercised restraint. He left out the evidence that Elazar phoned the boardroom moments before the blast, because that could not be verified. And he decided not to link the treasure to the Jerusalem Temple. That sensational information was also unconfirmed.

Jordan would persist, and he was confident that ultimately the full truth would emerge.

As the layout editors were putting the finishing touches on the first edition and the headline writers were getting to work, Shaul Meltzer sauntered over to Jordan's desk and offered a conspicuous handshake. "Well done, Ben," Meltzer said, loud enough for several staffers to hear. "I knew I picked the right man for the assignment."

Assignment? I brought you *the story, jackass.*

Still, Jordan accepted the compliment. He watched as Meltzer sauntered back to his office, no doubt planning a promotional blitz for the following day.

Jordan rummaged for a number and dialed the phone. There was still no answer at the Ramsi residence. He looked at his watch—6:10 p.m.—and thought about going to check it out. He wanted to tell Raya personally, before she read the news.

"About that dinner," Leah said, resting a hand on his shoulder. "You promised."

Jordan spun in his desk chair.

"You've met your deadline," she added, with a subversive grin. "And I'd say you're entitled to celebrate."

Jordan looked at the phone, wavering. He could always try again later.

They dined under a pair of spreading eucalyptus trees, in a quiet Jerusalem courtyard. The shrimp bouillabaise was exquisite, the salmon pesto rich and aromatic, but Jordan and Leah had the restaurant to themselves. On the edge of the Orthodox neighborhood of Mea Shearim, the stylish new bistro committed the twin sins of staying open on Shabbat and refusing to keep kosher. Weekly pickets by the neighbors and the constant threat of bombings kept the crowds away.

Leah chose the place. She was rekindling something combustible, and he was finally catching on. Stripped of all diversions, Jordan took refuge in superficial conversation. It was something he never mastered.

"How's Mozie?" he asked, referring to the mutt they had rescued together from the pound.

"He's adjusting," Leah said. "He and the cat seem to have reached a mutual understanding."

He watched Leah smile through her merlot, then tease a long strand of linguine from her fork. He tasted the pink fish she offered on a spoon. After all this time, she was as alluring as ever.

She reached across the table and touched his hand.

"Mozie misses you, Ben," she said.

Leah ordered the tiramisu, but Jordan passed on desert.

She was achingly sensual. She wanted him almost as much as he wanted her. He remembered the hunger, the raw energy of desire unleashed. The whisper of a sigh and the cries of ecstasy. The bite of her fingernails.

Outside her apartment, he kissed her, pressing his hands against the small of her back. She pushed back.

She opened the door and took his hand, and he followed her in.

Chapter 14

When Jordan strode into the newsroom the next morning, colleagues huddled around his desk, slapped him on the back, pumped him for the inside dope—eager for details and opinions that didn't make it into print, tidbits they could use to impress their friends. Though they professed political neutrality, most were thrilled to see the likes of Meyer Elazar in the crosshairs.

Jordan imbibed the moment. Usually oblivious to his image, he was wearing a blazer, ready for the television cameras. His exclusive was at the top of the front page and spreading across the Web.

Inside his glass office, Meltzer was leaning back in his chair, talking on the phone, flipping news channels with a remote control. He flashed Jordan a thumbs up. Meltzer was also unusually well dressed.

Jordan's phone kept ringing, but he let voice mail take care of it. Readers would be calling by now—tipsters and cheerleaders and armchair critics, not to mention conspiracy buffs eager to offer their own convoluted theories. He would make time for them later.

In a corner of the newsroom, Jordan's photo flitted across a television screen. The morning newscasts were jumping on the story. Instant validation. Jordan joined a huddle to watch it unfold. The picture cut to the Ministry of Culture, where a government spokesman was briefing reporters.

"The Minister categorically denies having received any information about the reported dig in the Negev. It simply was not discussed when he met with Rabbi Elazar." The spokesman looked up from his prepared statement, wagging his index finger for emphasis. "Any implication to the contrary is false and irresponsible."

Jordan watched with a serious but unflinching expression. The strength of the denial was a little unsettling, but it was only natural that the government would fight back. No one expected confessions. And no one was disputing that the meeting took place.

The broadcast moved to a hospital outside Amman, where a Jordanian medical examiner was holding an impromptu news conference.

"I can confirm that Professor Ismail Ramsi's body was found two days ago in an automobile in a ravine not far from here. There was some delay in making the identification. His death was judged to be the result of an accident. The autopsy showed that Professor Ramsi was driving with a dangerously high level of alcohol in his system. He expired from massive head injuries sustained when his face struck the windshield."

A reporter shouted a question that the microphone didn't pick up.

"No," the medical examiner answered. "There was no indication of any injury or abuse unrelated to the crash."

Jordan's colleagues were watching him now, gauging his reaction. Jordan's expression was unchanged, his eyes focused steadily on the television.

The anchorman introduced a tape of Samir Salam, a top aide to the King of Jordan, who had spoken to journalists in Amman moments earlier. Instinctively protecting his source, Jordan suppressed any flicker of recognition.

"His royal highness the King would like it known that he does not, repeat, does not, accuse the Israeli government," Salam said in an even voice. "In the present political climate, none of us should be surprised by unfounded rumors and speculation." The reporters shouted follow-up questions, which Salam ignored.

Though he didn't show it, Jordan was beginning to feel queasy.

Someone changed the channel. A correspondent was conducting an interview, and the caption identified the interviewee as Yoram Kishon, a staff archaeologist at the International Institute.

"So you personally participated in the excavation in the Negev?" the reporter asked.

"Yes. I was there the whole time," Kishon said. "I catalogued every object we removed from the ground. My job was to organize the records—photographs, sketches, schematic diagrams noting the location where each artifact was found."

"What can you tell us about the so-called 'Silver Scroll?'"

"Nothing. There's nothing to tell."

"You mean they kept the secret from you?"

"No, I mean there's no such thing. It doesn't exist."

"How can you be sure?"

"If our team unearthed it, I would have known about it. I was at the Institute when they delivered the progress reports."

"Couldn't they have concealed it?"

Kishon's body language said it was a stupid question.

"It's hard to imagine how, or even why. Think about it. Something like that would have required extensive analysis. Delicate cleaning, chemical treatment, maybe translation. You could hardly interpret it on the spot. The moment it came out of the ground, no one would have had any reason to deviate from the routine."

Jordan swallowed heavily. *Yoram Kishon? Where the hell did they find him?*

"I kept a set of records," Kishon said. "I would be happy to show you."

The staff of *The Shofar* watched in awkward silence. Jordan could feel their discomfort, as if he had developed a sudden contagion. He guessed that some who congratulated him minutes ago were privately enjoying this.

Live, on Channel 6, the Prime Minister stepped out of his office, into a crush of cameras. He was seething, or pretended to be.

"The report in today's *Shofar* is a cowardly and scurrilous attack on the State of Israel by those who would give comfort to its enemies," the head of government declared. "It is a fabrication grounded in fiction. With the discovery of Professor Ramsi's car wreck near the Jordanian capital, it should be tragically obvious to everyone that Israel never arrested the professor.

"Coming from a stuntman like Mr. Jordan, it's no surprise. But I, for one, expect a higher standard of journalism from *The Shofar* and its editor, Shaul Meltzer."

Jordan's chest constricted, his mouth went dry.

"Jordan!"

It was Meltzer, working himself into a tremulous tirade.

Jordan crossed the newsroom with an unhurried stride, betraying no loss of confidence. Meltzer shut his office door behind them, so the gawkers outside could only guess at the rest. The editor was red in the face.

"I hope and pray you can explain this," Meltzer said. "Because if you think *I'm* going to bear a cross for *your* carelessness, you are badly mistaken."

"Can't you see? It's a cover-up," Jordan said.

"Then uncover it," Meltzer sputtered. "And do it in time for tomorrow's paper."

Had he screwed up? Was he set up? Was there a way out?

The desperate dialing began.

Samir Salam was "unavailable," as were Jordan's "reliable" sources in the Palestinian Authority and the King himself, who held Jordan in such high regard. The phone at the Ramsi residence went unanswered. He tried emailing Khalid Farouk, but he doubted the terrorist even checked the random accounts he had used in the past.

Though they pretended to be absorbed in other things, the writers who sat nearest to Jordan strained to hear what he was saying, transfixed by his plight.

Finally, a ray of hope: The mistress of the French representative confirmed her earlier account with unwavering clarity. Hidden treasure, that's what Guillaume had said. But to Jordan's chagrin, she refused to go on the record. Guillaume had left a grieving widow, and the mistress saw no point in exposing their affair.

Jordan got in the car and drove. The traffic at the checkpoints was agonizing, and he had to kill the air conditioning to avoid overheating the engine. July had intruded on October with a wilting vengeance.

When he reached the West Bank pharmacy, Mohamed was stocking toilet paper.

"What happened?" Jordan asked.

Mohamed avoided eye contact.

"It must have been a mistake," the brawny Palestinian said, putting another package on the shelf.

"A mistake?"

"Mistaken identification."

"But you were *sure,* Mohamed."

"It was hard to see."

Jordan felt the ground collapsing beneath him.

"Where's your brother?"

Mohamed looked up from his work, and Jordan could see fear in his eyes.

"Stay away from my brother," the boy said.

Back in the sauna of his rental car, with the heat set at full blast to bleed the engine, Jordan dialed more numbers. Surprisingly, Miriam Wiesman's phone rang endlessly. Jordan pictured the secretary alone in her home, withdrawing from the world.

He needed to talk to her.

By the time he got to her town house, there were police cars in the driveway, and an ambulance with flashing lights, and a satellite truck by the curb. He slammed his car door and ran toward the building.

At the front door, a police officer blocked Jordan, holding an arm against his chest. Someone inside was backing toward them, wheeling a stretcher. Jordan pressed to get through, but the cop restrained him. The stretcher rolled by on squeaky wheels.

It was carrying a body bag.

The next thing Jordan knew, there was a television camera in his face. "Tell us, Mr. Jordan, do you feel responsible?"

Jordan's body was numb, his mind uncomprehending. The question echoed from somewhere far away.

"Do you think your story drove Miriam Wiesman to suicide?" the T.V. reporter asked, with an accusatory thrust of the mike.

Jordan went back to the office, struggling to make sense of the secretary's death. He would write about it as honestly as he could. And he would squeeze whatever he could out of the medical examiner.

He ducked into the men's room.

Shaul Meltzer was standing over a sink—no, bracing himself against it. He looked up. His face, which had been flush with bombast earlier in the day, appeared drained and drawn. He spoke in an uncharacteristically quiet voice, a voice of resignation.

"I'm retracting the story," he said.

Jordan stared in disbelief.

"On what basis? You don't know that it's false."

"I know more than I wanted to. And I know that I can't defend you."

"What are you talking about?"

Meltzer reached for a paper towel.

"I should think that was obvious."

Jordan felt a stab of fear.

"Who's been spinning you?"

The editor mopped his forehead.

"Don't force the issue, Ben. If you have any instinct for self-preservation, I suggest you follow it."

"Damn it, Shaul, you're protecting the people who destroyed the Institute and murdered the Council."

"No, Ben, I'm protecting *you*."

"Bullshit," Jordan said, slamming his palm against the paper dispenser.

Meltzer looked at him.

"Aren't you listening? For your own sake, as well as mine, I'm telling you to drop it."

"Drop it? How can I drop it? My credibility is on the line."

Meltzer dried his hands and tossed the paper towel in the trash.

"You're screwed, Ben," he said, walking out. "We're both screwed."

In time for the evening news, Benjamin Jordan was suspended indefinitely. Meltzer issued a statement disowning the story and blaming the writer's "overzealousness." Jordan's efforts to salvage credibility had yielded nothing. On the airwaves, the right wing was unleashing a venomous assault. In their prosecution of Jordan, they brandished Meltzer's admission as Exhibit A.

"Take it from his editor: This reporter can't be trusted," a member of Elazar's political party declared. "Clearly, Benjamin Jordan is in bed with the Palestinians."

Refusing to accept defeat—or worse—Jordan tried Ramsi's widow one last time from his desk in the newsroom. With the phone ringing in his ear, he glanced at Meltzer's glass office, where the editor was pacing behind his desk and pausing every few seconds to dictate instructions. Leah was taking notes. The buzz was that Meltzer had assigned her to write "the real story," part of his effort at damage control.

A new email popped up in Jordan's mailbox, from an address similar to the one Khalid Farouk had used before. Jordan clicked to open it.

> You disappoint me, Benjamin. You not only failed, you made matters worse. My people must know that I had nothing to do with the bombing of the museum, that I did not murder those Palestinian children. I expect you to set this right.

Another new message, from the executive vice president at the network.

> Ben, regarding that meeting, we'll let you know when we're ready to reschedule. The boss wants to wait and see how things shake out.

Jordan signed off. Utterly demoralized, he waited for the elevator. He stepped inside without looking back and pressed the button twice. Someone stopped the door from closing.

"I'm sorry, Ben," Leah said, without getting in. "Shaul asked me to investigate the dig in the Negev. I tried to say no, but . . . . "

Jordan nodded and pushed the button.

For the first time since the incident at the checkpoint, Jordan returned to his apartment. If the threat remained, he was beyond caring.

The refrigerator was empty, save for some spoiled milk and a few shriveled oranges. He opened a bottle of cheap red wine and drained a glass before sinking into the couch.

Clearly, someone had twisted Meltzer's arm—wrenched it out of its socket. And scared him to his core.

Unless . . . .

What did Meltzer know? What had he been told?

Meltzer had buckled—that was all. Wasn't it? The editor was no closer to knowing the truth now than he had been the night before, when the presses started rolling. Maybe, in time, the facts would justify his retreat. Or maybe the facts would slip away under the politicians' covering fire, leaving only the fog.

Jordan cringed at the possibilities.

He stared at the telephone, hoping it would ring, hoping his Jordanian source would summon him to an interview, where everything would become clear.

Tell us, Mr. Jordan, do you feel responsible?

The question haunted him. Was it possible that his reporting on Meyer Elazar had pushed Miriam over the edge? Was it possible that his reporting was wrong? The image of the grieving secretary consumed him.

He thought of his parents, and he felt the weight of their legacy. Through their lives, they had given him a mission in life, and he felt himself faltering.

He thought of his readers, the people who had jammed his phone with messages when the day began, when the story was still true and he was too important to take their calls. He owed them an ex—

A window shattered in a violent crash, and the light in the apartment cut out. Fragments of broken glass sprayed across the room, and the tabletop lamp smashed to the floor. Jordan rolled off the couch and flattened himself against the rug, bracing for the next fusillade.

In the darkness, he held his breath and listened. Limited options raced through his brain—dash for the door, seek refuge deeper into the apartment, or stay down, below the line of fire.

But all that followed was the sound of the street, drifting through the broken window. Jordan lifted his head and looked around. A rock had landed beside the lamp.

Reader mail.

He plucked a sliver of glass from his hair and brushed himself off. He looked out the window, but whoever had hurled the missive had vanished in the night. Dazed, Jordan walked into the bedroom, tripping over a pair of stray shoes, bumping into an overflowing laundry basket. The answering machine on his night table was blinking. He lay down on the bed and stared at the pulsing red light.

He hit the play button.

"Mr. Jordan, it's Doctor Safran, at the hospital — "

Jordan hit "delete."

"Ben, it's Leah."

Delete again.

"Mr. Jordan, it's Miriam Wiesman."

Jordan sat up with a start.

"I'm sorry to bother you at — "

The voice was familiar, yet different. There was less anxiety, less underlying angst.

He hit "rewind" and listened to the time stamp. The call had come in two days earlier, at 4:16 in the afternoon.

"Mr. Jordan, it's Miriam Wiesman. I'm sorry to bother you at home, but they said you were out of the office. You know, I, I'm sorry you had to see me in such a pathetic state, when you visited. I must seem incredibly foolish, longing all these years after a frozen heart, mourning something that never was, pouring it all out for a total stranger—a reporter, of all people."

She sounded calm, centered, self-possessed. She didn't sound like a woman in danger of taking her own life, or someone with illusions waiting to be shattered.

"But I think I can face it now, face it and look forward. I'm not saying it's going to be easy, but . . . but I know you're not interested in all that. Anyway, the reason I called is, I hope you figure out what happened. And I remembered the name.

"You know, the name on the file that Meyer took from the office. I'm embarrassed that I couldn't remember it before. I think I must have blocked it out. If it's still of any use, the name was Cavanaugh. C-A-V-A-N-A-U-G-H.

"Good luck, Mr. Jordan. If there's anything else, you can always phone."

Part II

Chapter 15

Ann Arbor, Michigan

A cold drizzle coated the foliage, dampening the autumn hues. Catherine Cavanaugh trudged across the campus, deadened by the chill. For a moment, an oak leaf caught her eye—disconnected, fluttering, falling.

The young scholar carried four overstuffed shopping bags, two in each hand, and one of them was beginning to rip. She had packed them neatly, lovingly, holding nothing back. Alone in a silent house, she had risen early for the task. She wept as she folded the white cable sweater, the one her mother wore on winter nights. It reminded her of Northern Ireland's craggy coast. She smiled at the sight of a plain floral dress. Her mother bought it for commencement, the year Catherine received her doctorate.

Two weeks had passed since her mother slipped away, losing the struggle they had waged so long together. In the months following the diagnosis, Maeve Cavanaugh had offered many words of wisdom. She had spoken of love and marriage and widowhood, and her own unshakeable faith, but never anything as mundane as a sweater or dress. It was left to Catherine to divine her wishes—and, then, to find the strength to carry them out.

The tear in the paper bag widened as Catherine crossed Maynard Street, a block from Saint Pat's.

During the first year of the illness, when it was still possible, Catherine walked her mother to and from Sunday mass. But she never went inside. While her mother took communion, Catherine sat in a nearby coffee shop, nibbling on cranberry scones and drafting lectures.

In her late twenties, Catherine held a coveted assistant professorship at the University of Michigan, in the same town where she had finished high school. She had dreamed of Yale or Harvard, but when the time came she refrained from applying. She opted to stay close to her ailing mother. Though the burden of care took a toll on her research, her introductory course was oversubscribed. The undergrads seemed to sense that they came first. They appreciated her irreverent wit and provocative ideas.

Jealous colleagues credited her looks.

Nature had blessed her with a cover girl's features; life had animated them with sincerity. She abhorred makeup, ignored fashion, rejected pretense. She was built for a beach on the Cote d'Azur, though the windswept dunes of Lake Michigan were more her element. She lectured in jeans.

Father Devaney recognized her as she stepped into the church, struggling with the bags. But before the spry old man could reach her, the heaviest bag gave out, spilling its contents in the aisle. Catherine bent to pick up the clothing, and the priest knelt beside her.

"Catherine, it's good to see you. How are you holding up?"

"Better than my shopping bag, Father," she said with a sniffle. "Thank you for asking."

"Here, let me," Father Devaney said, gathering it up.

"They were mother's," Catherine said. "Nothing fancy, but I thought someone might put them to use."

"Someone will be very grateful. And so am I."

"Thank you, Father. And thank you for all your kindness. You know, she could always count on you, to raise her spirits."

Devaney smiled his kindly smile, and grasped her hand with surprising power.

"The Lord can be a comfort, if you let him. The Church is always here for you, Catherine."

Catherine blinked back a tear and smiled.

"I have to get to class," she said, and hurried out.

Catherine left her religion in a Belfast cemetery.

On false suspicion, the Irish Republican Army had executed Connor Cavanaugh, a stern but loving dad and one of their own. They accused him of Protestant sympathies. They said he betrayed the cause of independence and the Catholic Church.

To teach an indelible lesson, they put a bullet in his forehead and dumped his body in the wildflowers along a country lane.

The murder of her father shattered Catherine. In school, she was shadowed by the lies about her father, shunned by her classmates.

Only her brother, Ian, kept her from giving up. Ian was three years older, and, when responsibility fell prematurely on his shoulders, he rose to the challenge. He found a second job at a meatpacking plant so Catherine would have time for her schoolwork. He was always ready with a smile, a laugh, a joke, a compliment.

"Catherine, you're the prettiest girl in all of Belfast," he never tired of saying.

In church, Ian sat beside his mother, grasping her hand, giving her the courage to hold her head up.

Then Ian, too, stopped smiling. Something was troubling him. Something was tormenting him.

He didn't confide in Catherine, but he didn't need to. Before long, there were hints and rumors.

Catherine tried to reach out to Ian the way he had reached out to her, but she didn't know how. She told him to visit Father Donegan. Father Donegan would help.

One day, as Catherine was walking home from school, two older boys fell in beside her. They began with taunts and escalated to pushing and shoving. One of them grabbed her, pulling back her arms. The other tore open her blouse.

Beyond the terror, beyond the humiliation, she felt guilt and shame, as if she believed them when they called her a slut and a whore.

Her brother came to the rescue.

"Let go of her," he said.

The other boys turned on her brother.

"What's it to you, faggot?" one of them taunted.

"Faggot," the other said.

Her brother threw the first punch.

When the scuffle was over, Catherine helped Ian get up. She ripped off a piece of her torn white blouse and pressed it against his bloody lip.

They walked home together. She was crying against his chest, and he was holding her protectively.

Much later, Ian opened up to her in tears of shame. He was consumed by unspeakable desires. His behavior was a mortal sin. He was struggling to reconcile his personal truth with God's truth, and it was impossible to do. The Bible was clear.

The third time he confessed, the priest said he was an abomination in the eyes of the Lord.

Catherine had no answers. She hugged him and told him she loved him.

A few days later, Ian went elsewhere for reconciliation. A short walk from home, under a slate sky, he stood in the path of an oncoming train.

From the clothesline behind a neighbor's house, Catherine had seen him walking alone along the tracks. She had seen him stop and stand perfectly still as the signal bells rang and the whistle blew. She had seen him spread his arms, as if to embrace his deliverance.

At the final moment, she had been running toward him, screaming.

Catherine's mother insisted it was an accident. She prepared to bury Ian beside his father, in the shadow of their church. But Father Donegan refused. In committing suicide, Ian had committed an unpardonable sin. According to the archdiocese, he had forfeited his right to a Catholic burial.

Catherine's mother fled with her to the United States, to Michigan, where Uncle Billy had a job at an automotive plant. After three years clerking at a supermarket and studying for the American certificates,

Maeve became a nurse at the university hospital, the same hospital where she died.

The loss of faith left a void that Catherine struggled to fill. It helped explain her academic specialty, something her mother never understood.

The lecture hall was almost full when Catherine shuffled her notes and tapped the microphone. Two hundred undergraduates settled into their creaking seats, stashed their knapsacks, and opened their notebooks. Catherine surveyed the audience, deciding where to begin.

Her eyes fixed momentarily on several students in the tenth row seated with hands joined and heads bowed in prayer. The unusual display distracted her with curiosity, but when they looked up, she launched into the day's lecture.

"Today, I'd like to discuss Herod the Great, one of antiquity's master builders," she began. "His legacy includes some of Israel's most important archaeological sites—the Herodeion citadel, the mountaintop fortress Masada, the classical port city Caesarea, the palace at Jericho, and Jerusalem's Temple Mount, among others. His greatest achievement, the reconstruction of the Temple, was also his most ephemeral. It stood for less than a century before the Romans razed it. As ancient Hebrews worshiped there, modern Jews revere its ruins. The Western Wall endures as Judaism's holiest shrine.

"But before we focus on the archaeology, a bit about the man. Who was this Herod, who left such a lasting imprint? He was, quite literally, king of the Jews, though he never trusted his hold on power. To put it politely, he was a paranoid, brutal megalomaniac, and there was no escaping his rage. To snuff out domestic opposition, real and imagined, he slaughtered countless Jews. He saw conspiracies all around and tortured people into confirming them. He murdered his wife Mariamne in the mistaken belief that she was sleeping with one of his closest advisors. He also murdered the advisor. But his madness only intensified. He ordered two loyal sons to be strangled, because he feared they were in too much of a hurry to succeed him. He installed a golden eagle, a graven image, over the gates to the Temple. When devout Jews toppled it, Herod had them burnt alive.

"But pity poor misunderstood Herod. The world remembers him best for a crime it's doubtful he ever committed.

"I'm referring of course to the Gospel of Matthew, Chapter 2, Verse 16, about Herod's actions following the birth of Jesus. As you recall, the wise men from the East had brought word of a newborn king. Borrowing a page from Egypt's pharaoh, in the Book of Exodus, Matthew tells us that

Herod issued a death warrant for all the male children of Bethlehem age two and under.

"As Connolly has written, it sounds like something Herod would do—yet it's hardly plausible. Think about it. Herod's other horrors are thoroughly chronicled by the historians of the age. This one appears only in Matthew. It isn't even mentioned in the other Gospels. Ripping babies from their mothers' arms should have provoked open rebellion, one of the greatest crises of Herod's reign—not such yawning silence. I admit, it makes for a good story, but we can safely categorize it as biblical fable."

A student in the middle of the tenth row raised his hand, and Catherine called on him.

"Yes, Bryan, you have a question?"

Bryan rose to his feet. He had sandy blond hair, cut short and neat, and a boyishly smooth face, and he carried himself with upright posture. He took a moment to find his voice.

"Did you say *biblical fable*, professor?"

"Yes, that's right."

"Professor, I've been sitting through your lectures for several weeks now, listening respectfully, but in good conscience I can no longer keep silent. You seem to reject the scriptures. And you seem to make no room in this class for those of us who believe."

The class erupted in exclamations of protest and murmurs of surprise, but Catherine asked for silence.

"Ladies and gentlemen, Bryan has the floor."

"Thank you, professor. My message is simple. The Bible is the Truth and the Word and the Testament of the Lord. You and the other secular humanists at this university have no place distorting its meaning, or subverting its authority. I speak for 176 members of the Campus Gospel Fellowship: We won't be marginalized any longer, and we're putting you on notice. If the faculty doesn't hear us in Ann Arbor, the politicians who write the checks will listen to us in the state capital."

Catherine's students sat at rapt attention, wondering how she would respond.

"Thank you, Bryan, for speaking your mind," Catherine said, calmly. "I'm sorry if you feel I've been disrespectful. I want you to know that I begrudge no one his faith. In fact—in fact, I envy it. But this is a class on biblical archaeology, and I'm a biblical archaeologist. Our aim is to employ science and reason and scholarship in the search for answers. We're searching for truth, Bryan. And if you believe in truth, you have nothing to fear from the search."

Bryan scowled. "My fear is reserved for God," he said.

Catherine looked at her student and caught a glimpse of her brother.

Ian knew the fear of God. And Ian believed. He believed every word, including the words that cut him to his core. If he didn't believe, he'd still be with me . . . .

She stepped from behind the lectern and faced her critic.

"If the Gospels were gospel, the task would be simpler, Bryan. But unfortunately for all who struggle to understand, the Bible is not the final word. So we reach deeper."

Bryan rose again, an expression of outrage barely masking his glee.

"That's exactly what I'm talking about," he said. "You reveal yourself to be a critic of the Lord, not a student of His word."

"Maybe you can help me, Bryan. What, exactly, is His word?"

"His word is plain," Bryan said, raising a bible. "It's between these covers, for all who care to read."

Catherine nodded in reflection.

"Is it in the Gospel of Mark, Chapter 5?"

"As sure as the Son rises, professor."

"Help me, class, who can summarize the opening passage of Mark 5?" Catherine asked. "This isn't a test; you can refer to the book."

A dozen hands shot up. Catherine pointed to a crew-cut student toward the left of the auditorium, a tall teenager in a varsity sweater. "Andrew, thank you."

Andrew stood and opened his bible. "Jesus arrived by boat in the land of the Gadarenes, and a wild man who lived in the tombs ran to him. The man was possessed by demons. And Jesus ordered the demons to leave his body."

"Did the demons obey?" Bryan asked.

"The demons made a deal," Andrew answered. "They agreed to give up the man's body if Jesus let them possess a nearby herd of pigs. But, as soon as the demons invaded the pigs' bodies, the herd ran over a cliff, into the sea, and drowned, presumably taking the evil spirits with them."

"A miracle," Bryan said, to a chorus of amens from the students seated closest to him.

"Perhaps," Catherine said. "How about the Gospel of Matthew, Chapter 8? Who can summarize Matthew's account of the same event?"

Catherine pointed to a woman in the front. "Angela, go ahead."

Fingering the gold cross that hung from her necklace, Angela read for a moment before speaking up. "The devils went into the pigs, and then the pigs rushed into the sea and drowned."

"Back up, a bit, if you would," Catherine requested. "What does Matthew say happened when Jesus first reached the shore?"

Angela read the verse to herself, and a look of distress crossed her face. She looked to Catherine for guidance.

"It's okay, tell us what it says."

"It says—it says Jesus was met by *two men* possessed by devils who came out from the tombs," Angela mumbled.

"How many?"

"Two."

"Two men possessed by devils," Catherine repeated. "Twice as many as Andrew found in the Gospel of Mark. So, which account are we to believe, Bryan? Did Jesus perform two exorcisms that day, or only one?"

Bryan's face flushed.

"That's very clever of you, professor, but twisting a pair of verses doesn't prove anything."

"Oh?"

"If you looked closely, you'd see that Mark's story took place in the land of the Gadarenes, and Matthew's took place in the land of the Gergesenes. We can accept both versions without choosing between them."

"Both versions?" Catherine asked. "Very well. How about Mark 10 and Matthew 20? When Jesus and his disciples were leaving Jericho, how many blind men begged for help? Did two men regain their sight, as Matthew says, or just a lone beggar named Bartimaeus, as Mark tells it?"

Blank stares from the audience.

"Let me make it easier," she said. "What Jewish holiday did Jesus and his disciples observe at the Last Supper?"

"Passover," several students shouted.

"You're right," Catherine said. "And you're also wrong. Three of the Gospels say it was the Passover meal, but the fourth Gospel says the Last Supper took place *before* Passover.

"And while we're on the subject, what of Judas? We all know that Judas betrayed Jesus, because the Bible tells us so. But what became of Judas? Was he so wracked with guilt that he hanged himself, as Matthew reports? Or should we believe what we're told elsewhere in the New Testament: That he bought a plot of land with the money he was paid for betraying Jesus, and later fell to his death in some kind of accident?"

"These are details, professor," Bryan stammered. "Far be it for us to second guess. None of this changes the larger truth. What we need to focus on are the teachings of Christ."

Catherine looked at her student and pictured herself in a Belfast church.

Like you, I embraced Him. I knelt before the altar, grateful for His sacrifice, secure in his love.

Much as I was comforted by my own father's love.

And now I have neither.

"Bryan makes an excellent point," Catherine said. "The core of the New Testament is the word of Jesus himself. So let's forget the biblical narrative for a moment and examine Christ's own words. And let's cut to the heart of the matter. When Jesus was on trial for his life, accused of blasphemy, and Jerusalem's high priest asked if he was the Son of God, how did he respond?"

Catherine scanned a sea of expectant faces, including Bryan, who saw where she was going and was powerless to change the course.

"If you go by Mark," she said, "Jesus replied with a simple declaration: 'I am!' But if you believe Luke, Jesus dodged the question with a sarcastic retort: 'You say that I am.'

"One question, two different answers. Both the word of God," Catherine said.

Bryan groped for something to say, but Catherine preempted him.

"I grant you, those weren't the last words. There were more. But even at the climactic moment, as Jesus hangs from the cross, the Gospels leave us guessing.

"In the Gospel of John, Jesus expires with the mortal words, 'I thirst ... It is finished.' In the Gospel of Luke, Jesus departs this world affirming his faith in God. 'Father, into your hands I entrust my spirit,' he says. Some versions of Luke, but not all, include a compassionate plea for the executioners: 'Father, forgive them, for they know not what they do.'

"But Matthew and Mark conclude with a starkly contrasting image, the messiah in despair: 'My God, My God, why hast thou forsaken me?'"

Many of the students looked impressed, and some of them appeared unsettled by the exercise.

"The inconsistencies don't end there," Catherine said. "As Jesus died, the earth shook, rocks split, and graves opened. Saints were raised from the dead. The curtain inside the Temple spontaneously tore from top to bottom. Darkness fell over the land at midday and lasted for three hours.

"That's the Gospel according to Matthew. It has all the subtlety of a Hollywood extravaganza.

"Mark and Luke agree on the three hours of darkness and the torn curtain. But they make no mention of the earthquake, the splitting rocks, or the graves giving up the dead.

"John omits the special effects altogether. No darkness at noon, no torn curtains, no walking dead. No telling how the author of the fourth Gospel missed those details.

"And consider what happens later, in Jesus's tomb, when it's discovered that his body has vanished.

"This is the story of the Resurrection, *the central event in Christian theology*. And here again, *the Gospels conflict*.

"Matthew and Mark describe Mary, mother of Jesus, and the other Mary, Mary Magdalene, going to the tomb and encountering one divine messenger, who explains that Jesus has risen.

"Luke describes a larger group of people—not just the two Marys, but also Joanna and some other women from Galilee—meeting *two* divine messengers in the tomb.

"And John—John gives us a third version of the story. John tells us that, after visiting the tomb by herself, Mary Magdalene runs to two of the disciples and tells them that Jesus's body has been taken. The two disciples rush to the tomb, find it empty, and leave. They seem to assume the body was removed, as Mary Magdalene said. But Mary Magdalene stays by the tomb, weeping. Alone, she looks into the tomb, and meets two divine messengers, who ask her why she's crying.

"Then Mary turns around—and comes face to face with Jesus."

Catherine paced the stage.

"It's not surprising that there are discrepancies," she said. "It would be surprising if there weren't. None of these accounts was written during Jesus's lifetime, and none of them can be taken as eyewitness testimony. The scholarly consensus is that the earliest of the Gospels, the Gospel of Mark, was first committed to writing two generations after the crucifixion. *Two generations.* That's a long time to remember his exact words. And I challenge any of you to quote, verbatim, what I told you this very day, this very hour, about King Herod, before Bryan led us on this illuminating digression."

Catherine scanned the room again, meeting only blank stares.

"Come on, people. Here you are, sitting with notebooks open, scribbling away, and none of you can repeat my lecture verbatim?"

No one rose to the challenge.

"Bryan, you were listening carefully. How about you?"

"I'm just a humble Christian, professor. I wouldn't compare myself to the apostles. And I wouldn't compare your lecture to the teachings of Christ."

A scattering of heads nodded in agreement, and Catherine seemed to concede her misstep.

"You're right, of course. My mistake. But the bottom line is, Christianity demands faith. If you've got faith, you don't ask for proof. If you need proof, you can't count yourself among the faithful. And if you search for proof, you better be prepared for what you find."

"The Devil can cite scripture, professor. We're putting you on notice: The blasphemy must stop."

Blasphemy? You accuse me? I was so faithful that I sent Ian to Father Donegan, and Father Donegan sent him to hell.

Bryan stood up again, and his friends stood with him. They filed out of the tenth row, into the aisle, and started walking toward the exit.

Catherine watched their protest in astonishment. Elsewhere in the auditorium, a handful of students rose from their seats.

Her indignation grew. They weren't just criticizing *her*; their literal approach to the Bible was a condemnation of her dead brother.

"We're not done here," she said, trembling.

My brother Ian is buried behind a prison, among the criminals and lost souls, because the churches of Belfast refused his body.

The protesters kept walking. *Walking on Ian's grave.*

In a quavering voice, Catherine called after her departing students.

"God gave us more than a book," she said. "He gave us hearts and minds and flesh and blood. The capacity to think for ourselves, the capacity to love. If we are true to ourselves, and if He created us in his own image, how can we be wrong? Can somebody please tell me? Can you? Because I'd like to know."

The last of the protesters left the auditorium, and the doors slowly closed behind them. The rest of the class sat silently staring at Catherine.

She looked around self-consciously, and she looked down at the lectern. She realized she had lost control. She was afraid her last question had sounded like an argument, or a parting shot, though in reality it was a heartfelt plea. Her hands were shaking.

She was flustered and embarrassed.

"That's all for today," she said, quietly.

She gathered her papers and stepped down from the podium. Avoiding eye contact, she walked toward the exit. As she approached the rear of the auditorium, she noticed a man in tortoise-shell glasses and a brown tweed jacket sitting in the last row.

He was the chairman of the tenure review committee, a man who could make or break her career, and he was taking notes.

Chapter 16

From another seat in the back row, Benjamin Jordan watched with fascination.

He watched Catherine's shoulders sag as she exited, and he thought he saw a trace of tears.

In her wake, some of the students seemed troubled by the doubts she had sown, and others sounded as if they were worried about her.

She wasn't the retiring, abstruse sort he had imagined. She was much more intriguing. For all the cool control she had shown as she dismantled her critic, she had let the student get to her. She had revealed passion and vulnerability, and the outward signs of an inner struggle. But Jordan couldn't begin to guess her importance to Meyer Elazar. He wondered why she had been ignoring his messages.

He followed the professor into the hall and caught up with her as she approached the stairs.

"Excuse me, Professor Cavanaugh—"

She turned around as if shaken from a dream and looked at him with puzzlement.

"I'm Benjamin Jordan, from Jerusalem," he said.

For an unguarded moment, she showed a glimmer of attraction. She tried to pull herself together as she shook his hand.

To Jordan's surprise, his name didn't seem to register.

"I'm from *The Shofar*," he volunteered.

"I'm sorry, have we met?" the professor asked.

"I've left several phone messages at your office, and sent a few e-mails over the past week," Jordan said.

"Oh, I'm terribly sorry. I really haven't kept up. It's—it's been a difficult time," she said. "What's a reporter for *The Shofar* doing here in Michigan?"

Jordan smiled, as if the answer was self-evident.

"Looking for you."

She looked startled, and even more off balance, if that was possible.

"What for?" she asked, studying Jordan more closely.

"Let me buy you a cup of coffee and I'll explain."

In the eyes of the Jerusalem establishment, Jordan remained a spectacular screw-up, or worse. He had made a mistake—even he saw that now. Samir Salam had explained, belatedly.

Two days after the press conference that drove a nail in Jordan's reputation, the wily Jordanian caught up with him in Jerusalem's Israel

Museum. Jordan had gone there to think, as he did from time to time. He was staring at a wall-size carving that depicted the sack of the Jewish city Lachish by the Assyrians in 701 B.C.E. The victorious king Sennacherib had commissioned it to memorialize the event. As the ancient tableau illustrated, the conquering army impaled many of the Jews and hoisted their bodies on spikes before leading the rest into captivity. Jordan looked without seeing—his mind was somewhere else. But he soon became aware of an elderly tourist at his elbow. The disguise was so convincing that Jordan couldn't see through it—until Samir began reminiscing about a Red Sea cruise.

They wandered through the exhibit halls, past stone sarcophagi and bronze spearpoints, conversing in hushed tones.

"What the hell happened?" Jordan demanded. "How could you do that to me?"

"There was a misunderstanding," Samir said. "There was indeed a Silver Scroll—of that you can rest assured. But it had nothing to do with the dig in the Negev."

Jordan was incredulous.

"But you said — "

"No, I didn't," Samir countered, defensively. "I might have implied, but you surmised."

Jordan didn't know if he was angrier with himself or his source.

"Then where the hell did they find it?"

"It was sitting in a storeroom at the Institute, for God knows how long."

"You can't be serious."

"It was embedded inside the handle of a ceramic jug. And it might have stayed there forever. The jug itself was a common type, used to store olive oil, I'm told. But someone moved it to a workbench to prepare it for use in a display, and a janitor accidentally knocked it to the floor." Samir grinned mischievously. "Imagine his horror—and his surprise as he picked up the pieces."

"Why didn't you tell me?"

"I'm sorry, Benjamin. I didn't know. Our mutual friend didn't tell me. He didn't think it was significant."

"Damn it, Samir. What about your news conference? You cut my nuts off."

"All I said was that the King does not accuse the Israeli government. Don't be naive, Benjamin—you can hardly expect him to make such an accusation." Samir winked, maddeningly. "But that doesn't mean it isn't true."

"Let me guess," Jordan said. "This janitor, his name was Ehud, and he died in the explosion?"

"How did you know?"

Jordan shook his head in disgust.

"What about your eyewitnesses, the kids from the pharmacy who supposedly saw Ramsi arrested?"

"The Israeli army can be very intimidating. Believe me, the boys saw what they saw."

"The goddamn body showed up in Amman."

"What does that prove?"

"Come on, Samir."

"As the medical examiner said, there was a delay in making the identification. I tried to reach you the night before your story ran, but your cell phone was off and your voicemail was full. I hope she was worth it."

It was hardly the kind of story the discredited reporter could take to his editor, and it didn't account for Meltzer's weirdly frightened behavior, so Jordan had chased his only lead—all the way to Ann Arbor.

They sat in the back of the coffee shop, waiting for their cappuccinos to cool. The place smelled of oatmeal cookies and damp wool sweaters. Rain pelted the glass storefront, soaking the students who scurried past.

Catherine was looking into Jordan's eyes, curiously, but he was taking his time, taking her temperature. Trying to be sensitive. He took a long sip of cappuccino. He put it down and met her gaze.

"You heard about the explosion at the Institute?" he asked.

She looked down and away.

"Horrible," she said. "Just horrible."

"And the aftermath?"

"I heard that Israel struck back at terrorists in Lebanon."

Jordan nodded sympathetically. *She hadn't been following the news.*

"I'm trying to piece together what happened, what the context was," he said. "The main thing is, I'd like to know about your connection with Rabbi Elazar."

She looked confused, as if the question didn't make sense.

"Why?"

"Someone close to the rabbi gave me your name," Jordan said.

To match the name with an identity, Jordan had searched the Internet for occurrences of "Cavanaugh" and "Elazar." His search turned up the schedule for the annual meeting of the Academy of Biblical Archaeology—four years earlier. Both Cavanaugh and Elazar had been panelists at the Zurich conference, albeit at different sessions. Catherine Cavanaugh of the University of Michigan, then a mere doctoral candidate, had participated in a seminar on the use of satellite imagery in archaeological exploration—spotting lost trade routes and other man-made anomalies beneath the present-day topography.

Tapping into an academic database, Jordan was able to obtain a copy of her dissertation. She had filled 247 pages analyzing ancient pictograms carved in the rock of the Jordanian desert. Jordan was disappointed to find it had nothing to do with the subject at hand.

Then he read the footnotes. Cavanaugh had interviewed Meyer Elazar.

So at least they were acquainted.

"Who was this 'someone close to the rabbi'?'" Catherine asked.

"The rabbi's secretary. She left your name on my answering machine two days before she died. Apparently, it was written on a file that the rabbi removed from his office the last time he was there."

Catherine stared in disbelief.

"What was in the file?" she asked.

"I was hoping you could explain."

"I don't see how. I only spoke to Rabbi Elazar once in the past three years, and that was a good six months before the bombing."

"What did you talk about?"

"We chatted about Mordecai Mandel."

"A mutual friend?"

Catherine laughed—more at herself than at Jordan. "He died in 1883, quite obscure. I'm researching a book about him. At least, I was, before I had to put it on hold. And I called Rabbi Elazar to get his input."

"What about?"

"Some information and leads I had developed."

"Such as?"

She looked at him with suspicion, as if sensing a threat.

"Mr. Jordan — "

"Ben."

"Mr. Jordan," Catherine continued, impatiently, "please forgive me if I feel no compulsion to discuss my research."

"I don't blame you. I would feel the same way. Your work is competitive, just like mine. But it could be more important than Mordecai Mandel."

"I used to think that myself. I'm sorry you had to travel such a long way for so little, but — "

"Just tell me this: Was it related to the Silver Scroll?"

Catherine looked at him blankly.

"I don't know anything about that," she said, and there was no questioning her sincerity. She was already rising from her chair. "Thank you for the cappuccino. I hope you have a safe trip. Now, if you'll excuse me — "

"How about the Copper Scroll? Did it have anything to do with the Copper Scroll?"

Catherine froze. She was curious—that was obvious—but, more than that, she was troubled.

"Would you care to explain?" Jordan asked.

"No, I think you should," Catherine replied.

Jordan gestured for Catherine to sit, and the professor sank back into her chair.

They stared at each other, bound by mutual interest.

"I'm listening," the professor said.

"I've been told that the Institute discovered an artifact, a silver scroll. Like the Copper Scroll, it described fantastic treasures and their hiding places. Apparently, it was written after the Copper Scroll, after many of the treasures of the Copper Scroll had been dug up and reburied in safer locations. My source believes it points the way to the lost treasures of the Temple . . . assuming anyone could interpret it."

The blood drained from Catherine's face, and pale anxiety rushed in.

"Do you have a copy of this silver scroll?" Catherine asked.

"No."

"Do you know anyone who does?"

"No, I don't."

"Do you have any idea what it says?"

"Only what I've told you."

"I see. Well, thank you, Mr. Jordan. I'm glad we had this chance to talk."

Catherine was rising again, reaching for her coat.

"Wait," Jordan pleaded. "What have I said?"

"I have to go," Catherine said. "I'm sorry, but I can't help you."

"Wait—what does it mean?" Jordan asked.

He reached for her sleeve, but she was already gone.

Jordan followed her into the street and watched her dart through the traffic. A passing car threw up a sheet of water, splashing him. The windbreaker he had packed was little use against the downpour.

Jordan stood on the sidewalk as the cars rolled past. He had gotten the sense that she was interested—or was that personal?—but it turned out she was scared. He had hit a wall, and he was less than optimistic about breaking through. Still, Catherine Cavanaugh's nervous, skittish reaction was further validation: He was on the right track.

And now he had something new to go on. The focus of the professor's research and the subject of her last communication with Meyer Elazar was a man who died in 1883. The man's name was Mordecai Mandel.

Jordan fumbled in his pocket and pulled out a soggy campus map.

Chapter 17

An hour later, after a couple of false starts, Jordan was deep in the stacks of the Harlan Hatcher Graduate Library, searching through aisles of musty books. Despite the absence of dust, it seemed that most were rarely disturbed. But it was just his luck that the one obscure volume he needed had been missing from both the undergraduate and the departmental libraries. Oddly, the librarians had no record of it ever having been signed out. It was possible that the book had been shipped to a warehouse to make room for titles people actually used, they said.

It was also possible that the brief biography of Mordecai Mandel, published in 1896, had been placed on the wrong shelf. It was so easy to lose a book in a library. File it just a few feet out of place and for all practical purposes it disappears.

The graduate library was his last chance. He studied the note he had jotted from the short entry in the computerized catalog, the only reference to his subject.

> Jerusalem merchant, 1827-1883, accused of fraud against British Museum.

Jordan crouched and followed the call letters across the second shelf. He was getting close.

Where *The Mandel Manuscript* belonged, there was a gap in the collection, just wide enough for a slender volume. He searched the rest of the shelf, then the rest of the bookcase, satisfying himself that it was missing.

Dejected, Jordan turned his back on the uneven rows of authors and titles and sank to the floor, leaning against the bookcase. He closed his eyes, lost in thought, and sapped by the jet lag. The century-old biography wasn't exactly required reading. What if the professor had it? He made an educated guess that she would be reluctant to share.

His eyes focused on a cart parked at the end of the aisle, loaded with returns. He leapt to his feet and pored over it. Nothing. Energized, he prowled the stacks, sifting through other cartloads of unsorted books.

At last, a slender volume caught his gaze. The title was embossed on the spine: *The Mandel Manuscript*, by Randolph Rempel Jamison.

Jordan claimed his prize. He turned it over, and over again. The leather binding was brittle with age, cracked like the paint on an antique portrait. The gold lettering had lost its luster. Yet, remarkably, here it was after all these years, waiting to tell its story.

Jordan found an empty carrel and closed the door. The private study looked out on the law school's gothic spires, but Jordan was oblivious to the view. He opened the book. Surprisingly, what followed was not a traditional biography at all, but a modest essay, printed at personal expense by an author no publisher would back. Jordan began to read.

This account is dedicated to the memory of Mordecai Mandel. To my eternal shame, I nearly shrank from writing it. Long before his hour of fame, and infamy, I counted him a friend. Many afternoons, we sat together in the dinge of his Jerusalem shop, sipping his tea, smoking his tobacco. On the other side of a faded curtain, his daughter greeted the customers with warmth and charm, and an unfailing grace that seemed sadly out of place. In the back office, I listened while Mordecai talked – about the misfortune that led him to David Street, and the ambition that would lift him beyond. We were an odd pair, an Anglican churchman and a Russian Jew, but we were neighbors in Jerusalem.

All of this helps explain why I stayed silent during the events in question more than a dozen years ago. Readers may ask why I come so late to the subject. I have no satisfactory answer. The years have left me old and frail, in failing health, and at last the shortness of time stiffens the spine. I write now in the modest hope that future generations might see the matter more clearly – if they remember it at all.

I arrived in the old city in the spring of 1877, to begin my ministry at Christ Church, beside the Tower of David. Like the pilgrims who filled our pews, I thrilled to walk the crowded streets. In the Arab souk, merchants in flowing robes sold sandals as timeless as the prophets, and spices befitting wise men from the East – cinnamon, cardamom, and curry. The air was heavy with pungent smells – pomegranates spoiling in the heat, and butchered lambs, hanging from hooks. Just a few short steps from the church, there were tables heaped with pistachios, and pushcarts filled with honeyed sweets. And every day, as I took my walk, I passed a storefront stacked with trinkets. The window displayed icons of the Virgin Mary, and wooden crosses of all sizes. Mordecai Mandel was a Jew, but he understood the tourist trade.

When business was slow, Mandel stood in his doorway, greeting passersby. Inside, he stocked a wider selection – oil-burning lamps made from clay, supposedly as old as the Old Testament, and stone chips, priced at three pounds sterling. If pressed, Mandel would settle for half that amount. The faithful left convinced they had gotten a bargain – on genuine pieces of Golgotha.

People believe what they will, and Mandel was a master of persuasion.

The real treasures occupied a shelf toward the back. These were relics Mandel had purchased from the Bedouin—glass perfume bottles dating to Roman times, figurines of the Canaanite fertility goddess, Greek coins worn dull with age. The Bedouin had pried them from the dust.

At first, Mandel and I exchanged pleasantries, in the manner of people only vaguely acquainted. From time to time, I steered souvenir-hunters in his direction, cautioning them appropriately. Mandel thanked me by name. Then one day he stopped me in the street.

"Father Jamison, I have something to show you. A rare and beautiful discovery."

Inside the shop, Mandel unwrapped a truly marvelous object, a silver chalice, simple in design, tarnished by time, immediately evocative of Jesus and the last supper. It was too fantastic to be true.

The Jew could read my mind. "It's not the Holy Grail," he said, sheepishly. "At least, I've no basis to suggest it. But it dates to the 1st Century, perhaps even the time of Jesus."

I held it to the light, inspecting the workmanship.

"How do you know?" I asked.

"From a coin found beside it."

"Thank you for showing it to me," I said, handing it back.

"It belongs in a church, Father. A position of prominence. Why not your own?"

The question engaged my imagination.

"It would grace any altar," I replied, "but I can hardly justify the expense."

"Never mind what it's worth. Give me the satisfaction of keeping it close to home, where I might see it from time to time. It's yours for £10."

Mandel was pleased to repay past favors, and I could hardly refuse. I took the chalice with me and returned the following day with the shopkeeper's money. The next Sunday, and every Sunday after that, I used the goblet to administer the sacraments.

You can imagine my surprise when, two months later, a visiting Londoner took note of the relic as we chatted after mass. "I bought one just like it," he remarked. "In the artist's workshop in Safad."

"How can you tell it's the same?" I asked.

"From the silversmith's mark," the Londoner said, pointing to a pair of inconspicuous initials. "He wanted seven pounds, but he gave it up for six."

Annoyed, I confronted Mandel—and instantly regretted doing so. He was mortified, and his embarrassment was painful to see. "On my soul, Father, I didn't know." He reached into a drawer and took out £10, which he thrust into my hands. "Keep your money, and keep the chalice," he insisted. "But please, accept my apology."

Thus began our friendship.

Mandel was a child of the *shtetl*. As a boy, he considered himself privileged, but that was an illusion. For Russia's peasant Jews, there was no security—only gradations of wretchedness. Even then, Mandel was a dreamer. One night, he sat upon a haystack, studying the constellations, and drifted off to sleep. He awoke to the thunder of hoofbeats and the smell of smoke. Cossacks were rampaging through the village, plundering homes, savaging livestock, torching houses. A cacaphony of drunken, violent shouts filled the night. Paralyzed with fear, powerless to resist, he watched the *pogrom* unfold. Several of the revelers dragged his bearded father from the house and sheared him like a sheep. They threw him in manure and urinated in his face. Then they drowned him in a watering trough.

Mandel could hear them kicking the dead man's body, cursing that he had succumbed too quickly.

The eldest of Mandel's three sisters ran naked and screaming from the back door, but two of the attackers ran her down. When they finished, they finished her with a saber.

The rest of the family was trapped inside—his sisters, his grandfather and a newborn niece. Men the young Mandel recognized as Christian neighbors barred the windows and lit the roof. He prayed his kin were already dead. Instead of an answer, a tortured cry rose from the flames. The voice belonged to his mother.

The boy burrowed into the haystack. He heard a torch land in the hay, and he felt the spreading heat. But the dampness left over from the afternoon's rain protected him. The fire petered out.

My friend wept without tears as he told his story.

"Why did they do it?" I asked.

Mandel laughed at my ignorance and naivete.

"How do you explain the violence that one man does to another?" he asked, rhetorically. "What accounts for evil, or hatred?"

I must have looked dissatisfied, because he offered a more literal explanation.

"They did it because we were Jews," Mandel said. "They did it because their church taught them we killed Jesus."

My friend spoke politely of "their church," as if it were somehow different from my own. Still, his answer hit me like a fist. As I caught my breath, I thought of correcting Mordecai. It wasn't the Church's teaching. It was the Bible, the word of God, that recounted the trial and conviction of our Lord by a court of Jews. But there was no point in debating the fine points.

"How shameful," I said, "that your people should be held to blame for the actions of their forebears."

Mandel repeated his cynical laugh.

"You mean the *alleged* actions of our forebears," he said, disputatiously. "But hasn't it always been so? In the Dark Ages, my father's Polish ancestors were slashed and burned by an army of crusaders. The crusaders hoped to win God's blessing before reclaiming the Holy Land. Centuries later, members of my mother's family were tortured by the Inquisition. Those who survived the dungeons died at the stake. Can you imagine the horror — as the smoke filled your lungs, and the flesh crackled and popped?"

The shopkeeper shook his head ruefully.

"You see, Father, we Jews are no strangers to the fire. I wouldn't be surprised if someday, it consumed us all."

In the fall of 1881, it was ambition that consumed my friend Mandel, a burning desire for wealth and success and recognition. He was never meant to be, or content to be, a shopkeeper, and the pain of a social snub caused his discontentment to boil over.

It was the latest in a string of indignities. As a young man, Mandel had the misfortune to fall in love with the daughter of an affluent Viennese family. They met in Jerusalem, where she was touring and he was seeking a new life, away from the persecutions of his native land. Anna and Mordecai were both Jews, but they had little in common. They married over her family's objections, and her parents never relented. For all their self-importance, Anna's parents suffered a reversal of fortune and died in debt, leaving her nothing. In time, Anna realized she had traded a life of European sophistication for one of sweat and dust. The romance soured.

Hoping to regain his bride's affection, Mandel reached for a foothold in the society she left behind. He gambled on a series of rash investments and fell on his face, repeatedly. Persuaded that modern engineering could make the desert bloom, he bought shares in an agricultural enterprise. The irrigation equipment failed, the barren land yielded only losses.

With ample justification, Mandel doted on his loyal daughter, Rivka. In the fall of 1881, he contrived to introduce her to a visiting university student, the son of a prominent Berlin physician. He was exuberant when they fell in love. He was devastated when the physician vetoed the match. The son left Rivka heartbroken.

Wounded, Mandel was in a dangerously wishful frame of mind when a pair of French adventurers approached him weeks later with a tantalizing business proposition. They had stumbled upon a clue to an ancient Egyptian burial ground in a valley west of the Nile. They knew Mandel was a respected figure in the antiquities trade. For an investment of £200, Mandel could keep a tenth of any riches they discovered. It was a generous offer, but then, Mandel's reputation would give the expedition credibility with other investors. Late one night, by the light of Mandel's flickering oil lamps, the Frenchmen unfolded a set of tattered maps and explained their plan. They were prepared to spend as long as a year digging. There were considerable risks, but the potential payoff was incalculable. The shopkeeper had less than a day to consider their proposal; they would depart the following afternoon to meet their lead sponsor in Cairo, a Greek diplomat. Excitedly, Mandel drained his savings but came up £50 short.

The next morning, Mandel rose with the sun and visited a prosperous neighbor who traded in wine, a circumspect Italian named Aldo Campagnoli. Campagnoli was reluctant to invest. But by sheer insistence, and a measure of embellishment, Mandel persuaded his neighbor to put up the difference. Then he saw the Frenchmen off.

Day after day, week in and week out, Mandel mused about the treasures they might discover and the fame those would bring. He debated with himself the merits of selling the artifacts outright versus exhibiting them commercially. When he was in an especially good mood, he spoke of donating his share to a museum, or at least making a loan of it.

After three months, Mandel grew impatient. After six months, he was wracked with worry. After seven months had passed with no word from his partners, Mandel sent inquiries to the Nile village that was to serve as the expedition's base. No one in the town had heard of the pair. Neither had the purported sponsor in Cairo.

Mandel plunged into a melancholy blackness.

On a Wednesday afternoon in September of 1882, as shadows fell across David Street, a Bedouin shepherd pushed aside the curtain in the rear of Mandel's shop and woke the proprietor from one of his increasingly lengthy naps.

"What do you have for me today, Nadim?" Mandel grumbled.

The shepherd looked apologetic.

"Only this," he said, offering a ragged bundle of loosely rolled leather.

Mandel yawned.

"No glass? No coins?"

"No, *effendi*."

If business weren't so slow, Mandel would have been disappointed. Nadim was one of his better suppliers, and it had been many weeks since he last visited. The boy had keen eyes, and abundant time to scour the parched hills and valleys.

"Let me see," the Jew said, more out of courtesy than genuine interest.

He reached for the bundle and laid it out on a table, but it was so long that it draped over the edge and onto the floor. Mandel tried to press the brittle material flat, but it cracked. The shepherd shrugged his shoulders, as if to disclaim responsibility for the condition of the merchandise.

Mandel leaned over the table to study it more closely. It looked like a religious scroll, but the writing was barely discernible. The ink had faded, and the letters bore an unusual form. In some places, the writing was little more than a black smudge. From the few words Mandel could recognize, he guessed he was looking at part of an old Torah, a collection of the five books of Moses used in Jewish worship. Discarded Torahs were not uncommon; Jewish law required that damaged scrolls receive a ritual burial.

"Where did you find it?" Mandel asked.

"In a cave, *effendi*. I was looking for a sheep."

Mandel looked at the scroll again. Torahs were inscribed on parchment. Oddly, this text was written on leather.

"I'll give you four pounds," Mandel declared.

The boy furrowed his brow and pulled in his chin. "Four pounds!" he exclaimed, with the usual indignation.

As usual, the boy was right, and Mandel knew it. A European collector might pay as much as fifteen.

When the haggling ended, a jubilant shepherd left Mandel's shop clutching six pounds, two shillings, and a perplexed merchant stooped to gather his discovery.

In the weeks that followed, I saw less and less of Mandel. He withdrew from friends and customers alike, leaving his daughter to mind the store. When my concern impelled me to intrude upon him, I found him hunched over the ragged manuscript, even more disheveled than usual, scribbling elaborate notes. Deep into the night, he stayed closeted in his cramped office, rubbing the leather with whiskey, or soaking it in oil to accentuate the writing.

I begged him to explain, but he asked me to be patient. The French confidence men had humiliated Mandel, and he was loath to risk further embarrassment—particularly where I was concerned.

Unbeknownst to me, Mandel struck up a correspondence with several eminent scholars. In February and March of 1883, a series of biblical authorities visited Mandel's shop. The last came all the way from Prague.

After the Czech departed, Mandel welcomed me happily. He actually hugged me with joy.

"Father, can you believe it? The experts agree. It predates any other by at least 1,500 years."

"What is it, Mordecai?"

"Genesis, Father. The Book of Genesis! It's the oldest one known."

"How can they tell, Mordecai?"

"The writing, Father. The writing!"

Mandel spread part of the manuscript before me and pointed with a stylus. "Characters like these haven't been used since the 6th Century B.C. – not since Nebuchadnezzar conquered Jerusalem and banished the Jews to Babylon."

My heart was glad for Mandel, and I congratulated him. If what he said was true, this relic of his would be a blessing for all mankind.

"Have you any idea what people will *pay* for this, Father? They tell me it could fetch hundreds of thousands of pounds!"

I had not thought to put a price on it.

Three months later, Mandel was touring the intellectual capitals of Europe, presenting his famous manuscript to assemblages of scholars and potentates, inviting libraries and museums to bid on it. He traveled from Prague to Munich to Vienna, then to Paris and Amsterdam, and finally to London. He arrived in triumph, heralded by the press, celebrated by people of rank and nobility. The newspapers speculated as to who would buy "The Mandel Genesis," and at what price. The Louvre was rumoured to be negotiating an offer of £800,000.

Meanwhile, professors and religious leaders debated the object's authenticity. The debate was far from academic.

Shockingly, Mandel's Genesis differed from the version at the bedrock of Judaism and Christianity.

Both versions began the same:

"In the beginning, God created the heaven and the earth. And the earth was without form, and void; and darkness was upon the face of the deep."

But where the standard bible had God creating the sun and the moon and the stars on the fourth day, the Mandel Genesis said God spent the fourth day making grass and trees.

According to the Mandel version, God created the celestial lights on the third day, before he progressed to plants.

There was another glaring inconsistency. In the standard version, God devoted the fifth day to creatures of the sea and sky, and the sixth to beasts of the earth. The Mandel Genesis reversed the order.

Those were the most conspicuous discrepancies, but the Mandel Genesis also contained numerous variations of word and phrase.

As Mandel soon learned, even minor inconsistencies had monumental implications. Suddenly, far from being etched in stone, the word of God seemed mutable. The world had ample reason to reject his discovery.

Some critics dismissed the Mandel text as a forgery conceived in greed. Others denounced it as an atheistic plot. Still others accused the Jew of conspiring against Christianity – an illogical accusation, given that Genesis belonged equally to the Hebrews. Surprisingly, the Vatican and the Church of England stayed out of the debate – perhaps for fear of losing it.

By August of 1883, the experts at the British Museum had reached a consensus: The manuscript was genuine. Determined not to lose to the French, the director of London's preeminent museum secretly procured £1,000,000 from the Chancellor of the Exchequer to effect the purchase. In his hotel suite, Mandel and the museum curators toasted their imminent success.

But news of the pending deal appeared in a London paper, and the French were quick to retaliate. They didn't raise the bid, as Mandel might have anticipated. Instead, they withdrew from the contest, branded Mandel a fraud, and ridiculed the British experts for believing him.

Thrown on the defensive, Mandel's allies at the museum stood their ground, even as members of Parliament raised a hue and cry about the public expenditure.

Then the French ambassador in London distributed a statement taken from a Jerusalem merchant, an Italian-born wine trader named Aldo Campagnoli. Interviewed by French investigators, Campagnoli attested that Mordecai Mandel defrauded him of £50. The wine trader recalled that Mandel had induced him to invest in a phony archaeological venture just three years earlier. Still bitter, Campagnoli said the promise of Cleopatra's treasure overcame his natural skepticism.

As the news spread, Mandel's efforts to explain were lost in an uproar of condemnation. Former allies turned on him. Church leaders proclaimed his manuscript an obvious sham. Cartoonists lampooned him as a hook-nosed Shylock. Politicians called for criminal prosecution. Mandel's fashionable hotel demanded immediate settlement of his debt, which he was unable to pay.

At a safe distance, I kept my silence.

Lacking funds to return to Jerusalem, Mandel wrote his daughter, begging that she locate the Bedouin who sold him the scroll. As futile and dangerous as the mission seemed, the girl joined a caravan and rode to a string of nomadic encampments in the Judean Desert. She found her answer — but lacked the courage to communicate it. The shepherd Nadim had been robbed and murdered two months earlier.

Discredited and destitute, Mandel lost touch with his family.

One day in the winter of 1883, he checked into a rooming house in a seedy section of Brighton. According to the inquest, he stood in front of a mirror, lifted a revolver to his ear, and pulled the trigger.

The infamous Genesis scroll was auctioned in London to pay Mandel's debts. It went to an unidentified bidder — the sole bidder — for the poetic sum of 6 pounds, two shillings. It was never seen again.

To this day, the establishment dismisses Mandel's manuscript as a hoax. If his name endures, it is only as an object of derision.

But I knew better. I was in Mandel's shop the afternoon he purchased the curiosity. I listened to him boast about the bargain he had wrung from an unwitting shepherd. Am I to believe the Bedouin fabricated the document? Or that anyone invested such effort, only to settle for a pittance? For that matter, why would someone with truly devious ambitions choose Mandel as his pawn?

Over many months, I saw Mandel struggling to interpret the text. Was this, too, a ruse?

Mandel was blinded by greed, but he had vision enough to see the danger in controversy. If he had authored the Genesis scroll, he would have produced something less threatening, something that conformed to established beliefs. I know this because, even before he left for Europe, he fretted about the textual inconsistencies and the reaction they could provoke.

As for the Egyptian fraud, I knew the truth, which Mandel confided in me. He was a victim, not a perpetrator.

Yet, to my perpetual disgrace, I stood apart from the debate. I was afraid to stand up to men of fragile faith and small imagination, afraid of guilt by association, afraid to contradict my church. I had the cowardice of my convictions.

I will take that burden to my grave.

After Mandel died, I paid my respects to his daughter. She mentioned the silver chalice Mandel sold me, and the £10 he returned when I impugned his character. I told her I still used his gift for the Eucharist. Whether he intended to cheat me at first, I never knew. But Rivka knew. She saw her father buy the goblet from a Damascus trader — for the impressive sum of £20.

Jordan closed the book and stretched the cramps from his legs. Night had fallen on Ann Arbor, and a freezing rain glazed the trees. The journalist pondered the tale. He pitied the pathetic shopkeeper. Better than most, Jordan could imagine the catcalls and jeers Mandel must have known. Clearly, Mandel was a flawed messenger. But the world had paid a price for its pettiness. From the vantage point of the 21st century, Jordan saw that Mandel's text was in all probability authentic. In the 1940s and '50s, the Dead Sea Scrolls had come to light through eerily similar circumstances.

The tragedy of it all infuriated him. A life ruined. An amazing discovery lost. A crime against history, and posterity. The Mandel Genesis should have inspired humility. Instead, the arrogance of orthodoxy reasserted itself.

Jordan thought of the auction, and the single unidentified bidder. But his mind centered on a more pressing mystery: *What did Mordecai Mandel have to do with a bombing outside Jerusalem?*

Catherine Cavanaugh held the key. She had learned something about Mandel that inspired her to contact Meyer Elazar. Whatever that was, it was on Elazar's mind less than 48 hours before the destruction of the archaeological institute, when the rabbi was seen removing a file on Cavanaugh from his office and rushing to meeting with a senior member of the Israeli government.

Then the institute exploded and Elazar disappeared.

What prompted Cavanaugh to call Elazar?

Jordan looked at the book, and realized he had no way of signing it out. On impulse, he reshelved it—several feet from its proper spot.

Chapter 18

Catherine sat in the semi-darkness of her office, chewing the end of a ball-point pen. The bulb of her desk lamp cast a halo, the only light. It was almost 8:30, and the corridor on the second floor of the museum building was deserted. Her nerves felt as tense as the springs in her worn leather chair, which squeaked as she leaned back.

She was still in shock. The Israeli journalist's story boggled her mind. All the more so because he missed the point.

How many people knew? What would they do?

It was too much to make sense of all at once. A cascade of emotions washed over her. She grieved for Meyer Elazar, who had been something of a mentor early in her training. She remembered his bemused look when she appeared in his office, a brash young student offering to assist one of the leading figures in her field. She remembered the stern manner in which he interrogated her, asking why she wanted to be an archaeologist. And she remembered his sympathy—or was it empathy?—when she answered, quietly, *"To find a reason to believe."*

The rabbi had leaned across his desk, addressing her in a gravel voice. "That's a dangerous reason to dig," he said.

She had another reason, equally compelling, if not more so, but she kept it to herself.

To find a reason not to believe.

She recalled leaving the rabbi's office in embarrassment, thinking she had been foolish and naive.

A week later, she received a letter from Professor Nuri Hafetz, who was about to undertake an important excavation in Jerusalem. He couldn't pay her, but he could arrange for her to stay with some friends for the summer. Would she like to volunteer? For some mysterious reason, the rabbi had taken it upon himself to make a call.

In the weeks that followed, she had been the rabbi's guest at speeches and seminars, and even a few cocktail parties. Some of the other students questioned her friendship with Elazar. How could she condone his reactionary politics, they demanded. Catherine pleaded ignorance. She was too absorbed in her work to think about politics—or so she convinced herself.

In time, politics intruded in ways that were impossible to avoid. Elazar's name appeared in the headlines, and his face was on the front page. She began to distance herself from the influential rabbi, unconsciously at first, then self-consciously. She made excuses to decline invitations, and spoke up only half-heartedly when friends or colleagues tried to demonize Elazar. Yet, she still accepted the occasional big favor—such as the time Elazar nominated her to speak at a conference in Switzerland.

Even now, the memories gave her pangs of guilt. But they were nothing compared to the anger.

The disloyal protege was an ambitious scholar, and she couldn't help but feel betrayed. She had confided in Meyer, and no one else. She had shared exclusive details of her unpublished research. She had reached out for help—not just for the benefit of his advice, but also to make amends for her behavior toward him.

Elazar had scoffed. "Don't waste your talent," he told her. "Surely you can pursue something more substantial."

Though the criticism hurt, she could accept it. She could even reject it and move on. What she couldn't handle was the *duplicity*. If the Israeli journalist was to be believed, Meyer had lied.

The lead she had been pursuing wasn't a dead end, after all. And Elazar had held back crucial information—even as he betrayed her secret to others.

The springs of her desk chair squeaked with outrage.

She could have been poised for greatness. Instead, she was struggling just to keep her career on track.

She flogged herself for not pushing harder to finish her biography of Mandel. In the academic rough and tumble of "publish or perish," she felt her shelf life expiring. From the outset, she had pinned her hopes of winning tenure on this project, and she came to believe she would make a contribution to knowledge.

But if what Benjamin Jordan said was true, she was in danger of being overtaken by events. Her obscure, underexposed subject seemed at risk of being drawn into the media glare. Even if she managed to complete it, it would take months, perhaps years, to find a publisher. If she submitted it to a journal, it could take just as long to slog through the peer review process, as petty, jealous experts critiqued her work.

Assuming she lived that long.

It was an involuntary reaction, a bit of dark sarcasm, but the more she thought about it, the more she worried. Meyer was dead. Murdered, along with his closest colleagues. And what for?

For the fruits of her research?

She felt a surge of panic. She held her breath and listened to the stillness. Drops of frozen rain strafed the glass.

The old steam radiator hissed and crinkled, then sputtered into silence.

She told herself she was overreacting. With deliberate calm, she ignored the adrenaline coursing through her veins. Harnessing her paranoia, she decided to safeguard her work. She hadn't told Elazar everything. She had developed a theory, but before she could explain it, Elazar had cut her off with criticism.

She turned on her laptop computer and clicked her way to the unfinished draft of her book. Concentrating on a plan restored her sense of control. With a few quick commands, she saved the draft to a compact disc, and protected it with a password. With a few more keystrokes, she saved several files of notes and transcripts, and confirmed that they had been copied successfully.

Then she clicked to her privacy software and wiped all trace of the original files from the computer.

The CD was supposed to be her back-up archive. Now it was her safe deposit box. She ejected the disc from its drive. She swiveled in her chair and scanned her bookshelves. One of the thicker volumes, *The Riverside Shakespeare*, caught her eye. She slipped the disc between the pages of King Lear, Act IV, Scene ii, and restored the book to its shelf.

She opened her file cabinet and flipped through the tabs, searching for the critical folder, which contained a legal pad of her handwritten notes and a cassette tape. She must have misfiled it. She thumbed through the files again, slowly, to no avail.

The adrenaline returned, colder than before.

She ransacked her desk. Where could it be? There were only two possibilities, unless . . . .

The first possibility was that she left it at home. The second was that she left it at her uncle's cabin in the woods of northern Michigan, on remote Loon Lake, where she occasionally retreated to write in solitude.

The third possibility . . . was too disturbing to take seriously.

Catherine turned off her desk lamp and locked the office door behind her.

Chapter 19

The walk home ordinarily took 15 minutes, but Catherine was in a hurry. Never mind that the sidewalks were slippery from the sleet. She drew the hood of her anorak tight and tilted her head against the wind. Her muscles clenched, numbly. She looked over her shoulder, but the roads were almost empty.

She lived on a quiet side street, in the smallest house on the block, a weathered bungalow. A dormer window protruded from her attic bedroom, and a covered porch framed the front door. A curtain of spruce trees shielded it from the neighbors.

Preoccupied with the missing file, Catherine hustled down the pebbled drive. She jangled her keys and opened the door.

The house was warm and dry—and sadly lifeless without her mother. In happier days, the smell of pea soup or the sound of a kettle whistling might have greeted her, but those were merely memories. She hung her coat on the antique rack and kicked off her Timberlands. She switched on a light and headed straight for the den, which doubled as a study. Urgently, she rummaged through the cabinets.

The folder wasn't there.

Damn.

She looked out the window at swaying trees and leaves whipped by invisible gusts. It would take three hours to get to the cabin on the lake—and another three hours to get back in time for the next day's departmental meeting. She couldn't afford to miss it; she was already on notice for having skipped the last two.

She had pulled her share of all-nighters over the years. Still, she dreaded the prospect of driving through the night. She was tempted to crawl under a down comforter and curl up with a novel, but she realized she was too distracted to rest. Better to dress warmly, fill a Thermos and get going.

Floorboards creaked beneath her feet as she climbed the stairs. She clicked on the light. The bed looked inviting, but she went to the closet. She picked out a plaid flannel shirt and a dry pair of Levis and set them on the bed. She wriggled out of her turtleneck, folded it neatly, and laid it on the dresser. She slipped out of her jeans. Her reflection in the mirror was a photographer's study, the contrast of a pale, slim torso and a black lace bra.

She tensed. She heard a noise downstairs, or thought she did. The sound of hardwood creaking. She listened.

All she heard was the ticking of a clock and the wind in the trees.

The house was still.

With a conscious effort, she shrugged it off.

She swept the hair from her eyes and stepped into the tiny bathroom. She felt a headache coming on, and it showed. She reached over the sink and opened the medicine cabinet, looking for a Tylenol. She popped a chalky tablet on her tongue, cupped some cold water from the faucet, and swallowed. She closed the medicine cabinet and looked in the mirror. She noticed with embarrassment that there was a tiny piece of lettuce stuck between her teeth.

Had that been there all afternoon? And during coffee with that reporter?

She started to open the cabinet again to get some floss, but she stopped in mid-motion and pressed it shut.

That's strange.

She looked in the mirror, and she looked over her shoulder, through the bathroom door, into the bedroom.

It was brighter than usual.

The lamp on her night table was on.

Only she didn't remember turning it on. In fact, she remembered turning it *off* the night before, as she did every night, when she put down her book and rolled over to go to sleep.

The lamp had come on again when she came upstairs a few minutes ago and flicked the main switch for the bedroom, the one for the ceiling light. The two lights were on the same circuit.

But if the switch on the night table lamp was left in the *off* position, as usual, the switch on the bedroom wall couldn't make it turn on.

Puzzled, Catherine walked over to the night table. She switched the lamp off. The book she had been reading was sitting there, just as she remembered—spread open face down to keep her place, on top of a pile of lecture notes.

She picked up the book and turned it over.

She felt a surge of panic.

She had read that page, that entire chapter, at least two nights ago.

Had somebody been in my room? Had somebody been nosing around my night table?

My lecture notes?

She heard the wind in the trees and the ticking of the clock.

She picked up the phone and dialed 911.

"I think somebody's been in my house," she said.

"Is this Maeve Cavanaugh?" the emergency dispatcher asked.

"Catherine Cavanaugh."

"Okay, Ms. Cavanaugh, what makes you think there's been an intruder?"

She could have been wrong about either the book or the light—but not both.

"I just got home, and things don't look right . . . ."

"Is it possible the intruder is still in the house?"

Still in the house?

"I don't know—yes, I think so."

"Can you get out of the house?"

"I—I'm upstairs."

In my underwear.

"Okay, Ms. Cavanaugh. What I want you to do is stay on the phone with me, and we'll have some officers over there soon."

Six minutes later, there were two police officers in her bedroom, and two more making a sweep of the house.

A humorless bodybuilder in his 20s—he had introduced himself, and she had already forgotten his name, but there it was on his nameplate, Officer Briggs—put on a latex glove and opened her night table drawer.

"Do you notice anything amiss?" he asked.

"No, I don't," she said with embarrassment.

He was almost as young as her students.

"Is anything missing from the house?" he asked.

"Well, yes."

"What?"

"I'm not sure. Just some papers and a cassette tape. I mean, I'm not sure they were here before."

"Are those items valuable?"

She didn't know how to answer.

Another officer stuck his head in the bedroom.

"We've searched the closets, the basement, under the bed in the other room. Everything's neat and tidy. And the backdoor's locked tight."

"What about the lamp?" Catherine asked. "I know I turned it off before I went to bed last night."

"Do you think you could have fallen asleep with the light on?" Briggs asked. "Or just forgot turning it on again in the morning?"

The cop was humoring her.

"That doesn't explain the book," she said. "The book was open to the wrong page."

Officer Briggs picked up her copy of *Harry Potter and the Chamber of Secrets.*

"I wouldn't have left it open to the part about the spiders in the woods," Catherine said, "because I was already at the part about the ghost in the bathroom. Moaning Myrtle."

"Scary story," Briggs said. "Kept my little brother up at night."

"My mother liked it, too," Catherine said. "She got it as a present in the hospital."

Briggs put the book down.

"I'll tell you what, Mrs. Cavanaugh. Let's you and I walk through the house together and see for ourselves."

Chapter 20

Ann Arbor

Jordan peered through the windshield wipers, straining to catch a number on a mailbox or house. He needed answers, and he didn't intend to wait for them.

What was the professor hiding?

Slowing to a crawl, he saw police lights flashing beyond a row of spruce trees. He inched closer, his heart in his throat. Two cruisers were parked in front of a modest brick bungalow.

Catherine Cavanaugh's address.

The shock spread from the pit of Jordan's stomach through his aching body to every nerve and capillary. He hit the brakes and gripped the steering wheel.

Images came flooding back of ambulance lights flashing in front of Miriam Wiesman's house, and her body bag wheeling past him, strapped to a stretcher. Jordan didn't believe Elazar's secretary had committed suicide. He believed she had been murdered.

He cut his headlights and pulled over, watching the house, trying to decide whether to go in for a closer look. In his fear for the young professor, he felt something else. Something personal.

The first cruiser backed out of the unpaved drive, grinding pebbles beneath its tires. The cruiser's brake lights came on, its emergency lights stopped flashing, and it slowly drove away. A minute later, the other cruiser followed.

Relieved, but doubly curious, Jordan pulled into the driveway. He parked beside an old Jeep Cherokee and cut the ignition in his minivan, the only vehicle the rental agency had left.

It looked as if every light in the house was on.

He slammed the door to the minivan and dashed through the rain to the shelter of the porch. He rang the bell and waited. Through the windows, he could see a coat hanging on a rack, and a pair of hiking boots. One coat and one pair, he noted.

He thrust his hands in his pockets and pulled in his elbows, unaccustomed to the chill. He rang the bell again, to no avail. He stepped off the porch and looked at the house. It had a quaint, lived-in quality. A gap-toothed pumpkin grinned from the railing, and a birdfeeder trailed sunflower seeds. Light filtered through the lace curtains of the dormer window.

The rain matted his hair and ran into his eyes.

He saw movement in the house. Catherine was coming down the stairs, toward the door. He stepped onto the porch.

Instead of opening the door, she called out angrily from behind it.

"What do you want?"

"I was reading about your friend, Mordecai," Jordan said, raising his voice to make himself heard. "I'd like to know how a 19th Century shopkeeper fits into my story."

"Yeah, well, you're not the only one."

"What happened?"

"Someone broke into my house. Maybe it was you. Maybe you wouldn't take 'no comment' for an answer."

"It wasn't me. But you're right—I won't take 'no comment' for answer."

"I think you're the reason this happened," she said, and even through the door he could tell that she was shaking. "Whoever it was, you led them to me."

A look of horror clouded Jordan's face.

"If I could find you, so could they," he said.

"But who? And why?"

"You tell me, professor. I'm still standing here in the dark."

A gust of wind blew rain in his eyes.

"We need to talk, professor."

She unlocked the deadbolt and opened the door a crack. She made no effort to mask her distrust.

"Give me your wallet," she said.

Jordan handed it over, frowning. She took it and shut the door. She flipped through the contents, examining his credit cards and identification.

"A professional would have thought of that," Jordan said.

"Maybe. So tell me, Mr. Benjamin Jordan, of Jabotinsky Street, Tel Aviv, would anyone at *The Shofar* vouch for you?"

"Call and find out," he said.

"I think I will," she said, and left him on the porch.

He stood alone in the cold. Did she think he was bluffing?

He looked at his watch. It was 10:56 p.m. in Michigan, not yet 6:00 a.m. in Tel Aviv. Would anyone answer the phone in the newsroom?

Five minutes later, she returned.

"The switchboard operator said you couldn't be on assignment for the newspaper because you were indefinitely suspended."

"She's right," Jordan said. "I came here at my own expense. Not just to get my job back, not just for my name, but for answers."

His words hung in the air and blew away on the wind.

Catherine opened the door.

"Why did they suspend you?" she asked.

"I'm not really sure. Maybe because I made a stupid mistake."

"Are you sure you aren't making another?"

"I don't think so."

"Do you always knock on closed doors in the middle of the night?"

"If that's what it takes."

"Well, you're a little late."

She opened the door wider and let him out of the cold.

"Do the police have anything to go on?" he asked, as she shut the door behind him.

"They think I'm imagining the break-in."

"Was anything taken?"

"I'm not sure. There's one other place it could be, all the way in Northern Michigan, and if I don't leave now, I won't make it back in time for my morning meeting. I'm already falling asleep."

"I'll drive," Jordan said.

She looked at him warily, then she seemed to warm to the idea. She glanced out the window at his mommy-van.

"Besides," Jordan said, "how can you resist such hot wheels?"

She looked him in the eye and grabbed her coat.

Chapter 21

Northern Michigan

Jordan fell in line with the late-night truckers heading north on the highway, until the tail lights and the raindrops fell away, leaving open road.

Catherine stared out the window, withdrawing from the danger she felt, and the sense of violation. Withdrawing from Jordan, too.

She was drawn to him, but she didn't trust him. He was a reporter. But that wasn't all. In light of past experience, she didn't trust men—or her own judgment about them. For a while now, it hadn't been an issue. She had been too preoccupied with her mother's illness.

Her mother said that was an excuse. Her mother said she was using it to avoid the challenges in her own life, like the book she couldn't bring herself to finish.

Jordan took his eyes off the road and looked at her.

"I can't help you if you don't help me," he said. "What did you tell Meyer Elazar?"

"Fortunately, I didn't tell him everything."

"Does he know that you held something back?"

"*Does* he? You mean '*Did* he?'"

"I'm not ready to think of him as dead. They haven't found his body."

"What?"

"There's evidence suggesting Rabbi Elazar was somewhere else when the Institute exploded," Jordan said. "Just before the bomb went off, he seems to have phoned the museum to confirm that the other Council members were all present."

"Were they?"

"All but two of them: a Palestinian and a representative of the Vatican. Both confidantes of Elazar. Both mysteriously dead."

She couldn't believe what she was hearing. She couldn't feel her extremities.

"So who would know what I told Meyer? And who would be after my research?"

"I can only guess. I know Elazar was in touch with a senior member of the Israeli government. And I know the dead Palestinian, Ramsi, was in contact with the Jordanian government."

"How about the Vatican's representative? Could he have told the Vatican before he died?"

"I don't see why not."

"And if a reporter has gotten this far, there's no telling who else is on the trail," Catherine said.

"If it's any consolation, I'm not usually the last to know," Jordan said.

"Sorry, I didn't mean it that way."

"I know," he said. "It's been a tough day, and I've made it tougher for you."

He turned to her with an expression of genuine concern. "We have a long way to go, and you have a meeting in the morning. Get some rest if you can."

"Thanks," she said, with a nervous smile.

She closed her eyes and curled up in the passenger seat, drained by the stress, hiding from the fear, retreating from the questions. Grateful that somebody else was driving. She slept, oblivious to the squeak of the windshield wipers.

He woke her when they reached the exit, and she guided him through a small lakefront fishing village, down twisting country roads, past rustic cabins, onto an old dirt logging trail. The minivan bumped its way over the rutted terrain. The woods pressed in on them, leaving only a river of sky. A lonely cloud sailed low over the treetops, ghostly white against the clear sparkle of stars.

The forest thinned, and they entered an abandoned orchard. Branches arched overhead like skeletons' fingers.

"Apples and cherries," Catherine said. "I used to pick them as a child."

Jordan slowed to a stop. A deer was blocking the road. The high beams bounced off its retinas, which glowed like the eyes in a flash photo. The doe looked straight at them. It looked nothing like a proverbial deer frozen in the headlights. It looked proud and confident, standing its ground. It watched them for a moment, then lost interest and walked off into the trees.

Somewhere in the darkness, an owl hooted.

The cabin capped the crest of a small hill. Jordan parked beside it and stepped out of the car, stretching his limbs. The air filled his lungs, cold and crisp and purifying. He felt invigorated.

Shivering, Catherine opened the door and flicked on a light. Jordan followed her into the cottage. She went straight to the kitchen table and rummaged through a pile of papers. She opened an accordion folder and thumbed through the contents.

"It's all here," she said, with palpable relief. "We can go back now."

Jordan's shoulders sank. He looked exhausted—and exasperated.

Catherine put down the folder. For the first time since he showed up at her door, she focused on Jordan. She noted the shadow of stubble across his rugged features, and the lean, raw power of his body. She was struck by the depth of emotion in his eyes, and something intangible—an air of natural confidence and inner pain.

"I could use a cup of tea," he said.

"Of course," she said, apologetically. "We can stay and rest for a while."

She set a pot of water on the stove and excused herself, disappearing into the bedroom, where Jordan glimpsed the foot of a quilted four-post bed as she closed the door behind her.

Jordan stared at the folder lying on the table. Unlabeled, it gave no hint as to its contents. He resisted the impulse to open it. He looked around. A fieldstone fireplace with a broad hearth and wrought iron implements dominated the room. Beside it stood a pile of neatly stacked birch logs. Simple bookcases lined the walls, which were finished with roughly hewn pine boards. The room was decorated with hunting artifacts — duck decoys, a deer's antlers, and a trophy bass, mounted over the fireplace. There were two couches of tartan plaid, and between them a table cut from the trunk of a giant oak. A braided oval rug covered a swath of the floor.

Jordan sank into a couch. He surmised that the large windows across the room opened onto a porch, but it was hard to tell in the dark.

He felt his eyelids surrendering to the lure of sleep, until the teapot whistled from the galley kitchen. Catherine emerged from the bedroom in gray Michigan sweats and served him a steaming mug.

"I hope you don't mind instant coffee. It's all I could find."

"Perfect," he lied.

She threw a few logs in the fireplace and lit some kindling. The birch bark caught fire.

She lay down on the couch across from him and sipped a cup.

"So this is where you go to escape?" he asked.

"The perfect hideaway, isn't it? I come here to write."

The fire popped and crackled. Jordan watched the flames dance hypnotically.

"Alone?" he asked.

"I work best alone."

"What made you stop work on the Mandel book?"

"I was here, working on it, when I got the call. It was the last time I was here. I remember her voice on the phone, so calm, so brave, trying to reassure me. My mother had taken herself to the hospital. She was alone when she got the diagnosis. And there was so little time . . . . While she was still alive, it was hard enough to keep up with my teaching."

"Did she ever see you teach?"

"Never."

"I think she would have enjoyed it."

"I'm not so sure."

"That was quite a performance you gave in class."

"You were there?"

"Too bad I'm not a drama critic."

Catherine laughed. "I assure you, the lesson I had planned wasn't nearly as interesting."

"Who is this student, Bryan, who challenged you?"

"Bryan Jennings, part of a growing movement on our campuses and in our politics. I thought his contribution today was enlightening."

"Where I come from there are lots of Bryans. They tend to drive the course of events."

"I almost envy them," Catherine said. "Their passion, their conviction, their clarity. Their devotion to a cause. They go through life with so few doubts, so few burdens. Just as the New Testament teaches: 'The truth shall set you free.'"

"Yes," Jordan said, "but have you noticed? Their Truth has a tendency to take others prisoner."

Catherine gazed into the fire. "I've noticed."

"In a way, Mordecai Mandel was a prisoner," Jordan said, glancing at the folder on the table.

She studied the folder, which was lying exactly as she had left it, on top of a copy of National Geographic, obscuring half the cover photo of Jerusalem's golden Dome of the Rock.

"Are you a religious man, Benjamin?"

"You have to understand," Jordan said. "I grew up in the Holy Land."

"So?"

"No, I have no use for religion."

"Why?"

"Do you want me to be blunt?"

"I do."

"From what I've seen, Karl Marx got it wrong. Religion isn't the opium of the people. It's the LSD."

"What do you mean?"

"Opium numbs and tranquilizes. LSD inspires psychedelic visions—and violent delusions. It drives people to acts of destruction—and self-destruction. It seduces people with the promise of enlightenment, but it robs them of the ability to think for themselves."

"That's an awfully cynical way of looking at it."

"As I said, I grew up in the Holy Land."

The conversation drew her in.

"What about Jesus's message: 'Love thy neighbor'?"

"Jesus taught that "Love thy neighbor' was the *second* most important commandment. The *most* important commandment, Jesus said, was to love God. And look where that got us. For the love of God, the New Testament says, the Jews demanded Jesus's execution. They accused him of blasphemy. For the love of God—and for rejecting the son of God—Jesus condemned the Jews. For the love of God, he left a legacy of hatred and persecution, every bit as powerful as his message of brotherhood."

"Do you believe there's a God?"

"I'm willing to keep an open mind," Jordan said. "But for me, believing begs the question: Who created Him?"

"How about the Old Testament? You never found the Bible to be a source of wisdom, or inspiration?"

"I did."

"What changed?"

"I read it."

"And?"

"No wonder people have been fighting over the Promised Land for thousands of years. Just look at the way God gave the land to his Chosen People. He didn't just give it to them, he commanded them to go and take it, despite the fact that it was already occupied. And he commanded them to exterminate the prior occupants. 'You must not leave a soul alive,' he said. So the Israelites marched from city to city, slaughtering all the Canaanite inhabitants—men, women and children. As a child, I was taught that Joshua fought the battle of Jericho, and the walls came tumbling down. They don't tell you that the battle of Jericho was part of a murderous campaign—the first genocide."

"God was afraid the Canaanites would corrupt the Chosen People," Catherine said. "He feared that they would inspire the Israelites to worship pagan gods, and practice child sacrifice."

"Yes, but if he wanted to save the children, why did he have them slaughtered? It was a divinely sanctioned Holocaust, minus the crematoria. At one point, God warned the Israelites not to complete the genocide so quickly. He was afraid the wild animals that fed on the corpses would grow too numerous. 'Love thy neighbor' is a noble ideal. But the God of the Bible has a way of turning 'Love thy neighbor' into 'Us versus Them.' That's where he and I part ways. Does that make me a cynic? You be the judge, professor."

Catherine rose and walked to the table. She picked up the folder and pressed it to her chest. She felt his compassion and idealism, a kindred spirit. She sensed courage and honesty, and a wounded soul. She wondered if she didn't sense a deeper connection.

She looked at him again and saw a stranger.

"How do I know if I can trust you?" she asked.

"You don't. You have to take it on faith."

She turned her back on Jordan and looked out the window, into the darkness. Silently, she debated with herself, leaning one way, then the other.

She sat on the edge of the couch and put the folder between them, on the trunk of the ancient oak.

"When I was researching Mandel, I looked for members of his family," she said. "It was a tedious search—birth certificates, obituaries, the list of Holocaust victims at Yad Vashem.

"He has one surviving descendant: A great great-grand-daughter, now in her eighties. Harriett. I visited her at a nursing home here in the United States. She was happy to see me, all smiles. Gave me a hug, invited me to sit with her. Then she asked me about my father. She thought I was a niece who died in 1979.

"It was heartbreaking, really. One moment she seemed clear-headed and engaged, highly intelligent. The next her face went slack, she became vacant and confused. Again and again, I explained who I was, why I was visiting her. She smiled, nodded, and kept calling me 'Laura.' That was her niece's name.

"I tried to get her to talk about family history, about Mordecai Mandel. For a day and a half, all I heard were occasional fragments of random memories. I was at a loss. So I decided to read to her from *The Mandel Manuscript*, by Randolph Rempel Jamison. I was about five pages into it when she interrupted.

" 'It's too bad Mordecai kept his discovery to himself,' she said. 'It's too bad he never shared it with the world.'

" 'He tried, but the world didn't want to listen,' I told her.

" 'He didn't try. He wanted to. He planned to. But he was scared,' she said.

" 'Do you know what happened to it?' I asked.

" 'He left it to someone, someone who believed in him. Someone who stood by him during the worst of it. That's what he said in the letter.' "

" 'I thought it was sold at auction, after his death,' I told her.

"She looked at me, indulgently, like a parent gently correcting a child. 'My dear Catherine,' she said, 'you're getting it all mixed up. It was the *Genesis* scroll that was sold at auction. To an anonymous bidder, for 6 pounds, 2 shillings. Exactly the sum Mordecai paid for it when the Bedouin boy brought it to his shop.'

" 'Was there something else?' I asked.

"She was looking at me expectantly now, a teacher leading a pupil to an obvious conclusion. She nodded, wisely, perceptively, almost playfully, chiding me. At that moment, she seemed completely lucid. She seemed to grasp the entire situation.

"'You missed the most important part,' she said.

"There *was* something else, Ben. Mandel had purchased *another* ancient document from the Bedouin. He planned to share it with the world *after* selling the Genesis scroll, after he had established his credibility. He expected it to be a stunning encore. But when he was reduced to the status of a laughingstock, the issue became moot. If the establishment rejected his initial find, imagine how it would react to an even more startling claim.

"Mandel was convinced that this other scrap of writing would shake one of the world's great religions to its foundation. Or so he said during boastful moments.

"Other times, perhaps more soberly, he said his hand was weak, that the evidence he possessed was just a tantalizing tease, that the ultimate, earth-shaking proof remained beyond his reach.

"The ultimate proof was hidden. *Hidden with the treasures of the Temple*, which were spirited out before the city fell to the Romans. And where would one even begin to look for those?

"The family kept silent, unwilling to risk more humiliation. Even after the Dead Sea Scrolls were discovered, making Mandel's Genesis seem much more credible, the family held its secret about his other lost relic. Maybe they didn't believe Mandel's boasts. Maybe they believed, and feared the consequences. Still, they passed the legend from one generation to the next, unwilling to let it die.

" 'And after all that, it would have died with me,' Harriett said.

"She stopped talking, and I prodded, gently. 'Which religion?' I asked. She looked puzzled. I tried to be clearer: *Did Mandel ever say which religion this missing relic would undercut?*

"She struggled for a moment. 'You'll come for Passover this year, won't you, Laura?' she said. 'I'm making matzoh ball soup. You always loved my matzoh ball soup.'"

"And just like that, she was gone, the connection broken. I came back the next morning and read to her again, but I couldn't get past matzoh balls and potato latkes. At the end of the day, I had to get back to Michigan. I would have visited her again, if I had time. But I think she told me all she knew.

"And here's my record of it," Catherine said, pointing to the folder. "My notes of the interview, and my tape recording. Plus some later observations of my own."

Jordan touched a finger to his lips, pensively.

"What do you believe?" he asked.

"I'm certain Harriett believed every word of it."

"What did Meyer Elazar believe?"

"He thought Mandel was a pathetic fool, not to be taken seriously. Or so he said. When I returned from interviewing Harriett, I called Meyer for advice. I told him the story. I asked if he knew anything about Mandel's secret second discovery, or the family legend. Meyer said I was wasting my time. He sounded irritated that his protégé was pursuing such nonsense, as if it reflected poorly on him. In retrospect, he protested too much."

"You know, it's possible that Elazar knew nothing of the Silver Scroll at the time," Jordan said. "It's possible he had no idea that treasures of the Temple might yet be recovered, and with them, Mandel's 'ultimate proof.'"

"What difference does it make? When he got the news, he should have shared it with me. He owed me that."

"Do you think he wanted the glory for himself?"

"Meyer wasn't motivated by ego. He acted on principle. He could be a stubborn old goat, but he was a pious man. He was wholeheartedly committed to Israel and Judaism."

"What if Israel and Judaism were threatened?"

"Israel and Judaism have always been threatened."

"What if something threatened to shake them to their very foundation?"

Catherine didn't answer.

Jordan leaned toward her.

"Supposedly Mandel left this other document to someone who stood by him," he said. "Any idea who that was?"

"I have a theory."

"Are you going to share it with me?"

Catherine hesitated. "Have you thought through the implications?" she asked.

"I'm starting to. But I'm reminded of what a wise professor said: 'If you believe in truth, you have nothing to fear from the search.'"

The largest of the logs collapsed in the fireplace, kicking up a shower of sparks. She closed her eyes.

"I don't know, Benjamin. I just don't know."

He awoke beneath the quilt of her four-post bed. The early morning light filtered through the trees, erasing the frost from the windowpanes. He turned to his side, half expecting to see her, to feel the warmth of her body, but he was alone. He had fallen asleep in his clothes, and the other side of the bed lay undisturbed.

The hardwood floor was cold and unforgiving. Barefoot, he went in search of her. The living room was empty, and the fire had turned to ash. But the dawn brought a dramatic view. The house overlooked a lake, about a mile across, ringed by sloping woods and blanketed by a low covering of clouds. The orange, red, brown, and green of the woods bled together like watercolors and reflected in the rippled surface.

He found her outside, sitting on the edge of a weathered deck, her back to the cabin. Through a gap in the trees, she was watching the lone figure of a man in a distant rowboat, fishing.

"I wish I could stay here," she said, without turning around.

"Did you sleep?"

"I needed to think."

"What did you decide?"

"I wish you luck, Benjamin. But you're on your own."

A breeze rustled through the birches. Across the lake, the tiny fisherman reeled in his line and cast it again.

"It was your story before it was mine," Jordan said.

"Send me a copy."

"I may not be able to do it without you."

"You may be right."

"How else can you make peace with Meyer Elazar?"

"It's too late for that," she said. "I need to get home."

She stood up as she spoke.

"It isn't that easy," he said. "You think you'll be safe? You think they'll leave you alone?"

"I have a class to teach."

"Catherine, don't be ridiculous. You can't hide, and you can't go on avoiding— "

She shot him a look of indignation.

"I need your help," he said.

"That may be. But I don't need yours."

Chapter 22

The West Bank

The helicopter swooped low over the hilltop and banked sharply to the right, hitting a patch of turbulence that left Goren's lunch in his throat.

"General, you're an easy target. We should maintain a higher altitude," the pilot said over the intercom.

"No, circle back," Goren said. "If I'm going to order it, I'm going to witness it."

The helicopter banked again, and Goren leaned out the door, restrained by his shoulder harness, looking down at the red-tiled rooftops. The roar of the engine and the rush of air filled his visored helmet.

Through the open door, he had a clear view of the hilltop settlement and the ground forces advancing toward it from the valley below. Soldiers hiked up the mottled slopes, and tanks scraped clouds of dust from the dirt access road.

"Is that the synagogue?" Goren asked, pointing.

"Yes, that building over there," said the major seated beside him.

The first of the tanks entered the main square. The settlement looked like a ghost town.

"The ground commander is waiting on you, sir."

Goren looked over the hills to the southwest, across miles of Palestinian territory, toward Jerusalem. Until the day before, when the army forced them out, the settlement had been home to a few hundred chronically embattled Jews.

"Get on with it," he said.

The lead tank swung its gun barrel toward the synagogue, tilted it up a notch, and fired. The tank rocked back on its treads as the flat roof and outer walls of the synagogue collapsed on a cushion of smoke and dust.

"What a waste," Goren said. "What a tragedy."

The settlers wanted it this way—they didn't want Palestinians living in their homes, or defiling their temple—but the only upside Goren could see was that he was done protecting them. No more Israeli soldiers would die so that a handful of Jews could maintain a symbolic presence.

I could be in Tel Aviv right now, watching my grandson trip over a soccer ball, or accidentally kick it into his own goal, and instead I'm here, watching Israeli soldiers blow up a Jewish temple.

He could smell the smoke rising.

On the ground, the tank turned 90 degrees and fired a shell into a row of garden apartments.

Where does it end?

The ground commander's voice crackled through Goren's headset.

"General, we're taking sniper fire from the school."

Goren looked down and saw his men scrambling toward defensive positions. One of them was wounded in the thigh, trying to drag himself to safety.

Another soldier rushed to the wounded man's aid and supported him with his free arm, using the other to fire into the school. As Goren watched, a bullet tore through the rescuer's neck. The two soldiers tumbled together.

"Take out that sniper now!" Goren shouted.

A nearby Apache helicopter swiveled and blasted a hellfire missile into the school. The earth shuddered.

"I thought the last of the holdouts was pried loose yesterday," Goren fumed.

"He must have been hiding," the ground commander said.

"Finish the job," Goren said. He leaned toward the pilot. "Lieutenant, I've seen enough."

On the ground, a trio of tanks fired round after round into the red-roofed buildings, raising a cloud of smoke as Goren's helicopter climbed to the west.

At an airbase outside Tel Aviv, a young colonel named Lipman met Goren on the helipad and escorted him to a black Chevy Suburban. He climbed in after the general, and a security man shut the door.

"How did it go?" Lipman asked.

"It was a goddamn sacrilege. And we lost one of our boys."

Goren's face was flushed, and he was sweating profusely.

"I'm sorry," Lipman said.

The Suburban started rolling, and Lipman raised the partition that separated them from the men in front.

Goren exhaled heavily and tilted his head back, spent with exhaustion.

"You'll be briefing members of the cabinet in an hour," Lipman said.

"Do you have the report we discussed?" Goren asked.

"No, General. Mossad is stalling, or blowing us off."

"Goddamn it, if Avi Arad and his staff think I'm going to forget about the fiasco in Lebanon, I want you to light a burner under their asses. They assured me the air strike was a no-brainer, and I expect an explanation. You saw the newspaper story—that bastard Farouk was mocking us."

Lipman, Goren's closest aide, maintained the calm of someone who had weathered the general's storms.

"Arad's people say the reporter who accused us of bombing an orphanage is a known Palestinian sympathizer. They say he can't be trusted."

"Of course he can't. His own editor conceded as much when he sacked him, and retracted that bullshit story implying that the government blew up the museum. But even reckless sons of bitches get some things right."

"I do have some new information, General. You know my friend at the American embassy? Well, over drinks, I happened to bring up the Lebanon fiasco, and our frustration with Mossad."

"Fishing without a license."

"My CIA friend owed us, and he prefers that we owe him. He got their National Security Agency to search its communications intercepts, and it seems Arad had sent an agent to visit Jordan's editor, Shaul Meltzer. They have a recording of the agent reporting back."

"What did they hear?"

"Meltzer promised to deal with Jordan. Meltzer promised that, going forward, Mossad could have confidence in the paper's coverage."

"Jordan's story didn't accuse Mossad of anything, did it?"

"No, General, it didn't say a word about Mossad."

"Then why is Avi Arad, the head of Mossad, getting a reporter fired?"

"Maybe he was worried about the next story."

Chapter 23

Detroit

Jordan tucked a newspaper under his arm and looked for a seat in the departure lounge. It was standing room only. He read the front page while waiting for his flight to board, but none of it registered.

Catherine had closed the door on him, on the story, and on the reality of the situation. He'd given her a day to change her mind, but she insisted her mind was made up. Short of camping out on her doorstep, what could he do?

She was ambivalent—that was clear. Even if she was holding back, she wanted him to pursue the story. She had shared the secret of Mordecai Mandel, at least part of it.

Jordan almost convinced himself that he was doing her a favor by leaving Michigan. Whoever was watching her was watching him. Maybe they would follow him and leave her alone.

Without the benefit of her help, he was left with only the outline of a plan. Mandel had possessed something far more important than the Genesis scroll, something he believed would shake one of the world's great religions to its foundation—or at least cause tremors.

Whatever it was, it described something even more profound, which was buried with the Temple treasures. Something the old lady, Harriett, had referred to as "the ultimate proof."

It seemed clear that the prospect of acquiring the ultimate proof had inspired the assassination of Elazar's fellow Council members and the destruction of the Institute. Now, whoever possessed the Silver Scroll could seek the treasure and the greater prize free of competition or interference.

Without the Silver Scroll, the closest thing to a treasure map, Jordan had no way of finding either. But Mandel's missing relic might tell the story. According to the old lady, Mandel had intended to unveil it as a stunning encore. Instead, in disgrace, he had entrusted it to someone who stood by him. Jordan intended to find that someone.

"Flight 9731 to London, now boarding all rows."

Jordan scanned the terminal, looking for a familiar face. Looking for Catherine.

He handed the attendant his boarding pass and walked down the ramp.

Chapter 24

Ann Arbor

Adam Keller, dean of the faculty, dismissed his secretary for the evening and ushered Catherine into his office.

"Thanks for coming in," the dean said, gesturing toward a maroon leather couch. "I thought it was important for us to talk."

Anxious and curious, Catherine sat down. It was the kind of couch—low, deep and awkward—that put the visitor at an immediate disadvantage.

"If it's about the department meeting the other day, I'm sorry I couldn't be there, or at those other ones. It's just that—"

"Not at all," Keller said, waving his hand. "I'm sure everyone understands."

He poured them each a sherry and sank into an armchair.

In his late fifties, Keller exuded erudition, sophistication, and success. He was said to be in line for the university presidency. With his dark business suit and trim physique, and a touch of gray accenting his handsome features, he could pass as a corporate CEO, which was a useful quality when he cultivated the university's major donors. Though he was trained as a biblical scholar, he had an impressive command of multiple fields, including classical history, economics, and the fine points of Big 10 football. His greatest talent was reserved for a more nuanced game: academic politics.

Keller put his feet on the cocktail table, leaned back in his chair, and pressed his fingertips together.

"Listen, Catherine, something's come up, and I think it's too good to pass up."

Catherine listened.

"I don't need to tell you how few openings there are in your field. You didn't choose it for its practicality. Well, there's a tenure-track opening right now with excellent long-term prospects. I think you should take it. Of course, we'd miss you terribly, but it's a rare opportunity, and it would be selfish of us to stand in the way of your career. You'll need to decide quickly."

"Where's the job?"

"Westphall State, a real up-and-coming program, and with your talent, you could carve out a real leadership role," he said, with improbable enthusiasm. "They hope to win accreditation next year. In time, if you publish well, you could use it as a springboard to a top school."

"Isn't that somewhere in Nebraska?"

"Iowa. They need somebody now, and the dean, Mike Freitag, is an old friend of mine. I told him he couldn't find anyone better. It comes with a substantial signing bonus, which I took the liberty of arranging—negotiating—on your behalf. And a generous budget for research."

"But I *have* a tenure-track position. Here at the University of Michigan."

"I don't need to tell you that a junior position around here is like Cinderella's coach. Pumpkin Time sneaks up awfully fast, and hardly anyone marries the prince. You need to look to the future, Catherine. Trust me on this."

"I'm willing to take my chances," she said.

Keller rubbed his face with one hand and sat up straight, thinking. He leaned forward, facing her.

"I'm sorry, Catherine, but I don't want you to harbor any illusions. It wouldn't be fair. No one wanted to say anything during your mother's illness, but under the circumstances . . . . Well, you understand."

"No, I don't."

"The tenure committee has been tracking your progress. I tried to warn you, Catherine. None of the members believes you can overcome your lack of published scholarship."

Her world was spinning, breaking apart.

"I know that's disappointing, but we all have to face facts and adjust our expectations, from time to time. If you look at it objectively — "

She tried to stop the spinning, to look at it objectively. She braced herself against the leather couch . . . . Then, across an unnatural distance, she saw.

"He's gotten to you, hasn't he? Bryan Jennings of the Campus Gospel Fellowship is threatening to make political trouble for you. And you don't even have the courage to come out and say it."

"What are you talking about?" the dean said, not very convincingly.

"Don't bullshit me, Adam."

They locked eyes, and Keller looked away, blinking.

"Sonofabitch," he whispered, burying his head in his hands. "I'm sorry Catherine, honest I'm sorry. I thought I could shield you from the worst of it."

"I didn't think he could squeeze that hard."

Keller drained his sherry in a gulp.

"From what I hear, you demolished him," Keller said. "He was hoping to score some points, make himself heard, win the presidency of his organization, and you left him completely humiliated. I have to hand it to you, you never did anything half-assed."

Catherine's panic was fading, and the instinct to fight was taking over.

"I won't go," she said. "I can't give in to this."

"You can't stay."

"What are you talking about? This is a university, for God's sake. The faculty can't railroad me out of here over a religious controversy. That's insane."

"It's not about your teaching, Catherine. It's about *us*. He knows about *us*."

She looked at the dean, too stunned to respond.

He knows about us?

"How could he know?" she whispered.

"Who knows? It's a small community. People talk, people snoop. He can't be the only one, but he's the only one with a hard on."

"What could he possibly prove?"

Keller looked sheepish.

"Who could have known way back then that email was so indestructible?"

"Stand up to him, Adam. Call his bluff. People have overcome far greater embarrassments. It's ancient history anyway."

"He's already written to Barbara, all righteous and moralistic, like he's doing her a favor, warning her that he might make an issue of it, quoting the Ten Commandments. *'Thou shalt not allow thy husband to screw his students and get away with it, blah blah blah.'* She wants you gone."

She studied the line of his powerful shoulders, uncharacteristically burdened, and the anxiety in his eyes. She remembered the old mixture of passion and fearlessness, confidence and humor, and searched for a trace of it.

"Come on, Adam. You're not the first professor who ever fell in love with a graduate student."

He looked away.

"It's more complicated than you think."

"How complicated can it be? Assuming this was an aberration, Barbara will forgive you. We were wrong, and I'm deeply sorry. But we can't undo it. All we can do is apologize, and make amends."

Keller poured himself another sherry. His expression went from grim to funereal. Catherine barely recognized him.

"So it wasn't an aberration," she said softly.

"There's more to it," he said. "I was hoping you'd never find out."

Her shoulders went slack, and she slumped further in the awkward couch.

"Do you know Marilyn Rivers?" he asked.

"The one who teaches at the University of Texas?"

"The very same."

"Her husband did his medical training here."

"When Rivers finished her doctoral work at Stanford, and some remarkable field work in the Upper Galilee, she wanted to come to Ann Arbor. A majority of the department's senior faculty wanted to bring her here. They wanted to give her *your* job. Of course, it wasn't your job at the time. You had applied for it. But she was the top choice."

Catherine was getting queasy.

"They would have given it to her. But I intervened. I persuaded them to hire you. I never could have done it if you weren't a strong candidate. But they thought Rivers was stronger. As you might have sensed, there were some lingering resentments."

She felt suffocation, a personal implosion.

"Why, Adam? Why did you do it?"

"Why did I do it? I did it because I wanted you, I needed you, I couldn't bear to lose you. I was afraid I was going to lose you forever. I did it because even after all that time, I couldn't stop dreaming . . . .

"I did it because I thought I owed you that much, that it was the least I could do, for all the pain. Not just for your sake, I suppose, but to ease my conscience.

"I wish I could take it back," he said. "No, that's a lie. I would never take it back."

"And now you tell me that I don't even belong here."

"No matter how you look at it, Catherine, we're screwed. They'll say you got your job by sleeping with me. And I'll stand accused of much more than a momentary lapse or marital indiscretion. They'll say I abused my authority."

"And they'll be right," she said.

"I'm sorry, Catherine. I'm sorry I brought this on you."

"We brought it on each other."

"You didn't know I was married."

"Not at first."

"Take the job, Catherine. Make the most of it. Make a name for yourself that no one can take away. Find something important. Or write something memorable, and undeniable. Not that dull Mandel biography. Write something worthy of your talents, and the rest will follow. I'll help you any way I can."

She left in a daze, thunderstruck by life's sudden reversal.

She walked unconsciously until she came to a hard wooden bench and stopped to rest.

She wanted to stand and fight and accept the scandal. It would be her penance. But she couldn't do that to Adam. She couldn't bring herself to blame him.

Taking the job at Westphall was out of the question—not only because it meant *going* to Westphall. She couldn't accept it because Adam had arranged it.

She realized that wherever she went, people would wonder: Why hadn't she made it at Michigan?

She thought of Adam's advice: Find something important; write something memorable.

She thought of Benjamin, chasing *her* story, determined to get to the bottom of it. With or without her.

She thought of Bryan Jennings and Meyer Elazar, determined to get the better of her.

She thought of Mordecai Mandel, silenced, defeated and forgotten. Crying out for redemption. She had been avoiding him, or something larger. His unfinished work had become her own.

She looked up, at the stained glass window, the altar, and the cross. She was sitting in the last row of her mother's church.

She remembered the light in her bedroom, and the book on her night table.

In a voice only she could hear, she screamed in terror.

Chapter 25

An Aegean Island

Dawn reached across the sea, bathing the hillside in pink and gold.

Meyer Elazar sat beneath an olive tree, lost in thought. It had been another sleepless night, grappling with the task at hand, and he had come to watch the sun rise. Maybe the salt breeze would clear his head.

Below him, the sparsely wooded slope stopped at a cliff's edge. Below that, he could hear, but couldn't see, the rhythmic advance and retreat of the waves. The blue water seemed tranquil, except where jagged rock formations just offshore rose to challenge it.

He wondered, how many sunken wrecks lay hidden beneath the surface? He had been here before, thousands of years ago, on his way home from a far-away war. In an age of heroes, when gods fought among men. The gods had blown him off course. A midnight storm tossed his ship, splintered the mast, and swept him overboard. Somehow, he washed ashore, the sole survivor. He was a leader of men, responsible for his crew. And they had died so he might reach his destination.

On the island, a sorceress sheltered him and kept him in bliss. Until, like the hero Odysseus, he returned to the real world to regain what was his.

That was in his youth, in his imagination.

Life at the present-day monastery of Saint Constantine was hardly blissful. But it was serene. It had an otherworldly quality, like an out-of-body experience.

The island was a picturesque anachronism, less than three miles square and virtually uncorrupted by life on the mainland—since the German occupation. Goats roamed wild in the hills, and grapes ripened on the vine. At the far end, where the land rose gently from the sea, a village hugged the coast of a crescent cove. A dozen fishing vessels bobbed at their moorings, and several others headed out to sea, carrying on a tradition as old as the *Iliad* itself. One of them had brought him here.

Sheets of white linen billowed in the sea breeze, hanging from clotheslines. There were no cars to speak of, only a few vintage pick-up trucks, because there was nowhere to drive.

He felt a strange kinship with the place, a common heritage, which went beyond his love of Homer. On their way from the boat to the monastery, they had stopped beside a pile of stones. It marked a mass grave. In retaliation for a campaign of sabotage, which culminated in the sinking of a German patrol boat docked in the cove, the Nazis had machine-gunned 18 villagers—and the monks of Saint Constantine.

Perched atop a promontory, the centuries-old monastery occupied the island's high ground. Its architecture gave expression to the Greek Orthodox Church, which long ago diverged from Rome. A sky-blue dome crowned a whitewashed octagonal base, surrounded by four smaller, lower domes. A nearby tower echoed the design.

In recent years, the order of Greek Orthodox monks had returned to reclaim the monastery from decades of abandonment. They began by restoring the cross atop the chapel, and finished by enclosing a satellite dish behind one of the outbuildings. The accommodations were Spartan yet functional. His own thick-walled quarters were scarcely large enough to fit a wooden cot and a desk, but he required nothing more.

He rose, stretching his legs, and moved closer to the cliff's edge. Seabirds floated in the air and on the water, buoyed by the waves.

He thought of earlier days, diving off the coast of Caesarea, and amid the coral of Eilat. He thought of Mishka, bobbing in the surf, grinning broadly beneath her mask.

Mishka, torn from him so soon.

And their daughter, barely three years old.

The pain and anger flared anew.

Part III

Chapter 26

London

Jordan exited the underground at Tottenham Court Road and stepped into a flap of pigeons. The afternoon rush was beginning. Men and women in trench coats walked briskly toward the station, some toting precautionary umbrellas. A taxi driver honked his horn at a Jaguar's swift maneuver.

Jordan walked a block down Great Russell Street and, at a rapid clip, climbed the broad stone stairs to the entrance of the British Museum. He darted through a crowd of schoolgirls coming the other way, past throngs of tourists consulting their maps and guidebooks.

In 1883, the British Museum had been poised to pay £1 million for the Mandel Genesis. The museum had examined the relic thoroughly, and the index to its archives showed that it saved the original notes and correspondence of the curators who dealt with Mandel. Jordan hoped the file contained a name—someone who believed in Mandel, someone who stood by him at the height of the scandal.

Someone Mandel later entrusted with a far more important artifact.

The building was closing in less than an hour, and Jordan was determined not to lose the day. Resisting the lure of the galleries, he found his way to the center of the museum, a vast and ornate reading room. Under a dome of blue and gold, suffused in gray light from the skylight at its apex, table after table of students and scholars sat quietly absorbed in their specialized research.

At the counter, a pretty redhead took his request and sent him to wait at a numbered table. Only 45 minutes to closing time.

The redhead paused to talk with another museum employee, a tall young man with slicked-back hair and a narrow black tie. She spoke in a whisper but gestured with animation. They smiled and laughed, quietly. She didn't seem to grasp the urgency of Jordan's mission.

His eyes wandered the room impatiently. At the next table, an elderly gentleman of sprawling girth tweaked his walrus mustache and peered through bifocals at a stack of papers, delicately lifting pages from one pile to another. He rubbed his hands together, as if preparing to sample a delicacy. Behind the walrus, a pert blonde in a smart tweed coat brushed her hair from her eyes and looked up from a hefty tome. She looked at Jordan and straight through him, completely engrossed in her work. Several aisles over, an olive-skinned man in a pin-stripe suit sat down, glanced his way, and began to read the inside pages of a broadsheet newspaper.

A museum attendant carried a cardboard box toward Jordan's table—and kept walking. She delivered the box to a young man in a U2 T-shirt and blue jeans sitting at the far end of the room.

The pretty redhead was nowhere in sight.

The brochure Jordan picked up on the way in included a map of the exhibit halls, which he began to study. He was surrounded by a treasure of cultural riches, from stone relics of prehistory to the sublime sculpture of the ancient Greeks, from the funerary art of Egypt to the armor of medieval Europe, from intricate Islamic paintings to bold African carvings. But all that really interested Jordan were some mundane records of the museum itself that dated to the 1880s.

The redhead caught his eye and motioned for him to approach the desk.

"I'm very sorry, but the records you requested aren't available at the present time. They're being used."

He looked around the room, trying to guess who shared his exceedingly unlikely curiosity.

"Do you know when they'll be available?" he inquired.

"Regrettably, there's no way of telling."

"Can people check them out?"

"Nothing leaves the museum. Patrons must return everything by the end of the day."

Jordan prepared to bide his time.

"However, the records you're looking for have been signed out by a member of our staff. Staff members can hold them indefinitely."

"May I speak to that person?"

"I'm sorry, we don't do that."

Jordan leaned across the counter and gave her a plaintive look. "If I don't see these papers, I'll miss my deadline, I'll lose my job, my mother will be tossed out of a nursing home, my puppy-cat Cuddles will starve, and they'll put me behind bars for robbing piggy banks, because I have a doctorate in early modern prehistory but no practical skills. Would you consider making an exception?"

"Let me see what I can find out."

She opened a museum phone directory to the "W" page and scrolled down a column of names with her index finger. Then she dialed the number. Jordan did his best to discreetly read the upside-down name.

"It's Claire in the reading room. Is he in please?" the redhead asked.

From Jordan's angle, it looked like she had pointed to "Waverly, Nigel."

"Gone? For the day? Very well then, thank you."

Claire hung up the phone.

"I'm sorry, but he's out until tomorrow. Maybe you'd like to try again then."

"There's one more thing. Do you have copies of London newspapers from the 19th century?"

"That would be the British Library. I'm afraid they'll be closing shortly as well."

Jordan thanked her and left the reading room.

From a public phone, he dialed the museum operator. In short order, he learned that Nigel Waverly was an assistant curator of East Asian glass and ceramics. He was expected to return the next morning. Jordan wondered if he got the wrong name.

Why would an expert in Chinese pottery be interested in Mordecai Mandel?

With five minutes left before closing time, he decided to salvage something from his outing. He made his way to the Greek galleries to take in the Elgin Marbles—chipped and broken friezes removed from the Parthenon of Athens. In one of them, a bull destined for the sacrificial altar struggled to escape its fate. But before Jordan could fully appreciate the sculpture, it was closing time, and the security guards began clearing the hall.

Jordan exited the museum as night was falling and headed toward the underground.

He was looking forward to a night of undisturbed luxury—a hot shower, a plush robe, a comfortable bed. Maybe even room service. But above all, a chance to recharge his batteries and ease the aches of accumulated injuries. In a small act of expense account rebellion—he still had his company credit card—he had booked a room at Claridge's. A room with mahogany, marble, and that most peculiar British indulgence, the heated towel rack.

From the museum, Jordan went directly to Claridge's, where a Rolls Royce and a BMW idled with the taxis by the entrance. The uniformed doormen welcomed him into the lobby, and a luggage porter went to retrieve the duffel bag Jordan had checked hours earlier, on his arrival in London.

Jordan waited by the front desk, worrying about Catherine, second-guessing his decision to leave Ann Arbor. Bag in hand, he crossed the lobby toward the elevators, eager to get to his room and phone Michigan. He stepped into the elevator and the attendant pressed eight. The door closed and the elevator began to rise.

In the few seconds it took the doors to close, a picture etched itself in Jordan's mind. It registered gradually, like the image on a sheet of photographic paper floating in a darkroom bath. It was the image of an olive-skinned man in a pin-stripe suit, standing in the Claridge's lobby. By the time the elevator passed five, Jordan had placed him in another context—the reading room at the British Museum.

Who was the man in the pin-stripe suit?

Why was he following me?

Jordan got out on the seventh floor and found his way to the stairs. He bounded down them, taking the last set two at a time.

Am I being irrational?

Moments later, he was standing in traffic, hailing a taxi, asking the driver to take him someplace cheap. Someplace that didn't demand a credit card.

Someplace that wouldn't insist on swiping his Visa and creating an electronic trail, Jordan thought.

The driver looked from his passenger to Claridge's and laughed under his breath. The taxi left the familiar environs of downtown London and seemed to get lost. It slowed to a stop in a dark and grimy part of town, outside the Royal Prince Hotel.

Instead of going inside, Jordan walked half a block, past a liquor store and a newsstand, a sleeping wino and a sickly prostitute, and slipped into a phone booth. He looked around to see if he was being watched, but no one stood out. He tried Ann Arbor, where it was early afternoon. No luck. Catherine's office and mobile lines went to voice mail, and home kept ringing.

He pictured the man in the pin-stripe suit. Either he was another museum patron with expensive taste in hotels, visiting London from out of town, or he was shadowing Jordan. And if he was shadowing, what were the odds that his intentions were benign?

Was he involved in the destruction of the archaeological institute, or the suspected break-in at Catherine's home? Was he trying to beat Jordan to the objective, or was he trying to stop Jordan altogether?

Jordan ducked into the Royal Prince Hotel.

Greeting him with bloodshot eyes, the desk clerk handed him a pair of depleted towels along with the key. To say the Royal was past its prime generously assumed it ever had one. But the Royal settled for cash, and not much at that.

The barely furnished room smelled of stale tobacco and cheap whiskey, and the sheets had the chlorine aroma of industrial-strength bleach. The thin mattress sagged in the middle.

The endless ringing of Catherine's phone rattled him. It was still ringing in his head when he collapsed on the bed. He was worried and worn out. His head throbbed, and his wounds ached.

He lapsed into a fitful sleep. The flashing neon of the liquor store played against the window shade, adding to his subconscious unease.

The first noise he heard was a scream, followed by another. He struggled to think clearly.

"They've got guns!" someone shouted.

A burst of gunfire confirmed it. Jordan bolted upright and looked around. There was nowhere to run or hide. He heard hurried footsteps down the hall, and the sound of a scuffle.

Instinctively, he understood.

He hurled his body at the door and held it shut with all his strength, feet spread wide on the floor, hands outstretched and pressed high against the wood.

There were more screams and gunshots. The screams were unintelligible, but the voices sounded Israeli. They sounded as if they were trying to warn him, even as they were silenced. Someone shook the doorknob to Jordan's room and banged his shoulder against the door. The door opened a crack, but Jordan fought back and forced it shut.

He was alone in the room, but he felt that lives depended on him—not just his own. If only he could hold back the terrorists, and buy the others some time. He imagined himself in the body of someone bigger and stronger, a wrestler. He summoned all his inner power.

Rifle butts crashed against the door, splintering the wood. Jordan held his ground. In the hall, the lead intruder stepped back and pointed his rifle at the door. There was nowhere for Jordan to go.

The rifle exploded in automatic fire, and dozens of bullets ripped through the door. The bullets tore through Jordan's chest and abdomen, knocking him backward onto the bed. He felt no pain.

His last thought was of the people he had failed to protect.

A man masked in a nylon stocking stepped into the room. He stood over Jordan's body. He watched, casually, as Benjamin Jordan's blood soaked the mattress and formed a puddle on the floor.

The room at the Royal glowed red and purple from the neon liquor sign, giving Jordan's body a macabre tint.

He awoke with a start, thoroughly disoriented.

He was at the Munich Olympics, where Palestinian terrorists had invaded the Israeli athletes' dorm.

No, he was on the kibbutz, in the bunk with the other boys, and he was the only one awake.

No, he was in London, where a seedy hotel served as refuge.

The door to his room was intact and locked; the sheets were soaked with perspiration. It had been an old, recurring nightmare, though years had passed since he last experienced it. The bogeyman of his youth was back to taunt him.

The fear cut too deep, the pain was too personal, to fully acknowledge, so Jordan had relegated it to the recesses of his subconscious.

He felt he was there, in Munich, one of the unarmed Israelis confronting the terrorists of Black September. While the rest of the Olympic Village slept, he was blocking the door with his body, trying to keep the intruders away from his teammates. Some of the Israelis put up a valiant but hopeless fight. Two were killed, and two escaped. The rest were taken hostage.

Usually, in the dream, Jordan died in the dormitory, defending his teammates. Other times, others died so that Jordan's nightmare could go on. After a day of threatened executions, he and his fellow hostages were transported by bus to helicopters and flown to an airfield where, as the terrorists demanded, the German authorities had positioned a jet to fly them out of the country. German snipers watched as two of the terrorists inspected the plane. Aboard the helicopters, the Israelis waited, bound and blindfolded. It was night, but the glare of the klieg lights pierced the darkness.

A voice spoke in German over a loudspeaker. Jordan couldn't understand the words, but the harsh, gutteral language evoked an almost primal fear in each of the Jews.

A single shot cracked the night, then a cacophony. Klieg lights exploding in a shower of sparks, which Jordan could sense if he couldn't see; machine gun fire in all directions; the plink of bullets penetrating the metal skin of the helicopter, the shatter of a windscreen. Voices shouting in German and Arabic. An Israeli muttering a prayer, and others joining in.

A terrorist pulled the pin on a grenade and tossed it on the floor. Jordan could hear the metallic clang as the grenade bounced and rolled under a hostage's seat.

Then, in daylight, the aftermath. The copters were charred wrecks. None of the hostages survived. How many times had Jordan imagined himself in their place?

He was exhausted, but there was no point trying to sleep.

Chapter 27

London

Jordan was standing at the front door to the British Library when it opened the next morning, and shortly after that he was seated in a dark cubicle, listening to the whir of the microfilm machine and watching the film blur past. He hit fast-forward, then rewind, zeroing in on the proper dates.

In the summer of 1883, *The Times* of London had devoted a string of articles to the strange saga of Mordecai Mandel. Most of them appeared on the inside pages. If someone had stepped forward to defend Mandel, there was a decent chance he'd appear in the coverage.

"Curious Relic Unearthed in Jerusalem," the first headline announced inconspicuously. It was dispatched from Prague, where the correspondent described the mixture of excitement and skepticism that greeted Mandel at the outset of his European tour. "The parchment resembles Genesis, but deviations in the text raise questions about its authenticity," the story reported.

Jordan read the account and moved on.

"Ancient Scroll in Paris," the second installment declared. "It appears to predate by centuries any known biblical text," the story said. "If Mr. Mandel's manuscript is to be accepted, we must do no less than rewrite the Divine order of Creation."

"Mr. Mandel Arrives From Amsterdam," The Times reported on July 26. "The gentleman from Jerusalem is considered one of the Holy Land's leading antiquarians," the story said. "An intrepid adventurer, he is said to be at home among the Bedouin, who guide him on his explorations of the Judean wilderness."

Jordan smiled inwardly at the hype.

"Mr. Mandel Meets With Top Scholars, Presents His Artifact," the next piece related. "We shall subject the Mandel Manuscript to the most sophisticated analysis modern science and letters can perform, and only then shall we pronounce judgment," Dr. Charles Salisbury, chief curator at the British Museum, was quoted as saying.

"Validation For Mandel Manuscript," the newspaper announced on August 22. "One of the greatest archaeological finds of the 19th Century," Dr. Salisbury proclaimed. "It would be a cause of embarrassment to every British subject if the Mandel Manuscript should repose anywhere but London."

Toward the bottom of the article, a quote from Mandel made Jordan pause.

"I should not be surprised," Mandel said, "if other ancient writings should surface, shedding further light on matters of long-held belief."

"Bidding War For Mandel Manuscript," the paper revealed two days later. "*The Times* has it on good authority that the chancellor of the exchequer has appropriated the sum of £1,000,000 for the purchase of Mr. Mandel's Genesis. We are told Mr. Mandel has every expectation the French will respond to this development by raising their bid."

"Denunciation of Mordecai Mandel," the paper blared on August 27. "One of the greatest hoaxes of the 19th Century," the French ambassador to the Court of St. James's declared. "The British should know better than to trust the Jew. But let them pay."

"Mr. Mandel's Deceit" followed in early September, featuring the tale of the Italian wine trader Aldo Campagnoli.

"A Clever Forgery," published September 6, was the final chapter. "Mandel has perpetrated a cunning, shameless fraud," Dr. Salisbury capitulated.

As a footnote, Dr. Salisbury denied that the British had been about to offer £1,000,000. He suggested that Mandel planted the story to elicit a higher bid from the French—and instead invited his own undoing.

Jordan read the last article twice, searching for clues, but nothing caught his attention. On the whole, his reading confirmed what he already knew.

All that remained were some letters to the editor.

"We shall not again underestimate the treachery and resourcefulness of the Hebrew race, particularly where large sums of money are at stake," an R.L. Caldwell of Dover wrote.

"England has witnessed an assault upon all we hold sacred and true. It should come as no surprise that, in the end, God's word prevails," the Rt. Rev. James Geraghty of Twickenham opined.

"The shopkeeper from Jerusalem has conspired against faith, just as surely as the Hebrews of old killed the Son of God," Peter Coughlin, M.D., of London wrote.

"Pity Mordecai Mandel, but pity his critics more. Mr. Mandel leaves England in disgrace. Those who hound him remain in an even less enviable condition, a state of willful ignorance," an S. Belk of Oxford wrote.

"Shame on Charles Salisbury and our other vaunted experts for falling for such patent nonsense," a Wm. Westerly of East Anglia wrote.

Jordan stopped and reversed.

"Pity Mordecai Mandel, but pity his critics more," S. Belk of Oxford wrote.

Jordan had nearly skipped over it, but now he reexamined each word of S. Belk's letter.

> Mr. Mandel leaves England in disgrace. Those who hound him remain in an even less enviable condition, a state of willful ignorance. I have examined the Mandel Genesis, and I believe that it may yet be the genuine article. Mr. Mandel alone knows the truth, and perhaps he can find solace in it. For his benighted critics, there is no consolation.

Jordan reviewed what the old woman, Harriett, had told Catherine.

"He left it to someone who believed in him. Someone who stood by him during the worst of it."

Jordan could picture Mandel clinging to Belk's letter like a lifebuoy in a storm. It was hardly a ringing endorsement, but it was more than anyone else seemed to throw Mandel's way.

Jordan made a copy.

So who was Belk?

Jordan returned to the hard-bound newspaper index and scanned the volumes for the 1880s. The most promising mention of an S. Belk dated to March 1883, several months before Mandel's arrival in London.

"Professor Sedgwick Belk of Balliol College, Oxford, will speak on Tuesday at 3 o'clock," the notice said. "He will present theological, historical and naturalistic interpretations of the plagues visited upon Egypt in the Book of Exodus."

Jordan looked at his watch. He wanted to get back to the museum in time to examine its file on Mandel, but there was more to do here.

He read half a dozen additional references to Sedgwick Belk, which offered no further enlightenment. The last time Belk published anything of his own was in 1881, long before any possible bequest from Mandel.

Jordan turned to the most tedious task of all, combing legal notices published in the winter of 1883 for any reference to an auction of Mandel's possessions. He hoped that if the auction was advertised in the papers, and if the auction house was still in business, and if it kept records going back more than a century, he might somehow identify the other manuscript's anonymous buyer. He had a hunch—nothing more—that the identity of the buyer would get him one step closer. It was a long shot, and the agate type left him so bleary eyed that he was afraid he would miss it. If his strategy failed, his recourse would be to go from auction house to auction house, taking shots in the dark.

Then he spotted it, deep inside *The Times* edition of January 17, 1884.

"In liquidation of debts," the 19th Century classified ad began. "Three lots of silver flatware, late of Cheswick Hall. Two lots of family portraiture, oil on canvas, 1690-1833. Two lots of porcelain, British manufacture. Of separate provenance and recent notoriety, one leather scroll, 'The Mandel Genesis.' Thomas H. Begley & Sons, Auctioneers, 161 Quincy Road, London."

Jordan searched the London phone book and the Internet but found no trace of the auction house. He left the library and hailed a taxi.

"Take me to 161 Quincy Road," he told the driver.

After a considerable detour, the car turned onto Quincy Road. The driver slowed and noted the numbers.

"That would be 161," the driver said, pointing.

Sandwiched between a music store and a video shop, 161 Quincy was an Indian carry-out called the Delhi Deli.

The driver looked at Jordan for instructions.

"I lost my appetite," Jordan said.

Instinct told him that Belk was his man. But there might be other possibilities.

He didn't want to cut any corners—not after that last debacle.

"Make it the British Museum," he said.

He entered the museum warily, taking mental photographs of the faces in the crowd. He didn't think he had been tailed, but if anyone was shadowing him, they might be staking out the place, expecting him to return.

He still hadn't reached Catherine.

He joined a queue at the reading room desk. There were three people in line ahead of him. When it was his turn, he handed over his request form.

Claire, the young woman who had helped him the day before, gave a forced smile.

"Hello again," he said. "The Mandel file. Can you see if it's available?"

"Right, please have a seat and we'll be with you shortly, Mr."—she paused to read the name Jordan had written on the form—"Mr. Barnes."

She seemed uneasy.

Jordan sat down off to the side and made a careful survey of the room. Claire talked on the phone, cupping the handset as she spoke. He caught her looking at him, and she quickly looked away.

Jordan looked around. Something seemed odd. He didn't know what, but he didn't like the feel of it.

He waited several long seconds until Claire turned her back to him. Then he wasted no time getting out of the reading room.

He looked back over his shoulder to see two men cut in front of the line and engage Claire in an urgent discussion. Claire turned to where Jordan had been seated and a look of surprise crossed her face.

The two men scanned the room, evidently searching for Jordan, but they were an instant too late.

Jordan found his way through the galleries and down a staircase to an employee men's room, where he slipped into a stall. He shed his newly acquired overcoat, donned the tweed hat he had tucked in a pocket, and perched a pair of drugstore eyeglasses low on the bridge of his nose. It wasn't much of an exit strategy, but it was all he had prepared.

The door to the men's room opened and two men walked in. Jordan held his breath.

They stood in front of the urinals.

"I heard on the radio they found his body in an alley, in a trash bin," the first said as he unzipped. "Shot in the face."

"Did you ever work with him?" the other asked.

"No, they said he specialized in porcelain . . . Nigel Somebody-or-other."

Jordan stifled a gasp.

Waverly murdered?

Why?

"The police seem to think the killer is here at the museum. Judging by their presence, they seem to suspect a member of the staff."

Or a patron who shared an extremely obscure interest.

One urinal flushed, followed by another.

Jordan hung his overcoat in the stall and fled the men's room. Approaching the main doors to the museum, he saw an unusually large complement of security guards, who he assumed were augmented by police in plain clothes. He hesitated, gauging the flow of people funneling through the exit.

He spotted a woman in her 30s with three young children and he slipped beside them, trying to look like the father.

As he got closer to the door, a guard studied him critically and scowled. Jordan smiled and nodded and kept walking. He felt eyes watching his back, but he kept his own fixed paternally on the children.

Then he was outside in the gray light of day, and he had to restrain himself from breaking into a run.

Chapter 28

Oxford

"Sedgwick Belk," the Oxford don repeated, peering over his reading glasses. "That's a name you don't hear very often."

"I suppose not," Catherine said.

"And why, might I ask, does he interest you?"

Horace Giles of Balliol College, Oxford, seemed to be studying her with suspicion. In the moon-faced academic's medieval lair, she was glad she had done her homework. She had run Giles's name by a former student, now doing graduate work at Oxford, and he had told her what to expect.

Professor Giles was said to hoard knowledge the way some people collected stamps. He would part with the rare ones grudgingly, and only if he expected to get the better end of the trade. Yet there were also occasions when ego took over, and he could not resist showing off a particularly exotic item in the collection, thereby hinting at the wealth he kept to himself.

His was an odd disposition for a teacher, but he was reputed to participate very little in the shaping of young minds. It was said that his infrequent encounters with students seldom failed to remind him—or them—of his superiority. Once in a rare while, however, an exceptionally confident or cynical student went away thinking that maybe there was not so much Giles kept to himself.

As the old don peered over his reading glasses, Catherine wondered: Was he suspicious—or jealous with anticipation?

"I'm writing about 19th Century biblical scholarship," Catherine said. "Belk seemed like one of the more unconventional thinkers of the day. But then his own writing fell silent, while he was still a relatively young man."

"Indeed it did," Giles said.

"They say that you're the authority in such matters."

"Indeed I am."

"Do you know if he left any papers, journals, unpublished manuscripts . . . ."

"Ahhh," Giles nodded. "The scholar's endless quest for originality. To plow unbroken ground, however barren or inaccessible it may be. To unearth rocks and pebbles, if that's all there is, and declare them gems. That's what the Ivory Tower demands, isn't it?"

Giles looked through the leaded glass of his window, into the gothic courtyard below. Catherine followed his gaze. The stone buildings predated the imitations in Ann Arbor by 800 years, give or take a century.

"Are you saying that Belk left nothing but rocks and pebbles?" Catherine asked.

Giles frowned. "Not at all. Indeed, I suspect Belk's papers would be a fertile field." Giles arched an eyebrow. "Maybe even the stuff of which careers are made."

Something in Giles's manner hinted that it was the first time he had given the subject any serious thought, and that he was trying to hide his ignorance.

"What do *you* expect to glean from them?" Giles asked.

"Another point of view."

"Indeed," he said, watching her, clearly unsatisfied with her response.

"And a last, desperate shot at tenure before I abandon my feeble career and become a hostess at McDonald's," she added.

Giles laughed.

"I didn't think they had hostesses at McDonald's," he said.

"Indeed," she said.

Giles laughed again.

"Alas," he said. "It seems the Ivory Tower's loss may be McDonald's gain."

"You know, I'd settle for very small stones," she said. "Even gravel."

"I wish I could help, but Belk left us nothing. He simply left."

"Where did he go?"

Giles unwrapped a small fragment of his collection.

"Strangely, he dropped everything in 1884 to visit the Holy Land. He never said what he was looking for or what he hoped to accomplish. And he never returned."

"What do you make of it?" Catherine asked.

"Who's to say?" Giles said, watching her. "It was almost as if he embarked on his own personal crusade. Perhaps he got religion."

"Did he leave a family?"

Giles seemed to note the limits of her knowledge.

"He left a bloody probate mess, that's what he left. He inherited the family's ancestral title and lands from his uncle six months before he departed. The seat in the House of Lords, the estate at Pamet Roads, all of it. And after he disappeared, it took 19 years for title to pass to his nephew. Without a body, how could anyone be sure the Earl of Pamet was dead?"

Indeed, Catherine thought.

"How disappointing," she said, even as her thoughts turned to Pamet Roads. "Thank you very much, Professor Giles. If you ever need a table at McDonald's, allow me to return the favor."

"Hold the pickles," he said with a wink.

They rose and shook hands.

"What a remarkable coincidence, your coming today, don't you think?" Giles said.

"Why so?"

"Yours is the second inquiry I've received today that takes me back to the 1880s."

Catherine struggled to maintain her composure.

"This morning it was Scotland Yard," Giles said, gauging her reaction. "They were asking about a man from Jerusalem named Mordecai Mandel. Evidently a curator at the British Museum developed a sudden interest in Mandel shortly before he was shot."

"Killed?"

"Quite."

Catherine couldn't hide her discomfort.

"You know their lives intersected, don't you?" he said.

"Hmmm," Catherine said, with studied ambiguity.

"As I said, a remarkable coincidence."

Chapter 29

Catherine bought a newspaper at the station and riffled through it while she waited for the train. She found a short story on the murder of Nigel Waverly. She focused on the fourth paragraph.

> Police are seeking to question a Michael Barnes, of unknown address. Sources say Mr. Barnes had been trying to obtain unspecified records that were in Mr. Waverly's possession before his death. The records have gone missing, and theft is considered a possible motive in the killing.

What the hell am I doing?

The quaint, academic mystery of Mordecai Mandel had become a deadly affair. And yet she felt more alive than ever. She was driven by pride and anger, and a reawakening of ambition. Her mother was right: For too long, she had muffled her dreams in fear of failure.

There was no way she could abandon them now, no way she could admit defeat. Westphall State was not an option.

The students who walked out of her class had walked on her brother's grave, but they had done her a favor. They had reminded her of Ian, and the tragic injustice. The righteous wrong inflicted by the church, and a sister's guilt for sending him to Father Donegan.

The priest had called him an abomination in the eyes of the Lord, and Ian had believed.

"Is this seat taken?"

Catherine looked up and gasped.

"You really should be more observant," Jordan said.

She wasn't sure if she was more thrilled or furious.

"What are you doing here?" she asked.

"I thought I'd look into an advanced degree. Do you think they'd let me in?"

He sat down beside her.

"I'm glad you're safe," he said.

"There was another killing," she said.

"I know."

They looked at each other for a long time without speaking.

"I thought you were letting go of all this," he said.

"That wasn't possible," she said.

"I was wondering how long it would take you to figure that out."

"Does that make us rivals?" she asked.

"How about partners?"

The conductor announced that Catherine's train was boarding.

"It's a shame, your leaving as I'm arriving," he said.

"What's your plan?"

"I thought I'd look up one of the dons at Balliol College, the one who occupies the position once held by Sedgwick Belk. I thought he might know something about Belk. I called some experts, and they all said he's the man to see."

Catherine groaned.

"You know Professor Giles?" he asked.

"Indeed," Catherine said.

"What's he like?"

"I think he would consider you the most remarkable coincidence yet."

"Huh?"

"It's a long story."

He looked at her ticket.

"And you've got a train to catch."

Catherine zipped her duffel.

The sun was sinking over the English countryside as the train lurched out of the station. Catherine settled into a window seat. She put her newspaper on the empty one beside her and watched Oxford's medieval chapels fall away.

Jordan moved the newspaper and took a seat.

"How far are we going?" he asked.

She looked at him with surprise. *Such boldness. Such nerve.*

She felt a deep sense of relief, which she quickly suppressed.

"To be determined," she said. "By way of Pamet Roads."

"Ah, the ancestral estate of Sedgwick Belk," he said. "A bit off the beaten path, but according to its Web site it's open for tours."

She was impressed by his resourcefulness—almost awed by it. In short order, he had connected Mandel with Belk, independently arriving at the same conclusion she had guarded so jealously for so long, even from Meyer.

"Maybe the current lord of the manor can fill in some blanks," she said.

They sat in silence for a while, enjoying the shifting view of hills and meadows. The train rocked and swayed in a steady, reassuring rhythm, carrying them deeper into the night. Speaking in low voices, leaning toward each other intimately to avoid being overheard, Catherine told Jordan about her meeting with Giles, and Jordan recounted his trip to London.

He sensed that something else was weighing on her, a personal problem. But she didn't volunteer, and he didn't press. Unconsciously, she rested a hand on his wrist.

"I still don't know what's going on," Catherine said. "I don't know what we're up against."

"Someone is after the treasures of the Temple, and Mordecai Mandel's 'ultimate proof,'" Jordan said. "Based on your conversation with Elazar months ago, they believe the Silver Scroll can lead to something earth-shaking. To clear the path and cover their tracks, they've wiped out the Institute and its governing council."

"With the possible exception of Meyer Elazar," Catherine said.

"One of my sources thinks Elazar is behind it."

"That's crazy."

"That's what I thought. At first."

"What else do you have to go on?"

"The man who tailed me in London looked Mediterranean," Jordan said.

"That doesn't narrow it down much, does it?"

"No. He could have been Arab, Israeli . . . ."

"Or southern European?"

"Or southern European."

"But we're not talking about a single individual, or a handful of people, are we?"

"No," Jordan said. "We're talking about a sophisticated organization with international reach."

"Given what little we know, who would have the most at stake?"

Jordan thought it over.

"Considering that Islam wasn't established until the 7th Century, and considering that Mandel's 'ultimate proof' dates at least as far back as 1st Century Jerusalem, I would surmise that Christians and Jews have the most to lose."

"I agree," Catherine said. "And I would go one step farther. Considering the 1st Century time frame, and the fact that Christians and Jews share the Old Testament, I would posit that Mandel's discovery most likely relates to events of the New Testament."

"That sounds logical to me," Jordan said.

"Who is this Waverly, the murdered curator?" Catherine asked.

"I don't know. Probably just someone the conspirators used to get the British Museum's files on Mordecai Mandel. Maybe they bribed him, or blackmailed him. The interesting thing is, these records were available to the public. The only reason I can think of for stealing them is to subject them to some kind of forensic analysis. Or maybe to prevent *anyone else* from seeing them."

She unfolded the newspaper article. "What do you know about a Michael Barnes?" she asked.

"He's one of the most brilliant journalists of his generation. Good looking, too."

"You know him?"

"It was a name I put on a form in the reading room of the museum."

"Well, for all your brilliance, they say you're a suspect in the Waverly killing."

"That's not very sensible of them. If I were the killer, why would I go back for the records a second time?"

"Maybe you were trying to establish an alibi."

"Then why would I run?"

"Maybe you weren't so confident in your alibi."

"Technically, the paper has lawyers to get us out of these situations, but . . . ."

"But technically you're not actually on assignment for the newspaper right now."

"The man the police want is Michael Barnes," Jordan said.

"They'll see through that soon enough. What if they arrest you?"

"I have—what's the expression?—'prior commitments.' So let's not give them the chance."

Chapter 30

Pamet Roads

The village of Pamet Roads was mostly tucked in for the night when the two travelers disembarked from the train and left the station on foot. By the moonlight, they could see the outlines of old farmhouses, low hedges, and gnarled oaks. There was a chill in the air.

They were traveling light, and Jordan carried the bags. He had Catherine's duffel, his laptop, and a knapsack containing clothes and other basics he purchased on the fly, to replace the stuff he left at the Royal.

They followed a light to the end of the main street, and a pub called the Black Rabbit. The warm glow of a fire lit the taproom. Two men in their sixties sat drinking beer in the corner farthest from the fireplace, and a stout woman in an apron stood behind a bar, washing glasses. From his collar, one of the men was the village vicar.

"Jesus Christ, Father, I swear, marriage is like the bloody priesthood," the other said loudly, waving his pint. "Poverty, chastity, obedience . . . you'd think I married the bloody church."

"Maybe if you *kept* your vows," the proprietor scolded. "Now mind your manners, Tom, we've got company."

Tom sized up the strangers.

"Lizzie gets four stars in the Michelin guide," he volunteered. "Her biscuits are tougher than Michelins."

"Pipe down, Tom, or you can add another kind of 'abstinence' to the list," Lizzie said.

"Don't believe a word Tom says," she told the new arrivals. "My biscuits *are* Michelins. Now what can I get you?"

"A couple of beers," Jordan said. "And we're looking for a place to stay."

"I can put you in the barn," Lizzie said. "Forty pounds for the night."

Catherine fumbled for words.

"Don't worry," Lizzie said. "The only barnyard animal ever stays there is my brother-in-law, and he's in Durham. It's what we call the guest quarters."

"We'll take it," Jordan said.

The two retreated with their beers to a table by the hearth.

Lizzie brought them plates with biscuits and lamb stew. "Leftovers," she said.

They downed the biscuits, which lived up to their reviews. Jordan ate hungrily, while Catherine sampled the stew and politely stirred it on her plate so as not to give too much offense. Across the room, Tom grumbled into his beer, while the vicar, a small man with dark eyes, a bulbous nose and shattered capillaries, quietly nursed his own.

"If you're done, I'll take you to your quarters," Lizzie said.

They followed her behind the kitchen and up a flight of creaking stairs, through a trap door in the ceiling. From the rear, Jordan had a tantalizing view of Catherine's faded jeans and the way she filled them. Seamlessly.

The barn was a comfortably sized attic with high, sloping planks of knotted wood and aged, horizontal beams, like a ship's timbers, spanning the open space overhead. The walls were decorated with a hodgepodge of antiques—a naturalist's drawings of plants and birds, a huntsman's horn, and assorted farm implements from a bygone era.

Lizzie clicked on a floor lamp beside a large featherbed, which was heaped with a down comforter. She turned on a second lamp next to a couch. She struck a match and started a fire in the wood stove, and then she drew the window shade.

"The tub is through there," she said, pointing to the opposite end of the attic, which was partitioned as an oversized bathroom. "And there's plenty of towels in the chest. Unless there's anything else you'll be needing, I'll see you in the morning."

She descended the creaking stairs, closing the trapdoor behind her.

"You can have the couch," Catherine said.

Jordan looked from the couch to the bed to Catherine.

He set the bags on the floor.

"You can have the washroom," he said.

"No, you go ahead."

He took a shower and emerged in boxers, with a towel draped over his shoulders. A few beads of water clung to his chest. Catherine tried not to stare at his well-defined body. He was built like a soccer player, balancing speed and strength. The irresistible force rather than the immovable object.

He rummaged in his rucksack for a clean white T-shirt. As he pulled it over his head, she noticed the scars of his recent injuries across the muscles of his abdomen.

"How did you get those?" she asked.

"A Lebanese woman did it. Actually, several Lebanese women."

"Must have been your natural charisma."

"It was nothing personal. They just wanted me dead."

"Do you usually evoke that response in women?"

"They don't ordinarily act on it."

"What did you do to provoke them?'

The humor left Jordan's eyes.

"I showed up hours after the Israeli bombs fell and identified myself as an Israeli. They were angry and grief-stricken, and I understand their reaction . . . .

"But I admit," he added, "it wasn't my best opening line."

"As I recall," Catherine said, "you used something similar on me."

Catherine gathered some things and sought the privacy of the bathroom. She ran the hot water. The bathroom door refused to close completely, and she gave up, leaving it open a crack. She dimmed the lights and eased herself into the tub, an antique model that rested on four feet. She sank into the hot water and closed her eyes, hoping to wash away the world, but she couldn't stop thinking about Jordan. She saw the jagged line of a scar, and she was sure it reflected a deeper wound. She wondered what it would take to heal it. In her mind's eye, she traced the scar with her fingertips, slowly, delicately, barely touching.

Why had she been so hard on him?

She had spoken without thinking, and she regretted it. It was a subconscious effort to keep her feelings at bay, and it had failed.

He had entered her life forcefully, unexpectedly, turning everything upside down. She was afraid to let him in and afraid to push him out. She imagined him just outside, watching her, reading her thoughts, reaching out to her, opening the door . . . .

Jordan reclined on the couch, trying to get some rest. It seemed like the perfect place and the perfect moment, except that she was clearly uninterested. He heard the soft stir of water in a tub, the light splash of a body moving. He turned involuntarily. Through the narrow opening, he caught a glimpse of her back. He turned away.

He imagined her rising out of the tub, dripping water, turning toward him, opening the door . . . .

She opened the door.

Wrapped in a towel, she reached into her duffel and took out her version of pajamas. She ducked back in the bathroom and emerged moments later in Michigan sweats and a clinging tank top.

"Let's trade," she said. "I'll take the couch and you take the bed."

"No thanks, it's all yours."

"After your experience at the Royal, you deserve it," she said.

"I'm comfortable here," he lied.

She took the comforter off the bed and draped it over Jordan.

"Good night," she said, and she turned out the light.

They awoke at first light. Lizzie made them eggs and sausage and toast with marmalade, which they ate beside the fire in the taproom.

Alone in the far corner, Tom nursed a hangover and a cup of blackest coffee. It wasn't clear to either of them if Tom was Lizzie's husband, or just her best customer.

As Lizzie cleared the table, Jordan handed her payment for room and board, plus a generous tip. He asked for directions to the manor house, and she pointed the way, somewhat surprised at the question.

"What sort of man is the Earl?" Catherine asked.

Lizzie pondered the question, not sure how to answer.

"Have you ever heard of *noblesse oblige*?" Tom asked.

"Yes, of course," Catherine said.

"Well, then, that's the difference between you and the Earl," Tom declared.

"Now Tom," Lizzie scolded.

"How does he keep up his estate?" Catherine asked.

Tom laughed ruefully.

"With a little help from the state, that's how," Tom said.

"Not the state, the Royal Trust for Historic Preservation," Lizzie corrected.

"In other words, he's on the dole," Tom said. "Without the Trust, the lord without manners would be a lord without a manor. Alas, poetic justice was denied."

"What happened?" Catherine asked.

"The family wealth—the real wealth, anyway—was lost or spent long before Crendal inherited, and Pamet Hall itself seemed destined for sale. But the Earl wanted to keep Pamet Hall. He wanted to restore it to its glory, along with his family's wealth and prominence.

"Instead of managing the family business prudently, he expanded recklessly, cooked the books, and borrowed heavily against his inflated stock holdings. All to support a pretentious pose—polo ponies and chauffeured cars and fashion models at charity balls. Houses in London and St. Tropez, and an expensive refurbishing of Pamet Hall.

"You might have read about the scandal. When the stock collapsed, a lot of ordinary people lost their savings. I was one of them, like a goddamned fool.

"Crendal's lawyers kept him out of jail, but the creditors were closing in. To keep Pamet Hall in the family, his younger brother, who made an honest fortune, offered Crendal more than it was worth. But you have to understand, the estate is Crendal's heritage, the very essence of his pride. And the only thing that would burn Crendal more than losing Pamet Hall would be losing it to his brother."

He'd be right at home in the Middle East, Jordan thought.

"To keep it out of his brother's hands, Crendal made a deal with his own personal devil. The Royal Trust for Historic Preservation agreed to maintain the estate. In return, Crendal agreed to open it to the public. Even the living quarters, which were converted into a bed and breakfast."

"What became of Crendal?"

"The Earl kept title to the property. But he was left a guest in his own house, an exhibit in his own museum."

Tom grinned with a twinkling of satisfaction.

"Naturally, he despises tourists."

Lizzie volunteered Tom's transportation services, and they crammed into his battered pickup truck. With the windows rolled down and the loamy smell of morning heavy in the air, they passed the quaint storefronts and neatly tended gardens of the village's main street. They turned right, through the meadows.

Chapter 31

Pamet Hall

They drove down a long cobblestone lane through a tunnel of majestic oaks toward the manor house, a vast stone edifice with rows of mullioned windows marching smartly in procession, like the generations of nobility who inhabited it. Set amid terraced gardens, it commanded miles of fields and woodlands.

They rounded a fountain at the center of the circular drive, past a parking lot for guests, where a handful of cars were parked. Tom dropped them at the visitors' entrance, and they thanked him for his trouble.

The morning fog was lifting, and Jordan hoped it was a sign.

Somewhere nearby, a pack of dogs barked excitedly, while horses snorted and whinnied. They sounded eager to be let loose on the countryside. It was a bad day to be a fox in Pamet Roads, Jordan thought.

They entered through the west portico, into a modest foyer with a reception desk, a coat-check and a stand for umbrellas.

"Welcome to Pamet Hall," the elderly woman behind the desk said. She was wearing a badge that identified her with the Royal Trust for Historic Preservation. "Unless you'd prefer to wait, you can join the tour already in progress," she said.

Jordan paid for a pair of tickets, and they followed the woman through a drawing room with a coffered ceiling and classical busts, and a giant reproduction of Tintoretto's *Eve Tasting the Fruit of Knowledge* set in a Rococo frame.

They stepped into the Great Hall, a soaring gallery of oil portraits. It had a cathedral ceiling, articulated with wood, which predated the house's façade, and an enormous table fit for a banquet. The guide, a pretty young woman with exceptional poise, was lecturing a small group.

The gallery presented a canvas of British history. There were men garbed in puritan simplicity and powdered pomposity. Men in uniform, and men in vested suits, with watch chains hanging from their vests. There were women, pale and bloodless and plump and prim, and, most unnerving of all, painted in formal discomfort, a pair of children who evidently died too young to be represented as adults.

Jordan studied the faces of the late Victorian era, searching for the vanished Sedgwick Belk, assuming he'd know Belk if he saw him.

"The seventh and ninth earls—the stout ones over there—each served in the Cabinet," the guide said. "The current earl's great grandfather—that dashing fellow in the uniform—was wounded in World War I, where he was decorated for shooting a pair of spies. And the man who enlarged the house to its current proportions in the late 18th century owned some of England's finest distilleries. He's remembered today for his charity and rectitude."

Jordan tried to put himself in the Earl's shoes. As the portraits attested, the estate's current occupant could trace his ancestry through generations, and the weight of expectations must have rested heavily on his shoulders.

By contrast, Jordan had no birthright, no family treasures to remind him of his parents. As a child, all he had was a snapshot—and the faded memory of a lullaby. The words had deserted him, leaving only the melody.

But Jordan's legacy was no less haunting.

"Now, if you'll step outside, my colleague Frances will show you the gardens, in the finest tradition of English horticulture," the guide said.

Jordan hung back, and Catherine stayed with him.

"Do you think you could introduce us to the Earl?" Jordan asked the guide, as he and Catherine offered their business cards.

"I'm very sorry, but the Earl doesn't receive tourists," the guide said.

"We're not tourists," Jordan said.

The guide read his card.

"Is it for an interview then?"

"Something like that."

"May I state the subject?"

"Personal."

"He's not expecting you?"

"It concerns his family, but, naturally, if you think he'd rather learn about it after our article is published . . . ."

"I'll tell him you're here."

"Thank you."

Catherine looked pensive.

"What are you thinking?" Jordan asked.

"I should have come here a long time ago."

She looked from portrait to portrait, studying the faces.

"Just our luck we get the black sheep of the family," she said. She turned to Jordan, and realized she hardly knew anything personal about him.

"Do you have any brothers?" she asked.

"No."

"Sisters?"

"None."

"What do you parents do?"

"They died when I was an infant. I never knew them."

"I'm sorry," she whispered, with moisture welling in her eyes.

"I grew up on a kibbutz," Jordan said. "I had a friend, Daniel, who was like a big brother to me. An American who came to fight for us."

"Are you still close?"

Jordan's thoughts seemed to drift away.

"One day, when I was eight, Daniel left on a mission. There was no time to say goodbye, they later explained. The next day, he was shot. They would have buried him on the kibbutz, with military honors, but his family in America wanted him back home. Where they could visit his grave."

Jordan noticed that his story had affected her.

"And you?" he asked. "Any siblings?"

Catherine fought to hold back the tears.

"I had a brother named Ian," she said. "I miss him terribly."

The guide returned, looking surprised.

"The Earl will see you," she said.

They glanced at each other, concealing their excitement.

The guide led them up the grand staircase to the second floor and down a long corridor. She knocked on a mahogany door, and a voice within issued an inaudible greeting. The guide opened the door.

Lord Myles Crendal appeared to be in his mid-40s, with dirty blonde hair that hung rakishly over one eye, and slightly uneven cheekbones that gave him a vaguely dangerous aspect. He had the look of a man afflicted—by a noxious mix of last night's scotch and this morning's sunlight.

As he hung up the phone, his eyes took a moment to refocus, and then he focused on the tour guide.

"Thank you, my dear," he said, and he watched her turn and leave, his bloodshot eyes fixed firmly on her ass.

Jordan absorbed the man's habitat. The walls were trimmed with classical molding and lined with shelves of antiques—a pair of flintlock pistols, ornately inlaid with mother of pearl, a Samurai sword of gleaming steel, and two large-caliber bullet shells, tarnished with age, standing on tiered pedestals of black wood. There were jade Buddhas from the Orient, bowls made of blue and white porcelain, and a brass mariner's sextant, for navigating by the sun and stars.

But it was hard not to stare at the Earl's proudest trophy, which stared down at them from behind the desk. As other huntsman might adorn a rustic mantle with a moose or deer, the Earl of Pamet displayed the head of a Bengal tiger.

"Welcome to Pamet Hall," the Earl said with a forced smile, followed by a flicker of interest in Catherine. "To what do we owe the pleasure?"

"Thank you for seeing us," Catherine said. "We're researching one of your ancestors. We were hoping we could peruse any records you have that shed light on his life and work."

Crendal gave them a queer look.

"Belk, is it?"

Jordan and Catherine exchanged glances.

"I suppose he was the most interesting," Catherine said.

"Certainly the most eccentric. But hardly the most illustrious. I have some highly accomplished forbears, you know. You've probably heard that. Men of action and achievement, as my father often said. Yes, well . . . . But here you are, asking about that strange bird Belk, who wasn't even lord of this manor long enough to sit for a portrait."

"May I ask how you knew it was him?"

"Oddly, just yesterday I promised someone else a look. An Oxford professor."

"Giles?" Catherine asked.

"Yes. And he was most emphatic. 'Don't show anything to anyone else,' he said."

"Did Giles give you a reason for that?" Jordan asked.

"The old boy warned me not to entrust the family name to the wrong sort of people. He said he could lend his considerable prestige to any rare documents in my possession, enhancing their market value, while scholars of lesser reputation—or no reputation whatsoever—could have the opposite effect."

"I visited him just yesterday to get his advice on my own research," Catherine said. "There was no indication he had previously given your ancestor more than a passing thought."

"And what makes Belk so interesting to *you,* Professor Cavanaugh?" the Earl asked, with a sly and solicitous look.

"Naturally, the mystery of his disappearance is a big part of it—finding out what prompted him to leave this magnificent estate and sail to the Holy Land. Discovering what happened to him, and whether he found what he was looking for."

"Do you know?" the Earl asked.

"No, but with your help, we might be able to answer the question," Catherine said. "Wouldn't it be exciting? Aren't you curious? I think his contemporaries assumed he died before getting very far, but what if they were wrong? What if he lived, and died an old man in a faraway land?"

A ripple of unease crossed the Earl's face, and Jordan sensed that Catherine had made a tactical mistake. Based on what the Oxford don told

Catherine, Belk left no direct descendants. Crendal's line inherited the title and property through one of Belk's nephews. Despite the obvious lure of the mystery, and the implicit suggestion that it involved something valuable, Crendal might worry that their research would lead to a rival heir.

"You think he might have lived, and left a family?" the Earl asked.

"I think that's highly unlikely," Jordan said. "The more interesting question is what he was looking for, and what became of it."

At a minimum, Jordan thought, a direct descendant of Belk could present a costly and embarrassing legal claim. On a deeper level, the search could threaten more than Crendal's hold on the land. It could threaten his very identity.

"I'll have to think it over," the Earl said, inspecting the business card that identified Jordan as a member of the press. "We'll talk again, maybe after I've kept my promise to Professor Giles."

"I understand," Jordan said. "It's hard to argue with Giles. He's used to getting his way."

The Earl digested that fact with a twist of indigestion.

"Maybe the best thing would be for me to consult an expert of my own," Crendal said.

"That's very sensible of you," Jordan said. "In the meantime, should we submit a request to the Royal Trust? They might want to play a role. In fact, they might claim some authority in the matter."

The flesh beneath Crendal's left eye quivered.

"I don't think any of us want to involve them," he said. "I think we should take this first exploratory step privately, the three of us. Provided you treat it as off the record."

Jordan looked at Catherine, and she answered with her eyes.

"Show us where to begin," Jordan said.

Chapter 32

The Earl escorted them to a room on the third floor. The walls were lined floor to ceiling with mahogany bookshelves and row upon row of leather-bound, gilt volumes. A ladder leaned against one wall for access to the top shelves. The center of the room was occupied by a trestle table with four spindly chairs. A wooden trunk sat beside the table with bands of iron and an old-fashioned hasp for a missing padlock.

"These are Sedgwick Belk's papers, awaiting Professor Giles," the Earl said. "None of them is to leave this room. Now if you'll excuse me for a short while, I have a call to make."

They nodded their assent and got to work.

The papers at the top documented preparations for Belk's journey to the Holy Land—receipts for clothing and other provisions, confirmation of passage on a ship, arrangements for maintenance of the manor in his absence.

They read each page carefully and set it in a pile. The documents in the trunk seemed to be stacked in roughly chronological order, with the latest on top.

They studied an exchange of letters with the college about Belk's departure and potential return. His resignation was perfunctory, devoid of explanation. The college informed him that he would forfeit any chance of reinstatement if he stayed away more than two years.

Deeper they plowed, until Catherine's hands almost trembled with excitement. She read the page a second time and handed it to Jordan. He felt an eerie shiver.

It was a sheet of aged, flimsy stationery, stained and slightly torn, still creased where the author had folded it. The writing was slanted and irregular, as if penned by an unsteady hand.

27 December 1883

My Dear Lord Belk,

The Torah teaches us that God commanded the Chosen People to keep his Words as frontlets between their eyes, and to bind them upon their hands and doorposts.

Please accept the enclosed as tokens of Respect and Gratitude, for I have no further use for them. I convey them as they were conveyed to me, pried from the dust of Antiquity.

I trust that you, Sir, will discern their inner meaning, and be guided by it.

Faithfully yours,

Mordecai Mandel

They looked at it in silent reverence.

"It was dated the day he died," Catherine said.

"It proves you were right," Jordan said. "Mandel gave Belk the artifact he intended as his encore."

"Mandel boasted that it could influence religious beliefs," Catherine said. "He said it described something extraordinary buried with the Temple treasures in the 1st Century."

"And Belk appears to have gone in search of the treasure."

"But where are Mandel's enclosures?"

Whatever Mandel enclosed for Belk had become separated from his letter.

They reached back into the trunk. In short order, Jordan found a clipping of Belk's letter to the editor criticizing Mandel's critics, and a handwritten draft of the same. There was also an invitation from Charles Salisbury of the British Museum to meet Mandel and examine his manuscript with a select company of experts.

They pored over letters from students, lecture notes, household bills. Deeper still, there was a paper in which Belk offered an explanation for Noah's flood. He theorized that the deluge occurred when a narrow strip of land linking Europe and Africa, near the straits of Gibraltar, gave way, allowing the waters of the Atlantic to rush in and flood the Mediterranean basin. It had an unmistakable similarity to modern theories centered on the Black Sea and the Bosphorus. But an accompanying note showed that it had been rejected for publication.

Distracted by the contents of the paper, Jordan almost failed to notice the date. It was written three years before Mandel arrived in London. If Mandel's enclosures were here, they were badly out of sequence.

A maid brought sandwiches, but they didn't stop to eat. An hour later, they reached the bottom.

"They're not here," Catherine said, defeated.

"He probably took them to the Middle East," Jordan said.

"Let's focus on the letter," Catherine said. "*God commanded the Chosen People to keep his Words as frontlets between their eyes, and to bind them upon their hands and doorposts.*"

"I think it's clear that Mandel was alluding to phylacteries," Jordan said.

Catherine pictured the miniature boxes with leather straps, and imagined a devout old Jew tying them around his wrists and forehead before wrapping himself in a prayer shawl. They consisted of little black cubes, about two inches in each dimension, affixed to broader and flatter blocks that served as their base. The boxes ordinarily contained bible verse.

"Agreed," she said. "Or he could have been referring to mezuzahs."

"Either way."

Jordan pictured the hollow cylindrical ornaments that Jewish families then and now displayed in their doorways. Like phylacteries, they were designed to hold tiny sheets of scripture.

"When you think about it, they would have been ingenious devices for hiding information or smuggling messages," he said.

"And now they're gone."

The corrupt smell of cigar smoke wafted into the room, and Lord Crendal strode in, with just the slightest wobble. He had a stogie clenched in his teeth, and it appeared he had been drinking.

"So, what have you learned?" the Earl asked, sinking into a chair.

"Your ancestor was an extraordinary figure, and quite under-appreciated. The papers make that clear," Catherine said.

"What's to appreciate?"

"He was an independent thinker, who rejected the conventions of his day. He could see a multiplicity of perspectives. In religious tradition, he saw geology, biology, the whole sweep of natural history—"

"Fascinating," the Earl said, looking deeply into her eyes, feigning an appreciation for her analysis, lowering his gaze. "So, what do you suppose it's worth?"

"In the realm of scholarship, there's no way to put a price on it," Catherine said.

"How about in the realm of Sotheby's, or Christie's?"

"I'm not qualified to say. But Benjamin and I would like to continue our examination. There's enough to write a book."

He looked at her inscrutably.

"I should think you might be missing some chapters," the Earl said, drawing deeply on his cigar.

"You're right," Jordan said. "The archive is incomplete. Are you sure that's all there is?"

"It is what it is," Crendal answered. "What were you hoping for?"

"For instance, there's a letter from a man who attained some notoriety in his day, referencing enclosures. But the enclosures aren't there."

The Earl exhaled, and the smoke was tinged with gin.

"Tell me more," he said.

"The man who wrote to Belk was a Jewish shopkeeper, from Jerusalem," Jordan said. "He was accused of trying to defraud the British Museum by selling it a fake artifact. They drove him out of London in disgrace. But he felt a bond of some sort to your ancestor, and wrote him a letter of deep personal thanks. That was the day he checked into a flophouse and put a bullet in his head."

Crendal grimaced. The mere association seemed distasteful to him.

"Let me see," he said.

Jordan handed him the leaf of aged, flimsy stationery covered in Mandel's unsteady scrawl.

"It's part of what makes Belk such an interesting figure," Jordan continued.

The Earl read the letter and narrowed his eyes. He inhaled deeply, and the end of his cigar glowed a fiery orange.

"So this is part of the paper trail that leads to Belk and whatever else," he said, pointing with his cigar. "Flimsy, isn't it?"

He lowered the smoldering end of his cigar to within millimeters of the letter's edge.

"Everyone loves a mystery," Crendal said, looking at Jordan. "Sometimes a mystery is better than the truth."

"For all we know there's a pot of gold at the end of that rainbow," Catherine said.

"Or a sleeping dog," Crendal said. "Sometimes it's better to let them lie."

The cigar was nearly touching the paper.

"Give it a chance," Catherine said. "Give us a chance."

The edge of the page was beginning to blacken.

Crendal smiled at Catherine.

"Let's sleep on it," he said. "Why don't you spend the night at Pamet Hall, as my guests, and we'll discuss it over breakfast."

He put the cigar between his teeth and took another puff.

"As you know, I'm expecting Giles the day after tomorrow," he added.

They ate dinner with the other overnight guests in a formal dining room. The crystal chandelier tinkled like a wind chime in an unseen draft, and a burble of conversation filled the room.

The waiters served rare roast beef *au jus*. Catherine looked at her plate and saw visions of a hunt's bloody conclusion.

"You're not eating?" Jordan said.

"I prefer mine cooked," Catherine said.

Jordan summoned a waiter and sent Catherine's dinner back to the kitchen.

Catherine whispered in Jordan's ear.

"I think Belk would have removed the contents of the ritual objects and kept them at hand for easy reference."

"Or would he have kept them someplace safe?"

"Hmmm."

The waiter served Catherine a well-done cut, but she ignored it. She was listening to an elderly gentleman in turtleneck and tweed, who was holding forth at an adjacent table. She recognized him from the tour.

"The guide was a lovely girl, but she airbrushed history," he told his friends. "For all her talk of charity and rectitude, it was slavery that built Pamet Hall. Profits from the slave trade, shipping Africans to the West Indies."

When the coffee had been cleared, Jordan escorted Catherine to her room. The Earl had placed them on separate floors. Jordan remembered Catherine's sensitivity the night before, and he assumed with chagrin that she had specified the arrangements.

"When we see the Earl in the morning, we'll do our best to win his trust, and buy some time," Jordan said.

"Well, goodnight then," she said, opening the door. She hesitated and turned to look at him.

"If you need me, I won't be far," he said.

She forced a smile and closed the door.

Chapter 33

Jordan found his own room one flight up, at the end of the corridor. Amid the dark luxury of his paneled bedchamber, he thought fate might be compensating him for his night at the Royal. The Earl had even provided a bottle of brandy, already open, to hasten his dreams. But he was in no mood to enjoy it.

He thought of Catherine in her Michigan sweats, and the clinging tank top, which left just enough to the imagination.

He sat beside the fire in a deep leather armchair. The darkness of the unlit room matched his mood. He turned the problem of the missing items over and over in his head, but he saw no solution.

The little black boxes were meant to stay sealed. By ancient custom, they contained excerpts from Exodus—the Tenth Plague, most terrible of all.

His mind wandered through the labyrinth of Pamet Hall to the Great Hall and the faces on the walls. The portrait of charity and rectitude.

It was slavery that built Pamet Hall, the man at dinner had said.

Suppose he found what he was looking for, and suppose Mandel was right about its significance. How would people respond to the message? How would they respond to the messenger?

Some people clung to their illusions, even when the truth was right in front of them. The truth could be too uncomfortable. Easier to blame the messenger than to accept the message.

Jordan had lived that lesson.

In a manner of speaking, he had opened the box . . . .

He was back in Connecticut, outside a big bland house with a neat green lawn, stepping out of a station wagon with fake wood siding. He was 13 years old.

Several years had passed since his buddy Daniel gave his life for Israel, and Daniel's parents had sponsored an exchange program. The Friedmans were struggling to come to terms with Daniel's death, and to memorialize him in a way that was faithful to his sacrifice. They bought plane tickets for eight children from the kibbutz to visit America and arranged for the children to stay with Jewish families in their community. The idea was that kids from the Connecticut suburb would later visit the kibbutz, but that never happened. Jordan figured he was the reason.

He stayed with the Friedmans, in the room that once belonged to Daniel. He was with them for Passover.

When it was time for the holiday dinner, everyone crowded into the dining room. Daniel's teenage sister, Allison, and his grandparents were there, along with some neighbors named Anderson, and Rabbi Berman and his wife, from the Friedmans' temple.

The table was set in fine china and silver, with a wine-stained copy of the Passover *haggadah* at each setting. There were piles of *matzah*, chopped apples and honey, chopped liver, and congealed lumps of pureed fish called *gefilte* fish.

Mr. Friedman began by asking the Rabbi to say a few words, and the Rabbi warmed to the task. He explained that they were gathered to tell the story of the Jews' Exodus from slavery in Egypt. With a nod to the Andersons, who were African American, the Rabbi said it was only fitting that Jews celebrate Passover with friends of other faiths and backgrounds.

Reading from the *haggadah,* they all joined in singing.

When Israel was in Egypt's land,
Let my people go!
Oppressed so hard they could not stand,
Let my people go!
Go down, Moses,
Way down in Egypt's land,
Tell ol' Pharaoh,
To let my people go.

For Jordan's benefit, the Rabbi explained that slaves in the American South had sung the same song while they prayed for deliverance. The Jewish Exodus gave them hope and inspiration.

As the youngest child present, Jordan was called upon to read the Four Questions. "Why is this night different from all other nights?" he began. He asked the traditional questions in a clear, steady voice.

Reading from the *haggadah*, Mr. Friedman told the famous story, recalling that once Jews suffered in cruel bondage to Egyptian taskmasters. Moses asked Pharaoh to let his people go, but the wicked Pharaoh stubbornly refused. So God sent a series of plagues upon Egypt. After each plague, Moses repeated his plea, but Pharaoh hardened his heart against the Jews. Finally, God inflicted the most terrible plague of all. Passing over the houses of the Israelites, God killed the firstborn of every Egyptian family.

At last, Pharaoh gave in, and the Jews fled in such a hurry that there was no time for their bread to rise. But almost as soon as the Jews were out of his sight, Pharaoh changed his mind. He sent his army chasing after them.

Trapped between the Pharaoh's onrushing chariots and the Red Sea, the Jews looked doomed. Then, in the greatest miracle of all, God parted the waters to let the Jews escape—and drowned the pursuing army.

The Rabbi cleared his throat. Though it was a Jewish holiday, he said, it celebrated universal values, freedom and equality, and God commanded the Israelites to tell their children the Passover story so they would never lose sight of these basic human rights.

Jordan's expression must have given him away.

"Ben, you look surprised," Mr. Friedman said. "This can't be the first time you've heard the Passover story, is it?"

There was a long, awkward silence while Jordan formulated an answer.

"I like your version better," Jordan said, diplomatically.

"Is there another?" Mr. Friedman asked.

Jordan tried to dodge the question, but Mr. Friedman maintained eye contact.

"There's the original," Jordan said.

"What do you mean?"

"The Book of Exodus."

"Didn't we just cover that?"

"Rabbi?" Jordan said, deferring.

The Rabbi didn't know what to say.

Daniel's grandfather jumped in jovially and tried to get Jordan off the hook. "Now, Ben, you're only responsible for four questions. That's why they call them The Four Questions. Let's eat."

Mrs. Friedman rose to serve dinner, but Mr. Friedman motioned for her to sit.

"I want to know what's on Ben's mind," Mr. Friedman said, with more eye contact.

"Do you have a bible?" Jordan asked.

Mr. Friedman left the dining room and returned with a seldom-opened copy of The Five Books of Moses. "Hebrew and English," he said.

Jordan flipped through it, trying to find his place, conscious that everyone's eyes were upon him. After an uncomfortably long interval, he found it.

"The very day the Jews left Egypt, God told Moses how to observe Passover, and this is the way God put it: 'Any bought slave may partake, provided you have circumcised him.' *Any bought slave.*"

"What's that supposed to mean?" Mr. Friedman asked.

"I think it means the Jews had slaves," Jordan said. "I think it means it was okay with God if, after escaping slavery in Egypt, the Jews kept slaves of their own."

"No, that can't be," Mrs. Friedman said. "Tell him, Rabbi."

The Rabbi looked like he had suddenly come down with a severe case of heartburn. Which was strange, since he hadn't even touched his *gefilte* fish.

"Just look at the Ten Commandments," Jordan said, flipping ahead in the Bible.

" 'Remember the Sabbath day and keep it holy,'" he read. " 'You shall not do any work—you, your son or daughter, your male or female *slave*, or your cattle, or the stranger who is within your settlements.'"

Mr. Anderson looked at Jordan in disbelief. "That's not the way I remember it," he said.

"Then there's 'Thou shalt not covet,'" Jordan said, plunging ahead. "'You shall not covet your neighbor's house: you shall not covet your neighbor's wife, or his male or female *slave*, or his ox or his ass, or anything that is your neighbor's.'"

"I don't know where you get this reference to male or female *slaves*," Mr. Anderson said. "The Bible I know refers to *'manservants'* and *'maidservants.'*"

"Maybe those are old-fashioned English words for slaves," Jordan said.

"I think they're altogether different," Mr. Anderson said.

"Well, maybe," Jordan conceded. "But there's more, lots more."

Mrs. Friedman looked stricken.

"It's right here, in Exodus 21, right after the Ten Commandments," Jordan continued. He showed it to Daniel's grandfather, who read it aloud.

" 'When you acquire a Hebrew slave, he shall serve six years; in the seventh year he shall go free without payment . . . . If his master gave him a wife, and she has borne him children, the wife and her children shall belong to the master, and he shall leave alone. But if the slave declares, 'I love my master, and my wife and children: I do not wish to go free,' his master shall . . . . pierce his ear with an awl; and he shall then remain his slave for life.'"

Everyone looked at Jordan in astonishment. It was so quiet they could hear the Rabbi's stomach gurgle.

"Benjamin, I think you may be confusing the institution of slavery with indentured servitude," Mr. Andersen offered. "Indentured servants go free after they work off their debts."

"Maybe the boys do," Benjamin said. "But not the girls. Look: 'When a man sells his daughter as a slave, she shall not be freed as male slaves are.'"

"That's horrible," Daniel's younger sister, Allison, said.

"And when it comes to slaves who aren't Hebrew, not even the boys go free," Jordan said. " 'These shall become your property: you may keep them as a possession for your children after you, for them to inherit as property for all time.' "

"I don't believe it," Mrs. Friedman said.

"There's more," Jordan said. "If a man murders another man, the penalty is death. But if a master kills his slave, it's like it isn't even a crime. As long as the slave doesn't die within a day or two, the master *'is not to be punished . . . because the slave is his property.'* "

Mr. Friedman looked incredulous. Everyone looked incredulous.

"I'm sorry," Benjamin said to no one in particular. "That's what it says."

"Then what the hell is the point of the story?" Mr. Friedman demanded. "I mean, what about 'Let my people go' and all that?"

Mr. Friedman directed his question at the Rabbi.

"Do you want to tell him, Benjamin?" the Rabbi said, in a tone of respectful encouragement.

Jordan took a deep breath. "You see, in the Bible, Moses didn't really say, 'Let my people go.' "

"Are you kidding?" Mr. Friedman said.

"In the Bible, *God* said it. God was giving Moses a message to take to Pharaoh. The thing is, there was more to it. What God said was, 'Tell Pharaoh to let my people go *so they can worship me.*' "

"I don't get it," Mr. Friedman said.

"For God, it wasn't about the evils of slavery. It was about worshiping Him."

Jordan could tell that they didn't understand.

"Remember the part about Pharaoh hardening his heart after each plague and refusing to let the Jews go? Well, that's the problem. In the Bible, *Pharaoh* didn't harden his heart. God did it for him. God *made* Pharaoh resist when Pharaoh was ready to give in: 'But *the Lord* hardened Pharaoh's heart, and he would not let them go.' "

"That's nuts," Mr. Friedman said. "Why would God do that?"

"God explained. God wanted an excuse to flex his muscles. He wanted to show everyone how powerful he was."

Jordan looked for the quote. But before he could find it, the Rabbi recited from memory.

" 'Then the Lord said to Moses, 'Go to Pharaoh. For I have hardened his heart and the hearts of his courtiers, in order that I may display these My signs among them, and that you may recount in the hearing of your sons and of your sons' sons how I made a mockery of the Egyptians and how I displayed My signs among them—in order that you may know that I am the Lord.'"

"What about the parting of the sea?" Allison asked. "You mean it was just God showing off?"

"Allison!" her mother scolded.

"It was no accident that the Jews found themselves with their backs to the sea," the Rabbi said. "God arranged it that way. The Bible says the Israelites had been making good progress on their journey out of Egypt when God told them to *turn back* and camp by the sea. God *wanted* Pharaoh to go after them. One last time, God hardened Pharoah's heart against the Israelites. Why? God tells us:

" 'So that I may win glory for myself at the expense of Pharaoh and all his army.' "

There was a long, dumbfounded silence.

"Well," Mr. Anderson said.

"Hmmm," Mr. Friedman said.

"Ummm, is everyone ready for soup?" Mrs. Friedman asked.

Jordan spoke up.

"Rabbi Berman?"

"Yes, Benjamin?"

"What I don't understand is . . . ."

"Yes?"

"Why did all the Egyptian children have to die? They didn't do anything wrong."

Rabbi Berman looked at him sadly.

"That, Benjamin, is a very difficult question."

In the lonely luxury of his Pamet Hall guest room, Jordan reached for a snifter and poured the Earl's brandy. He swirled it in the glass.

He pictured a devout Jew, an Orthodox Jew, engrossed in prayer, with phylacteries strapped to his wrist and forehead. The little black boxes contained snippets of scripture. Traditionally, passages from Exodus.

On the awesome power of God, and the death of the firstborn.

The phylacteries that Mordecai Mandel bequeathed to Sedgwick Belk supposedly concealed something else, a secret that challenged one of the world's faiths. A secret still hidden.

Jordan raised the brandy to his lips, but he didn't drink.

The image of phylacteries stuck in his mind, like a face out of context. He had seen a pair just recently—he was sure of it. Or something that resembled phylacteries.

Displayed like trophies in a place of pride.

No, not trophies—*pedestals*.

He put down the brandy.

There had been a pair of antique bullet casings on a shelf in the Earl's study, standing on black wooden blocks.

Was it possible?

Chapter 34

It was past 2:20 a.m., and Catherine was tired of tossing and turning. She felt a sense of lonely isolation, like a cold draft.

Her accommodations, recently refurbished, were charming and romantic, and shockingly expensive according to her guidebook on Great Britain. The room was lit with elegant sconces and a blazing fire, and reflections of the flames danced in the gleaming brass of the andirons. The bed was shrouded in a silken canopy, accented with red and gold drapes. An antique mirror framed in gold hung over the mantle. Yet there was something ominous about Pamet Hall.

She thought of sneaking into Jordan's room and surprising him, but thought better of it.

The old house made noises . . . or was that a knock at the door?

She froze. She listened again, and she heard a light rapping at the door to her room. Before she could answer, the knob turned and the silken canopy fluttered.

"Ben?"

"No, it's Myles," the Earl of Pamet said. "May I come in?"

She sat up in bed and pulled up the covers, holding them against her chest.

"What is it?" she asked, as the Earl stepped into the room.

"I'm sorry to wake you," the Earl said. "There's something I think you should see."

"About Belk?"

"In my study," Crendal said. "I didn't want to wait."

"What about Ben?"

"Ben wouldn't get up," Crendal said. "Apparently my brandy got the better of him."

"Give me a minute," Catherine said.

The Earl stepped into the hall, and Catherine pulled on some clothes.

Jordan treaded lightly down the vacant corridor, past closed doors, to the back stairs. He tried to move quietly, but it was impossible to silence the scuffs and echoes of his feet against the floor. He reached the second floor and traced his way to the main corridor. There, the Persian rugs—long runners of silk and wool—muted the sound. Stationed along the walls, occasional suits of armor and marble statuary cast disconcerting shadows.

Jordan tested the door to the Earl's study. It opened without a struggle. He stepped inside, gently closing the door behind him.

He felt his way in the dark to the Earl's desk, and turned the switch on the lamp one click, to its dimmest setting. The curtains were open. Jordan couldn't see out, but if anyone happened to be looking in, they could watch his every move. He wondered how much light leaked out of the study from the brass banker's lamp, into a moonless night. He reached to close the curtains—and stopped.

He weighed the risks. Was it better to avoid interruption, or to prepare for it? There was no clear answer. Jordan drew the curtains.

A clock in the corner said it was just past 2:20 a.m.

He turned to the shelf with the twin, tarnished bullet casings. As best he could judge, they dated to World War I. Maybe they belonged to the Earl's great grandfather, the one who shot the enemy spies.

The brass shells were sitting on small pedestals of black wood. The pedestals looked like phylacteries.

With a deep breath, Jordan picked the shell on the right off its pedestal.

The shell was engraved in a jeweler's script: "Ypres 1917."

The name of the bloody battle conjured images of horror—brave young men climbing out of trenches, into machine-gun fire, instantly torn to gore. Human scarecrows hanging in barbed wire. Soldiers choking on poison gas, their faces contorted in agony. Corpses rotting face-down in the mud, a feast for the rats.

Jordan turned the hollow brass casing lengthwise and looked inside, into the blackness from which the bullet had fired. It was empty. He set it down on the shelf.

He picked up the second shell. It bore the same inscription. It was empty, too. He set it beside the first.

He felt a rush of adrenaline, and it took force of will to steady his nerves. He lifted the first pedestal from the shelf. It fit easily in the palm of his hand. On closer inspection, it was made of hardened leather, not wood, and it weighed less than its volume would suggest.

If it was a box, it didn't open voluntarily. He inspected it closely, searching for seams. He noted a minute trace of residue that looked like glue where the cube met its base.

Catherine followed the earl down a long corridor to the far wing of the second floor, which apparently served as his private residence. They passed a familiar mahogany door.

"Isn't that your study?" Catherine asked.

"The next door on the left," the Earl said.

He opened the door and ushered her inside with a gallant gesture.

"My private sanctuary," he said.

A fire was burning in a marble fireplace, and a Chippendale couch was arranged beside a cocktail table. A bottle of Perrier Jouet was chilling in a sterling ice bucket, and two crystal champagne flutes were standing on a tray.

"What did you want to show me?" Catherine asked, taking a half step back.

"Over here," the Earl said, gesturing to the cocktail table.

A cloth-bound album was set out beside the champagne.

"Go ahead, take a look," the Earl said, as he closed the door.

She wanted to get out of there, but the album called to her.

She sat down, and the Earl sat beside her.

She opened the album as he poured the champagne.

It was a collection of antique photographs, members of Crendal's family. She flipped ahead to the bookmarked page. The sepia-toned image showed a man with a trim mustache and the burning eyes of a half-crazed genius, or maybe a poet. Catherine stared at the picture. The subject reminded her of Edgar Allan Poe.

The calligraphy inscription identified him as Professor Sedgwick Belk.

Was that all? Just a photograph?

She smelled cigar smoke and gin, and she felt the Earl's breath on her cheek. He was leaning toward her, looking over her shoulder . . . .

Ignoring him, she turned the page. The next picture featured a group of children.

She felt his lips on her neck, kissing her.

Recoiling, she pushed him away.

"You know we're drawn to each other," he said. "You can't resist."

"I'm flattered, really, but I'm with Benjamin."

"You can be honest: You never imagined that you'd be here like this with someone like me, an English noble."

"Sorry, I think you're confusing me with someone else."

His eyes gleamed with drunken intensity.

"Don't you want my help?" he said.

She looked at him with disgust and started to leave.

He rose up, blocking her, locking her in an embrace, forcing his mouth over hers.

Anger and shame welled up like bile, as they did that day in Belfast, when the boys ripped open her blouse.

She bit Crendal's lip, and he cried out in pain, loosening his grip.

"Bitch!" he cried, smacking her in the face.

Stunned, she grasped his shoulders—and kneed him the groin.

He tripped over the table, sending crystal and silver crashing.

In the adjacent room, Jordan spun around, knocking over one of the antique bullet casings.

He heard Catherine's scream, and a crash of furniture.

He left the phylactery and ran from the study, into the hall.

Catherine was fleeing toward him, holding a champagne bottle by the neck. Distressed and disheveled, she rushed into his arms.

"I'm getting you out of here," Jordan said.

The Earl staggered into the hall. He dabbed at the blood dripping from his lip. He looked at the two of them with smugness and spite.

Jordan took a step toward him, angrily, as a door opened down the hall. One of the guests stuck out her head.

"Come on, Ben," Catherine said, pulling Jordan away.

The Earl called after them.

"You'll never know," he said. "You'll never know what happened to Belk."

Chapter 35

Ten minutes later, they were out in the cold, moonless night, trudging down the long cobblestone drive through the tunnel of oaks, away from Pamet Hall. Jordan was carrying the bags.

"Can't we call someone to come and get us?" Catherine asked.

"Not a good idea," Jordan said.

"I'm sorry, Ben. It's my fault."

"Don't apologize. Just keep walking."

"Now I'll be lucky to get a job at Westphall State," Catherine said with gallows humor. "I should have slept with the son-of-a-bitch."

"No, but I should have fractured his face."

The wind rustled through the oaks, and the moon peeked through the clouds, only to disappear again.

"Owww," she said, tripping on the cobblestones, grabbing Jordan's arm.

"You should have worn more practical shoes," Jordan said, breaking her fall.

"Next time I'm at Pamet Hall, I'll remember that."

Jordan knelt beside her and brushed the hair from her face. In the moonlight, he saw that she was bruised.

"Here, let me," he said. He unzipped his knapsack and took out a plastic bottle. He poured some water on a plush white monogrammed facecloth and pressed it against her cheek.

"Where'd you get that?" she asked.

"It was in my room."

"That's stealing," she teased. "If murdering a museum curator and assaulting an earl in his own house weren't trouble enough, now we really are in trouble."

"Here, put these on," Jordan said, fishing her Timberlands out of her bag.

She glanced back, toward Pamet Hall, as she laced them up.

"I've blown our chance, Ben. I've ruined everything."

"I promise, you did not."

"Now we'll never learn the secret of Mordecai Mandel's ultimate proof. I'll never publish, and you'll never get your reputation back."

"I believe we will."

"I admire your optimism, but let's be honest."

"Catherine, we're not leaving empty-handed."

"I can see that. Did you steal the bath towels, too?"

Jordan took her face in his hands and looked into her eyes.

"I found the phylacteries," he said.

She searched his eyes, looking for evidence of a joke, but he was deadly serious.

"Where are they?" she asked.

"Sitting on a shelf in Crendal's office."

"I don't understand. You want to *go back?*"

"While you were enjoying a nightcap with the Earl, I was in his study. I found the phylacteries beneath a pair of antique bullet casings, serving as miniature pedestals. I doubt Crendal even knew what they were. They could have been sitting there since his great-grandfather's time. You see, Sedgwick Belk had put Mandel's missing texts back inside the phylacteries, and he had sealed them shut. As if Belk were keeping faith with Mandel, keeping Mandel's legacy intact. But I used a razor blade from the Earl's desk to break the seals. I removed the enclosures. *I have the enclosures*."

"What are they?'

"A stack of inscribed parchment sheets, no larger than a matchbox. All stuck together. And another thing, which you'll have to see for yourself."

"Do you know what they say?"

"I didn't have time."

"Will Crendal notice they're missing?"

"If he sobers up, he may notice that the bullet shells have been disturbed. And if he notices that the shells have been disturbed, he'll figure out the rest."

"We've got to get out of Pamet Roads," Catherine said. "We've got to get out of England."

"We need to go somewhere safe, where we can hide and figure out what we have."

Behind the manor house, in the Earl's kennel, a dog started barking, and others joined in.

Jordan extended a hand and helped Catherine to her feet.

"It's about five kilometers to the station," he said. "If we hurry, we can make the first train out."

"Do you think we should go somewhere out of the way, like the Scottish Highlands, or the northern coast?"

"That would make it harder for someone to sneak up on us, or watch us unobserved, but it's easier to disappear in a big city. Besides, I think you had it right the first time. We need to get out of the U.K., before the authorities or anyone else can block our exit."

"Then there's only one place to go—the one country that wouldn't send you back. The one country where the law shields you from extradition."

"Israel."

"Yes, so stop dawdling," she said, picking up the pace.

An hour out of the station, as the train cut through fields of baled hay and grazing cows, Jordan walked back up the aisle from the dining car, bumping against arm rests and carrying a pair of Cokes.

"Here," he said with a frown, handing one to Catherine as he sank back into his aisle seat.

"What's the matter?" she asked.

"There's a new terrorist threat, so they've heightened security at Heathrow and Gatwick."

"That means tighter screening of passengers."

"And baggage."

"Do you want to chance it?"

"The high-speed train from London to Paris, under the Channel, takes two and half hours. If we took that instead, we could fly out of Paris tomorrow."

"That would give the police more time to figure out that you're the man from the museum. Or for Crendal to file charges."

"They may be looking for us already. The question is, where are they least likely to spot us?"

They transferred trains outside London and switched buses twice to avoid unwanted attention, then made a loop of Harrod's on foot. On a busy street corner in Knightsbridge, by the light of a streetlamp, Jordan flagged a taxi. "Waterloo Station," he told the driver, holding the door as Catherine climbed in. He opened his wallet and thumbed through the contents.

"Do you have enough money for the cab?" he asked, in a low voice.

"Yes, more than enough."

"And a credit card for the ticket?"

"Mine and my mother's, which I didn't get around to canceling."

"Good," he said, handing her a scrap of paper. "Now, if for any reason I don't show up, get yourself to Jerusalem, go to this hotel, and ask the manager, Ari, to give you his best room without entering you in the registry."

He started to close the door, but she held it open.

"What are you talking about?" she said.

"There are countless surveillance cameras at the terminal, and we shouldn't be seen together. If they're looking for either of us, they'll be looking for me. So I'll meet you on the other end, at Gare du Nord in Paris."

She looked at him with astonishment.

"Trust me," he said.

"And if that doesn't work?"

Jordan shrugged.

"You'll figure it out. But whatever you do . . . ."

"Yes?"

"Don't go to Westphall State."

Before she could answer, he turned his back and vanished into the crowd.

She looked out the rear window as the taxi pulled away from the curb, but Jordan was gone.

She told herself she trusted him. Of course she trusted him. In his confrontation with the Earl, he had seemed hell-bent on revenge. He had clenched his fist with an anger that bordered on jealousy.

Or was he simply covering his tracks, and improvising an exit strategy?

Either way, Catherine gaped at his audacity—and his execution. He had carried it off brilliantly. So brilliantly he made lying and stealing seem virtuous.

But what, exactly, had he carried off?

What was in the phylacteries?

What if she never saw him again?

The concourse at Waterloo Station looked like an enclosed street, with a grand façade of brick and stone facing inward, opposite shops with multicolored signs and awnings. Under its glass sky and metal trusses, she felt like an extra on a set. She tried not to look into the cameras.

Inside the Eurostar terminal, she scanned the queue at the security check, searching for Jordan. She made it to the head of the line, and he was still nowhere to be seen. She glanced at her watch. In minutes, the train would be boarding.

A businessman in a double-breasted suit was standing several feet away, talking on a mobile phone, and he was taking an uncomfortable interest in her. She tried to ignore him—even as she tried fruitlessly to get the gist of his conversation. She thought she heard a few words in Italian.

She put her knapsack on the X-ray belt and passed through the metal detector. Uniformed guards searched her bag, tested her shoes for explosives, and passed the wand over her body, pausing at the buttons on her faded jeans. A security woman studied her passport, patiently comparing the face in the photo with the passenger.

Catherine feigned annoyance to camouflage any outward sign of anxiety.

"Would you please come with me?" the woman said.

No!

"Sure," Catherine said.

The woman led her into a small, featureless room with a table in the middle. Another security officer, a sallow woman in her 40s, was standing behind the table, looking at a video screen. She looked at Catherine for several seconds, studying her face.

"Is there anything you want to tell me about your companion?" the officer said.

"Companion? I'm traveling alone."

The officer smiled a patronizing smile.

"What's his relationship to you? Boyfriend?"

"I don't know what you're talking about."

"I can help you, if you want my help," the officer said. "It's your choice."

What did they know?

"Is he a violent man?" the officer asked. "Is he a danger to others?"

Catherine felt a drop of sweat slide down her spine.

"What are you talking about?"

"That's a very nasty bruise," the security officer said, pointing to Catherine's cheek. "Domestic violence is nothing to trifle with. If you need help escaping a bad relationship, there are places you can go. I've been there myself."

Catherine almost laughed with relief.

"Thank you for your concern," she said, "but I'm going to Paris."

At Gare du Nord, the sleek bullet train disgorged its passengers into an enormous shed.

Catherine stopped beside by a pile of suitcases, pretending to study the departure times posted on an overhead display.

Where the hell was Jordan?

At the end of the platform, she saw a tall blonde woman with stiletto heels greet the man in the double-breasted suit. He gave her a deep kiss, and they walked off, arm in arm, toward the escalator.

She spotted Jordan across the crowded concourse. He gestured subtly toward the exit, and they each made their way to the taxi stand along the Rue de Maubeuge.

"Mademoiselle, may I share your ride?" he said, with an accent so bad it made her laugh.

Chapter 36

Pamet Hall

It was another cloudy, moonless night in Pamet Roads, and just past the dinner hour the Earl of Pamet sat beneath his Bengal tiger, in a chair comfortably molded to his body through years of wear, surrounded by the peculiar assortment of heirlooms that gave expression to his character. He fancied himself a hunter, a warrior, an adventurer, an imperialist—a man to be feared and respected—even if all these trappings of courage and violent physicality came with the house. If fate placed him in dangerous circumstances, it went without saying that he would meet its test with the same fearless strength his forebears had displayed.

Only on this night, the Earl's wrists, forearms, ankles, and waist were strapped to his chair with duct tape, and he was stripped to his soiled underwear.

"I told you, I don't know where they are," he whimpered. "I don't know, I don't know, I don't know . . . ."

His uninvited guests wore black ski masks, like IRA gunmen, but there was no trace of Ireland in their voices.

The first was tall and powerfully built; the other, shorter and thicker. They had arrived after most of the staff left, on the one night of the week when the estate was closed to overnight guests. They had been interviewing him, off and on, for the better part of four hours, and their work remained incomplete. They had progressed from the location of Belk's papers—the trunk now sat beside them in the study, its contents already thoroughly examined—to every detail of his recent visitors' stay. Every question the American and the Israeli had asked, every comment they had made, every object that had caught their eye.

Crendal provided little resistance—How could he resist?—but when his memory faltered, they enhanced it with a slightly modified respirator mask made of clear plastic, much like those used in hospitals and ambulances. The mask formed an airtight seal around Crendal's fractured nose and mouth.

After the intruders found the letter from Mordecai Mandel to Sedgwick Belk, and interpreted its meaning, they began probing Crendal for the missing enclosures. When he failed to respond under duress, they told him exactly what they were seeking, even drawing a sketch of a phylactery to help him, but the Earl remained blank.

There had been a moment, no more than a second or two, when the Earl might have fought back—a fleeting instant in which to make the most pivotal decision of his life, guided by little more than instinct or reflex. That was when they first intruded. He thought of reaching for the samurai sword and taking his chances against their guns. But he had hesitated, and the moment had passed. Once restrained, he was at their mercy.

"Will you tell me?" the tall one asked again.

Crendal shook his head back and forth in terror, tears streaming down his face. His answer, through the mask, was a muffled "I don't know."

The interrogator gave the signal—a finger across his throat—and the shorter man shut the valve on the plastic mask.

The Earl's eyes bulged, and he squirmed and jerked involuntarily. His every autonomic impulse was fighting to breathe. The agony of suffocation was exceeded only by the fear—pure, primal, and physiological. Worse than death, it was the extended, onrushing imminence of death. Unlike other forms of torture, however, it was no test of endurance. It was simply unendurable.

His face contorted in agony, and as he clung to consciousness, he saw a soldier in the Great War dying an excruciating death, beyond the help of any medic. The sight made him want to run, to escape the poison gas, but the only escape was through the machine-gun fire.

Then it hit him. He saw his salvation in a bullet.

His world faded to white.

They undid the mask and waited for him to revive. Then they began the process anew. His head rolled, and vomit dribbled down his chin.

"Will you tell me?" the interrogator asked.

Crendal nodded weakly. Raising his head, he pointed with his nose. "Over there," he said in a faint rasp.

The interrogator leaned toward him menacingly. "You mean you've been holding something back?"

A look of horror filled Crendal's eyes. "No, no," he sobbed.

The interrogator went to the bookshelf and swept aside the memories of Ypres 1917. He lifted one of the pedestals, and it hinged open like a box.

Crendal grinned like a man who had cheated death and found God.

"Its empty," the interrogator said.

Crendal stared in disbelief. He felt like a man condemned to the fires of hell.

The interrogator opened the second ancient phylactery.

"Empty," he said.

Crendal invoked the Lord's name in vain.

The interrogator put the phylacteries in the trunk with Belk's papers. He returned his attention to Crendal.

"Where are the contents?" he asked in a quiet, unyielding voice.

"I don't know, I don't know," Crendal whimpered through his tears.

"What was inside?"

"I swear, I don't know . . . ."

The interrogator looked at the clock.

"We're running out of time, Lord Crendal. Do you know what that means?"

Crendal's eyes widened.

"They must have taken it," Crendal said. "That's it, the American bitch and that Israeli reporter must have taken it! It's that simple."

"What did it say?"

What did it say? What could he say?

The interrogator signaled to his partner, rubbing his thumb against his fingertips. The shorter man clamped a hand over Crendal's right hand, flattening it against the armrest, so Crendal's fingers protruded over the end. Then he produced a cigarette lighter.

"This will hurt, and I would not expect it to heal," the interrogator said. "Again, where are the contents?"

Crendal stared at the cigarette lighter, poised an inch beneath the tip of his index finger. They didn't bother to gag him; there was no one left alive at Pamet Hall to hear his complaints.

"No, don't do it, don't do it," he pleaded.

The interrogator nodded, and the flame of the disposable lighter enveloped Crendal's fingertip. The searing pain silenced his scream.

The stocky man held the lighter in place for a good ten seconds, and when he pulled it away, Crendal's finger was on fire. Crendal watched it roast, the flesh melting and charring and filling his nostrils with a sickening stench.

"Where are they?" the interrogator asked.

His jaws clenched shut, Crendal mutely shook his head. The fire burned itself out, leaving him with a smoking, bony ruin of a fingertip, like a sausage left on the grill.

"You're not holding something back again, are you?"

"I don't know," Crendal whispered.

"Now would be a good time to remember."

The interrogator pointed to the samurai sword, and his partner lifted it off the wall. He tested it on the drapes. At the mere touch, it effortlessly cut the fabric.

The stocky man lowered it until it just barely touched the tape on the back of Crendal's left wrist.

"It won't grow back," the interrogator said.

Crendal wailed in desperation. "I'm telling you, I don't know! I can't tell you what I don't know. What do you hope to accomplish? What?"

The stocky man raised the sword.

"It's in the kennel!" Crendal screamed. "Look in the kennel."

The interrogator spoke in a low voice. "I think you made that up," he said.

Crendal broke down. "What do you want me to do?" he asked.

"Tell me something."

Crendal looked at him, not sure what he should say.

"The stables! Go check the stables!"

The interrogator kept looking at him.

"London! It's in London!" Crendal insisted.

The interrogator nodded, and there was a blur of steel. Crendal's left hand landed on the floor with a dull thud. The stump of his wrist spurted bright red blood onto the Persian rug.

He screamed in pain and stared in horror at the irrevocable mutilation. The sudden, cold-blooded finality of the injury was more than he could comprehend. His mind went into shock, and his body followed.

"One last question," the interrogator said. "Why are your former guests going to Paris?"

Crendal looked at him and sobbed, "I don't know."

The interrogator nodded. He spoke quietly, soothingly, almost benevolently. "I believe you," he said, and he removed his hood. He grinned through crooked teeth.

From the edge of delirium, Crendal looked into his eyes, and understood.

There was another flash of samurai steel, and Crendal was falling, rolling on the floor, looking up at his own headless body.

Chapter 37

Paris

From the balcony of their hotel room near the Louvre, Jordan could see the city lights reflected in the river Seine as it snaked its way under stone bridges, past the Ile de la Cité and the towering glory of Notre Dame.

"I always wanted to visit Paris," he said.

"You really should step inside, where no one else can see you," Catherine said.

With a sigh, Jordan shut the French doors to the balcony and drew the curtains.

"Now that we're finally alone," Catherine said, "are you going to show me what you stole?"

"First, I need to check in."

He put his laptop on the writing desk and booted it up. He scrolled through his email. He recognized an unusual address and clicked.

> Where is the next story, Benjamin? My patience is wearing thin. Can I count on you to follow through, or should I share my information with another reporter?

Jordan typed a quick reply to Farouk, not knowing if it would be read.

"Making progress. Need more time."

Impatient, Catherine found the remote control and turned on the television. She sat on one of the two double beds and flipped channels. They had arrived in the middle of the night, and their bags still lay on the floor, where they had dropped them minutes ago.

On CNN, the news readers were talking about a plane crash in the Philippines, with 159 passengers and crew presumed dead. A powerful hurricane in the Caribbean was lashing Cuba and sending people into a panic along Florida's Gulf coast. In the West Bank, Israeli forces had bombed the home of a 30-year-old man they identified as a Palestinian terrorist. And, in the English countryside, an ancestral estate fit for royalty was burning.

Catherine turned up the volume.

Flames leapt from the roof and windows of the Great Hall and engulfed the west end of the house, farthest from the Earl's private study. Spouts of water poured from fire hoses into the historic portrait gallery, but the rural firefighters and their limited apparatus seemed badly outmatched. Against the blackness of night, the awful beauty of the flames looked made for television.

"Local officials say the fire appears to have been deliberately set—possibly to cover up a spree of grisly murders at the 17th century manor house," the correspondent said.

Catherine lifted a hand to her cheek, and Jordan watched gravely.

"One of the confirmed dead is Lord Crendal, the Earl of Pamet, scion of one of England's oldest families," the correspondent continued. "Crendal was best known for his role in a corporate scandal that cost investors hundreds of millions of dollars. Authorities have no idea just yet who murdered the Earl and two members of the household staff, but they say his death was gruesome. He was found decapitated, and there are signs he was tortured."

"Oh my God," Catherine exclaimed, bending at the waist in a whirl of emotions—fear, revulsion, even sympathy for Crendal. She struggled to keep herself from picturing his last moments.

"That could have been us," she said.

CNN cut to celebrity news and the breakup of a Hollywood starlet from her on-again, off-again boyfriend, an alcohol-abusing rock star.

"If you hadn't stolen the contents of the phylacteries, Ben, they'd be in the hands of the killers by now."

"And if you hadn't resisted the Earl's charms, we'd still be at Pamet Hall."

"So what did we accomplish?"

Jordan reached into Catherine's knapsack and pulled out a tin of breath mints. From inside the tin, he removed a small, airtight, clear plastic bag.

The bag contained a miniature stack of parchment, almost the length and width of a matchbox, several sheets deep. The parchment was covered in unusually fine writing, smaller than the print in a newspaper stocks table. To the naked eye, the individual letters were difficult to read.

"It's been in my knapsack the whole time?" Catherine said.

"Since the train to London, when you got up to use the rest room."

He reached back into her knapsack and took out her hardcover copy of the bestseller, "A Leaf in Autumn." He opened the book and removed an envelope of fine linen stationery, embossed with the return address of Pamet Hall. From inside the envelope, he withdrew another clear plastic bag.

It contained a small square of gold foil, folded in on itself as if to fit in its former hiding place. The gold appeared to be engraved.

"Unbelievable," Catherine whispered. "Absolutely unbelievable."

Jordan set the artifacts on the desk.

"I'm almost afraid to touch them," she said. "Almost."

Jordan reached into his own bag and fished out other purchases—a blunt tweezers, a large magnifying glass, a box of cotton swabs. He slid them across the desk to Catherine.

She opened the bag containing the gold foil. She slowly unfolded the foil, taking care not to damage it. The delicate operation took several minutes. The gold was somewhat thicker and more durable than she expected; perhaps it was an alloy. The creases were permanent, and the sheet refused to lie flat. She put it back in the plastic bag and inserted it between pages of the book to press it open. Crude but effective.

It had been folded four times, and the lines of the folds divided it into 16 rectangles, which crisscrossed two distinct columns of writing etched in the precious metal.

"How could they achieve such fine print?" Jordan asked. "For that matter, how could they read it?"

"I think you're looking at the high art of early spy craft," Catherine said, picking up the magnifying glass.

The text was written in archaic Hebrew, similar to that of many Dead Sea Scrolls. She read at length without interruption, taking notes on a pad of hotel stationery as her excitement mounted.

She handed the lens to Jordan.

"What does it say?" he asked.

"See for yourself."

Jordan struggled to interpret the writing. He focused on the first verse.

"'In the Valley of Achor'—no, 'in the *ruins* in the Valley of Achor'—'under the steps which go eastward . . . a strongbox of silver . . . seventeen talents by weight . . . .

"'In Kohlit, the piled ruins of Kohlit, offering vessels . . . and ephods."

He gave her a quizzical look.

"Ephods?"

"Vests," Catherine said. "They were worn by the high priests."

Jordan looked at her in amazement.

"Is it . . . ?"

"The foil describes the locations of 64 caches of hidden treasure," Catherine said. "Some of the descriptions mention enduring landmarks, such as the Kidron Valley east of old Jerusalem. Others refer to places mentioned in the Bible—such as Secacah and the Zered canyon—whose whereabouts are matters of conjecture. Still others refer to place names that ring no bells whatsoever, such as the ruin called Kohlit."

"Is it a copy of the Silver Scroll?" Jordan asked.

"Unfortunately, no. It's a copy of the Copper Scroll, describing the original hiding places, before the riches of the Temple were dug up and reburied."

"Damn."

"It's still important," Catherine said. "Its very existence is telling. The fact that someone produced a facsimile or forerunner of the Copper Scroll, etched in gold, should end the debate about the Copper Scroll's authenticity, and the reality of the treasure."

She set the gold foil aside and put the bag of parchment under the magnifying glass. She wanted to put each of the parchment sheets in a bag of its own, so they could examine them individually, but she hesitated.

"What are you thinking?" Jordan said.

"At some point, these will need to be carbon dated. The ink will be tested, the parchment will be subjected to DNA analysis, and all of it will undergo whatever experiments future generations of scientists may devise. So, I'm wondering, can we separate them without doing harm?"

"Hmmm. It seems to me the harm has already been done. I doubt Mandel and Belk, and God knows who else, showed such delicacy in the 1880s. I doubt I was so delicate in the Earl's study, though I took care to hold them by the edges. Just be careful."

It was the easy answer, and she wondered if Jordan was rationalizing in his eagerness to unlock the mystery. But, in her own eagerness, she didn't argue.

She used the tweezers to place the sheets in separate bags. She numbered the bags with a marker as she worked. She put the first sheet under the lens and began reading through the clear plastic.

The first sheet was an excerpt from Exodus. Catherine recognized it as one of several markedly different versions of the Ten Commandments that appeared in the Bible. This was a lesser-known version, not the standard Decalogue memorialized in schoolrooms and American court battles and represented on twin tablets as if it were somehow more sanctified than the others.

This passage contained no discussion of honoring thy mother and father, or coveting thy neighbor's wife, or committing adultery, or bearing false witness, or stealing, or killing. But this version was the only one the Torah expressly identified as the Ten Commandments. According to Exodus, Moses, taking dictation from God atop Mount Sinai, recorded it on two stone tablets.

The passage began by ordering the Israelites not to mix with the prior inhabitants of the Promised Land, whom God targeted for elimination:

> *You must demolish their altars, smash their sacred pillars, and cut down their sacred poles. You are not to bow in worship to any other god, for the Lord's name is the Jealous God, and a jealous God he is. Avoid any alliance with the inhabitants of the land, or, when they go wantonly after their gods and sacrifice to*

them, you, any one of you, may be invited to partake of their sacrifices, and marry your sons to their daughters . . . .

It concluded with instructions in the proper manner of ritual sacrifice.

You shall not offer the blood of My sacrifice with anything leavened; and the sacrifice of the Feast of Passover shall not be left lying until morning. The choice first fruits of your soil you shall bring to the house of the Lord your God. You shall not boil a kid in its mother's milk.

Catherine struggled to grasp the significance. As far as she could recall, the language tracked the Hebrew Torah closely if not identically. Nothing new, nothing special.

Jordan got nervous just looking at her.

"What is it?" he asked.

"It's an excerpt from the Ten Commandments. In other words, the sort of scriptural snippet one could find in any phylactery. Or in your trusty Bible."

She slid it across the desk for Jordan.

She turned to the second page. Her eyes widened. She saw immediately that the second page had nothing to do with the Torah, and nothing to do with what preceded.

"What do you see?" Jordan said.

"It's as if the first page, quoting the Ten Commandments, was merely camouflage placed on top to disguise the rest of the contents, in case the phylactery fell into the wrong hands. But the second page—the second page is the beginning of a letter."

She scribbled notes as she read. In places, it was far from legible; entire words and phrases were smudged out or obliterated.

Jordan looked over her shoulder.

"The writing isn't so different from modern Hebrew," he said.

"No, it's quite similar. The challenge is that the text is in such poor condition. It probably aged more in the past century, in the damp British climate, than during the previous two millennia, when the desert climate preserved it."

For more than two hours, they labored to interpret it, passing pages back and forth, recording their work on Jordan's laptop and on the pad of hotel stationery.

When they finished, the clock read 3:11 a.m.

"I may not have captured the archaic syntax, Ben, but I've tried to make it as clear as I could."

She handed Jordan her handwritten translation, gaps and all.

MY FRIEND YONATAN,

A FORTNIGHT HAS PASSED SINCE WE LOST THE TEMPLE. MANY OF OUR FRIENDS ARE DEAD OR CAPTURED. MY FATHER IS KILLED, BY MY OWN HAND. IN THE END, HE STOOD IN OUR WAY.

YOUR BROTHER JUDAH, OF STRONG ARM AND UNCONQUERABLE SPIRIT, HAS FALLEN OR BEEN TAKEN PRISONER, I KNOW NOT WHICH. HE STOOD ALONE IN THE NARROWS OF THE TUNNEL TO BLOCK OUR PURSUERS AND DEFEND OUR ESCAPE. HAD HE FAILED, YOU WOULD NOT BE READING THIS.

WITH THREE OF MY MEN, ________________________, I HAVE RETREATED TO THE CAVE ABOVE THE WADI – YOU KNOW THE PLACE. BUT THE ROMANS ____________________, AND NOW WE ARE TRAPPED. FOR ME, IT MATTERS NOT. I AM ALREADY MORTALLY WOUNDED.

DO NOT ATTEMPT TO RESCUE US, BECAUSE RESCUE WOULD BE FUTILE. DO NOT GRIEVE FOR US, FOR WE DIE WITH FULL HEARTS. AND DO NOT FEAR, FOR WE WILL NOT BE TAKEN ALIVE.

JERUSALEM IS LOST, BUT THE FUTURE IS NOT. YOU MUST LEAD THE RESISTANCE. YOU MUST CONTINUE THE FIGHT UNTIL YOU LEAD OUR PEOPLE TO FREEDOM. YOU MUST RETAKE THE CITY. OR YOU MUST DIE TRYING.

WE HAVE MADE AMPLE PROVISION FOR __________. AS YOU KNOW, BEFORE THE TEMPLE FELL, LARGE QUANTITIES OF GOLD AND SILVER AND MANY OTHER TREASURES WERE SMUGGLED TO SAFETY. I GIVE YOU MY COPY OF THE KEY TO THEIR WHEREABOUTS.

THERE IS MORE THAT YOU SHOULD KNOW. THOUGH THE HIGH PRIEST FORBADE US, WE

TOOK THE TEMPLE CHRONICLES AND OTHER SACRED TEXTS–AS MANY AS WE COULD CARRY ON THAT FINAL FLIGHT.

WHY THE HIGH PRIEST FORBADE US, I DO NOT KNOW. MAYBE HE REFUSED TO SEE WHAT WAS COMING. PERHAPS ________________. PERHAPS GOD'S WRATH WAS MORE THAN HE COULD FACE. WE COULD SEE, AND WE CHOSE TO ACT. WE CHOSE TO PRESERVE THE HISTORY OF THE JEWS, TO PREVENT OUR ENEMIES FROM ERASING OR REWRITING IT. FOR WITHOUT THE PAST, THERE CAN BE NO ___________.

WE MANAGED TO SAVE, AMONG OTHERS, THE WRITINGS OF HANAN, ELEAZAR, ________, CAIAPHAS, AND ZADDOK.

IT WAS ALMOST AS IF MY FATHER WANTED IT ALL TO GO UP IN FLAMES, OR TO BECOME BURIED IN THE TEMPLE'S RUBBLE.

FEW PRIESTS HAVE BEEN PRIVILEGED TO READ THESE CHRONICLES, AND I WAS NOT AMONG THEM. I CONFESS MY CURIOSITY. IF IT WERE POSSIBLE, I MIGHT HAVE STOLEN A LOOK. BUT THERE WAS NO TIME. WHO KNOWS? MAYBE THEY WOULD UNLOCK THE MYSTERY OF MY ENIGMATIC GRANDFATHER CAIAPHAS AND EXPLAIN WHY HE BECAME A PENITENT RECLUSE. MAYBE THEY WOULD EXPLAIN WHAT HAPPENED WHEN HE CAME DOWN FROM ________ AND WHAT HE WITNESSED WHEN ____________________.

BUT I LEAVE THIS WORLD NONE THE WISER.

WE HID THESE PRECIOUS SCROLLS SECURELY AS WE FLED, WITH THE CACHE OF OFFERING VESSELS BURIED ______________. KEEP IT __________.

MY FRIEND, DO NOT BE CONTENT TO FOLLOW THE OTHER LEADERS. THOUGH ONE

HAS WISDOM, ANOTHER COURAGE, AND A THIRD RUTHLESS CUNNING, ONLY YOU POSSESS EACH OF THESE QUALITIES IN SUFFICIENT MEASURE TO SUCCEED.

I BELIEVE YOU ______________.

_____________________________.

THE BEARER OF THIS MESSAGE IS BRAVE AND TRUSTWORTHY, AND IF HE HAS DELIVERED THESE WORDS, THAT IS PROOF ENOUGH OF HIS RESOURCEFULNESS. YOU WOULD DO WELL TO GIVE HIM A PLACE OF RANK BESIDE YOU.

______ WISH I COULD LIVE TO SEE IT REBUILT, AND TO STAND WITH YOU AGAIN BESIDE THE ALTAR.

MAY GOD __________ HIS COUNTENANCE UPON YOU.

AARON BEN MATTHIAS

The professor and the journalist looked at each other numbly.

"Is this how Howard Carter felt when he opened Tutankhamen's tomb and found it full of gold?" Jordan asked.

"Or is this how Mary Magdalene felt when she visited Jesus's tomb and found it mysteriously empty?" Catherine answered.

"The letter mentions Caiaphas, the high priest of Jerusalem named in the Gospels."

"Caiaphas, who presided over the trial of Jesus."

"Caiaphas, who turned Jesus over to the Romans and urged he be executed."

"Caiaphas, lightning rod for 2,000 years of persecution of the Jews."

Caiaphas.

"The letter depicts him as withdrawing into a life of penitence after witnessing an event or events unknown," Jordan said.

"And it says he left behind some sort of monograph that might yet be recovered."

Jordan thought back on long afternoons at the Israel Museum, which exhibited an ossuary engraved with the name Caiaphas. The Jewish high priest had long been recognized as an historical figure, just as real as Pontius Pilate, the Roman governor. But Jordan could never bring himself to believe that this stone bone box belonged to the very same Caiaphas who walked the pages of the New Testament, the man depicted as such a malevolent force in dramatic reenactments, from Easter plays in medieval times to Mel Gibson's popular movie. Any tangible connection to the Christian passion had seemed beyond the grasp of Jordan's mind or body.

And this was more than a connection.

"Did you know that Caiaphas became a penitent recluse?" Jordan asked.

"There's never been so much as a hint of that in the known record," Catherine said. "I think we have what you journalists would call a world exclusive."

"What would have given Caiaphas such a guilty conscience?"

"The letter implies it was something he witnessed."

Jordan looked at her.

"It's hard to avoid the obvious, isn't it?" he said.

"If the Gospels are to be believed, Ben, Caiaphas was a witness to the last days of Christ."

"And the death of Christ."

"And, potentially, whatever came next."

Catherine swallowed heavily.

"Just hypothetically now, if I saw something miraculous, something that made me believe I had condemned the Son of God, I might have trouble sleeping, too," she said. "Face it, Ben: *This letter can be interpreted as supporting, circumstantially, the central article of Christian faith."*

She was almost giddy with the kind of nervous energy one feels taking in a magnificent view from a terrifying height. Never had the historical record inched so close to the heart of the Gospels. Never had she personally come so close to overcoming her skepticism. And she had participated in the discovery. She held it in her hands, and was one of only two living souls to share its secret.

She was so caught up in the excitement that she barely stopped to consider what it might mean to a Jew.

"You're jumping to conclusions," Jordan said. "Let's slow down and look at this from all angles."

"Go ahead."

"As one of Jesus's accusers, Caiaphas could credibly attest to the man's divinity. I'll grant you that. And, as a religious leader, he could credibly *discredit* the story of the Resurrection, too."

"Why?"

"At a time when all of Israel was waiting for the messiah, Catherine, how plausible is it that a man of God would ignore such a sign from God?"

"What would you expect him to do, shout from the rooftops? His people, the same people who rejected Jesus, would have accused him of blasphemy. The Romans probably would have crucified him, just as they crucified Jesus, for challenging the Roman gods and the divine supremacy of the Roman emperor."

"Hell, Catherine, Caiaphas could have witnessed anything," Jordan said. "We can't just assume it was the Resurrection."

"You're right, of course. But the letter says he left a chronicle, apparently some sort of memoir. And Aaron ben Matthias himself speculates that this memoir, which Aaron personally rescued from the besieged Temple, could tell us what Caiaphas saw. That must be why Mandel called it 'the ultimate proof.'"

Jordan studied her handwritten translation.

"The letter from Aaron ben Matthias to the Jewish rebel Yonatan doesn't say where the chronicles were hidden."

"No, but it says they were deposited with a cache of offering vessels. Presumably, this is one of the caches initially buried by the Jewish resistance—one of the caches described in the Copper Scroll," she said.

"And, if my reporting is right, the treasures of the Copper Scroll were dug up and reburied in the days or weeks after Jerusalem fell."

"And, if your reporting is right, Ben, Meyer Elazar and his colleagues at the Institute came to possess a Silver Scroll, which provided a key to the later hiding places."

Jordan got up and walked to the windows. She could see the tension in his back.

"I wonder," she said. "Did the men who held the key know what door it might open?"

She thought about Aaron ben Matthias, who rescued the Temple chronicles with ignorant zeal. If he had known the stakes, would he have acted differently?

She thought of Aaron's unnamed messenger, entrusted to carry the secret to another leader of the resistance. The messenger must have been equally bold to leave the refuge above the wadi and run a gauntlet of Roman soldiers.

As best Catherine could figure, the message was never delivered. It remained locked in the phylacteries, buried along with its bearer. Maybe he escaped the Romans, only to perish in the Judean desert. Maybe he ended up in another cave, in another gorge, where he crawled to die of heat and thirst—lost and forgotten for 18 centuries, until a Bedouin stumbled upon his bones.

Stumbled upon his bones, and found the phylacteries, which made their way to Mordecai Mandel and Sedgwick Belk.

And what became of Aaron ben Matthias, the author of the letter? He had vowed that neither he nor his men would be taken alive. Did they draw lots, like the Jewish holdouts at Masada, the mountaintop fortress, to determine which of them would slay the others and then take his own life? If so, how would the last man standing commit suicide? There were no bullets to end it instantaneously. Would he cut his wrists, or fall on his sword? Would he have the courage to leap from the mouth of the cave into the ravine? Or would he falter at the moment of truth, and die at the hands of the Romans, breaking under interrogation?

Thoughts of violent death inexorably brought her back to Lord Crendal. *Torture and decapitation*, CNN had reported.

"Do you think we're responsible for Crendal's death, and whatever he went through?"

Jordan turned around as if the non-sequitor yanked him back from some place far away.

"No, they would have killed him anyway, just like they killed Nigel Waverly."

Jordan answered in a matter-of-fact tone, as if the answer was unequivocal, but deep inside he wasn't so sure. He couldn't bring himself to dwell on the horror of Crendal's fate, which he wouldn't wish on anyone. It didn't take much imagination to picture himself in Crendal's place . . . .

"But, Ben, who are 'they'? Who are the killers?"

"I don't think we're any closer to an answer. At least three members of the archaeological council knew about the Silver Scroll. The representative from Rome could have told the Vatican. The Palestinian member clearly told the Jordanians. And Meyer Elazar seems to have informed an ally in the Israeli government. Those are just the known possibilities."

"But the torture, Ben. What does that tell you?"

"I wouldn't expect the perpetrators to sign their own signature, or leave their own calling card. At least I wouldn't count on it."

"There was a man on the train from London—I thought he might have been watching me. I think I heard him speaking Italian. Do you think there could be a connection to Nicolo Altieri, the murdered priest?"

"It's as good a theory as any," he said with exasperation. "But if they had tailed us to Paris, they could have gotten us by now."

The television was still tuned to CNN. Catherine zapped it with the remote. The tube went black with a greenish flash and a loud *zzzunk.*

The noise jarred Jordan's nerves. The sudden silence was uncomfortable. It made it too easy to hear himself think. He looked haggard and stressed and deeply distracted.

"We should try to get some sleep," Catherine said.

"Maybe later," Jordan said.

Catherine grabbed some of her stuff and disappeared into the bathroom.

Jordan turned on the television but muted the sound. He flipped channels absent-mindedly, stopping on music videos. He gazed at videos without music, neither seeing nor hearing.

Catherine reappeared in a white T-shirt that could have been one of his. She put a hand on his shoulder, but he seemed not to notice. She pulled down the bedspread and got into bed. She clicked off the lamp.

Jordan sank into a chair and looked out at Paris, toward the twin towers of Notre Dame. He had never believed in the life of Jesus. He had never even entertained the possibility that Jesus rose from the dead. In his mind, Christianity was a myth, a fiction—the Crucifiction. Even if one were inclined to believe, finding truth in the New Testament's contradictions required more than a leap of faith. As Catherine so ably demonstrated in her debate with the student, Bryan Jennings, it required a feat of mental gymnastics.

Jordan thought the story of the trial and execution of Jesus could be explained in political terms, as an attempt by early Christians to distance themselves from the unruly Jewish majority and ingratiate themselves with Rome. In an age of Roman domination, the emerging sect would have courted destruction if it blamed Rome for the death of its savior. Therefore, the Gospel writers placed the moral burden squarely on the Jews of Jerusalem and their figurehead, the high priest Caiaphas.

The accusation that Jews killed Jesus had inspired centuries of persecution. Now it appeared Caiaphas himself might have something to say about it.

What if he confirmed the charge? And what if he concluded that the man the Jews condemned truly was the Son of God?

An eternity ago, beside a lake in Michigan, Catherine asked Jordan if he had thought through the implications. *Mandel was convinced that his scrap of writing would shake one of the world's great religions to its foundation,* she had said.

But that had been an abstraction.

Chapter 38

Paris

She found him at dawn, asleep in the armchair. She gently woke him.

He dragged himself to the shower and pulled on clean clothes but his eyes remained bloodshot and bleary. He turned on CNN.

"Are you up to writing?" Catherine asked. "Because if you're not, I can start on a draft and — "

Jordan looked perplexed.

"What do you mean?" he asked.

"I don't know if you want to sit down at the keyboard together, or take turns, or divide the story into sections . . . ."

"What story?"

"*Our* story. I still don't know where we should publish it, but . . . ."

"We have no story."

"No story? Benjamin, we're sitting on one of the greatest stories ever told. Caiaphas, the Jewish high priest, died a penitent recluse after condemning Jesus—and witnessing something extraordinary. We've got to get it out, tell the world."

Jordan looked troubled.

"Not now."

"What are you waiting for, the Second Coming? Ben, the whole world will be talking about this story. It will open people's minds. It will open people's hearts. It will make skeptics reconsider. And you'll be more famous than Woodward and Bernstein."

"Not yet."

Flustered, Catherine was losing patience.

"After what you've been through, Ben, I can understand your caution, but — "

"It's not caution. Publishing would be cautious. Yes, we'd become the center of controversy. People would attack our credibility. They'd probably attack *us.* And we'll need to deal with that when the time comes. But publishing now would be the cowardly way out."

"I don't get it."

"We have what we have. We might have some trouble explaining how we got it, but I'm assuming the experts would authenticate it soon enough. The problem is what we *don't* have. We don't have the Caiaphas Chronicle. And without the Silver Scroll to point the way, we have no way of finding it. We have what we have, but we don't really know what it means."

"It goes a long way, Ben."

"It doesn't resolve anything."

"That doesn't have to be our problem."

His eyes showed a flash of anger.

"It will be everyone's problem, if we don't first make it our own."

"Are you sure you're looking at this objectively, Ben? Are you sure you aren't being protective of the Jewish faith?"

"Instead of what—casually tossing a match in the tinder of anti-Semitism?"

"Why don't we trust the public to read it, and interpret it for themselves? After all, isn't that what journalists do?"

She read the key passage aloud, but Jordan cut her off.

"Don't you see what's happening? We're in a race for the truth. For the answer. For the *whole* story. Others are trying to get there first, to claim it for themselves and control it—quite possibly to suppress it. If we go public now, you're right—I'll be famous, and so will you. The story will make our careers. But we'll lose whatever shot we have at the larger story."

"So how do you propose to win?"

"I don't know."

"And what if something should happen to us?"

"Let's make sure it doesn't."

"That's not much of a plan."

"No, it isn't."

"What's next, then?"

Jordan pondered the question.

"I'd like to see Notre Dame, and the Louvre, and stand atop the Eiffel Tower," he said, wistfully. "I'd like to see them with you."

"Benjamin," she said quietly, "you know we can't."

"Then how about breakfast? Will you join me for breakfast? We can spend an hour in Paris together before heading to the airport—if you're still coming, that is."

She couldn't bring herself to say no.

Jordan collected his computer and the artifacts. He carefully loaded them into his knapsack and turned up the volume on the television to make the room seem occupied.

"I have your phone," she said, putting it in her purse.

"Did you take your notes?" he asked, as she stepped into the hall.

"Yes, of course."

He closed the door behind them and hung out the "Do Not Disturb" sign. They were two steps down the hall when he stopped. He turned around and went back. He retrieved the pad of unused stationery from the desk.

"We might have left an impression," he explained as they got in the elevator.

Three stories down from the hotel room, half a block away, parked between a fire hydrant and a silver Audi, the driver of a black BMW pressed a finger to his ear. The vibration of the glass in the hotel window tickled an invisible laser beam, which transmitted the couple's vocal emanations to a small recording device on the BMW's dashboard. The tape was running.

The driver adjusted his earpiece. Moments ago, Cavanaugh and Jordan had been arguing in English. Now a television announcer was making a commercial pitch in French.

The driver was tempted to keep listening, but the sound of the hotel room door closing was his cue to move on. He pushed a button, turning off the laser beam. He closed his car window and placed the recording device in the glove compartment, next to a 9-millimeter compact handgun. Looking toward the hotel entrance, watching for his targets to emerge, he turned the key in the ignition.

Chapter 39

An Aegean Island

Meyer Elazar gazed at the face of Jesus.

It was long and pale and Northern European, with a thin nose and slightly hollow cheeks, and the obligatory covering of facial hair. Yet it was unnaturally devoid of character or personality, as if these were somehow inaccessible. In a strange paradox, its featureless quality was part of what made it distinct.

The body that hung from the cross was slender and smooth, expressing the power of human weakness rather than muscular strength or masculinity. A faithful vision. Take away the cross, and the crown of thorns, and he remained instantly identifiable.

But that was merely a testament to artistic convention.

Elazar wondered, What would he have looked like in the flesh, this Jew from Galilee?

More like an Arab than an Aryan, he guessed, based on geography.

Staring at the icon, Elazar was struck by the thought that the Church deliberately flouted one of God's fundamental commandments: *Thou shalt not worship graven images.*

Elazar had taken refuge in the cool shadows of the chapel to meditate, and to reflect on the puzzles of the Silver Scroll. He had been working on it feverishly, trying to crack its secrets, forsaking sleep and regular meals.

Twenty-four clues to 24 hiding places. Twenty-four troves of treasure. And one of them contained something so profound it would shake one of the world's great religions to its foundation.

That was the legend of Mordecai Mandel, passed down through generations. Recounted by Catherine Cavanaugh—lovely, brilliant, innocently idealistic.

Ahh, Catherine, beautiful Catherine, so much like my Mishka. Still digging for a reason to believe? Take it from me, it's a desperate quest. Haven't you read your Christian Bible? Blessed are those who believe without proof.

And cursed are those who search for it, if life has taught me.

Live in doubt, dear Catherine. Savor your uncertainty. Abandon the search. But live your life. For the holes we dig can swallow us in darkness.

Chapter 40

Paris

They sat at a sidewalk café, trying unsuccessfully to enjoy the moment.

Catherine ate a croissant as Jordan devoured a spinach crepe. The aroma of coffee hung in the air, mingling with the auto exhaust.

She had pulled her hair back and covered it in a silk scarf, and both of them wore sunglasses. Jordan's face was covered in a shadow of stubble. He scoured the *International Herald Tribune*, but the fire at Pamet Hall had happened too late for the morning paper.

The air was cool and the sun was bright—too bright for the emotional hangover each nursed. Unconsciously, she squeezed the purse sitting on her lap, reassuring herself.

"Without the Silver Scroll to guide us to Caiaphas's eyewitness account," she said, "I don't see what more we can do. We're stranded, like a sailboat on a windless sea."

"Then it's time to start paddling."

"Aren't you afraid?" she asked.

"Yes, of course," he said. "Most of all, I'm afraid of failing."

"You set the bar so high, I don't see how we can succeed."

"I don't see how we have a choice."

She stirred the cream in her coffee, but it was slow to mix.

"How do you live with the fear?"

Jordan closed his eyes, reliving the stoning in Lebanon, the red dot in his rear view mirror, the shattering of his apartment window. The murder of Nigel Waverly, followed by the even more grisly death of Lord Crendal.

He thought of Miriam Wiesman waiting a dozen years to plan a trip to Eilat, a trip she never got to make.

"I wish we could explore Paris," he said.

"Let's get back to the hotel," she said.

They left the café walking.

She felt a slight bump, like she was being jostled, and a tug. Then the weight of her handbag slipped away.

She turned in time to see a man in jeans and a gray sweatshirt running away.

"My bag!"

It took Jordan a fraction of a second to process what was happening. Before she could object, he was in full sprint.

"Ben, no!"

He dashed between an elderly couple, around a baby carriage, through a family of tourists, out of the way of an oncoming bicycle, which veered aside and wiped out. The thief was darting through traffic to the screech of brakes and the blare of horns.

Jordan sprinted after him, narrowly dodging a Peugeot and a white delivery truck. The thief stole a fleeting glance back over his shoulder. He turned right down a side street. When Jordan rounded the corner in pursuit, the thief was turning left at the end of the block. Jordan was losing ground. His lungs burned, but he pushed himself even harder, ignoring the knapsack that burdened his movement.

What was in the handbag?

Her handwritten translation of the letter?

Surely her passport.

He turned left after the thief and barreled ahead, drawing curious stares. The thief was nowhere to be seen, but from the onlookers he left in his wake, Jordan deduced that he had taken a right at the corner drugstore. Jordan followed.

He found himself in a long, narrow alley that ended in a T-intersection, between buildings with mansard roofs, facing a chain-link fence and a wooded lot. There was no sign of the thief, no rippling wake of humanity to read. Had he ducked into one of the apartment buildings that backed onto the alley? Had he kept going? Was he lurking?

Breathing hard, Jordan stopped. He bent over, bracing his hands against his burning quads.

What did she have in that bag?

As best he could recall, her blue passport and the notes she had taken in the hotel room.

As best he could recall, the artifacts themselves were safe in his knapsack.

On his back.

In a deserted alley.

The buildings seemed to close in on him. The shadows behind the fences and trash bins seemed suddenly menacing. He heard a noise behind him, a door opening and closing. An old woman letting out a cat.

Without the passport, Catherine was stranded.

Jordan walked deeper into the alley and peered around the corner, first to the left, and then to the right. He took a half-step back.

To the right, two car-lengths away, a black BMW sedan was blocking the service road. The man in the gray sweatshirt and jeans was leaning into the driver's window, talking to the driver. Catherine's handbag dangled from his left hand.

Jordan tried to see into the car, but he couldn't see through the foliage reflected in the windshield.

The man in the gray sweatshirt passed the driver the handbag and gave him a jaunty wave, as if saluting *au revoir.* The thief turned and took a stride toward Jordan, seeming to look straight at him.

He was just a teenager.

The teen's face seemed to be forming a look of surprise when a spurt of blood burst from his chest.

Before Jordan could process the gunshot, the dead body dropped to its knees.

The driver's hand reached out with a silenced handgun and fired a second shot into the teen's head.

Jordan stumbled backward, into an aluminum trashcan, and pivoted as the lid clattered to the ground.

The BMW started moving.

Springing from standing start to full sprint, Jordan raced down the alley, between the buildings with the mansard roofs, into the cross street, knocking over a table where two old men were playing checkers. He swerved into traffic, and back onto the sidewalk, slamming a waiter balancing a tray of drinks.

He ran past storefronts, through traffic lights, around random corners, past the point of exhaustion, beyond pain, and he didn't look back.

When finally he stopped, in the doorway of a butcher shop with naked rabbits hanging in the window, he was drenched in sweat. He waited a minute, breathing fiery gulps of air. There was no one on his heels.

Where's Catherine?

Where am I?

What the hell happened?

Patrons of the establishment looked at him curiously. A middle-aged woman carrying a grocery bag used her free hand to steer a little girl clear of him, frowning as they passed.

He had to find Catherine. He had to warn her. He searched for his phone, but it was missing. Catherine had been carrying it.

It was in the stolen bag—and so was hers.

He read the street signs and referred to the map in his tour book. He was a long way from the boulevard where he had left her. As he stood on the sidewalk in the autumn breeze, the dampness of his sweat left him cold.

He started back toward the café, walking at a brisk but normal pace.

That must be what happened to Waverly. A handoff in an alley, and a bullet for his trouble.

It took Jordan almost 15 minutes to reach the spot where Catherine's purse was snatched. She wasn't there. He retraced their steps to the café. He looked from table to table.

Where else could she have gone?

The hotel was the obvious answer, but now that they had been tracked it was also the most dangerous. He found a pay phone and dialed the hotel. No answer in the room. No message at the desk. He didn't know whether to feel relieved or hopeless.

He had talked about visiting Notre Dame, or the Louvre, or the Eiffel Tower, any of which could make a logical rendezvous point. Unless . . . .

Maybe she was still on her way to the hotel.

If so, he had to intercept her. But how could he do that without walking into the same trap? He analyzed the problem as if they had simply gotten separated and needed to find each other. He refused to let any other explanation enter his thinking.

Chapter 41

An Aegean Island

Meyer Elazar's mind wandered through the twilight in search of an abandoned well in the courtyard of a house that once belonged to a widow named Rebekkah. It was a reference point in the Silver Scroll's clue to the seventh cache, but it meant nothing to him.

The shadows grew long in the cool recesses of the chapel.

He studied the cross on the wall above the altar. The nails that pinned Jesus to the wood were driven through the palms of his hands. The rendering was faithful to the Gospel of John, which alone among the Gospels told the story of Thomas. Until Thomas stuck his finger in the wounds where the nails had gone, the doubting disciple refused to believe Jesus had risen.

The icon was faithful to John, but it was historically inaccurate, Elazar thought. When the Romans crucified, they drove their nails through the wrists. The flesh, bones and sinews of the hands were too fragile. Under the weight of the condemned, they would rip free of the cross.

"Have we made a convert of you yet, Rabbi Elazar?"

The voice belonged to Father Gregory, head of the Order of Constantine.

Elazar smiled wanly. "I hope you're having better luck in the Sinai."

The monk sat beside him. He had a steady, serious presence, with hands folded calmly in his lap. His face was a cross between Lincoln and Rasputin—sad, noble, hypnotic. His eyes were set in dark, hollow sockets, and deep lines like the curves of a cello ran from the corners of his nose to the headwaters of a coarse beard. A small white crucifix hung from his neck against the plain black cassock of a Greek Orthodox priest.

"Our teams are digging for the second and twelfth caches," the monk reported.

"I wish I could join them," Elazar said, with a wistfulness that turned bitter.

The monk scowled.

"It's too dangerous, Rabbi. We can't take the chance."

The rabbi spoke in a gravel voice, his Rs growling.

"You take a far greater risk."

"Rabbi, we could hardly do otherwise."

There remained a strained formality to the relationship between rabbi and monk, for there was nothing natural or easygoing about the circumstances that had thrown them together. Respectfully, Gregory called Elazar "Rabbi," and Elazar addressed the Greek as "Father," though the appellation always struck Elazar as blasphemous by the standards of the New Testament.

Matthew, Chapter 23, if memory served.

"Do not call any man on earth 'father,' for you have one Father, and he is in heaven," Jesus said.

"You could let it rest in peace, Father Gregory."

"No, we couldn't—no more than you could. Unlike the Church of Rome, or the government of Israel, which jealously guard their earthly power, we seek the truth, wherever it leads."

"Hmmm," Elazar growled, skeptically. "When Croesus, king of Lydia, was trying to decide whether to attack his enemy, he consulted the Delphic Oracle. The oracle told him that if he attacked, he would destroy a great empire. Croesus attacked, and the prophecy was fulfilled. The kingdom he destroyed was his own."

The monk looked away.

"Rabbi, don't wear yourself out. This is a marathon, not a sprint."

"It's a 26-mile sprint."

"I should leave you alone."

With a slight bow of his head, the monk withdrew.

When Gregory was gone, Elazar stepped into the twilight. He walked toward the cliffs to watch the moon rise over the water. The whitecaps gleamed in silvery reflection.

He hadn't gotten used to being dead. All in all, it was a disturbing experience.

The Greek Orthodox priests of the Order of Constantine were gracious hosts, and he could never repay them for what they had done. But he longed for Israel. He wondered if he could ever return.

The Order had rescued him so abruptly that he felt he was being kidnapped. In those first terrifying seconds, he assumed he was being taken hostage by Palestinian militants, to be held for a political ransom his government could never meet—the release of prisoners, or the abandonment of land. He was ready to die for his people—he had long since made peace with the possibility, and he almost expected it—but he had a feeling it would be neither quick nor painless.

In those first terrifying seconds, he realized ruefully that some Israelis would welcome his death. He worried that the causes he fought for would suffer for his absence, and he worried that Israel would have the poor judgment to pay his ransom. He worried, too, that young Israeli soldiers would die trying to rescue him. Whatever they thought of his politics, they would do their duty.

But all of those fears were unfounded.

The reality was worse.

It began a few minutes past 6:00 a.m. on a Sunday. He was on his way to see the Minister of Culture about the Silver Scroll when several men—ordinary Israelis, by appearance—grabbed him off the street and hustled him headlong into a white van. They moved like terrorists—or bodyguards manhandling a head of state into a bulletproof limousine at the sound of gunshots. They moved so suddenly and forcefully—and he resisted with such determination—that he still felt the bruises. The action was so swift and tightly choreographed that it appeared there were no witnesses.

He wondered if this had something to do with the Silver Scroll, which had been his preoccupation only moments earlier, but he quickly ruled out any connection. The secret was too closely held.

As the van sped off, one of the men looked at him earnestly, with an expression of sincere concern.

"Rabbi, you're in grave danger," the man said.

Elazar remembered laughing nervously, thinking this was a ridiculous statement of the obvious.

Perceiving Elazar's misapprehension, the man tried to clarify.

"We're trying to save you," he said.

Elazar looked more closely at his abductors. There were no weapons in sight.

"Rabbi, there are people who want you dead," the man said.

Elazar thought of political enemies—Arab and Israeli—who had wanted him dead since 1985, if not earlier.

"Is that a fact?" Elazar said.

The man looked at him soberly.

"Your own government is planning to assassinate you."

The van turned a corner and sped through a bone-rattling pothole.

Elazar was confused. He didn't know what to believe. He wasn't about to accept his abductors as his saviors. But no one was restraining him.

"Come with us," said the man. "Let us show you."

"Let me out."

"Give us three days, then decide for yourself. Three days, for the rest of your life."

"Stop the van," Elazar insisted.

Elazar's interlocutor spoke to the driver. The van stopped.

"It's your choice," he told Elazar. He opened the door a crack.

Elazar gave his abductors a quizzical look.

"Why would my government assassinate me?" he asked.

"Because what you know poses a greater threat than guns or bombs."

Within two hours, Elazar was below deck on a boat sailing from a port in northern Israel to a destination undisclosed. They had politely asked him to wear a blindfold, and, for reasons he didn't truly comprehend, he had agreed.

"Who are you?" he asked his interlocutor.

"You can call me Alex," the man replied.

"That doesn't answer my question."

"For our own protection, that's all I'll say. In case you choose a separate way."

It was then 8:11 a.m. The Council was scheduled to assemble at the Institute at eleven—in just three hours—with Elazar presiding. It was Elazar's meeting. He had hoped to hold it two days earlier, on Friday afternoon, but he was delayed by a meeting with the Minister. When he and the Minister adjourned, it was nearly sunset, the beginning of Shabbat. The Minister asked him to meet again over breakfast Sunday, before the Council gathered.

Altieri and Ramsi had forced his hand. They were his closest allies on the Council, his wisest advisers, the only two he had trusted with the secret of the Silver Scroll. Of course, one or two others at the Council knew of the scroll's existence. But only the three of them knew its content, that it was a map to mind-boggling riches and precious relics—in all likelihood, the treasures of the Temple.

And only Elazar knew the deeper secret: That among those treasures lay hidden a potentially profound religious revelation. Catherine had supplied that piece long before it meant anything—before anyone had any reason to believe the treasures of the Temple could be unearthed. The rabbi had not yet seen fit to share it with his confidantes.

The treasure was trouble enough. They had been stewing over it for weeks. The tension had reached the breaking point.

They sat in Elazar's office Thursday, late into the night, angrily debating their options. Elazar believed they should keep it to themselves. He believed they should investigate secretly and find what they could before widening the circle. He proposed that the true object of the search be concealed even from the archaeologists in the field. He believed the situation would spin out of control if the story got out.

Altieri and Ramsi disagreed. They thought it was inevitable that the secret would get out. And then they would be accused of hoarding the knowledge to advance their own careers or personal agendas. People would say they were no better than the scholars who monopolized the Dead Sea Scrolls. Sunshine was the only solution, the only way to preserve credibility, they argued.

"You announce this and the Holy Land will become as pockmarked as the moon," Elazar countered. "Everyone and their brother will dig. It will frustrate our efforts."

"I agree, it's an unfortunate course," Ramsi said. "But the alternative is worse."

"How could it be worse?" Elazar said. "It will be out of our hands."

Altieri looked closely at Elazar.

"Is there something you aren't telling us, Meyer?" he asked.

Elazar already regretted involving his friends.

"We announce this, and we'll all live to regret it," he said.

"Maybe it's not our decision to make," Altieri mused. "Maybe we should consult the others."

"The others? What do the others know?"

Elazar had spoken with contempt. The rabbi saw the shock and disapproval on Altieri's face. He looked at Altieri fearfully, recognizing that his friend had crossed a mental bridge.

"The last time I checked, Meyer, this was an international council. It's not your personal fiefdom. Or ours, for that matter."

"What are you saying?"

"I'm saying that you should submit the question to a vote of the full Council. And, if you don't, I will."

Elazar's expression turned grim. He considered divulging the deeper secret, on the theory that it might change their thinking. But that would only make matters worse. What could he do? They had him over a barrel. He would have to persuade the Council to see it his way—that was the only solution. And, to do that, he would have to reclaim the moral high ground that had just eroded beneath his feet.

"I'll respect the decision of the Council," he said with bitter finality.

And so he had intended. But, overnight, his disagreement with Altieri and Ramsi fermented into distrust. One was Roman Catholic, the other Palestinian. He questioned their motives. He wondered if there was something *they* weren't telling *him*. He wondered what they knew.

He decided to consult the Minister of Culture, a conservative member of the cabinet who generally saw things as he did. They had been friends and allies since Elazar's days as an apolitical academic, when he was still a husband and father and their children played together. The Minister rearranged his schedule to see Elazar at his office in the Knesset. It was Friday afternoon.

The Minister urged him to keep it secret—all of it.

"Don't trust anyone," he counseled.

When Elazar demurred, the Minister grew insistent.

"It's much too important, Meyer."

"I've already committed to consult the full Council," Elazar said.

"Meyer, for God's sake, cancel the meeting," the Minister urged.

Elazar looked out the window. Shabbat was almost upon them. He excused himself, with a promise to return Sunday morning, before the Council meeting.

He had broken his promise.

As his fellow Council members assembled that Sunday morning, Elazar was aboard a ship of strangers, rolling with the waves. The motion might have made others sick, but Elazar was always at home on the sea.

"I'm expected at the Institute at eleven," he told the man who called himself Alex. "I should call and let them know I won't be there."

"I'm sorry, Rabbi, but that would jeopardize everything," Alex said. "It's a long journey, so you might as well rest. You can take your blindfold off, but please, don't leave your cabin."

Alex left the tiny cabin, leaving Elazar alone. Elazar removed his blindfold. His quarters were spare and windowless. He tested the door. It was not locked. He lay down on the hard bunk and took the man's advice.

Some time later, a sharp pounding on the door roused Elazar from sleep.

"Rabbi, rabbi, we need you topside."

When Elazar reached the deck, the sun was nearing the height of its arc, and there was no land in sight.

Alex handed him a phone.

"We just got word, Rabbi. There's a plot to blow up the Institute. There's no time, no choice: You need to warn them."

Elazar dialed.

Now, standing in the darkness of an Aegean night, looking out at the moonlit waves, Elazar recalled with anguish his call to the Institute moments before the blast. He tried to warn his colleagues. Crossing miles of ocean, the signal was weak.

"Get out, get out," he shouted into the phone. "There's a bomb."

They seemed not to understand.

He remembered asking if all were present, if all were safe.

"Is everyone okay? Is everyone there?"

He remembered hearing that Altieri and Ramsi were missing. He was ashamed he had gone to his government without them, ashamed of his distrust, though their absence seemed to validate it.

The warning came too late. The connection went dead, and he couldn't get it back. Half an hour later, Alex brought a radio to his cabin. Together, they listened to news reports of the explosion.

The world presumed Elazar was dead. That was just as well, the monk argued. It reduced the odds of someone killing him.

By the time they reached the island, there was no need for the blindfold. The abductors decided they could trust Elazar. They donned hooded cassocks before disembarking. They disguised Elazar as one of them. A small cross dangled from his neck as they walked by night from the crescent cove to the monastery of Saint Constantine, a single file line of phantom silhouettes.

Elazar was tired and out of breath when they escorted him into a dining room with a coarse wooden table and two benches. The thick walls were whitewashed stucco, bare except for a crude icon of the Madonna with child painted on weathered wood. There were no glass panes in the windows, only shutters, and they were closed.

A gaunt, bearded monk brought him a wooden plank with pears, cheese, and dark heavy bread. He introduced himself as Father Gregory.

"I'm glad you're safe," he said. "We need you."

"Who are you?"

"We are the Order of Constantine," Father Gregory said, earning a blank stare from Elazar. "We date to the reign of the emperor Constantine, early in the 4th Century. I'm flattered that you've never heard of us."

"I can't say I have," Elazar admitted.

"For all that time, we have stayed in shadows, working by stealth. The Order is dedicated to one mission and one mission only: To find the truth about Christ."

Father Gregory studied the rabbi's inscrutable reaction.

"I believe we have a common interest," the monk said.

Elazar had the disquieting realization that Father Gregory knew his secrets and much more besides.

"Go on," the rabbi said. Elazar wanted him to get to the point, but Father Gregory launched into a discourse on the Order's distant origins.

"To understand us, you need to return to 4th Century Christendom, the time of Constantine. It was a time when memory became shrouded in myth."

As Elazar well knew, Constantine unified the Holy Roman Empire and founded the city of Constantinople in the East. He also murdered his wife and son. But his greatest legacy was embracing a minor religious sect known as Christianity and making it the Empire's official religion. It was Constantine who forged one of the Church's central doctrines, defining the nature of Christ's divinity.

"No doubt the history is familiar to you," Father Gregory said. "When Constantine came to power, Christian theology was fractured and unformed. Influential bishops fought to mold it, espousing competing views. They struggled with a conundrum the Gospel writers had left unresolved: Was Jesus on earth a man, or a god? As a god, was he distinct and separable from God, his Father—like Zeus and any of his pagan progeny, such as Apollo and Aphrodite? Or were Jesus and the Father somehow one and the same, a unified God?

"In pursuit of political cohesion, Constantine demanded doctrinal agreement. So in the year 325 he convened hundreds of leading churchmen in Nicaea and compelled them to produce an answer. The result, three centuries after Jesus, was the Nicene Creed."

Even the rabbi could recite it.

"I believe in one God the Father Almighty, Maker of Heaven and Earth, and of all things visible and invisible: And in one Lord Jesus Christ, the only begotten son of his Father before all worlds; God of God, Light of Light, very God of very God; begotten, not made, being of one substance with the Father, by whom all things were made; who for us men, and for our salvation, came down from heaven, and was incarnate by the Holy Ghost of the Virgin Mary, and was made man, and was crucified also for us under Pontius Pilate. He suffered and was buried, and the third day he rose, according to the Scriptures, and ascended into Heaven, and sitteth on the right hand of the Father: and he shall come again with glory, to judge both the quick and the dead . . . ."

"To this day, Christian worshipers recite it so faithfully, in each of its varied translations, that you would think the words were given, if not by God, then by Saint Paul, or Matthew, Mark, Luke, or John," Father Gregory said.

"But that was just part of Constantine's imprint. Three centuries after the death of Jesus, it was Constantine who turned the cross into the symbol of Christianity. He claimed to have seen a cross of light in the noon sky on the eve of his decisive battle, along with the message, *'In Hoc Signo Vinces'* — 'By This Sign Conquer.'

"Years later, his mother Helena toured the Holy Land as his emissary. According to legend, she discovered a string of biblical places and relics, including the True Cross, the tomb of Jesus, and the physical remains of the three wise men from the East. Later, Constantine built the first Church of the Holy Sepulcher on a rock identified as Golgotha, the hill where Jesus was crucified.

"These legends took on a life of their own. They gave people a new connection to Christ. To this day, they serve as magnets for pilgrims and tourists, and scalding touchstones in the turmoil of the Middle East.

"But some 4th Century theologians privately disapproved. They worried that the focus on Jerusalem's holy sites distracted from the universality of God. And they worried that humans were muddying God's waters. To separate fact from fiction, one of them clandestinely founded this order.

"In his spirit, and in the spirit of Jesus Christ, we dedicate ourselves to the search for Christian truth in all its purity."

Gregory looked to Elazar for a sign of recognition.

"What if the truth isn't Christian?" Elazar asked.

"We are committed to following the truth wherever it leads, and revealing it to the world. We hope you'll help us."

"Why do you need my help?"

"Is there anyone more qualified to locate the treasures of the Silver Scroll?"

Elazar felt the blood draining from his head.

"I'm sure there is," he said, his rumbling voice reduced to a mumble.

"You're very modest, Rabbi Elazar. Of course, there is more. We must, all of us, consider the messenger."

Elazar wasn't following.

"If the truth is Jewish—if it supports the Jewish view—our Christian friends will be more than capable of delivering the message," Father Gregory said. "But if the truth is Christian, who would speak with greater credibility than an eminent, Orthodox, Zionist Jew?"

Chapter 42

Paris

In a cyber café on the Rue des Halles, Jordan took a corner seat with his back to the wall, so no one could see his screen or escape his range of vision. He pulled the keyboard closer and logged onto his email.

He searched for the messages that counted, hoping for word from Catherine. He recognized an unusual address and clicked.

> Benjamin, you have exhausted my patience, and you have proven that my confidence was misplaced. Perhaps another reporter will succeed where you have failed.

Farouk.

"I'm getting close," Jordan replied. *"If anyone else starts asking questions, they could put the story at risk."*

He scrolled through screens filled with spam, growing angrier by the second. He looked at his watch.

The computer froze, and Jordan couldn't unfreeze it. Exasperated, he shut the machine down and restarted it. It took minutes to come back to life. Jordan reopened his mailbox. Amid come-ons from the likes of FoxyKittensXXX and C1alis V1agra Bulk Orders, he spotted something from AnnRxxx123. Was it too much of a reach to think that might be a reference to Ann Arbor? He opened the message.

> Enter our sweeep stakes and win free trip to Paris. Gus the magic word and win dinner for too at restarant of your choise.

The message included a hotlink. Jordan clicked on the link, but it was dead.

It looked like any of countless cons by semi-literate hacks, but Jordan looked more closely. The reference to Paris was hard to ignore.

"Gus the magic word."

Was he really supposed to guess? Or was "Gus" the magic word? If it was some kind of code from Catherine, what was she trying to tell him?

Who was Gus?

He had a maddening sense that the answer was hiding in plain view. Then it hit him, and he was afraid she had made it too obvious. He wanted to bolt out of the café, but there was more to read.

He spotted another kernel of wheat amid the chaff, and he held his breath. The subject line mentioned a Red Sea Cruise.

> *Inshallah,* you shall find what you need. Let us pray together. Thursday, as before.

It seemed like the answer to a prayer, a message from Samir, or maybe from the King himself. What did he need? More to the point, what did Samir think he needed? The answer to both questions was plain—the text of the Silver Scroll, which could lead to the treasure and redeem his reputation—but Jordan didn't dare raise his hopes.

"Thursday, as before."

Tomorrow, at a mosque in Jerusalem.

Before leaving, Jordan checked the news on the BBC's Web site. He typed in "Pamet Hall" and "Crendal." Whatever euphoria he had just suppressed fled of its own accord.

> Authorities are searching for an American professor of biblical archaeology who was a guest at Pamet Hall the night before the devastating fire.
>
> Catherine Cavanaugh was eager to obtain access to the estate's vast collections of art, antiques, and historical documents, including the illustrious family's archives, sources tell the BBC.
>
> Cavanaugh was traveling with a man believed to be Michael Barnes, already wanted for questioning in connection with the violent death of a curator at the British Museum. The proprietor of a bed and breakfast where the couple stayed on their way to Pamet Hall said the pair left a generous tip but never volunteered their names.
>
> Police suspect the name Barnes is an alias. They are preparing a composite drawing of the man based on witness descriptions and video from a museum security camera, though the video is said to be of poor quality.
>
> A breakthrough in the investigation came from an Oxford don who claimed to have been visited by Cavanaugh two days before the ghastly killings.
>
> Cavanaugh had been employed at the University of Michigan, but a university spokesman said she was no longer on faculty. The spokesman wouldn't say whether she quit or was fired. However, a university source said Cavanaugh was recently informed that her work was not of sufficient merit to earn her a tenured position.
>
> In other developments, police confirmed that the Earl's body was mutilated before he died . . . .

Accompanying the article was a University of Michigan press office photo of Catherine trying to look serious, suppressing a smile.

Now she was the one who was radioactive. Sought by the authorities, stalked by killers, missing in Paris. He had to find her first—they had a flight to catch.

The question was, which flight? And how would they get through security?

Working online, he booked multiple reservations, a total of four flights on four different airlines to four different destinations, all departing within a one-hour window from the airport in distant Nice, along the Mediterranean coast. He used the names Cavanaugh and Barnes.

Then he looked up flights out of Paris's Orly airport. He found one that fit the bill, scheduled to depart 55 minutes before the first of the diversionary flights from Nice. They would buy their tickets at Orly at the last possible moment.

If they were lucky, the ruse would throw their mysterious pursuers off the trail, but it wouldn't fool the authorities. Just the opposite: A last-minute booking would flag them at the airport, where Interpol would already be on the lookout for Catherine.

One more problem to solve.

He ran out of the cyber café toward the Paris Metro.

He exited the station in a throng of pedestrian traffic, all heading in the same direction. He wished he were truly one of them, a tourist out to see the sights, whose only cares were the long line ahead and the impossible number of places to visit in the time available.

He circled slowly, searching the crowd, wishing that the clue had been more specific. Catherine was nowhere to be found. He wondered if he had guessed wrong or misread the message about the magic word. An urgency entered his stride, and he pushed his way through the mass of humanity, oblivious to the complaints that trailed him.

The crowd parted for a moment, and he spotted her walking away. He elbowed his way toward her. He was almost close enough to lay a hand on her shoulder when she turned to her left.

Damn.

She wasn't Catherine, but she looked a lot like Catherine. Out of the corner of her eye, the stranger saw Jordan looking at her, and she smiled at him. She was clutching the strap to her handbag, which should have been a give away. Jordan noticed that the flap to the stranger's handbag was loose, and he got an idea. He waited for her to turn away. As stealthily as he could, he reached inside her handbag. In a deft movement, he extracted his prize and melted into the crowd.

He glanced down at a Canadian passport. It might do the trick—if the tourist didn't notice it was missing and report it lost.

A pair of hands grabbed him from behind and covered his eyes. Catherine whispered in his ear.

"Lucky guess," she said.

She fell into his arms, and their lips touched beneath Gustave Eiffel's tower.

Part IV

Chapter 43

Tel Marevah
Israel

The men moved under cover of night, approaching the hardscrabble hill from the west. They spoke no words as they passed through a grove of olive trees whose leaves shimmered hauntingly in the starlight.

There were seven of them, and they moved with discipline and coordination. They were dressed casually and unremarkably, carrying bags of equipment. They followed their leader, Father Gregory, whose lively eyes pierced the darkness.

From the distant road behind them, a passing motorist might have discerned their figures traversing the barren landscape. But the road was sparsely traveled, and as far as they could tell their progress went unnoticed.

As they neared the top of the hill, an iron gate blocked the way. With minimal exertion, one of them severed the chain that tied it shut. The ground crunched beneath their feet as they crossed another 50 meters.

A narrow chasm opened before them. Gregory motioned for them to proceed, and one after another they disappeared into the earth, waiting until they were underground to light their flashlights. Gregory stayed behind. He walked 60 paces to the northeast and found another crack in the ground. He blanketed it with canvas. Then he returned to the primary opening.

He stood alone under a swirl of constellations, silently praying for success. Their mission was to unearth the 18th cache, and he hoped the rabbi had sent them to the right place. Gregory privately doubted the rabbi's conclusion. Still, he deferred to Meyer Elazar's expertise, and would take no pride in proving Elazar wrong.

The clue from the Silver Scroll was unusually figurative, almost poetic: *"Near Marevah, where the prayers of the poor take flight."*

Gregory believed this metaphor was simple enough. He believed it denoted a place of worship in a poorer quarter of the city of Marevah—or, more likely, in one of its outlying settlements. But Gregory conceded that his logic led them down a dead end. Nothing remained visible of the city or its settlements, which had long since fallen into ruin and vanished from the surface of the earth. All that survived was a utilitarian network of underground chambers.

And that is where Rabbi Elazar had sent them.

If the rabbi was right, he was descending into a world where bats once feared to venture.

He draped a sheet of canvas over the opening in the ground and pulled it closed behind him to keep any light from escaping. He marveled at the skill with which the craftsmen of old cut steps in the rock.

When he reached the floor of the chamber, he signaled to the others, who lit their floodlights. They were standing in a cavernous space carved out of solid rock, soaring almost two stories in height. The walls of the chamber were straight and met at right angles, like the walls of a building. But where the surfaces should have been flat, they were pigeonholed from floor to ceiling with thousands of uniform compartments hollowed out of the rock, like boxes in an ancient corporate mailroom. The first chamber opened into others, which repeated the pattern.

Until his scouting mission days earlier, posing as a tourist, Gregory had subscribed to the theory that this was a tomb, and that the holes in the wall were receptacles for funerary urns. As he examined the walls, his first thought was that they must have used very small urns, and he wondered what they did with the excess remains.

Then there was a sudden flap of wings, and he was startled by the cooing of a bird loose in the chamber overhead. A feather floated to the floor. Gregory saw rows of pigeons sleeping in the pigeonholes, and he began to acknowledge the strength of the rabbi's argument.

Elazar contended the place was a breeding place for pigeons. The Bible usually referred to the motley creatures as turtledoves.

Whatever you called them, they played an important role in Jerusalem's religious life before the Romans destroyed the Temple in 70 C.E. The main function of the Temple was the ritual sacrifice of animals. From all over Judea, faithful Jews made pilgrimage to present burnt offerings to God. Those who could afford to brought cattle, sheep and goats. Others offered pigeons.

Though the tradition had disappeared from Jewish observance, the making of burnt offerings was central to the laws God set down in the Torah, and vast tracts of the sacred text were devoted to it. When a woman gave birth, or experienced irregular bleeding, which rendered her unclean in God's eyes, the path to purity included the offering of turtledoves. According to the Gospel of Luke, Mary and Joseph traveled to Jerusalem to sacrifice turtledoves after the birth of Jesus.

If anyone sinned unintentionally, the Torah said, the way to win God's forgiveness was to offer up a bull or goat.

The law incidentally assured that the priestly class would be well fed, since they shared in the fruits of sacrifice.

God was particular about the selection of ritual offerings. He generally insisted on unblemished livestock. He was also particular about the preparation. When sacrificing a pigeon, God instructed, priests must take care to wrench off its head, burn the head on the altar, drain the blood, tear the bird open by the wings—without tearing it apart completely—and toss its crop on the *east* side of the altar.

Gregory had reread these passages as he reviewed the rabbi's theory. He thought it curious that modern Jews ignored the sacrificial rites. As Gregory saw it, either the Torah was God's word or it was not. If it was, it demanded complete obedience. If it was not, it merited no more respect than any other human institution.

Gregory remembered something else. When Jesus visited the Temple as an adult and complained that it had become a den of thieves—when he angrily upended the tables of the moneychangers—he wrought similar havoc on the pigeon vendors, whose presence helped explain the need for moneychangers. People needed money to buy offerings.

Gregory saw no disputing that before the Temple fell, there must have been a huge demand for pigeons in Jerusalem. Was the cavern at Marevah the industrial poultry farm of its day? Was this where the prayers of the poor took flight?

If it was, the cache could easily elude them in such an extensive complex. They didn't have much time. Once they broke ground or altered the appearance of the stonework, they had to assume they had a single night to complete their search; when morning came and the tourists returned, someone was bound to notice they had been there.

It was impractical to dig up the entire floor of each chamber and clear the accumulated guano to the bedrock below. What's more, metal detectors would be inefficient, if not altogether ineffective, at probing behind the rock walls.

Gregory did a quick calculation and estimated that there were about 2,000 pigeonholes. How long would it take to search each of them? Any one of them might contain a false back.

"There are no bats," Brother Alex whispered.

"The cooing of the pigeons disrupts their sonar, scaring them away," Gregory said.

He kept coming back to the wording of the clue. If it truly referred to the columbarium of Tel Marevah, then it had to be sufficient. It had to contain all the information the intended recipient would need to unearth the treasure.

Where did the birds take flight?

During his scouting mission, Gregory had seen them leave the columbarium through a crack in the roof of one of the adjacent chambers—the first opening he had covered. That's where he planned to begin.

The team came well equipped. They were prepared to document their work with video and still photography. Though it was a hurried, illicit excavation, they planned to follow scholarly standards as closely as possible. Otherwise, anything they discovered would be permanently suspect.

Gregory led them into the next chamber, beneath the crack in the ceiling. They flooded it with light. In the pit of his stomach, he felt a sickening sensation.

Directly beneath the fissure in the ceiling, the floor of the chamber had been disturbed. The disruption was recent, since his prior visit. Whoever had been there had taken care to cover their tracks, and if you weren't looking for it you could easily miss it, but a hole had been dug and refilled.

It was roughly the size of a grave.

Gregory craned his neck and studied the wall. High above, where the walls began to narrow toward the opening and the pigeonholes ended, he spotted something out of place. One of the men took photographs with a zoom lens, and another kept the video camera trained on Gregory as he called for a telescoping ladder and clambered up for a closer look.

The stonework spanning six contiguous pigeonholes—three over three—had been vandalized and crudely restored. The fractures and scratch marks looked fresh and raw, bereft of the dirty patina the walls of the columbarium had acquired.

Looking closely at that section of the wall, Gregory noticed something else different about it. It was bordered by straight masonry seams, as if the whole section had once been removed and then replaced or reinserted. From the color and texture of the stone—and the dirty accumulation that coated it—he could tell that the straight cracks were old, nearly as old as the columbarium itself.

With a bare hand, Gregory pushed aside the partitions that separated the top three compartments. He unhooked a flashlight from his belt and probed the rear of the compartments.

There was a hollow space behind the fractured pigeonholes.

It was empty.

Chapter 44

Jerusalem

In the heart of the walled city, in the shadow of the Temple Mount, Jordan passed a patrol of Israeli soldiers carrying automatic rifles. Everywhere he looked, he saw uniforms and guns, which only made him feel less secure.

"Inshallah—God willing—*you shall find what you need,"* the email had said. *"Let us pray together."*

Before him stood the Wailing Wall, a place of pilgrimage for the world's Jews. With their backs to Jordan, several *hasidim* in black suits and black hats were praying at the wall, rocking in ritual submission. Above the wall, in the background, atop the elevated stone platform that once served as the Temple's foundation, Jordan saw the golden dome of the Dome of the Rock, one of Islam's sacred places.

Jordan knew from past experience that if you stood close enough to the wall—close enough to slip a folded prayer into a crack between the massive blocks—you could look up and see only wall and sky, and trick yourself into forgetting that an Islamic shrine occupied the holiest spot in the Jewish universe. But when you stepped back, the Dome of the Rock was still there, and the Temple was still gone.

Was there anywhere on earth where the weight of history weighed more heavily?

Jordan crossed the wide plaza in front of the Wailing Wall and made his way to a security checkpoint at the entrance to a ramp leading up to the enclosed platform. He felt like a criminal in a police state, furtively going about his business beneath watchful but unsuspecting eyes. It was noon, and the sun stared down pitilessly. There was no hiding from it.

To his right, high overhead, the shorn vestige of an ancient arch protruded slightly from the massive wall, hinting at the grandeur of Herod's design. The master builder had fashioned sheer retaining walls to separate the low ground from a rectangular enclosure more than three soccer fields wide by more than five soccer fields long. The Wailing Wall, or Kotelet, as it was known in Hebrew, was a segment in the middle of the Western Wall. Once, Jews had worshiped there at the indulgence of Muslims. Now, Israeli authorities controlled the Kotelet and the rest of the space around the Temple Mount, but Palestinian authorities administered the high ground. They knew it by a different name: the Haram al-Sharif, or Noble Sanctuary.

Jordan had persuaded Catherine to wait in a Jerusalem hotel in case he was walking into a trap.

His destination loomed overhead, the third most sacred shrine in all of Islam. Not the Dome of the Rock, but the Al Aqsa Mosque, at the south end of the Haram. Compared with the blue and gold magnificence of the Dome of the Rock, Al Aqsa's exterior was modest simplicity. Its lead plated dome was dull as gunmetal, the shape and color of a spent bullet.

The comparison had crossed Jordan's mind once before, years ago, when he and the King entered the mosque together.

Jordan remembered the occasion clearly. The trip to the mosque was unplanned, an impromptu impulse on the King's part during a diplomatic visit. At the end of a 90-minute interview, the King asked Jordan to join him. They arrived at the mosque unheralded and almost unrecognized, with what Jordan thought was a dangerously small escort of three bodyguards plus Samir. As Jordan knew, the King enjoyed moving about incognito to get a clearer sense of his people. But that wasn't his only consideration. He wanted to avoid making a political statement; his interest in visiting the mosque was strictly personal.

And there was something else. On the way to Al Aqsa, he allowed that being inconspicuous was often the best defense.

In front of the mosque, they stopped at the spot where in 1951 a Palestinian gunman fired three rounds into the head and body of Jordan's first King Abdullah. The killer considered Abdullah a traitor for seeking peace with the Jews.

Abdullah's grandson Hussein had been with him that summer day in 1951, and the assassin fired at Hussein from point blank range. The fourth bullet should have killed the future king. Instead, it struck a medal.

Hussein was wearing the decoration at his grandfather's behest.

For Jordan, the story was history, and it flashed through his brain like an antique newsreel. For the current King of Jordan, an heir to Hussein and Abdullah, it was his own past and quite possibly his own future. Standing outside the mosque, the journalist tried to read the monarch's thoughts, but the King moved on without saying a word.

At the door, the King had removed his shoes like any other worshipper and handed them to the attendant, who did a double take but overruled the verdict of his own eyes. It was about 1 p.m. when they knelt to pray.

"Let us pray together. Thursday, as before."

The email didn't specify a time. Jordan could only assume the hour would be the same. He walked up the ramp and passed through a security checkpoint. Then he passed through a gateway into the city within a city that was once the Temple precinct.

In the days of the Temple, an inscription on a stone tablet warned non-Jews to stay away under penalty of death. Now, no truly devout Jew would go where Jordan stood for fear of accidentally setting foot in what had been the Devir—the Holy of Holies—where only high priests were permitted.

Jordan thought of Ariel Sharon's visit to the Temple Mount, the spark that ignited the second *intifada*. He wondered how different things might have been if Sharon had been more devout.

He made his way to the mosque and took off his shoes, leaving them in the designated place. At the door, an attendant asked him if he was carrying any electronic contraband—a camera, tape recorder, or phone—but Jordan shook his head. Then he stepped into the mosque. The interior was far more ornate than the shell. A long, wide, high space was punctuated by several rows of decorative columns, and a mosaic lined the interior of the dome. From blinding sunlight, Jordan's eyes adjusted to the dimness. He slowly explored the mosque, discreetly studying both the faithful worshipers and the scattering of tourists. No one caught his eye, and no one seemed to pay him any particular attention. Not to worry; he was early.

He sat on the carpeted floor near the center of the mosque, his back to the door. From that position, it would be harder for him to see someone arriving to meet him, but easier to be seen. He tried to clear his head. All he could do was wait.

He sat at the intersection of three great religions, on a plot of real estate that had been endlessly changing hands. Hardly anything man built there lasted; Al Aqsa itself had been destroyed by earthquakes and rebuilt repeatedly through the centuries.

Jordan felt a sense of awe to be at the epicenter of so much history and spirituality and human conflict. But more than that, he felt a sense of tragedy. The Temple Mount was impressive, but fighting over it seemed such a waste. What did it matter if Abraham and Isaac had been there? Or David and Solomon? Or Jesus, assailing the moneychangers in the Temple? Or Mohammed, ascending to heaven?

They were gone now. They were everywhere, or nowhere. They would remain alive in people's hearts and souls whatever happened to these few acres. He could understand fighting over water, or farmland, or fossil fuels, or a militarily strategic piece of ground. Even over the house where you grew up. But this was futility.

Though tradition held that God resided on this very site, in the Temple of Solomon, the Scripture said otherwise. Jordan had researched it for a story. The day the Temple was dedicated, Solomon said it would be preposterous for God to live on earth, let alone in a structure built by human hands. "But can God indeed dwell on earth?" Solomon asked rhetorically. Then wise Solomon answered his own question: "Heaven itself, the highest heaven, cannot contain you; how much less this house that I have built!"

Then there was Herod's Temple, erected by a Roman puppet hundreds of years after Solomon's fell. How could anything built by Herod be holy?

Back when Israelis and Palestinians were still negotiating, still paying lip service to the concept of land for peace, the Temple Mount was the rock no one could crack. Like their Muslim counterparts, devout Jews refused to give it up. But, unlike their Muslim counterparts, they were afraid to set foot in the place.

It was a hopeless conundrum. Jordan was trying to be rational, but he knew the very effort was irrational. It was pointless to subject religious passions to the test of reason.

"But can God indeed dwell on earth?"

Jordan had almost forgotten why he was there.

He looked around, casually. He got up and moved. He saw no familiar faces, and no one sought him out.

Cloistered in her room at the Hotel Morad, Catherine flipped channels. The manager had sent up a basket of fruit and chocolate, but she was too tense to touch it. The room had a private roof deck with a magnificent view of the hills to the southeast, but she had promised to stay indoors. They were guests of the manager, Ari, an old friend of Jordan's from their days in the army. There was no record of them ever having checked in.

Jordan had assured her she was in the best possible hands, but that did nothing to alleviate her concern for him. She had tried to talk him out of going. She had a bad feeling about the anonymous email inviting him to pray. She was the one who thought it might be a trap.

And yet, his determination to go was on some level comforting . . . .

She felt guilty for admitting it to herself, but when they were in Paris, she had begun to doubt his commitment. She believed they had more than enough information to go public, and his hesitation had unnerved her. Was he avoiding the truth? Was he afraid to tell the world? Was he consciously or unconsciously protecting his people, his religion?

Clearly not.

Or only at significant risk to himself.

By 3 p.m., Jordan was losing patience. By 5 p.m., he was wracked by doubt and worry. By 6 p.m., he didn't know what to think. Had he read too much into the message? Had he gotten it wrong? Had someone been waiting all afternoon to pray with Jordan in some other mosque in some other city? Or had something prevented his contact from making the connection?

At sundown, the mosque filled with men there to say their evening prayers. They knelt and bowed, nearly pressing their foreheads against the floor in humble submission. It was hard not to feel a part of something much greater than himself, even as an interloper. But, as an interloper, it was hard not to feel intimidated by the power.

As the crowd grew, Jordan's hopes momentarily lifted. Then he felt a sense of alarm: How would anyone find him in such a dense throng?

No one did.

Within an hour, the throng dispersed.

Feeling lost and defeated, Jordan stepped out of the mosque. He wanted to find Catherine fast and make sure she was safe. He was so preoccupied that he started walking before he remembered he was shoeless. It took him a while to find his shoes, and for a moment he wondered if someone had walked off in them.

He laced up his right shoe and absentmindedly slipped his toes into the other. There was something in the shoe, and he felt it crumple.

It was an envelope.

Chapter 45

Jerusalem

"Go ahead, open it," Jordan repeated.

She reached out nervously and took it.

It was unmarked, and the envelope was ragged where Jordan had torn it without the benefit of a letter opener. She removed the contents and unfolded four pages.

The first was a color photocopy of a photograph of a badly tarnished sheet of silver metal, shown beside a metric ruler. Despite the tarnish, she could see that the metal was engraved with two columns of precise writing. The metal appeared slightly creased or corrugated where, she inferred, it had been unrolled somehow.

She handed the copy to Jordan.

The second page was a sketch of the first that stripped away all the visual distractions and showed only the writing—clear, archaic Hebrew. The third sheet translated the text into modern Hebrew. And the fourth was an English translation.

Twenty-four clues to 24 hiding places.

They were back in the race.

This was the Silver Scroll. At the Institute in Jerusalem, its discovery had turned friends and colleagues into adversaries, and then it had reduced the place to rubble. As far as they could tell, it had triggered a chain of violence stretching from Israel to America, and from England to Paris—the deaths of Altieri and Ramsi, the gunshot on the road from Ramallah, the suspected break-in at Catherine's home, the murders of Nigel Waverly, Lord Crendal and the Paris purse-snatcher. It had set in motion mysterious forces, and it had lit the fuse for a potentially explosive revelation.

If Jordan was right, the Silver Scroll could explain where the treasures of the Temple were deposited in 70 C.E. after they were moved from the hiding places described in copper and gold. And if the Silver Scroll led to the treasure, it would lead to the word of Caiaphas—potentially, to eyewitness testimony about something so humbling and awe-inspiring that it turned Jesus's chief accuser, the Jewish high priest, into a penitent recluse.

Catherine looked skeptical.

"How do we know it's real?" she asked.

Jordan seemed surprised by the question.

"Why would anyone fake it?"

"Maybe to throw us off, send us on a wild goose chase."

"But without it, we were nowhere."

"And now?"

Jordan studied the translation.

"Now," Jordan said, "we have the advantage."

"How do you figure that? The competition, whoever they are, have a huge head start. Most likely they've had access to this document since before the museum was bombed."

Jordan grinned.

"Look," he said, handing her the page. "There are 24 clues. That's a lot of ground to cover, assuming they could figure out where to search."

"So?"

"Only five of the caches include offering vessels."

Catherine's eyes lit up.

"And we know from the letter you extracted from Lord Crendal's study that the chronicles were originally buried with offering vessels," she said excitedly. "So we can assume that when the Caiaphas Chronicle was dug up and hidden again, it was buried with offering vessels. And that means we can narrow our search."

"Considerably," Jordan said.

"But Ben, so can the opposition. We lost whatever advantage we had in Paris, when we lost my purse. We need to assume they have my notes."

"Let me see that," Jordan said, grabbing the page.

He zeroed in on the five relevant clues.

The third cache. *The lion of Egypt stands guard over 100 talents of gold coins, 50 talents of silver coins, and six offering vessels.*

The fourth cache. *Where the caravan of the thieving trader vanished in the desert, 130 talents of gold coins, 90 talents of silver coins, and 15 offering vessels.*

The sixteenth cache. *In the Valley of Asher, entombed beneath the stone demon, 120 talents of silver coins, 100 talents of gold coins, and 26 offering vessels.*

The twenty-first cache. *Where the Timna road crosses the road to Kadesh Barnea, take ten paces toward the setting sun to find 300 talents of silver, 230 talents of gold, and 19 offering vessels.*

The twenty-third cache. *In Jezebel's tomb, 20 talents of gold coins and three offering vessels.*

Jordan felt as if he was back in school and he had just been handed a test for which he had not studied. As he scanned the problems, he realized he didn't have any idea how to solve them. With one exception.

"So, do you think the Egyptians will let us move their Sphinx?" he asked in frustration.

"I don't see why not," Catherine said. "As long as we put it back."

"Does any of this mean anything to you?"

"To a point. Start with the lion of Egypt. The famous Sphinx has been gone over thoroughly, and so has the ground around it. And it is well defended. Anyone who wants permission to excavate on the Giza Plateau has to navigate a political and bureaucratic minefield.

"A caravan lost in the desert? You might as well search for a grain of sand on the beach after a hundred-year storm. Assuming you knew which beach.

"The stone demon? The Valley of Asher is a stark and treacherous landscape. If it's home to such a statue, it's done a good job of hiding it. Hmmm."

"Yes?" he asked.

"It doesn't make sense."

"What doesn't?"

"The demon statue would have violated Jewish law."

"Right. It would have been a graven image."

"Exactly," she said. "Unless that was the point. Unless the Zealots thought such sacrilege would provide protective cover."

"What about the crossroads in the Negev?"

"Or is it in the Sinai? It could be anywhere in hundreds of square miles, maybe thousands. The vague description doesn't tell me much. But with access to the most expensive satellite imagery that's available commercially, we might be able to find it. If it was heavily traveled."

Jordan bit his lip.

"That leaves Jezebel's tomb," he said.

Catherine shook her head hopelessly.

"So where would you look for it?" Jordan prodded.

"The Bible is clear about this, Benjamin."

"And?"

"Jezebel had no tomb."

"What do you mean?"

"God demanded that she be denied a decent burial."

"Then what became of her body?"

"According to the prophet Elijah, God commanded that her remains lie 'like dung on the ground' so that no one could ever point to anything and say, 'This was Jezebel.'"

"Now I remember. She was on the losing side of a religious war, and her corpse was left as food for the dogs."

"That's right. The name 'Jezebel' has come to mean a wild, wicked temptress—the ultimate sexpot—but in the Old Testament, Jezebel's greatest sins were religiously motivated. She was Phoenician, and even after she married a king of Israel, she worshiped foreign gods. The worship of other deities was an abomination in the eyes of the Lord, and the Bible often equated it with fornication."

"As I recall, Jezebel was so devoted to her native gods that she killed prophets of the Hebrew god."

"Correct. The prophet Elijah retaliated by slaughtering Jezebel's prophets. Jezebel vowed revenge, but the Hebrew god triumphed in the end. Jezebel was cast down from a great height. When her servants went to bury her, all they found were her skull, her feet, and the palms of her hands. Her tombstone was the scorched earth."

"A monument to false righteousness."

"A monument to righteous zeal, and a warning to those who cross it."

Jordan hung his head.

"I'm sorry, Benjamin."

"We're going to need help," he said.

Catherine thought it over.

"We need Zev," she said.

Jordan raised an eyebrow. He knew the archaeologist Zev Galil by reputation only.

"You know him?" he said.

"Meyer introduced us," Catherine explained. "We got to know each other."

"He was a friend of Meyer?"

"No, I wouldn't say that."

"Can we trust him?"

"Yes, I think we can."

"You think?"

"I know."

"How?"

"Ben, we're going to have to trust someone."

Catherine zipped her duffel bag. "He lives at Kfar Devar," she said. "We can be there tonight."

Jordan looked around the deluxe room Ari had given them. He sighed. The hotel had room service. And a private rooftop patio under the stars. And a king-size bed, still neatly made. He picked up the phone.

"Ari, it's Ben . . . Yes, everything's great, the best, thank you . . . Yes, there is one more thing. May I borrow a car?"

Chapter 46

Northern Israel

Zev Galil was a benign grizzly bear of a man with a bushy brown beard that climbed his cheeks and nearly merged with his shaggy hair, leaving a gap just wide enough for his warm and smiling eyes. He had a gentle manner and a ready laugh. He was also a brilliant archaeologist. Jordan had seen him interviewed on television.

He was known as a war hero, but he made his mark in the shrouded realm of intelligence, and no one seemed to know exactly what he had done to merit his military rank and honors.

He had been a protégé of Meyer Elazar, but politics had come between them. Galil was a dove, and he passionately opposed the construction of Israeli settlements in the occupied West Bank. Elazar was a leading proponent of the policy. Just as the former American President Jimmy Carter raised hammer and nail to help build houses for the poor, Elazar put his rudimentary carpentry skills to work in Palestinian territory. In the parlance of Middle East politics, he was establishing "facts on the ground." Build enough Jewish homes on the ground, and soon the ground would become Jewish. That was the theory.

Galil didn't hesitate to argue with the rabbi about the settlements. When Elazar assigned Galil to one of the less desirable digs, some associates saw a political subtext.

Galil accepted his assignment without complaint and threw himself into it enthusiastically. As it turned out, Elazar had done Galil a great favor. Studying mundane traces of daily life in Israel's hills and valleys, Galil had produced pathbreaking research. His work cast doubt on the historical accuracy of the Conquest of Canaan as told in the Old Testament. The Bible described a string of burnt, blood-soaked cities in which Joshua and the invading Israelites "left no survivor, destroying everything that drew breath, as the Lord the God of Israel had commanded." According to the Bible, even the Canaanite livestock were put to death. The only mercy God showed was for the trees. Kill the people, but spare the trees, God commanded.

Yet Galil found evidence of peaceful coexistence, if not common ancestry.

Critics said his conclusions were influenced by his own political beliefs. They said he saw what he wanted to see.

"How did you meet him?" Jordan asked.

It was night, and they were driving through the highlands of Northern Israel. The kibbutz where Galil lived was in the country's northernmost tip, hours from Jerusalem, near the Lebanese border.

Catherine tried to remember their first encounter.

"We spent some time digging together."

Jordan smiled.

"He had a crush on you, didn't he?"

Jordan said it with amusement, not jealousy. Through the darkness, he could sense Catherine blushing.

"Nah," Catherine said, unconvincingly.

"Yes he did."

"Okay, maybe a little."

"And you?"

Catherine went from blushing to pensive.

"I suppose . . ."

"Yes?"

"I suppose I had a crush on Meyer."

They arrived as Galil was putting his children to bed, and the archaeologist gave them a friendly if bemused welcome.

"Cavanaugh!"

"Zevi!" Catherine exclaimed happily, disappearing in his hug.

She introduced Jordan, and the two men shook hands.

"An honor to meet you," Jordan said.

"Likewise," Galil said, and it was clear he meant it.

"This is Annie, and this is Jesse," Galil said, proudly introducing the four-year-old and the three-year-old. "Say goodnight, kids."

"Goodnight kids!" the four-year-old said gleefully, chasing her sister into the bedroom.

They sat in the garden of Galil's small cinder block house, beneath the lime trees and the wind chimes. Galil fixed a batch of lemonade. His wife was away visiting relatives and he wasn't much good in the kitchen, he said by way of apology.

"I'm guessing you didn't just happen to be in the neighborhood," he observed as he settled his oversized frame into a chair.

"We need your help, Zev," Catherine began, with more earnestness than she intended.

Galil straightened up and leaned forward.

She saw the concern in his eyes, the selfless willingness to help, and she felt a cold black cloud descend upon her. She had made a terrible mistake coming here, and involving Zev in whatever danger they confronted. She remembered blaming Jordan, unfairly, for beating a path to her door in Michigan, and now she felt she was the one being reckless. Jordan couldn't help seeking her out; she was already part of the story, whether she knew it or not. But Zev was an innocent bystander. Hell, he wasn't even a bystander.

She glanced toward the bedroom window, where Zev's children were sleeping. She rose out of her chair.

"I'm sorry, Zev, we never should have come here. It was a mistake. We'll leave right away, and with any luck, no one saw us."

Galil reached out with a powerful arm and grasped Catherine's hand, gently pulling her back down into her chair.

"Was it the lemonade?" he joked. "Because I can make iced tea, or at least iced water."

"She's right, Zev," Jordan said soberly. "We weren't thinking."

"You came here for a reason."

"Thank you, Zev," Catherine said, standing again, "but I'm sorry. Let's go, Ben."

Galil slouched in his chair, stretching his legs and folding his hands over his paunch with Buddha-like calm.

"You make it sound interesting," he said in a matter-of-fact way. "Am I entitled to a hint?"

Jordan and Catherine looked at each other, and Jordan nodded.

She handed Galil a handwritten copy she had jotted of the five key clues, barren of any context or explanation. Without changing his posture or expression, Galil studied the page, nodding occasionally, then moving his head as if in time to a song only he could hear. It was a very long song.

"Have another lemonade," he said. He rose out of his seat and went back into the house.

Jordan and Catherine looked at each other, perplexed. They sat down and waited, watching through the screen door as Galil rummaged through a cluttered desk and an overstuffed filing cabinet.

"Aha!" he proclaimed, fishing a page out of a file.

The song was still playing in his head as he stepped back into the garden and reclaimed his chair. From the stiffness of the white paper, it appeared he was holding a large photograph with its back to his visitors. He handed it to Catherine as offhandedly as if it were an ad in a magazine and he reached for his lemonade. It made him pucker. He snapped his fingers.

"Sugar. That's what I forgot."

Catherine looked at the glossy color photo, which was marred by paperclip scratches and a splotch of coffee.

It was a mosaic. A very large mosaic, judging by the sneakered feet in the corner, which gave it scale. Somewhere—it wasn't clear where—a vast floor was painstakingly inlaid with tens of thousands of tiny colorful tiles, which formed a picture. The picture was a richly decorated map. Catherine had seen something like it at Madaba, in Jordan, but this was larger, more detailed, and more tightly focused.

Over the Mediterranean port of Alexandria, a cobra reared its head. Near the present-day Cairo, three pyramids rose from the plain. Sailboats plied the Nile, and crocodiles bared their teeth along the riverbanks. The falcon god Horus soared over the temple at Edfu, and four statues of Rameses II enthroned in stone marked the colossus of Abu Simbel.

Oases of palm sprouted from the Sahara, and dolphins leapt from the waves of the Red Sea. In the Arabian Desert, a line of camels crossed the dunes. A monumental sphinx stood at the center of the mosaic, beside the pyramids.

And, at the southernmost edge of the map, at the frontier of ancient Egypt, there was a golden-maned lion.

Catherine handed the photo to Jordan.

"The lion of Egypt?" he whispered.

"Could be," Galil remarked.

"Where is it?" Catherine asked.

"On the western coast of the Red Sea. It was discovered a few years ago, but it was buried again in a storm and archaeologists have only recently gotten around to clearing it off and really studying it."

"Unbelievable," Catherine said.

Galil moved his drinking glass in an elliptical fashion, swirling the ice cubes in the lemonade. "Are you sure you wouldn't prefer iced tea?" he asked.

They talked late into the night under the lime trees while the four-year-old and the three-year-old dreamed. Catherine and Jordan told their story from start to finish and Galil listened without interrupting, swirling the lemonade in his glass until the ice cubes melted and he downed the bitter beverage out of sheer absentmindedness. When they were done talking, they looked to him for a reaction.

"It's quite simple," he said. "We've got to find it."

"I wish it were that easy," Catherine said.

"We can have a crew at the Red Sea ruins in a day or two. I'll bring some of my best students. They don't need to know the reason. With any luck, end of story. Except for the small matter of the treasure. We'll still have 23 loose ends to tidy up."

"What if the Caiaphas Chronicle isn't under the mosaic?" Catherine asked.

Galil stared into his empty glass, frowning.

"Let's hope it is."

The kibbutz had a guest house, but it was much too late for the weary travelers to get a room. Catherine curled up on Galil's couch, and Jordan stretched out on the floor. Before she closed her eyes, she glanced at Jordan, and she was pretty sure she could read his mind. He wasn't thinking about lions or mosaics or lost caravans. He was thinking about the bed at the Hotel Morad, big enough for two. Jordan smiled and rolled over.

They didn't sleep very long. At sunup, Galil excused himself, shepherded the kids out the door, and dashed out. He had some fieldwork to complete. The water level in the Kinneret had sunk to its lowest level in decades, revealing the ribs of an ancient boat buried beneath the muddy shoreline. Galil and his students were scrambling to stabilize and free it before the water level rose again. It was an extremely sensitive operation. The wood had acquired the consistency of a sponge with none of the resilience. Exposed to the air, the fragile remains could quickly disintegrate. Carbon dating told them the boat dated to the time of Jesus. It reminded the archaeologist of Rembrandt's *Storm on the Sea of Galilee*.

Galil explained that he was going to have to leave the project under the supervision of a junior colleague. She would be thrilled at the promotion. But she wouldn't be nearly as thrilled to learn he was taking half of her team. He was still trying to come up with a convincing cover story.

Jordan and Catherine ate an early breakfast of yogurt and cereal at the communal dining room, where Jordan borrowed copies of the morning papers. The impatient Farouk had threatened to leak his information to another reporter, and Jordan spread out the papers with dread.

He scanned *The Shofar,* but there was nothing on the front page. He flipped through the inside pages. He picked up another paper, *Maariv*. He didn't see anything about the bombing of the museum, or the Silver Scroll, but something else stopped him. "Terrorist Group Infiltrates Media," the headline on page 5 said.

> One of the nation's leading journalists may be an undercover agent for the Tears of God terrorist network, according to intelligence sources.
>
> The agent allegedly has been using his position to spy on the government and undercut it through false or distorted reporting, the sources said.

> A suspected terrorist who was apprehended in the West Bank is said to have described the agent's mission in a recent interrogation. The suspect claimed not to know the agent's identity.
>
> Intelligence services have quietly launched an investigation, which some editors interviewed yesterday denounced as a witch-hunt.
>
> "If what you're telling me about the investigation is true, it's a brazen attempt to intimidate the government's critics, and it could have a chilling effect," said one editor who spoke on condition of anonymity.

Jordan folded the newspaper and stared into his cereal bowl.

The article was attributed to intelligence sources.

It didn't take much to plant an anonymous story, and to cast someone in a suspicious light. Especially if that person was already under a cloud—like Jordan.

Maybe someone in the government was taking out an insurance policy, laying the groundwork to destroy whatever was left of his credibility, in case he wrote any more damaging stories. In case he dared.

Maybe it was a warning.

If members of the intelligence establishment spread the right lies, Jordan would be seen as worse than biased or incompetent. He'd be branded a terrorist. He could lose more than his international television audience; he could lose his freedom.

And everything he'd ever written would be reinterpreted through the prism of betrayal.

He felt a noose tightening around his neck.

If the article was a veiled threat, it packed an added, unintended insult. Staring into his cereal bowl, he saw dark visions, shrouded in haze. Memories—or imagined memories—of the terrorists who left him an orphan. The faces of his parents.

A deadly enemy pulling the trigger, taking them away.

"Are you okay?" Catherine asked. "You don't look so good."

Jordan managed a wan smile.

"Bad milk," he said.

They walked back through the kibbutz toward Galil's home, lost in their own thoughts.

The lush, palm shaded grounds reminded her of a campus she had visited in California. When the Zionist pioneers arrived in the years before the war, fleeing the rising power of the Nazis, the land had been a malarial swamp. Enduring mosquitoes, mud, and other miseries, the young Jews had drained the swamp. There were years of privation. But, in time, they established a thriving community. From the beginning, the Arabs resented the Jewish presence. But under the Arabs, this land had been useless. As it was often said, the Jews had taken the least desirable and made it the most.

Jordan and Catherine walked past an outdoor swimming pool with lap lanes and splashing children. To Catherine, it looked like a scene straight out of American suburbia. But she knew the serenity was deceiving.

To the north, an unseen enemy lobbed rockets over a ridge that marked the Lebanese border, raining random death and destruction on the surrounding countryside. To the east, the Golan Heights dominated the landscape. The flat farmland that spread out beneath the Golan seemed utterly at its mercy. For much of Kfar Devar's history, the Syrians had held the heights, which remained honeycombed with their bunkers. From below, it felt like the Syrians could practically peer through the kibbutzniks' windows. Just thinking about an enemy so close and so advantaged made Catherine nervous.

Many of the neat little houses on the kibbutz had thick-walled safe rooms where the residents were trained to take refuge in a terrorist attack. And there had been attacks. The gunmen came in the dark, moving from house to house.

Catherine knew the history all too painfully. Meyer Elazar's wife and child had died in just such a raid. Meyer probably would have died defending them, but he had been away on a dig.

The kibbutz had survived the external threats, but now its way of life was threatened from within. The younger generations were growing up and moving away, making it hard for the community to sustain its aging pioneers. And the violence was strangling the modest revenue the kibbutz had earned running a motel for tourists.

A short distance from the swimming pool, the Jordan River meandered past the kibbutz, scarcely wider than a stream.

"It's hard to believe this trickle of water sustains so much life," Catherine said.

Chapter 47

An Aegean Island

Meyer Elazar closed his eyes and imagined he was wading through an underground river. Its cool waters fed the hubris of the taunting Jebusites. It was at once their lifeline and the Achilles heel in their defenses. In his mind's eye, it carried him toward the seventeenth cache.

Where the brother of Abishai rested as he rose to power, 30 talents of gold coins and six jars of incense.

From a stone-walled cell at the monastery of Saint Constantine, Elazar immersed himself in the river's claustrophobic chill.

The brother of Abishai was Joab. That was easy. And Joab attained command of King David's army through a singular feat of heroism. It happened at the beginning of David's reign, when David marched from his base in Hebron to the fortified city of Jebus. From atop the walls, the Jebusites boasted that David would never enter their city. They were confident in their ability to outlast the Israelites' siege.

David promised that the first Israelite to go up into the city would be rewarded with command of his army. Joab claimed the prize, and Jebus became known as the City of David—Jerusalem.

How did Joab manage his ascent? The Bible didn't exactly say, but if you melded the accounts in 1 Chronicles and 2 Samuel, you could reach your own conclusion. According to 2 Samuel, David exhorted his warriors, "Everyone who is eager to attack the Jebusites, let him get up the water-shaft . . . ."

The implication was that Joab entered through the secret, subterranean waterworks that had been chiseled through the bedrock to bring water into Jebus from a spring hidden outside the city's walls. From the spring, the water flowed through a long man-made tunnel. Inside the city, deep underground, the tunnel intersected a vertical shaft that rose toward the surface.

If the shaft was Joab's route to victory, the clue to the sixteenth cache suggested there was a place for Joab to stop along the way—a ledge, a side-tunnel, a hollow in the rock . . . .

All of that was easy to deduce. The hard part was finding it. Parts of the waterworks had been cleared in modern times, and parts remained obstructed. Parts were open to tourists. It was entirely possible that the relevant section remained undiscovered. Equipped with a miner's helmet, Elazar had scraped and squeezed and crawled and rappelled through the waterworks in a former life, but now, for the life of him, he couldn't see the answer.

"Rabbi?"

Through the heavy wooden door to his room, he heard the muffled voice of Father Gregory.

"Yes, come in."

"Good afternoon, Rabbi Elazar."

"Good afternoon, Father Gregory."

"How goes your work?"

Elazar shook his head.

"It would be easier in the field, with you and your brethren."

The monk nodded sympathetically.

"I know," he said.

"What's the latest from the Sinai?"

"The second and twelfth caches have been moved to safety." The monk spoke with a trace of bitterness. "We can safely say such magnificent discoveries have never been greeted with such disappointment."

"And Marevah?"

The monk smiled weakly.

"You were right, Rabbi."

"But?"

"Someone else got there first."

Elazar closed his eyes and leaned over his desk, burying his forehead in the palms of his hands.

"All we can do is persevere," Gregory said. "We must pray they struck gold, and nothing more."

"If you were a betting man, Father Gregory, would you take those odds?"

"If I were a betting man, Rabbi Elazar, I would bet on you."

Elazar smiled wanly at the compliment.

"But I'm not a betting man," the monk added, "so I put my faith in God."

Elazar laughed at what passed for humor.

Gregory looked troubled—not quite ready to go, and not in any hurry to stay.

"What else?" Elazar asked.

The monk bit his lip. He seemed nervous, and conflicted. He sat on the edge of Elazar's cot, and in the cramped confines of the monastic cell, their knees nearly touched.

"We have more competition," Gregory said.

"Who?"

"A former associate of yours. And a journalist."

"Who?"

"A Professor Cavanaugh, from Michigan. And Benjamin Jordan of *The Shofar*."

"Catherine?"

Elazar felt the blood draining from his head. He looked flustered.

"Did you confide in her, Rabbi?"

"Did I — *No,*" he sputtered. "*She* confided in *me*."

"How serious a problem do we have?"

"*Problem?* She's not an adversary—she's an ally. Of this you can be sure."

Gregory looked dubious.

"I don't know, Rabbi."

"We should combine efforts, Father Gregory."

"You're that confident?"

"We could use such help."

"That may be. But I'm afraid it may be too late. If we made contact with them now, others would see us, and everything would be compromised. I'm sorry to say, your friend has put herself in extreme danger. People have been killed."

"Then we must help her," Elazar said with alarm. "You helped me. You can help her."

"If we can protect her, we will. At the moment, we're not sure where they are, or even . . . . "

Elazar swallowed heavily.

"We were watching them for a time in Paris, and overheard them in an outdoor café, so indirectly, we've already benefited from their efforts," Gregory said.

"You mean you *spied* on them?"

"We weren't the only ones."

Elazar was taken aback. Though he had nothing to do with it, he felt complicit. He felt like he had violated a trust. Could he really be surprised that the monks would go to such lengths? He tried to decide whether the ends justified the means. But the only thing that came through clearly was his curiosity.

"How have they done?" he asked.

"Surprisingly well."

"Have they found anything?"

Gregory hesitated, as if he feared the rabbi's reaction.

"They know what they're looking for," he said.

"What's that?"

"The eyewitness account of Caiaphas, high priest of Jerusalem."

Chapter 48

The Sinai Peninsula

Zev Galil squinted into the video camera and began narrating extemporaneously as he stepped barefoot across the dusty mosaic.

"I'm standing on a truly remarkable map of the Middle East unearthed three years ago here on the western coast of the Red Sea. With me and my students are Professor Catherine Cavanaugh and the journalist Benjamin Jordan, whose investigations have brought us here today.

"We're taping this event to establish a primary record of our work at this site, given the extraordinary circumstances and the unorthodox methods to which we must resort. For reasons that may soon become obvious, I have not explained the circumstances to the members of my team. Let me say that I accept full responsibility for any legal or ethical breaches this exploration entails, and I leave it to the public to decide whether those breaches were warranted.

"Did you get that, Hannah?"

Hannah, a lithe 19-year-old with a desert tan, looked up from the camera's eyepiece and gave Galil a thumb's up. "Keep going, professor."

Galil glanced at his watch, a clunky digital with a plastic band held together by black electrical tape. He was wearing a T-shirt and khaki shorts and a broad, floppy hat that proved he had neither style nor vanity. He unfolded a copy of the morning paper and held up the front page to the camera.

"The local time now is 11:14 a.m. The date is November 2. And we're about to begin."

It was a typically hot and cloudless day, and the deep blue sky matched the deep blue sea. The site was south of Eilat, inside Egypt, on the barren coastal plain between the red rock mountains and the shorefront beach resorts, where the main attraction was diving in the coral gardens. The mosaic appeared to have been part of a small palace, maybe a beach house for a wealthy Egyptian civil servant.

The team members and their caravan of SUVs and pickup trucks stood out against the landscape, and there was no concealing their presence.

"If any tourists come by, we'll do our best to bore them," Galil instructed. Hannah kept taping.

They had ruled out digging at night, reasoning that at such an exposed site it would look more suspicious.

Doron Druri, the archaeologist in charge of the site, was still waiting for his grant to be renewed, and on a typical day, he would have been working with no more than half a dozen assistants. The volunteers from Europe and the United States had left for the season.

"How did you get Doron off the site?" Catherine asked.

"I told him we needed him to fill in for us on the Kinneret, before the water rises," Galil said. "He owed me."

"And what did you tell your team on the Kinneret?"

"I told them Doron needed us to help out in a pinch on the Red Sea."

Catherine's jaw dropped.

"I know, it wasn't the best excuse," Galil said sheepishly.

Galil tiptoed around the edge of the mosaic to the southernmost point, where the golden-maned lion reared up, as if challenging a hunter.

"It's an unusually dynamic depiction," Galil observed. "See how different it looks from the seated lions at the Temple of Isis in Philae?"

Jordan didn't know anything about the seated lions of Philae, but he squatted beside Galil like a baseball catcher and admired the artistry.

"How could our heroes bury the treasure without destroying the mosaic?" he asked.

"A very good question," Galil said. "My guess is they dug from the side, coming in under it."

"Is that your plan?"

"Too time consuming," Galil said. He motioned to his students, and they set up some equipment near the lion.

"Ground penetrating radar," Galil explained, as the students began taking soundings. "Once they get a baseline, they'll run a grid."

Another student, a young man in his early twenties, was photographing the mosaic with a macro lens, methodically moving from frame to frame, documenting the way each individual tile related to its neighbors.

"Over here, professor," one of the students shouted excitedly.

Galil rushed to the radar monitor and inspected the readout.

"We have several significant anomalies," he said. "They're all within a radius of a few meters from the lion."

Catherine squeezed Jordan's arm, and the journalist clenched his fists in anticipation.

"Okay, let's lay it down," Galil directed.

Two of the students lifted tanks from the trucks and shouldered them like scuba gear. Each tank was attached to a tube roughly double the diameter of a garden hose.

"Spray away," Galil said.

The junior archaeologists began spraying thick white foam on the southern end of the mosaic, covering a triangular area that encompassed the anomalies.

"It takes a while to set," Galil explained. "In the meantime, the students will use ordinary hand trowels to cut a clean border around the outer edge, where the tiles stop, and remove some of the surrounding stone work. Unfortunately, the size and shape complicate matters."

"Did you invent this technique?" Jordan asked.

Galil grinned at the thought.

"No, I stole it from thieves."

The wait was excruciating. Jordan used the time to examine the rest of the mosaic. Catherine distracted herself with Zev's copy of the morning paper. Amid the daily dose of depressing information, one story was particularly upsetting. A fundamentalist Islamic court in Nigeria had carried out a sentence of death by stoning a young woman convicted of adultery.

"Can you believe the barbarity?" she asked. "How can people think this way?"

"It's really no different than the Law of Moses," Galil said.

"The difference is we don't enforce the absurd."

"If we obeyed our Torah, we, too, would execute adulterers—and brides found to be less than virginal on their wedding night."

He was right, but he was deliberately provoking her. Catherine rolled her eyes.

"Give me a break," she said, and she swatted him with the paper.

Galil took it from her and started to catch up on his reading.

The temperature must have been close to 100 degrees, but Catherine suddenly broke out in chills.

"Wait a minute, give me that," she said, and she grabbed it from him.

Galil shrugged and walked away. Like a pastry chef testing the consistency of a soufflé or meringue, he gently poked the hardening foam.

Catherine looked up from the newspaper, her mind racing as fast as her pulse.

"It's time," Galil announced.

The southern Nile valley was now coated with rubbery foam that stuck to its surface. Galil knelt at the point of the triangle, and his students lined up along two sides. Wielding tools that looked like oversized spatulas, they began to free the mosaic from its underpinnings. Then they positioned a large plastic tube across the foam, like a gargantuan version of the cardboard core to a roll of toilet paper.

The students grabbed the edges of the mosaic. On Galil's signal, they began to lift. They began to roll it up like a carpet, using the tube as a support. The foam held the mosaic together. For the first time in two millennia or more, the tiles peeled away from the masonry beneath them.

"Slowly, careful now. Okay, wrap it as you go."

Two of the students draped a sheet of rubbery material around the outside of the roll to cushion the newly exposed underside of the mosaic. Catherine seemed not to notice what was happening, but Jordan watched with fascination.

"Thieves, you say?"

"They've walked off with some precious mosaics like they were carpets in a bazaar."

Jordan got down in the dirt and lent a hand. When the crew had peeled back two meters of tile, Galil gave the signal to stop. Hannah circled the newly bared floor, taping it from a variety of angles, and the photographer clicked away.

Galil eyeballed the area, comparing it with the radar report.

"Let's dig," he declared.

Ordinarily, a dig like this would proceed with glacial deliberation. Galil's team had to compress weeks of work into hours.

The students pried away the thin stone slabs that formed the floor beneath the mosaic. The space below resembled a basement partially flooded with sand. It had been hollowed out of the bedrock, except for the wall facing west, which had been constructed of stone blocks. Many of those appeared to have fallen inward, allowing the sand to infiltrate over time.

On the floor of the pit, tossed on waves of sand, were more than a dozen clay jugs. They had short necks, handles like ears, and wide, stubby bodies. If they weren't sinking into the sand, most would come up to a man's waist.

Frowning, Galil lowered himself into the pit. With his hands, he swept the sand away from the most exposed of the vessels. He ran his fingertips across its surface, feeling for cracks. Then he peered inside it with a pen light.

"The third cache?" Jordan asked.

"No," Galil said. "The secret to avoiding heart disease."

Jordan looked baffled.

"Note the varied proportions," Galil said, pointing. "These with the slender necks are for wine and olive oil, and those are for flour or grain. If I'm not mistaken, this one still contains unprocessed whole wheat."

"What about the coins, the ceremonial vessels, the – "

"Looks like we've got the wrong address. The pottery itself is everyday stuff. It's unworthy of ceremony and hardly suitable for transporting coins. Still, the organic chemists will have a field day."

The students were giddy with amazement. But Jordan and Catherine were subdued.

"Couldn't there be something else inside the jugs, or under the sand?" Jordan asked.

"Pass me the metal detector," Galil said.

"Professor," one of the students called out. "I think you should see this."

In the distance, a white Humvee turned off the coastal highway toward the excavation, kicking up a cloud of dust.

Peering over the top of the excavation, Galil watched it approach.

"Okay, let's cover this hole," he directed. "No rushing about."

Galil climbed out of the crawl space. Two of the students pulled a tarp out of a pickup truck.

"Zev," Catherine said.

"Pin it down with stones, use the floor slabs if you have to," Galil said.

"Zev," Catherine said.

"Remember, just another boring day at the office, sifting dirt, sweeping the floor. No hurry, no worry."

"Zev," Catherine said, waving the newspaper.

"Yes, what is it?"

"Tell me about *sharia*."

"What do you mean?"

She showed him the story about the Nigerian death sentence.

"I need to know—did the tenets of *sharia* predate Islam itself?"

"Can this wait? Yossi, cover that corner," Galil said, pointing.

"Just answer the question."

"Hmmm."

"Well?"

"*Sharia.* It's safe to assume Islamic law was based on earlier traditions."

"First century traditions?"

"I don't see why not. Probably older. Why do you ask?"

"I think I've found the lost caravan, the fourth cache."

Galil stopped and looked at her. He thought for a moment.

"Yes—yes of course. I think you're right."

"Can you clean up here?"

"Yes, we'll take care of it. You and Ben take the Jeep. We'll catch up with you."

Jordan looked up from the far side of the pit, where he was sifting soil through a screen.

"Come on, Ben, we've got to get going," Catherine said. She walked toward the Jeep and motioned for him to take the driver's seat. It was clear she was in a hurry.

"What is it?" Jordan asked.

"The fourth cache. The caravan of the thieving trader. I believe we'll find it near Wadi Rum, in the Jordanian desert."

Jordan turned from Catherine to Galil and saw the seriousness etched on his face.

"You go," Jordan said. "I'll handle this."

"This is *my* sandbox," Galil said in a tone that was non-negotiable. "What do you know about making sandcastles?"

Jordan wavered.

"Zev, the people in that Humvee could be dangerous."

"Ben, my friend, the students and I will be as diverting as we can be. But now the search is riding on *you*."

Jordan conceded. He walked toward the Jeep, minding Galil's advice not to hurry or worry.

The Humvee was drawing closer.

"Wait, Ben," Galil said.

Jordan turned around.

"You'll need these," Galil said, and he tossed him the keys.

Chapter 49

An Aegean Island

Meyer Elazar imagined himself chained in a dungeon, preparing to face the Spanish Inquisition and the ultimate test of his belief. The solitude of his monastic cell had become a purgatory.

Since he was a child, in journeys of the imagination, he had walked in the footsteps of his ancestors, trying to answer the unanswerable: What would he have done if he were in their position, forced to undergo the same trials?

What if he were Job, and God had reduced him to rags, killed his family, and afflicted him with excruciating sores, all to test his faith and win a wager with Satan? Would he have renounced God?

What if he were Abraham, and God had commanded him to sacrifice his son Isaac? Would he have obeyed? Would he have bound Isaac, placed him on the pyre, and raised his knife—until God told him to stop?

For that matter, what if he were Isaac? Would he have forgiven Abraham?

What if he were a Jew under the Syrian king Antiochus, pressed to violate God's law by eating pork? Would he have eaten? Or would he have let Antiochus cut out his tongue, tear off his scalp, and roast him alive in a giant cauldron, like the heroes of legend?

And what if he were standing in a Nazi gas chamber, as they released the deadly pellets? With his last breath, would he have proclaimed the watchword of the Jewish faith? Or would he have cursed God?

It was impossible to answer these questions in the hypothetical. But even in the hypothetical, when Elazar was honest with himself, he failed God's tests. And that knowledge was itself a form of torment. It made the rabbi feel weak and unworthy, even fraudulent. Maybe it made him compensate.

When he was a young man, it made him dig for his religion, where others took it on faith.

Later, when the Arabs murdered his wife and daughter, his bitterness propelled him into a yeshiva, and ultimately into the rabbinate. It fueled his hatred of Israel's enemies, and his determination to fight for the Jewish state. But, in the privacy of his soul, he still suspected he would fail the test.

Now, the hypothetical had again become real, more profoundly than he could have imagined. Now, Meyer Elazar was playing a central role in an effort that could undermine Judaism and bolster Christianity.

If he and the Order of Constantine were smart enough and fast enough, and if they didn't waver in their pursuit, the Silver Scroll would lead them to the personal testament of Caiaphas, high priest of Jerusalem, presiding judge at the trial of Jesus. If Elazar was right, the moment was nearly upon them.

And then what?

For almost 2,000 years, the New Testament account of the death and resurrection of Jesus had inspired hatred and persecution of Elazar's people. It was the soil in which the Nazi ideology took root. It had helped bring Jews and Judaism to the brink of extinction.

And still Jews rejected the Christian scripture. Their very identity, their existence as a people, hung in the balance.

Maybe the Caiaphas Chronicle would discredit the Gospels. Maybe it would rise to the Jews' defense.

But maybe it wouldn't. Maybe it would lend credence to the New Testament.

If Father Gregory's intelligence was correct, whatever Caiaphas witnessed made him a penitent recluse. And Elazar was being asked to drag this reluctant witness into the light of day.

The Christian Bible was supposedly a testament to brotherly love. But Elazar knew that was a selective reading. The proof was seared in his memory—the New Testament words of Jesus himself, trying to overthrow the old order.

> *"If anyone comes to me and does not hate his father and mother, wife and children, brothers and sisters, even his own life, he cannot be a disciple of mine."*
>
> *"I have come to set a man against his father, a daughter against his mother, a daughter-in-law against her mother-in-law, and a man will find enemies under his own roof."*
>
> *"Do you suppose I came to establish peace on earth? No indeed. I have come to bring dissension."*
>
> *"I have not come to bring peace, but a sword."*

The point of that sword was aimed at the heart of Judaism. Though Jesus was born into a Jewish family, for refusing to accept him or his word as divine, Jesus condemned fellow Jews.

"Snakes! Vipers' brood! How can you escape being condemned to hell?"

"On you will fall the guilt of all the innocent blood spilt on the ground."

"Your father is the devil and you choose to carry out your father's desires. He was a murderer from the beginning . . . . and the father of lies."

Jesus's harshest words were directed at a particular segment of the Jewish establishment, the strict and ritualistic Pharisees, but that nuance was lost in the passion.

Though Moses declared that the Torah was the last word on God's laws, the followers of Jesus set out to supplant it. The New Testament mocked Old Testament teachings as "outlandish," including dietary laws, "which have never benefited those who observed them." It denounced circumcision as "mutilation" and called those who practice it "dogs." It dismissed the rules for observance of the Sabbath. It seemed to ridicule the Old Testament as a collection of "erroneous doctrines . . . interminable myths and genealogies."

It sought to topple the foundation of the Jewish religion, the Law of Moses, given by God at Mount Sinai. "Had that first covenant been faultless, there would have been no occasion to look for a second to replace it," the Christian Bible said. Instead, God "has pronounced the first one obsolete."

The Old Testament taught Jews how to deal with blasphemers. It prescribed zero tolerance. Their reaction to someone like Jesus would have been predictable, an article of faith, dictated by Deuteronomy:

Should a prophet or a pedlar of dreams appear among you and offer you a sign or a portent, and call on you to go after other gods whom you have not known and to worship them, even if the sign or portent should come true do not heed the words of that prophet or dreamer. The Lord your God is testing you to discover whether you love him with all your heart and soul . . . .

As for that prophet or dreamer, he must be put to death.

According to Gospel, when the Roman governor Pontius Pilate asked a mob of Jews what he should do with Jesus, their answer was clear.

"Crucify! Crucify!" they shouted. "We have a law, and according to that law he ought to die, because he has claimed to be God's Son."

And so the New Testament blamed an entire nation and its descendants for the death of God, as if it were within man's power to kill God. As if the Crucifixion were contrary to God's plan, or Jesus's mission, as Christians understood them.

Even more insidiously, the Gospel of Matthew had the Jews blame themselves: "With one voice the people cried, 'His blood be on us and on our children.'"

Meyer Elazar asked himself, what would happen if he found the Caiaphas Chronicle?

He looked at his hands and saw them dripping with blood. It was the blood of innocent Jews, spilled in the name of Jesus. It was, quite possibly, a mortal blow to Israel.

Chapter 50

The Jordanian Desert

They were driving on a wide red river of sand, between rust-colored cliffs sculpted by time. Once, the sand had been mountaintops. But wind and water had ground it to dust.

To their left, sandstone rivulets dripped from the cliffs, frozen like icicles after a premature thaw. To their right, thousands of horizontal striations marked millions of years.

The river emptied into a lake of red rippled sand, which lapped at the feet of jagged stone mountains. In places, the mountains had melted into pillars separated by deep, narrow crevices.

The afternoon sun probed the mountains' secrets, eerily illuminating some crags and hollows while leaving others in shadow.

"Circle to the left, through that gap," Catherine said, drawing on memory.

Jordan steered the Jeep toward the mouth of another tributary.

This was the land of the nomad. Passing through on endless journeys, from time immemorial to the not-so-distant past, the Bedouin would raise tents and campfires on the valley floor. Just as quickly, they would pick up and move on. Even their great tent cities rose and fell without a trace. They left the land as they found it, shaped by nature and unaltered by man.

Almost.

There was a time in the late 1990s when Catherine feared tourism would spoil it. As her Bedouin friend Ali explained in broken English, foreigners were drawn by "gravities." At first, she didn't understand. Nonetheless, she could see the tiny Bedouin village that sprang up at a gateway to the region—neat rows of small, trailer-like houses spanning the bottom of a narrow canyon—and she believed she could see the future.

The future was delayed. As violence returned to other parts of the Middle East, so did the desert's purity and stillness. It had won a temporary reprieve.

Jordan looked through his rear view mirror at the trail of tire tracks. He felt he had inflicted a wound, but he knew it would heal.

"I think it's up ahead to the left," Catherine said, searching for landmarks in the rock formations. "Okay, this is it."

By the time Jordan cut the engine, Catherine was running across the sand. The sun was low in the sky, and she cast an elongated shadow as she ran. From her shadow, she looked twelve feet tall.

The cliff ahead receded as it sank toward the desert floor, undercut by erosion.

Catherine stopped and craned her neck, looking up at the cliff's smooth face. Jordan caught up with her.

"Gravities," she said.

The cliff was defaced with petroglyphs—prehistoric graffiti.

High overhead, rows of weird symbols were carved in stone. They were an ancient form of writing, as yet undeciphered.

A few feet lower, but still out of reach, a herd of camels crossed the cliff. They were drawn crudely, as if by children—or Picasso. But the humps were unmistakable. Some of the beasts were carved in two-dimensional simplicity—outlines of side views showing two legs only. Others conveyed a rudimentary sense of depth and perspective, showing both the near and far legs in mid-stride. Those were carved as solid shapes.

The lead camel was shorn in half, its front end missing. A sheet of rock had fallen away. Whatever artistry covered that section of the cliff face was lost forever. Vanished.

There were human figures, too, barely more sophisticated than stick drawings. They appeared to be walking behind the camels. Two were rendered in sufficient detail to make conspicuous their maleness. One had his hands raised over his head. He was holding something in his right hand—some sort of curved stick. Maybe a switch for striking the animals.

The other man had his arms raised in similar fashion. His elbows were bent at right angles, his forearms perpendicular to the ground. His right hand held a stick. But his left arm ended before the wrist.

He was missing a hand.

He had been carved without it.

Where the caravan of the thieving trader vanished in the desert, 130 talents of gold coins, 90 talents of silver coins, and 15 offering vessels.

"Let me get this straight," Jordan said. "The primitives who made these carvings punished thieves by cutting off their hands?"

"No, that's not the idea," Catherine said. "What I'm thinking is, much later, in the 1st Century, when the treasure was buried, the authors of the Silver Scroll might have associated amputation with Arab justice. They might have viewed the one-handed camel-driver in the Arabian desert as a convicted thief."

In the shadows, Catherine didn't notice, but he was smiling with admiration.

"Let's dig," Jordan said.

They ran to the Jeep and grabbed the shovels.

The sun was sinking over the mountains, and the Jeep cast an abstract shadow. It crept across the undulating sand like a painting by Dali.

They started digging.

The sun touched a jagged peak and seemed to pause, bursting into fiery rays. Then it disappeared behind the mountain, leaving a yellow halo and a darkened valley.

He looked up at the glyphs.

"How old are they?" he asked between breaths.

"My guess is, the oldest date back tens of thousands of years."

Jordan whistled.

"Why so high? It was quite a reach."

"My guess is, the people who carved them had their feet on the ground."

Jordan marveled at the sweep of geologic time.

But he was beginning to notice it wasn't on their side.

The ground wasn't getting any lower. For all their exertion, their digging was getting them nowhere. Jordan stepped up the pace, but the sand kept collapsing into the hole. He threw himself into it with a vengeance, but all he had to show for it was sweat.

Panting with exhaustion, Catherine put a hand on his shoulder and leaned on him to catch her breath.

"It's no use, Ben."

He raised the shovel again and plunged it into the sand with a fury born of frustration. The desert undid his effort.

"It's okay, Ben."

He put a hand on hers, and bowed his head.

Behind him, the yellow halo had disappeared, and the sky was turning from blue to black.

"We'll camp for the night," he said with resignation.

"Here?" she asked.

Jordan looked around. He gazed across the great sand lake at the peaks rising from the far shore.

"No, it's too exposed," he said. "We'll find something more sheltered."

They chose a neighboring valley, where a cluster of rock formations formed a protective screen. In the desert air, under the flawless sky, the temperature quickly dropped. There was no moisture in the atmosphere to retain the heat.

Jordan scoured the valley floor for the dried out husks of the tiny bushes that dotted the sand. They were the only sign of life in the parched landscape, the only hint that somewhere, far underground, a trickle of the primeval floodwaters continued to flow.

He built a campfire, keeping it small to conserve fuel. Catherine spread heavy woolen blankets on the ground beside it. She unzipped their single sleeping bag and spread it over the blankets to form a makeshift quilt.

She tried her cell phone and closed it in frustration.

"Useless," she said.

They sat on the sleeping bag, drinking water from plastic bottles and eating granola bars. The moon was rising over the mountains. It was nearly a circle. It was blindingly white. It seemed so close, close enough to touch.

"I'm worried about Zev," she said.

"I know, so am I. But you'll see. He'll be here tomorrow to solve our problem."

"I'm not so sure."

Jordan threw another wisp of wood on the fire.

He looked at the luminescent dial on his watch. It had been 29 hours since they left Galil to tend to the jugs and entertain the approaching tourists. They had driven up the Egyptian coast and through Eilat, where they purchased provisions and stopped to rest. Then on to the Arava Crossing Point at the border between Eilat and Akkaba.

"Shalom! Peace! Bon Voyage!" the signs exclaimed in English, Hebrew and Arabic as they left the Israeli side. Dusty green trucks filled with live cattle were coming the other way, preceded by their smell.

Jordan held his nose and Catherine held her breath as they crossed a narrow paved strip through a fenced-off no-man's land marked "DANGER – MINES."

Then they were in Jordan.

Catherine watched the fragile fire burn on the desert floor.

"What if they weren't tourists?" she asked.

Jordan gave her hand a reassuring squeeze.

"Galil's students are Israelis," he said. "That means they're soldiers. When we left, one of them was hiding in the back of the pick-up."

"Hiding?"

"With an assault rifle."

Catherine shivered.

"If they weren't in Egypt," Jordan said, "he would have been wearing it."

Jordan laid their last wisp of wood across the fire. The dried-out, delicate twigs curled up in glowing tendrils.

They felt the stirring of a breeze, and against the perfect silence of the desert night, they heard countless grains of sand suddenly rearranging themselves.

The tendrils faded, and the last lick of fire flickered out in a wisp of smoke that vanished in the pristine air.

Surprisingly, the night seemed brighter.

Overhead, there were a billion blinking stars. There were a thousand times more of them than Jordan had ever seen, and they shone with unfamiliar brilliance. In the desert, the heavens were pure. They were unfiltered by the reflected light of man's creation. Freed from earthly pollution, it was easy to understand ancient man's intimate relationship with the stars.

It was easy to see them as deities, or to believe in a Divine Creator. Here was the evidence.

She lay back and looked up at the sky. He leaned over her and brushed his fingers through her hair.

"I'm sorry, it's not the Hotel Morad," Jordan said.

"No, it's not."

"And it isn't Pamet Hall."

"You're right."

"It isn't even the Black Rabbit."

"Oh well," Catherine said, without the slightest regret.

Slowly, he kissed her neck. She reached for his hand and their fingers locked.

She rolled over onto him and gazed into his eyes, which smoldered with celestial fire. He lifted his face toward hers, but she looked up, at the stars. He pulled her toward him, slowly but inexorably. Their lips almost touched, and they exchanged a spark. A breath passed between them.

Then they kissed.

A long, deep kiss.

She pulled away and rose up over him. Arching toward the stars, she lifted her shirt and sweater over her head and cast them aside. He unclasped her bra, and it fell away.

The night was cold, but neither of them noticed.

When they fell back in exhaustion, it felt like morning. But it was only midnight. For a moment, Jordan thought a great ribbon of cloud had marred their perfect sky. Then he intuited the explanation. The Milky Way had risen as never before, enveloping them in its cool white light.

She fell asleep in his arms, listening to his heartbeat.

Lying awake, looking at the stars, Jordan pondered eternity. He considered the vivid reality of the moment, and the ephemeral nature of life. He held Catherine close, clinging to the moment. He thought of countless generations that had slept beneath the same stars, stretching back through geologic time to the creators of the petroglyphs, and farther still.

He wondered if anyone had experienced the same emotions he was feeling.

And then, in the glow of the Milky Way, in the warmth of Catherine's body, he had a revelation.

When he awoke, the stars were gone, and the moon was a ghost of its former self. It was not yet dawn.

He leaned over and watched Catherine sleeping. He kissed her, a brush of the lips. Her lips formed a smile. She wrapped her arms around him and pulled him close, demanding a deeper kiss.

"Come with me," he whispered, and pulled away.

She opened her eyes as he buttoned his pants. He reached out a hand and lifted her to her feet. She was naked, even more beautiful than before. He tossed her the shirt and sweater, and she quickly got dressed.

He took her hand and they scampered up the nearest of the rock formations, a miniature mountain that rose steeply from the campsite. The sandstone had a surprising consistency. It was neither soft nor brittle. It was hard, like kiln-fired ceramics, and almost musical, with a hollow timbre that could amplify echoes. She sensed it would resound if struck. They climbed hand over hand, using what steps and rungs and ragged footholds nature provided. When nature failed to provide, Jordan reached back for her hand and hoisted her up with a powerful arm. His wounds no longer troubled him.

They were nearing the top. An orange halo was forming behind the mountains to the east, a forerunner of the rising sun.

"Ben?"

"I'm right here."

"Ben?"

"Keep coming. We're almost there."

He looked over his shoulder. They were one step ahead of the sun.

"Ben, there's something I — "

"Take my hand."

She reached out, and with a powerful assist, she was standing beside him on the mountaintop. The sun was just beginning to peek over the eastern ridge.

She looked down, for the first time since they had begun the ascent, and the view was dizzying. They were almost 200 feet above the campsite, and the Jeep looked like a toy beside their blankets. By force of will, she controlled her fear of heights and took in the panorama. She looked toward the north, searching for the red river of sand, but it was hidden beneath the cliffs. She looked to the west, and the neighboring valley. She looked toward the great sand lake, where the caravan of the thieving trader had vanished in the desert.

She let out a gasp.

"Ben!"

"You're missing the sunrise."

"Ben, look—it's Zev!"

"Huh?"

He looked where she was pointing. A caravan of four sport utility vehicles had parked beside the petroglyphs, and the team was clustered at the base of the cliff.

"I told you," Jordan said, hugging her.

One of the members stepped away from the group. He seemed to be studying the ground. He appeared to turn and speak to the others, and then he pointed at a pair of faint tire tracks crossing the desert toward the mountain gap that led to their campsite.

"That's not Zev," Jordan said.

"Sure it —"

She was raising her hand to wave, but he grabbed it in an inflexible grip and held it in check.

"That's not Zev," he repeated. "Quick, follow me."

They ducked down, behind the rocks, and started down.

"Don't rush," Jordan said.

She quickly discovered that mountaineering defied the laws of nature. Descending was much more difficult than climbing—and much more dangerous. Plus, you had to look down.

"I'm right here," he said. "Watch your step."

She used his body as a crutch.

"If not Zev, then who?"

"Let's skip the introductions."

They were halfway down.

She planted a foot on some loose stones, and it slipped out from under her. He broke her fall.

"You all right?"

She nodded and kept going.

At the bottom of the rock formation, they sprinted down a steep dune. The soft sand cushioned each footfall. They ran to the campsite and threw their bedding in the Jeep. Catherine picked her bra off the sand and hung it around her neck as they opened the doors and jumped in.

Jordan glanced at her attire as he turned the ignition.

"Nice," he said.

They left the campsite in a spray of sand.

Jordan drove north, toward the canyons that exited the mountains. Catherine looked back, but no one was following them. They passed beneath towering cliffs and through a gallery of nature's abstract sculpture. While Jordan glanced from windshield to rear-view mirror and back again, Catherine put on her bra with a series of Houdini-like contortions that didn't require removing any clothing.

A couple kilometers from the campsite, they left the mountains behind them. For a good 160 degrees, the desert stretched into the distance for as far as they could see. The terrain was almost flat. A scattering of small green shrubs helped reveal subtle changes in its contour. Jordan gunned the Jeep over a shallow dune.

The Jeep stopped.

Jordan slowly accelerated, but the wheels spun. He put it in reverse, but it merely rocked and settled back. He shifted into drive and gunned the engine, but all that produced was a fountain of sand.

"Take the wheel," he said, and he jumped out.

He tried pushing while Catherine hit the gas, but it didn't work.

"Wait," he said, as if she was going somewhere, and he ran from the Jeep.

He ripped delicate branches from the ground and ran back, stumbling in the sand. He stuffed the branches under the tires for added traction.

"Now, very slowly, hit the gas," he directed.

The Jeep rose out of the dune and started moving. Jordan ran after it. Catherine was afraid to stop, afraid of sinking back into the sand. She slowed to the equivalent of a light jog and opened the passenger door. Jordan hopped in.

"Steady, now," he said, looking over his shoulder.

They were alone.

In less than an hour, they met up with a two-lane highway. It was dusted with drifting sand and devoid of traffic. They turned onto it and headed north.

She tried her phone, but she was out of range.

At a gas station along the highway, Jordan dialed Zev's number. He could barely hear Zev's voice over the noise of passing cars.

"We're fine, Zev. What about you? Did you have any trouble?"

"Some mild indigestion. It will pass."

"Did you find anything?"

"Yes, wonderful things. But nothing we were looking for."

"What did you do with it?"

"We could hardly declare it at customs, so we hid it. We'll be with you tonight. We're about to cross the border from Eilat to Akkaba."

"Change of plans, Zev. Meet us at En Bokek. We'll get there as soon as we can."

The strain was audible in Jordan's voice, and Galil could hardly miss it.

"What about the lost caravan?"

"It's out of our hands, Zev. But I think I've solved the mystery of the stone demon. Let's hope that's the one that counts."

"Where?"

"I'll explain when we see you. Catherine said we'll need all of your technology."

"Take care of her, Ben."

"And you beware of strangers."

Chapter 51

An Aegean Island

"I can't do it," Elazar said. "I won't help you."

Father Gregory looked at him with a combination of sympathy and stern moral clarity.

"Rabbi, you can, you must. I know it's difficult. It's difficult for me, too. But, for the sake of your people, if nothing else, how could you do otherwise?"

"For the sake of my people, I won't be a part of it."

They walked along the cliff, and the waves crashed beneath them.

The Greek Orthodox monk stopped and looked over the edge.

"Rabbi, I don't believe it's an accident that you and I face this test together. I believe it's the Lord's will."

"Father Gregory, when you and I speak of the Lord, I'm not sure we speak of the same one. Jesus is not my savior."

"Rabbi, I, too, have struggled with this. There's no avoiding the question. What would happen if our search undermined the Gospels? What would happen if Jesus never rose? Would the Church fall? Would people desert it? Would people abandon Christ's teachings? Would they despair of salvation? Would it be the death of Christianity?

"Could we ever atone for our righteousness, our crusades, for centuries of violence in the name of Christ? And what would it mean to eliminate faith, to replace it with religion based on fact and reason alone?

"I'll tell you what I concluded. I believe we must seek the light, and we must embrace the light, as God gives us to see the light.

"I believe we must take our lesson from the Old Testament, which showed time and again the power of God's anger when his Chosen People rejected his signs. I believe we must look to God at Mount Sinai. By then, He had brought plagues upon the Egyptians, He had parted the Red Sea, and He had freed the Israelites from slavery. In fire and thunder, He had delivered the Ten Commandments, commanding the Israelites not to worship idols. Yet still the Israelites refused to see. At the foot of Sinai, they melted their jewelry to make a golden calf, and bowed before it. And God made the Israelites pay for their blindness and disobedience by taking 3,000 lives.

"If God could part the waters, how difficult would it be for him to send his son among us? And how could any of us reject his gift?

"Now, Rabbi, I know what you think. You are thinking that if we *prove* the Resurrection, the Jewish faith and the Jewish state will be discredited. You are thinking that Jews will again be blamed for killing Christ, and that a new wave of violence could be unleashed against them. You are thinking that Judaism, already threatened by assimilation, intermarriage, and a loss of identity among its children, could crumble from within.

"You may even imagine that the Islamic world would gain in its struggle with Israel. You may fear that this proof would drive a wedge between the Jewish state and its Christian allies, including its patron and defender, America. But —"

"No, Father Gregory, you're mistaken. I don't think we'll prove the Resurrection, because I don't think it happened. I'm concerned that we might find something that makes it *seem* more plausible, with similar consequences. Just look at Josephus. Hundreds of pages into his history, he devotes three sentences to what he calls the arrival of the Messiah. He says that Jesus worked wonders and was crucified and rose from the dead."

The monk sympathized.

"We can agree, Rabbi, that, although Josephus wrote during the 1st Century, this passing mention must have been inserted later, by Christian editors. They were trying to correct an inexplicable omission—the absence of any reference to Jesus in the most authoritative history of his time."

"But Father Gregory—crude as it is, people believe the fabrication."

"And that is exactly why you must help, why you *will* help."

"Father Gregory, have you gone mad?"

"Rabbi Elazar, you must save Israel from itself. This is something you can do, but we can't do it for you. While we stand here arguing, the government of Israel is trying to grab the evidence, most likely to suppress or destroy it.

"History has nearly forgiven the Jews for killing Christ. But history would never forgive them for destroying *proof* of Christ.

"There's a saying in Washington, Rabbi. They say the cover-up can be worse than the crime. None of us can afford another cover-up."

Elazar looked at him with bewilderment.

"Another?"

"The Gospel of Matthew describes the original. It tells us that Pontius Pilate posted Roman soldiers at Jesus's tomb, mindful of Jesus's prediction that he would rise from the dead. Sure enough, the guards saw the risen Jesus. They reported this to the chief priests of Jerusalem—and we can only assume the group included Caiaphas. The priests conferred with the Jewish elders. Then, they bribed the guards. They paid the guards to say that Christ's disciples stole the body during the night, while the guards slept at their posts."

"I know the story, Father Gregory. In return for the bribe, the guards promised to dispute any word of the Resurrection, to make sure the Jews didn't suffer any repercussions. Of course, the Jews have suffered ever since."

"Do we need you to find the relic, Rabbi? Probably not. If we can't find it ourselves, it seems increasingly likely that your friend Professor Cavanaugh will lead us to it.

"But, as I said before, we must, all of us, consider the messenger. It's not just that an Orthodox rabbi and ardent Zionist—one with undisputed archaeological expertise—would give the message greater credibility. It's that, by being the one to unveil this evidence, you could redeem the Jewish people in the eyes of the world, and you could inoculate Israel against the potential backlash.

"We, too, worry about the consequences. We wish the Jews no ill. We want to give you this opportunity, Rabbi. We want you to take it."

The rabbi's head was spinning. He looked out to sea and searched for a flaw in the monk's logic.

Father Gregory left him at the edge of the cliff and trudged up the hill to the monastery of Saint Constantine. He was impatient but confident. He believed Elazar would accept his reasoning. To do otherwise was unthinkable.

Chapter 52

The Dead Sea

The lights of En Bokek twinkled in the distance, but the distance was hard to gauge. The blackness of night hung heavily over the Dead Sea, isolating and disorienting. In the dark, the land, sea and sky blurred indistinguishably. Overhead, there were neither clouds nor stars, only an impenetrable haze.

They were driving south, with the water somewhere on their left and a looming presence on their right. A wall of cliffs and mountains stretched from Qumran, at the northern tip of the Dead Sea, past En Gedi and Masada toward the remote enclave where Jordan had arranged to meet Galil.

Ahead, there were neither headlights nor taillights, just the ambivalent highway, which made intermittent inroads toward the sea and then veered away. In time, Jordan recognized that the road was consistent. It was the shoreline that zigged and zagged.

They had descended to the lowest spot on earth, 1,306 feet below sea level, and Jordan realized it was no coincidence that the region tapped so deeply into the myth-shrouded past. The land was so hard and inhospitable that it remained almost undisturbed. On the flat-topped mountain Masada, it took little imagination to breathe life into the ruined fortress where a band of Jewish rebels held out against the Roman army. And the fortress wasn't nearly as haunting as the barren ground below. At the foot of the mountain, the raised outlines of the Roman encampments—square borders of piled earth and stone—remained neatly in place, as if the army had only recently moved on.

In En Gedi, there was a cave where the Bible said David hid from Saul. Farther south, in another cave, followers of the legendary Jewish rebel Simon Bar Kochba had taken refuge from the Romans in the 2nd Century. David left no trace, but Bar Kochba's followers left a bundle of letters, a time capsule for 20th Century archaeologists, proving the hero was real. And, in the caves of Qumran, overlooking the great salt sea, ancient writings lay hidden and preserved, until they resurfaced in the 20th Century and came to be known as the Dead Sea Scrolls.

Jordan believed there was more, much more.

In the Valley of Asher, entombed beneath the stone demon, 120 talents of silver coins, 100 talents of gold coins, and 26 offering vessels.

The sixteenth cache. If they were lucky, it contained the Caiaphas Chronicle and the end of their search, the final word on Jesus.

The Valley of Asher cut through the Judean Desert beyond En Bokek, inland from the Dead Sea's southern extremity. Jordan planned to be there at dawn.

They pulled off the narrow highway, into En Bokek.

"See if you can get Zev on the phone," Jordan said.

Catherine dialed, and Zev gave her directions.

"Be right there," she said, and she hung up.

They passed a high-rise hotel, which stood against a dark, towering wall of rock. En Bokek was a modern intrusion upon the hostile landscape, where even the water sustained no life. It was a small colony of hotels and motels beside what passed for a Dead Sea beach.

No one came here to swim. They came for the novelty of floating in the salt water, and for the reputed curative powers of the sun, considered a remedy for skin disease. Some used it as a stopping point on a visit to Masada.

Jordan imagined ancient travelers arriving at the shores of the Dead Sea, believing they had found life-giving water, a southern Galilee—only to discover the undrinkable truth.

Catherine pointed.

"Up there, on the right," she said.

Jordan turned into a small parking lot and parked beside a low, round building. They sensed instantly that En Bokek was becoming a ghost town. Just as it had given the Jordanian desert a reprieve, the region's resurgent violence kept the tourists away.

They locked the doors of their borrowed vehicle and walked inside.

Galil saw them before they saw him. He greeted them with crushing hugs and showed them to a table in the casual eatery.

They quickly caught up. Galil told them how he had hidden jugs filled with dates and walnuts, and about the Humvee they had seen approaching the mosaic.

"Curious tourists, that was all," he said. "So curious we couldn't get them to leave."

"Did you find out who they were?" Jordan asked.

"On holiday from Italy. Three middle-aged men. Very serious."

"How did you lose them?"

"I think it was my lecture about soil gradations," Galil said with a wink. "Either that, or the laxatives one of the kids put in the hummos we gave them."

"Zev!" Catherine scolded.

"What can I say?" he shrugged. "They needed loosening."

Jordan recounted their experience in the Jordanian desert—most of it. He was bitter and angry and deeply worried, and he was too exhausted to conceal it.

"Whatever was there, it was within our grasp," he said. "And they stole it, right out from under us. Who knows? That could be the end of it."

Galil debriefed them in a calm, objective manner, probing for every conceivable detail on the usurpers.

"Who do you think they were?" he asked.

"I don't know," Jordan said darkly. "Maybe tourists from Italy."

Catherine had another theory.

"I'll put my money on Meyer Elazar's allies in the government."

"Why?" Galil asked.

"I don't think they would allow the treasures of the Silver Scroll to fall into hostile hands. I don't think they would take any chances with a potentially explosive revelation. At the very least, they would want to be the first to know. I think that's why Meyer's first impulse was to conceal the scroll's existence."

Galil pondered the possibilities. His expression turned ominous.

"As you said on the phone, Ben, let's hope the next cache is the one that counts. Tell me about the stone demon."

"The rock carvings made me think of it," Jordan said. "I was thinking about the people who carved them, thousands of years ago. I was wondering what they looked like, and how they saw their world. I thought of prehistoric paintings on a cave wall in France, and the Neanderthals who painted them. I thought of fossils I had seen in museums. You know, I've spent a lot of time in museums.

"Have you ever wondered what happened before modern science, when humans uncovered the remains of extinct creatures? Dinosaurs, for example. How did our ancestors interpret these monsters? What myths did they create to explain them?

"Lying awake in the desert, I thought of one fossil in particular, a skull in the Israel Museum. Almost human, but inhuman. Frightening, like a gargoyle. You might even call it *demonic*.

"Naturally, when we read the text of the Silver Scroll, we thought of the stone demon as a statue or sculpture, an idol or totem. And that didn't get us anywhere, because as far as we know there's no such thing standing in the open today in the Valley of Asher.

"But what if the stone demon was a prehistoric man, entombed in an undiscovered cave, where the authors of the Silver Scroll saw him peeking out of his grave? What if the stone demon is a fossil?"

"Hmmm," Galil said, thinking.

"Suppose you're right," Catherine said. "How would we find it? How are we any closer?"

"It's actually a very useful theory," Galil said, brightening. "Begin with the assumption that there's an undiscovered cave. That leaves two scenarios. If the entire cave has caved in, we might identify it from the topography, but we would have a difficult time excavating. If, on the other hand, only the *entrance* has collapsed, sealing the interior space, we could not only detect its presence—we could clear an opening and get inside."

"How would you do it?" Jordan asked.

"Have a little faith. We have the technology."

"What about your crew?"

"Three of them are camping in the desert, near the Valley of Asher, awaiting your arrival. The others have gone for more equipment."

"And you?"

"I arranged some hotel rooms here."

"Good. Then we'll start in the morning?"

"Before the sun. Meet me in the lobby at 4 a.m."

Chapter 53

In bed, with the alarm set, Jordan wished he could stop time as easily as stopping the clock. He wished he could cling to the night, and hide from the answers the day might bring. He wished he could cling to Catherine.

She slid her hand under the covers and slowly moved it across his skin. Her touch was soft, teasing, hesitant. She felt his body respond. He held his breath, and she held him in her grip.

She brushed her lips against his ear.

"There's so much I'd like to know about you," she whispered. "Tell me something I don't know, something personal."

"You know me," Jordan said.

She squeezed.

"Since you put it that way," Jordan groaned. He started to speak, and stopped. "I was raised on a kibbutz, an orphan."

"So you said."

"After serving in the army, I spent some time as a commando."

She squeezed harder.

"You only get credit if it's personal, Ben."

He tried to catch his breath, but the emotional wounds reopened, more painful than before. He lay there, wavering, wrestling with his fears.

He started up again, haltingly.

"My father and mother were killed when I was an infant. He was a shadow and she was a lullaby. Half a lullaby, really. No words, just a melody."

"Go on," Catherine said, with an encouraging caress.

"All anyone would tell me was that they were patriots. They gave their lives for their people.

"One of the women of the kibbutz, Ellie Bromberg, gave me a picture. She made me swear I'd never show it to anyone. I would take it out when I was lonely. My father was tall and strong. My mother was beautiful. They were both so young. I could tell they were very brave. But I wasn't allowed to know the details."

Catherine put her hand on his chest.

"I wanted to fulfill their legacy, to live a life worthy of their sacrifice. To make them proud. By their example, they inspired me to push myself in everything I did.

"As I told you, I had a friend, Daniel, he was like a big brother to me. An American who made *aliyah*, who came to fight for us. Daniel died when I was eight, on a mission. No one would tell me those details, either.

"One day, years later, when I was in the army, I was on patrol in the West Bank. It was in Ramallah, during the first *intifada*. It was like a war zone. We entered a house, a Palestinian house, looking for weapons. And while we searched, this young mother was rocking her baby, trying to comfort him.

"She was singing a lullaby. *My* lullaby. The melody was my mother's. But the words were Arabic. *Arabic*. And I was hearing them for the first time.

"I remember going back to the kibbutz, and confronting Ellie Bromberg. She wouldn't answer my questions. There was a photo album on her bookshelf, and I grabbed it. She tried to take it away from me. I remember flipping the pages of the album, almost tearing them. I remember finding snapshots of my parents in America, and formal pictures of them at family events. I remember seeing them age before my eyes. I remember seeing pictures of them with their grown children and grandchildren.

"They weren't my relatives. They were *Ellie's*. And she wept with grief. She wept for me. Still, she refused to tell me the truth.

"Later, I tracked down one of Daniel's friends, a guy who served with him in the commandos. Like Daniel's, his uniform bore the black dagger insignia, a curved dagger, which I later learned was the mark of the Sicarii—assassins. This guy was with Daniel when he died, and on another mission more than seven years before that. The earlier mission was still some sort of state secret, but the broad outlines had leaked. He told me what happened.

"Daniel's unit was sent on a raid deep inside Lebanon. Their mission was to hunt down and kill one of the terrorists who masterminded the attack on the Israeli athletes at the Munich Olympics. And they had excellent intelligence.

"They caught him at home in bed in the middle of the night, and when he reached for a weapon, they killed him in his bed. Shot him to pieces. Silently.

"Unintentionally, maybe unavoidably, they also killed his wife, who was sleeping next to him.

"Then they heard a cry, a baby's cry. They found the infant in a crib, bleeding. He must have been hit by a ricocheting bullet. They administered first aid, but they were afraid he would die if they left him. They could hardly summon help. So they decided to take the child with them.

"Daniel and the other commandos took me back to Israel. Back to the kibbutz, where I was raised as an Israeli and a Jew.

"To answer your question, I was born a Muslim. The son of terrorists, who killed Israelis and died for the Palestinian cause."

Catherine gasped.

In the darkness of the hotel room, he felt his body slackening.

In the darkness of the hotel room, he was 17 again. He was infatuated with an 18-year-old girl who was so hot she sizzled in her army uniform, and they were planning a camping trip together. Her parents were among the elders of the kibbutz, and for some mysterious reason, they disapproved of him—intensely. The girl canceled the camping trip, and then she canceled their relationship.

In the darkness of the hotel room, he was 34 again, and in love with a woman he wanted to marry. She was brilliant and beautiful, the most talented writer he knew. They had everything in common, and everything to live for. But when he told Leah the truth about his parents, Leah refused to marry him.

In the darkness of the hotel room, fate had united him with Catherine Cavanaugh, who could make him forget the rest, and they were lying naked together.

He looked up, toward the stars, but the ceiling blocked his view.

He stared at the blankness of the ceiling.

Like his body, his emotions went slack. He was alone. Again.

"I'm sorry," Catherine said, and she kissed his cheek, as softly as a whisper.

He felt a hot tear drip down the side of his face. He didn't think he had it in him. Then he realized the tear was hers.

She kissed him again, kissing away her tear. Then she kissed his lips. She pressed her body against his, and in the darkness of the hotel room, the passion returned.

Chapter 54

Her head was resting on his shoulder, and he was finally drifting off to sleep.

"Are you awake?" she asked.

Jordan wrapped his arms around her and squeezed.

"What was it like as a child, Ben, being an orphan? How did you feel? I mean, how did you deal with it?"

Jordan sighed.

"It was a long time ago."

She brushed her lips against his ear again and whispered, "Tell me."

He sighed again, with eyes closed.

"I tried not to think about it. I guess I felt like an outsider. Sometimes, I felt like an outcast. At Passover, a time for families to gather and open their homes to strangers, I felt *angry*."

"Because you were alone?"

"Not just that. We studied the Passover story in school. I could relate to the part about Moses, being set adrift in a basket, raised in Pharaoh's palace. But I could also relate to the Egyptian children. I was angry about the needless killing of the children. I don't know why, maybe it was instinct or intuition, a sense of not belonging. Sometimes it seemed that I was the only person on the kibbutz who thought that way."

"That must have been hard."

"It made me stronger. It made me question things."

"Your religion?"

Jordan lifted his head.

"My religion? Why do you think of it as *my* religion?"

In the darkness, between the cool white sheets, he felt her flinch.

Chapter 55

An Aegean Island

Meyer Elazar sat in the midnight blackness of the chapel, staring at the cross. It reminded him of a sword.

In hoc signo vinces.

For centuries, his people had been violently persecuted. With the loss of Jerusalem, they had been scattered, left to the mercies of hostile hosts and neighbors. Time and again, the Jews had transcended persecution to find a comfortable place in the larger society. Time and again, their illusions had been shattered. They had been herded into ghettoes, and then they had been herded to the slaughter.

And yet they had survived as a people.

Now they had a state of their own. And, in a cruel irony of history, most of Israel's Jews had abandoned their religion in favor of secularism.

In America, land of freedom, the situation was even more perilous, the rabbi reflected ruefully. Like other minorities, Jews had risen above discrimination so successfully that they were in danger of disappearing into the larger culture.

Once, for a brief shining moment, the modern state of Israel had been regarded as an underdog, heroically battling for its survival, rallying the world's Jews to its corner. Now, in its deadly struggle with the Palestinians, Israel was threatened with a double-edged sword. It could fall victim to its weakness. Or it could fall victim to its strength. Even as Israel's enemies targeted innocent civilians, its enemies were painting Israel as the powerful aggressor. If the world's Jews accepted this view—if they saw Israel as perpetrator instead of victim—their increasingly tenuous identity as a people could be at risk.

And therein lay the paradox.

For centuries, the persecution of the Jews had been a key to their survival. It had reinforced their identity and kept them separate. It had prevented the dissolution of their traditions, and it had fired their will to survive.

Elazar wondered: Was persecution an essential part of the Jewish experience? Or was it the path to Judaism's destruction?

He was at a moral crossroads, torn by indecision. Whatever he did, he feared the quest for the Caiaphas Chronicle could unleash new waves of virulent anti-Semitism. If he helped bring the relic to light, its contents could confirm history's most damaging indictment of the Jews—and undermine the Jewish religion. Yet, if he stood by passively, Israel could play into its enemies' hands, with consequences even more devastating.

There was a third possibility, if he was willing to gamble. Could the relic undercut Christianity?

Not if Israel was the messenger.

Elazar was tired and distraught. He felt himself sinking deeper into confusion and despair. His reasoning and rationalizing were leading him in circles.

He thought of Father Gregory's words.

"I believe we must seek the light, and we must embrace the light, as God gives us to see the light."

There was something else the monk had said, equally compelling, and chilling in its truth.

"History has nearly forgiven the Jews for killing Christ. But history would never *forgive them for destroying* proof *of Christ."*

A ray of clarity.

Elazar had to acknowledge his respect for Father Gregory. The man was dedicated to the search for God. Though the monk was clearly hoping for a different outcome—what he would call a Christian outcome—he approached the search with wisdom and charity.

"We, too, worry about the consequences. We wish the Jews no ill. We want to give you this opportunity, Rabbi. We want you to take it."

Elazar sensed that he was no longer alone.

"Rabbi, I didn't expect to find you here."

Elazar looked up at the monk.

"I needed to think."

Father Gregory nodded.

"I went first to your room, looking for you. There are new developments."

The monk looked grim.

"Your friend Professor Cavanaugh is on her way to the Valley of Asher. And the Israelis plan to follow her."

"What does that mean?"

"If she's as smart as you say, it means she may find the Caiaphas Chronicle. And, if she finds it, the Israelis will take it. They will hide it, or they will destroy it. And they will have no choice but to eliminate anyone who knows of it."

"Catherine."

"Yes. I'm sorry."

"You have to save her."

"How can I? All we can do is watch, and pray."

"You can rescue her."

"Rabbi, you overestimate our capabilities."

"Father, you insult my intelligence. We both know you can do it. But you won't."

"Rabbi, you have my sympathy. But what would you have us do? Kidnap her?"

"You kidnapped me."

"You came of your own free will. Do you think she would do the same? Or would she see us as the enemy? Think about it. We show up in the Judean Desert, urge her to come with us, and to place not only her life but also the relic in our care. Put yourself in her place. How would you react?"

Elazar considered the difficulty.

"Father, if I were in her place, I would listen to someone I knew and trusted. I would listen to a friend."

"Rabbi, I'm not her friend."

"No. But I am."

"What are you suggesting?"

"Let me go. Let me lead the rescue."

The monk scoffed.

"It's too dangerous. And it wouldn't work."

"It might."

"I admire you for volunteering, but no."

"How else can you prevent the relic from falling into Israeli hands?"

The monk had no answer to that. As Elazar watched, he seemed to struggle with the imminence and finality of defeat. He seemed to waver.

"We may be too late," the monk said.

"Father, I *beg* you."

The monk bowed his head slightly and withdrew. As he exited the chapel, he stopped and turned to Elazar.

"You're a brave man, Meyer."

Father Gregory walked down a darkened corridor and opened the heavy wooden door to his monastic cell. Moonlight was streaming in through a narrow window.

God willing, the plan might work, he thought, with rising optimism.

The monk removed a small rug from under his cot. He unrolled it on the cold stone floor. He took off his crucifix and his hooded cassock. He knelt on the rug and bowed, until his forehead nearly touched the floor.

In humble submission, he prayed in Arabic.

He prayed to Allah.

Chapter 56

The Judean Desert

They drove south from En Bokek and then headed west, ascending from the salt sea into the hills of the Judean Desert. They left their cars along a lightly traveled highway.

They hiked in silence.

In the predawn light, Catherine felt tense and anxious. In darkness, she could be alone with her dreams. She could hide from the world, like a child under the covers. She could be alone with Benjamin. But the protective cover of night was slipping away.

Mere hours before, she felt connected to Jordan more powerfully than ever. Now, as the bleak beauty of the desert emerged from the dark, she felt a doubt awakening, like a lizard crawling out of a crevice.

She had known Benjamin as an Israeli and a Jew. Now she didn't know how to think of him. Was he Israeli, or Arab? Muslim, or Jew? Did it matter?

She was ashamed of her thoughts. And yet . . . .

And yet, the question went to the heart of their mission. Consciously or subconsciously, did he harbor a hidden agenda? Would he follow the truth wherever it led, with a journalist's unswerving neutrality? Or would he take sides?

And, if he took sides, which side would he take?

Given the chance, would he seek redemption for the murder his father committed against Israel? Did that explain his reluctance to tell the story of Caiaphas's guilty conscience, his sensitivity about a potential anti-Semitic backlash?

Or would he seek vengeance on Israel for killing his parents—along with countless other Palestinians? Would he bend the facts, if necessary, to paint Rabbi Elazar and the Israeli government as villains, vindicating the story he had already written along those very lines?

She chastised herself for her doubts. After all, he was still Benjamin.

Or was he?

She realized there was something else she didn't know. She didn't know his true name.

She wondered if he knew it himself.

The hills still blocked the sun, but each of them could feel the heat rising with the light. The land was wrinkled with age, and they let the wrinkles be their guide. It took them 30 minutes, most of it downhill, to reach their destination.

The Valley of Asher was a deep, narrow gorge, carved by the rage of countless flash floods. A dry riverbed snaked through the valley floor. A few hardy bushes marked the river's path, but otherwise the land was lifeless and bare, ranging in color from off-white to brown. The sun had baked it to a consistency between chalk and clay.

Three of Galil's assistants had started without them.

Amnon carried a backpack loaded with an unusual piece of equipment. He had a squat, powerful stance, which projected confidence bordering on cockiness. In his right hand, he held a dish-shaped receiver, which was wired to the machine on his back. In his left hand, he held another device, which looked like the end of a boom microphone.

Yossi was standing beside Amnon, monitoring a small display screen wired to the machine. He peered through round, wire-rim glasses, which contrasted with his narrow boyish face and gave him a scholarly look. His backpack was bulging with mountaineering equipment and a pair of folded shovels. He was in the army, and he wore his rifle slung over his shoulder.

Hannah, lithe and tan, was videotaping. She carried a heavy pack, too, but she seemed not to notice its burden. She was wearing a photojournalist's vest. She panned from Amnon and Yossi to an indentation high on the canyon wall to their left, where Amnon's receiver was pointed.

"What are they doing?" Jordan asked.

"Listening," Galil said.

"What for?"

"Emptiness."

The machine emitted a loud *ping*, and the sound echoed through the valley.

Yossi studied the display and shook his head.

"The sonar can find the hollow places?" Jordan asked.

"It's supposed to."

Galil greeted the students.

"Where are the others?" Hannah asked.

"They'll get here as soon as they can. We won't wait for them."

Yossi spoke up.

"If we find anything big, how will we move it?"

"As Abraham told Isaac on the way to the mountaintop, 'Trust me,'" Galil said.

"Behold the fire and the wood, but where is the lamb for a burnt offering?" Yossi recited. *"Don't worry, my son, God will provide."*

"Give me a set-up, Dr. Galil," Hannah said.

Galil spoke into the camera as he had done on the coast of the Red Sea, explaining the irregular nature of their search and taking responsibility for their actions.

They followed Amnon and Yossi deeper into the valley, around a bend. The walls rose steeply on either side until they became vertical or nearly so. The archaeologists scanned the cliffs for anomalies where the opening of a cave might have caved in.

It was a slow, stop-and-go process.

The sun rose overhead, and the temperature in the valley climbed above 110 degrees. They were perspiring heavily, but their perspiration evaporated almost instantly. By late morning, they had covered barely half a mile.

The ping of the sonar echoed in the valley, and as quickly as the echoes faded, Yossi pointed excitedly to the monitor.

"Again," Galil said.

They repeated the procedure.

Yossi looked up from the monitor, grinning.

"Confirmed," he said.

Overhead, to their left, at the next bend, the cliff formed a promontory that jutted into the valley. The top of the promontory was shaped roughly like a dome. There was a large dimple in the side of the dome where the soil and rock had sunken inward. About 10 feet below, on the cliff face, there was a shadowy hollow, taller than a man. It looked like the opening to a cave.

Jordan walked a few paces, looking at it from another angle. It was less than a yard deep. If it was once a cave, nature had sealed it.

"An earthquake might have done it, or the accumulated weight of time," Galil said, as if reading his thoughts.

"Is this it?" Catherine asked.

"Hard to say. It's certainly a candidate."

"What now?"

"We look for a less formidable candidate."

Jordan was relieved. The cave—if that's what it was—was as high as the top of a ten-story building. He was hoping for something closer to the ground.

Amnon and Yossi resumed the search. The others followed them deeper into the valley.

Catherine watched Jordan studying the landscape. She wondered what he was thinking. He noticed her watching him. He smiled, and she smiled back, but her expression struck him as forced. She seemed distant. He wondered if it was a delayed reaction to his secret. He wondered if she held it against him. He felt his past repeating itself, and his heart sank.

"Over here," Yossi said, consulting the monitor.

"Again," Galil instructed.

A ping echoed through the valley, and Yossi frowned.

"One more time."

Another ping, and Yossi shook his head.

They marched on. They passed the opening to a narrower ravine to their left. It was more like a crack in the earth than a canyon; in places, a person standing with arms outstretched could touch both sides at once.

"What about that?" Catherine asked.

"Tempting. But it's not the Valley of Asher," Galil said. "It's called the Wadi Abiram."

Within the hour, they reached the end of the valley. It blended into the slope of an imposing mountain. The walls of the canyon ended in twin ridges.

The heat was draining. Galil reminded everyone to drink lots of water.

They continued part-way up the slope to reconnoiter.

The domed promontory, formidable though it was, appeared to be their only candidate.

"What now?" Catherine asked.

Galil examined the topography, gauging whether it would be easier to approach their objective from above. The promontory connected to a small plateau that they could use as a staging area above the gorge. They could even camp there if necessary. But the Wadi Abiram intersected the Valley of Asher, cutting off the plateau from the mountain approach.

"Unfortunately, we can't reach the promontory from here," Galil said, pointing. "The Wadi Abiram would be too difficult to cross."

It was as if the surface of the earth had split open. The width of the Wadi Abiram varied, and it seemed to widen near the top.

Galil took out a phone and tried to reach the missing half of his team, but the phone didn't work, and he snapped it shut.

"That leaves two choices," he said. "We can return another day with equipment to bridge the smaller ravine. Or we can proceed from below."

Jordan pondered the dilemma. His thoughts turned to the day before, and the prize that had probably been stolen out from under them. He looked at Galil, and without speaking, they reached an understanding.

"Does anyone want to wait?" Galil asked, looking each of them in the eye.

They shook their heads.

"Then follow," Galil said.

He set a brisk pace as they hiked back through the valley toward the foot of the promontory. The loose soil shifted beneath their feet, and

Catherine had to concentrate to avoid twisting an ankle. She was tired and overheated, and the hard part was still ahead of them.

They passed the intersecting ravine, and Galil stopped, reconsidering. He walked a short distance into the narrow, winding gorge, and looked up.

Watching Galil perform his inspection, Jordan realized a person could drown in the desert. In heavy rains, rare as those were, the tight gorge would quickly flood.

Galil rejoined the group, shaking his head.

When they reached the base of the promontory, they looked up, respectfully, measuring the challenge ahead. Catherine felt a heady mix of excitement and anxiety. The cliff made her sunrise hike with Jordan the day before look like a walk in the woods.

I must be insane.

"Don't worry," Galil said. "You can keep your feet on the ground."

Amnon and Yossi took off their packs and readied their mountaineering gear. Amnon clipped a two-way radio to the neck of his T-shirt.

Hannah looked back expectantly, toward the path they had followed into the valley.

"They should be here by now," she said.

"There's not much we can do about it," Galil said. "The roads are probably blocked."

"'The fewer of us, the greater share of glory,'" Amnon said. He grinned at Hannah. "Take good video."

Amnon started climbing. Hand over hand, with hammer and piton and nylon cord, he made his way up the canyon wall. He drove metal hooks deep into the rock to support the weight of those who would follow. He climbed with confidence and a competitive spirit, enjoying the sport. Hannah kept the camera trained on him.

Catherine watched nervously, vicariously confronting the terrifying height.

Amnon stopped at the opening that looked like a blocked cave. He stepped onto the ledge that formed its doorstep.

"What do you see?" Galil asked into his radio.

With his hammer, Amnon probed the wall in the back of the recess. A cluster of rocks the size of fists broke loose and caromed over the edge.

"Watch out!" he shouted.

Jordan pulled Catherine out of the way and covered her, all in an instant. The others scattered, dodging the falling rocks, which crashed to the valley floor.

They crouched defensively and closed their eyes, waiting for more rocks to rain down. When none came, they looked up tentatively and dusted themselves off.

"Are you okay?" Amnon shouted.

"Careful," Galil replied by radio. "Just tell me what you see."

"A lot of loose rocks. We might be able to clear it."

"Good work. Now see what's on top," Galil said.

Amnon resumed climbing. He reached the top and hoisted himself onto the domed promontory. He looked at the spot where the side of the dome had sunk in. He stood, fearless and exultant. From his narrow perch, he could move no more than a step or two to the left, right or forward without plunging to the valley floor.

"Come on," he said, not bothering with the radio.

"What do you recommend?" Galil asked.

"Let me and Yossi attack the side while you work on the top."

Galil looked at Yossi.

"Up you go," he said.

"After you," Yossi said. "You're going all the way."

Galil took a shovel from Yossi's pack and strapped it to his own. He put on a harness and clipped himself to one of the cords dangling from the cliff. The cord looped up, through a hook Amnon had driven into the top of the promontory, and back down again. Yossi and Jordan gripped the loose end to support Galil's weight.

Galil tested his end of the cord. He looked at Jordan and the women. "You wait here until we're ready for you." Then he spoke into the radio. "Here I come."

He handed the radio to Jordan and started climbing. He was hardly graceful, but he was more than competent. Jordan watched the big man's head move in time to a silent symphony.

Amnon's advance work speeded Galil on his way. The piton loosened ever so slightly under his weight, but the movement was imperceptible. Jordan and Yossi made sure there was hardly any slack in the line, so that if Galil slipped, he wouldn't fall far. In a short time, he was calling from Amnon's walkie-talkie.

"You're on, Yossi."

Yossi donned his pack and clipped himself in. He tested the cord and prepared to climb. He paused, remembering something.

"Hand me my rifle," he asked.

It was a habit deeply ingrained in Israeli soldiers.

Hannah slung it over his shoulder, but it hung awkwardly. She tied it to the side of his pack. He tugged at the rope. He looked at Jordan, who was holding the other end, and judged him strong enough to support his weight. Then he scaled the wall.

His feet dislodged sand and bits of rock. The others stepped back, easily avoiding the cascading debris. Jordan released some slack as he backpedaled, but he kept a firm grip.

Yossi joined Amnon on the ledge inside the shallow recess. They had a brief conversation with Galil above, and Yossi relayed instructions to Jordan by radio.

"Find some shade if you can. But stand clear while we dig."

Jordan and Catherine retreated to the far side of the gorge and sat in the dirt. Hannah found the best vantage point she could and zoomed in on the action above, adding her own narration.

"The climb is a severe test of our team," she said. "It's hard to see how people would have reached the ledge on the cliff wall 2,000 years ago, or why they would have tried. But other caves and other expeditions have proven that ancient people accomplished similar feats, so we aren't about to give up. With more time and better equipment, there might be an easier way. But we can't afford those luxuries."

Yossi and Amnon set to work with shovels and bare hands. The rocks they dislodged fell in an intermittent avalanche. When Yossi and Amnon were safely beneath the overhang of rock, out of his way, Galil began digging into the dimple and dumping spades of soil over the edge.

A worried look crossed Catherine's face. She took the radio from Jordan and called the boys.

"Yossi, look up. Is the roof stable? Is there any danger of further collapse?"

Yossi tapped the ceiling of the recess with the end of his shovel.

"I think it's okay," he radioed back.

They kept digging. Jordan and Catherine watched in awkward silence. The debris began to accumulate on the valley floor.

"May I ask you something?" she said.

"I hope I can answer."

"It may sound stupid, but . . . ."

"Go ahead."

"I'd like to know your name."

The question caught Jordan by surprise. He didn't know what to say. He fumbled for an answer, and the fumbling made him self-conscious.

"I suppose —"

"Yes?"

The radio crackled in Catherine's hand.

"Repeat that?" she said.

"Tell Hannah that Amnon's ready for his close-up," Yossi said.

She looked at Jordan.

"I'll tell her," he said.

Jordan got up and walked over to Hannah.

"They're ready for you," he said.

Galil lowered a harness, and Hannah began her ascent. She climbed all the way to the ledge inside the recess, where Amnon grabbed her and pulled her in.

Between the piled rocks and the ceiling of the recess, they had cleared a gap almost large enough for a person to squeeze through. They could tell there was an empty space on the other side of the rocks.

Hannah lifted her camera toward the opening and pointed it inside. There was an awful vibration, the sound of a landslide, and a cloud of dust. Then the space within lit up.

Galil had broken through from above, allowing daylight to penetrate.

"What's happening?" Catherine radioed.

"We've broken through," Yossi said. "It's definitely a cave."

A fresh avalanche of rocks fell from the ledge as Yossi and Amnon expanded the opening.

"Enough," Galil shouted from above. "We can get in through the top."

"I'll meet you inside," Amnon shouted back, and he climbed toward the opening he had made.

"What's happening now?" Catherine radioed.

"We're going in."

"Send down a harness. I'm coming up."

Jordan looked at her.

"You know how to do this?"

"They have a practice wall at a gym back in Michigan."

"A practice wall?"

"I've been on it a couple times."

"A couple times?"

She gave him a look of determination, trying to brush aside her own doubts as well as his.

"Ben, I can't miss this. I won't."

Jordan helped her put on the harness and double-checked the clip. She handed him the radio and tugged on the rope. Their eyes met.

"Jordan," he answered.

She held his gaze.

"Like the country? Or the river that runs between two countries?

"What do you think?"

She answered with her eyes, looking for him to say more.

"I'll see you up there," he said.

She looked away, disappointed. She started climbing.

She thought about the biblical Benjamin. His father, Israel, had given him that name. But his mother had called him something else. Before she died delivering him, she named him *Benoni,* "Son of My Sorrow."

Catherine kept her eyes focused straight ahead at the cliff, or up toward her goal. From above, Galil shouted encouragement. From below, Jordan gripped the nylon cord and watched her ascend. She was terrified, but she kept climbing. She cut her hands and scraped her limbs against the rock, and dust filled her nostrils. The intensity of her fear heightened the exhilaration.

Three-quarters of the way up, her lungs and muscles burning from the exertion, she found a solid foothold and paused to rest. Against her better judgment, she looked back over her shoulder and down at the dry riverbed seven stories below.

The world began to spin.

Her foothold broke away from the cliff, and she lost her grip. She felt herself falling away. She grabbed at the cliff, but all she touched was air. She watched the rock face rush past.

A sharp, powerful yank broke her fall. She dangled from the nylon cord and banged her side against the rock. The bruising impact brought clarity. She swung away from the cliff like a pendulum and back again. She used her feet to absorb the impact.

"Hang on!" Jordan shouted.

He sounded far away.

The cord held her suspended, and he held the cord. Drawing on some newfound reserve, she stabilized herself and straightened out, holding the vertigo in check. She marveled at the power of the human mind to suppress panic in a moment of crisis. She focused on what needed to be done.

She resumed her climb. She was defying gravity, but she was leaning on Jordan. He kept the rope taut as she walked up the cliff face.

Suddenly, the whole effort seemed absurd. Hannah's earlier narration rang truer than before.

How the hell could cave men do it? Why would they try?

She stopped at the ledge. Yossi pulled her in and put a protective arm around her. She arrived just in time to see Amnon crawling headfirst through the opening between the piled rocks and the cave ceiling. He was on his stomach, and his legs were disappearing into the cave.

"Wait a minute, I'm stuck," he said, backtracking.

Catherine didn't feel like waiting. Driven by curiosity, she defied her fear and continued to the top, where Galil said it would be easier to get inside. He hoisted her onto the promontory.

As soon as she was safe, the pent-up panic came surging to the surface. Shaking, she hugged Galil for dear life. Then she sank into a crouch, lowering her center of gravity and narrowing her field of vision, so she could no longer see down into the gorge. She closed her eyes and took deep breaths. Cautiously, she opened her eyes. The world was no longer spinning.

All of her climbing, all of her exertions, had brought her to ground level. Above the gorge, on the far side of the chasm, the desert plateau stretched toward a rising landscape of hills and ravines. On her side of the chasm, the promontory joined a plateau that extended a couple hundred yards and then fell off abruptly into an encircling canyon. Beyond that interruption, the plateau continued monotonously into the distance.

She took off the harness.

Galil grinned at her.

"It looks promising," he said.

His digging had cleared a chute that slid down into the cave. When the packed earth gave way, gravity had done most of the work.

Using a rock as a hammer, Galil pounded a mountaineering hook into the top of the promontory's dome, near the hook that supported their climb. He tied a length of nylon cord around the new hook and dropped the end of the cord into the chute. They could manage without it, but the cord would make it easier for them to climb down the chute and back up again.

With a sweep of the arm, Galil gallantly gestured for Catherine to lead the way.

"The honor should be yours," he said.

She was touched by the gesture, but she didn't move.

"No, Zev, the honor belongs to Ben."

"So it does," Galil said, nodding.

"But wait—who will help him?"

She realized that there was no one left below to hold the rope for Jordan. They looked over the edge.

Jordan had begun free climbing.

But barely 20 feet off the valley floor, he appeared stuck, unable to find a fresh handhold, and unable to safely retreat. He was frozen emotionally as well as physically. He had no experience with this kind of climbing, and the height had an effect on him that he didn't expect. He couldn't even call for help. He was afraid to shout. To talk on the radio, he would have to let go of the cliff.

Galil took the rope that snaked through the hook and wrapped it around his waist. He pulled in the slack, until Catherine told him to stop. He sank to his knees to brace himself more effectively against any sudden jolt. Catherine shouted down to Yossi, who relayed a message to Jordan by radio.

"Zev's got you," Yossi said. "You can use the rope."

Jordan placed his trust in the big man and the tiny piton that stood between them. He let go of the cliff. The nylon cord supported his weight.

"Up or down?" Yossi asked.

Jordan looked up, and then down.

"Up," he shouted.

Copying Catherine's technique, he climbed slowly and methodically, hand over hand.

Galil strained under the burden but held his own. His face flushed red, and he exhaled deep, controlled breaths like a weightlifter in the middle of the clean and jerk. He closed his eyes in concentration. When it seemed Galil's lungs would burst and the bulging muscles in his neck would snap under the strain, Jordan stepped onto the ledge, and the tension went out of the line.

"What are you guys waiting for?" Amnon shouted from inside the cave.

The others joined him one by one. Jordan passed up the honor of going second, opting instead to catch his breath. Catherine lowered herself down the chute, which declined at enough of an angle that she could control her descent. Jordan came last, through the side entrance, crawling over the pile of rocks near the ceiling of the cave.

The hollow interior of the promontory formed a natural foyer. Beneath the plateau, the cave widened into a spacious chamber littered with large rocks. It sounded like the inside of a seashell. From the opening of the chute, a shaft of light pierced the interior, but it penetrated no farther than the entryway. The team members produced a few flashlights from their packs, and they systematically probed the chamber—floor, walls, and ceiling.

They were weirdly separated from the world. But Jordan felt in his bones that others had long ago preceded them. He sensed their faded presence. He felt he was part of a human continuum older than humanity itself. He felt the same awe and reverence he had experienced in the desert beneath the petroglyphs.

Catherine felt the safety of a cocoon. She felt that nothing could touch them in such a remote hideout. Then she remembered that others were searching for the same thing, and she wondered if there was any place she would ever again be safe.

Jordan half expected to encounter the blackened remains of a prehistoric campfire, the smell of soot, and the shadows of former occupants dancing against the walls. But the cave showed no signs of prior habitation. It wasn't even clear how it could have been occupied. The random litter of rocks left no room to sit or sleep.

On the far side of the chamber, the cave split into two narrower tunnels.

Amnon advanced into the tunnel on the left. He moved slowly, looking carefully before each step. The tunnel bent and sloped downward. He disappeared from view.

"It's blocked," he said, and the words echoed.

The others followed the sound of his voice. A short distance down the tunnel, portions of the walls and ceiling had fallen in.

"More evidence of seismic activity," Galil said. "You wouldn't want to be here during an earthquake."

Amnon shined his light between the fallen rocks. Hannah pointed her camera. Through the gaps, they could see that the tunnel continued on the other side of the obstruction.

"There's no telling how far it goes," Galil said. "For all we know, there's a back door."

Jordan pictured an opening high in the narrow gorge that bisected the plateau. For someone who knew where to find it, it might make the cave more accessible.

They retreated into the main chamber, and Galil led them into the second tunnel. It began wide enough for them to walk three abreast and quickly narrowed as it turned a corner. Then it emptied into another chamber. The space was more or less round, and smaller than the first, about 25 feet across and 15 feet high at its center. Yossi scoured the ground with his flashlight. It was flat and relatively free of fallen rocks.

"What's this?" Yossi asked, pointing with his flashlight, focusing a circle of light on the floor.

The others huddled around him. Galil got down on hands and knees and inspected it at close range. He looked up at their expectant faces.

His smile said "eureka."

He held it up for all to see. It was a scrap of leather—a tiny, insignificant, nondescript scrap, no more than an inch long by a quarter of an inch wide. It bore no markings. But it spoke volumes.

Someone had been there.

"It's hard to know what it was," Galil said. "Maybe part of a sandal, from the webbing that would strap around a man's calf. Of course, that hardly matters."

He put it in a plastic bag for later analysis.

He stood up. "Don't overlook any detail."

They lined up side-by-side at the end of the chamber nearest to the entrance and slowly crossed the floor in unison, like police looking for clues at a crime scene. Nothing caught their attention. They fanned out to inspect the cave walls.

Yossi studied a section of the wall to the right of the entrance. Heaped against its base was a pile of rocks, some of them quite large.

"Take a look at this," he said.

"Hmmm," Galil said. "It looks like someone put them there. Maybe that's why the floor in this chamber is so clear of debris."

"Look, the cave wall seems to slope back behind the rocks, like the eaves of an attic," Catherine said.

Jordan pointed a beam of light above the pile of rocks, and the others gasped.

A fossilized skull was embedded in the wall.

It was lying sideways, and tilted at a slight angle, as if awakened from a light sleep. It was clearly hominid, but grotesquely inhuman. Its hollow eye sockets gaped beneath the ridge of a massive, unified brow. What remained of its massive upper and lower teeth gaped, too, as if frozen in mid-scream.

"The stone demon," Catherine whispered.

Hannah zoomed in on it, capturing the image.

Jordan illuminated a wider section. Other fossilized bones protruded from the rock — a hint of ribs, the top of a hip, the knob of a femur. The stone demon had been lying flat on its back.

Galil examined the surrounding rock.

"It looks like his grave was once a ledge, a shelf in the cave wall," he said. "You were right, Ben. *Mazel tov.* The question now is, what's behind these rocks. Is the cache still intact?"

Jordan touched one of the rocks that blocked their way.

"It isn't going to be easy to find out," he said.

"Au contraire," Galil said.

He set down his pack and removed a piece of equipment. It was a small video monitor attached to a long, skinny, rubberized tube. The end of the tube had a tiny fiber optic eye. Galil set it up on the cave floor and evaluated the barrier of piled rocks. He picked his spot and threaded the tube into the opening.

Jordan looked at the equipment with surprise.

"Did you develop this?" he asked.

"Actually, it's designed for probing colons. It's an endoscope."

"I never realized you had such a nose for these things," Catherine said.

"I can't take credit. However, if we're lucky, it may tell us if the cache contains the writings before we go to the trouble of moving all these rocks."

The students perked up.

"What writings?" Yossi asked.

Galil exchanged glances with Jordan and Catherine. Each of them nodded.

"You've earned the right to know," Galil said. "We're looking for some documents removed from the Temple in Jerusalem before it fell to the Romans. In particular, we're looking for the memoirs of a fellow named Caiaphas."

"*The* Caiaphas?" Hannah asked, lowering her camera.

"The very same."

"The one accused of condemning Jesus?"

"With any luck, we may have something to say about that."

"Holy shit," Amnon said.

Under Galil's control, the fiber optic eye twisted through cracks in the rockpile. It encountered a blockage, which forced him to retreat. He started again.

"Have you had one of these?" Galil asked Jordan.

"A colonoscopy?"

"You ought to. It's very important."

"I'll keep that in mind."

"Who knows what they'd find in there," Catherine said. "Maybe you could do the honors, Zev, as soon as we finish here."

"Look at that," Galil exclaimed.

The electronic eye was looking down on the space behind the rocks. There were two rows of bulging bags.

"Could be goatskin," Galil said.

He moved the focal point from bag to bag. One of them had a tear in its side. Its contents were spilling out.

The scope captured a blur of gold.

Galil brought it into sharper focus. They could almost read the writing engraved on the coins. Galil maneuvered for a closer look. An engraving of a gold pomegranate filled the screen.

"Beautiful," Galil said. "I've never seen one like that."

He pointed the probe farther back. The screen turned greenish.

"Copper, or bronze," Galil said, manipulating the tiny camera. "I'd say those are your offering vessels."

The probe explored what looked like an ornate frying pan. There seemed to be enough pots and pans to prepare a banquet.

"For the burnt offerings," Galil said. "The Temple would have had storehouses full of these."

"What about the writings?" Amnon asked.

"Patience."

The probe advanced deeper into the hiding place.

"Holy shit," Zev exclaimed.

The probe surveyed the lid of a ceramic jar. It was round, and unadorned. It reminded Jordan vaguely of the stylized roof of Jerusalem's Shrine of the Book. The roof of the museum was no random design. It had been modeled after the jars that held some of the Dead Sea Scrolls.

Galil panned to the right. There was a second jar. Its lid was cracked. A small chunk of clay was missing. Galil maneuvered the tiny camera toward the opening.

"Parchment," he whispered.

Chapter 57

The Valley of Asher

Rock by rock, they dismantled the barrier that separated them from the sixteenth cache.

Their backs ached, and their hands were scraped raw. The task demanded more than brute force. It took concentration to avoid slipping and crushing someone's foot. Dust rose from the cave floor, filling their eyes and lungs. They coughed as they worked.

They rested in shifts, except for Jordan, who refused to stop.

"Take a break, Ben," Amnon said.

"No, that's okay."

Jordan bent over in a heaving cough. His stood up, hacking.

"Listen to him, Ben. Get some air," Galil said.

Jordan wiped sweat and grime from his brow.

"Maybe you're right," he said. "Besides, there's something I want to see."

"What is it?" Catherine asked.

"Just a hunch. I think there's an easier way out—or in. Shout for me when you get close."

Jordan left the chamber and stepped into the relatively fresh air of the tunnel. It soothed his burning lungs. He walked back to the main chamber and used his flashlight to find the passage Amnon had led them down earlier. He retraced their footsteps, stepping over fallen rocks. He reached the wall of fallen rocks that blocked the way. He probed the darkness on the other side with his flashlight. He inhaled deeply, and exhaled with a cough.

He sensed a foul odor coming from the sealed passage. It was the smell of guano. Bat guano. If there were bats on the other side of the fallen rocks, and only on the other side, then that branch of the cave must have a separate opening. He wasn't sure why it mattered, but something told him it did. Out of curiosity, as much as anything else, he tested one of the rocks that blocked the way, and pushed it aside. He tried a second, and a third. The rocks tumbled to the ground beside him. In a few minutes, he had cleared an opening just barely wide enough to squeeze through.

"We're getting close," Yossi said, peering into the space beneath the stone demon.

"Wait a minute," Hannah said.

Yossi and Amnon lifted another stone and dropped it in the middle of the chamber, where it landed with a resounding thud.

"Quiet!" Hannah shushed them.

"What?" Amnon asked.

"Listen. What's that noise?"

"I don't hear anything."

"There it is again."

Catherine exited the chamber, and the others followed. She hurried down the tunnel to the main chamber, toward the light from the two openings they had created. When they reached the main chamber, the noise was unmistakable. The sound of the rotors grew louder. Then it grew weaker. Catherine tried to gauge the helicopter's location, but the echoes in the cave distorted any sense of direction. The rotors grew louder again.

"They're circling, or moving up and down the valley," Yossi said.

"Could it be the rest of your team?" Catherine asked.

"In a helicopter? Not likely," Amnon said.

"Does anyone else know we're here?" Hannah asked.

"Hell, until this afternoon, we didn't know where *here* was," Amnon said.

"They'll see our ropes," Galil said.

"And the packs we left on the valley floor," Yossi said.

"And the harness I left up top," Galil said.

Yossi fingered his rifle.

"I'm going to take a look," he said.

"No, stay here. I'll go," Galil said.

The rotors grew louder and louder. The helicopter was hovering overhead. Galil hoisted himself up the shaft that led to daylight. Yossi headed for the ledge. From the hole in the cliff wall, Yossi took up a sniper's perch, but he couldn't see the helicopter. The promontory blocked his view.

"Ben, are you there?" Yossi radioed.

"Right here," Jordan replied.

"Where?"

"I'm exploring the other branch of the cave. How's it going?"

"We have visitors."

"Who?"

"I'm not sure. They're arriving by helicopter."

"Be right there."

"I think you should stay where you are, in reserve," Yossi said. "We may need you."

"You're armed?"

"Safety's off."

"Keep an open line."

Inside the cave, Amnon turned to Catherine.

"It's not about the gold, is it?"

"No, I don't think it is."

Galil reached the top of the shaft but tried to stay hidden in the shadows. The helicopter was right on top of them. It was an industrial model, the kind an oil company might use to reach its rigs. The noise was deafening, and the rotors kicked up a sandstorm.

The helicopter reared toward the flat top of the plateau, a ready-made landing pad, and the pilot gently set it down. Two large men hopped out, one after the other, ducking under the blades, and they turned to help a third.

A barrel-chested man in his 70s stepped out of the copter, his thin gray hair blowing madly in the wind. He raised his hand to his forehead like a visor, shielding his eyes against the sun. He squinted, and the wrinkles around his eyes multiplied like cracks through the ice of a frozen pond.

Galil looked like he had seen a ghost. He stuck his head out for a closer look, and slowly lifted himself out of the shaft.

The pilot cut the motor, and the rotors beat the air with a deliberate *thwap thwap thwap* as they lost speed. The ghost stooped to avoid decapitation and ran toward Galil.

"Shalom, Zev," he said.

"Jesus Christ, Meyer."

"I'm glad you're here, Zev. Catherine was smart to seek your help."

"What the hell?"

"Take me to her, will you?"

The two men who escorted Elazar made a move to follow him, but the rabbi held up his hand to stop them, and they stood by the copter.

In the bowels of the cave, Jordan looked back the way he had come, and forward, toward the unknown. Overhead, the ceiling of the cave was moving, and so were sections of the walls.

They were covered with bats.

The stink was putrid, and he lifted his forearm to block his nose and mouth. He probed the floor ahead with his flashlight. It fell away into blackness. A wide pit blocked the path where the ground had collapsed.

He turned toward the entrance, and crouched beside the wall of fallen rocks he had partially cleared. Impulse told him to rejoin the group, but reason recognized the wisdom of Yossi's advice. He held the radio to his ear and listened.

Galil went first. Using the nylon cord to control his descent, he slid down the shaft, into the cave. He scanned a semicircle of anxious faces, and spotted Yossi in the corner, his rifled leveled.

"Easy, now," Galil said.

"What is it?" Catherine asked.

"Exactly," Galil said, with an expression of utter bafflement.

Hannah held the video camera at her side, but it was pointed up at Galil, taping.

A pair of legs poked out of the shaft. Galil grabbed them and eased them to the floor. The rest of the barrel-chested body followed.

Catherine stared into the face of Meyer Elazar.

"Congratulations, Catherine. I'm proud of you," he said, with outstretched arms.

"You—you're supposed to be . . . dead," Catherine stammered.

"Yes, that was the idea. But it didn't work out that way."

Over the radio, Jordan heard the familiar gravel voice, and his eyes widened with recognition. He frantically tried to process the data.

"Son of a *bitch*," Catherine exclaimed. "You goddamn son of a bitch!"

The ferocity of her outburst startled the others. Elazar was taken aback.

"I trusted you. I trusted you with the legend of Mordecai Mandel. And you — you betrayed me. You ridiculed my research, and then, when you put the pieces together, you kept me in the dark. Goddamn you, Meyer."

Over the radio, Jordan could feel her anger, and he could see her tears.

"I'm sorry, Catherine. You're right—I kept you in the dark. You could say I betrayed your trust. But I did it for your own good. I didn't want it to come to this. I didn't want to put you in danger."

"You didn't want me to *know*. You didn't want the world to know," Catherine said, scornfully. "What now? You plan to steal it from us?"

"You don't need to forgive me, Catherine. But you must listen to me. Your life depends upon it."

"What, you've come to threaten me?"

Galil put a calming hand on her shoulder.

"Easy, now. Let's hear him out," he said.

"Not me," Elazar said. "The government. The government of Israel."

"What about the government?" Galil asked.

"They tried to kill me, but I escaped. I'm not sure they even know I escaped. But now, they're after you. They're on their way here, right now. They know what you're looking for. They know all about the Caiaphas Chronicle. And they aren't about to let it see the light of day."

"Why should I believe you?" Catherine asked.

"For the love of God, Catherine. If you ever trusted me, if you ever counted me a friend, believe me now. Come with me. Please. I'm trying to save you."

The rabbi's impassioned plea made a strong impression on the others. Their faces filled with fear.

"Do you think you can hide from them?" Elazar asked. "Do you think they'll let you walk away?"

"I'm not leaving," Catherine said.

"I lost Mishka, I lost my daughter, I lost my colleagues at the Institute. I couldn't save any of them. But I can save you. Don't make me live with your blood, too."

There were tears in the rabbi's eyes.

Catherine was shocked. She had never seen him cry. She had never seen him display any depth of emotion—except anger toward the Arabs. She had always assumed that part of him died with a toddler in a terrorist raid.

"I'm not leaving without the writings," she declared.

Galil breathed a sigh of relief. It was progress.

The rabbi's eyebrow arched.

"Then it's here," he whispered.

She didn't answer.

"Still digging for a reason to believe, Catherine?"

"I know, Meyer. It's a dangerous reason to dig."

"Leave it, Catherine. Let go of it."

"No."

"There's no time."

"Then let's stop wasting it."

Chapter 58

Yossi and Amnon pulled aside yet another heavy rock, and the tomb beneath the stone demon lay exposed. The sixteenth cache occupied a shallow pit that had been dug in the cave floor under the overhanging rock.

Catherine ducked into the eave and stepped down.

She lifted the first of the ceramic jars from its hiding place. She felt the light rustle of the ancient texts shifting inside it. She handed it up to Amnon, who handed it to Galil.

She handed Amnon the second jar, the one with the fractured lid, and he peeked through the opening. It was packed with tightly rolled scrolls, like parchment batons.

Elazar was waiting topside, where Catherine had banished him. She felt a pang of guilt. She felt he should have been there to see the relics disinterred.

She bent down and reached for one of the goatskin bags. She grabbed it by the neck, where it was tied shut. She tried to lift it. The bottom of the bag fell apart, spilling its contents. Brilliant gold coins sluiced across the floor.

"Leave them," Galil said.

Catherine scooped up some of the coins and slipped them into her pockets as context for the find, to corroborate the details in the Silver Scroll.

"Let's get the hell out of here," Galil said.

She grabbed a scrap of goatskin for carbon dating. She clambered over the rocks and took Hannah's outstretched hand, which was slippery with sweat.

"Did you get that on tape?"

"Got it," Hannah said.

"Good, then let's go."

They left the endoscope on the floor of the cave, along with Galil's pack. They raced up the tunnel, into the main chamber. Yossi was standing guard.

"Where's Ben?" Catherine asked.

"Staying out of sight, just in case," Yossi said. With a nod of his head, he pointed toward the other branch of the cave.

"Tell him it's time to go," Galil said, and he steered Catherine toward the chute.

She grabbed the dangling cord.

"Move," he said, pushing her butt from below as she climbed up the chute.

"Wait," Catherine said, stopping. "How will we raise the jars?"

"Keep going," Galil said. "When I tell you, gently reel in the cord."

She disappeared up the chute.

"Ben, are you there?" Yossi radioed.

Galil turned to Amnon.

"Give me your pants."

"Huh?"

"Off with them," Galil insisted. "I'd use my own, but my legs are too big."

Amnon didn't understand, but given Galil's tone, he did what he was told.

Hannah gave Amnon his long-awaited close-up and whistled mischievously. Amnon blew the camera a kiss.

Galil tied the ankles of the pants in knots. He slipped one jar into each leg, until it nestled snugly against the knot. The jars widened at the top, and at their widest point they were almost as wide as the legs, so it was a reasonably secure fit. Galil passed the end of the cord under the crotch of Amnon's pants and looped it back up. He tied it in a slipknot and cinched it tight.

"Raise it now, slowly," Galil shouted.

Atop the promontory, kneeling beside the opening, Catherine pulled up the cord hand over hand. The jars bumped against the side of the chute. She winced, but they didn't break. She reeled in the pants. She untied the cord and draped the pants around her neck, one leg over each shoulder, to free her hands. She dropped the cord down the chute.

"Next," she shouted.

Galil shoved Hannah up the shaft. The camera dangled from her neck, banging lightly against the rock. Hannah lifted her head into the sunlight. Catherine grabbed one arm and Elazar grabbed the other, and they hoisted her onto the promontory.

"Go," Galil told Amnon.

"You go."

Galil started climbing.

"Ben, are you there?" Yossi radioed again, from a different position in the cave.

Galil emerged from the chute, assisted by the others. The pilot started the engine, and the rotors whirled into action. Elazar's escorts rushed toward them, gesturing urgently toward the open desert.

A pair of jeeps was moving toward them across the plateau.

"Get in the copter," Elazar shouted at Catherine. He put an arm around her waist and swept her several yards toward the aircraft.

Catherine stopped and struggled.

"Not without Ben," she shouted over the roar of the engine.

"There's no time," Elazar said, dragging her.

Hannah zoomed in on the jeeps. They belonged to the Israeli army.

Catherine draped the pants over Elazar's neck and broke free of his grip. She sprinted toward the chute. The wind from the helicopter blades blasted them with sand.

Elazar signaled to his escorts. They grabbed Catherine's upper arms and lifted her backward toward the helo.

"I'll get Ben," Galil shouted.

The jeeps had stopped on the far side of the narrow gorge known as the Wadi Abiram, which formed a protective moat, and a dozen Israeli soldiers jumped out.

Hannah looked at them through the lens. They were raising their rifles.

Galil took a step toward the chute and fell to his knees. The soldiers had opened fire.

Galil clutched his chest and looked toward the helicopter, where Elazar's men where lifting Catherine onboard. She looked back at him.

"Zeeevvv!" she shouted. The roar of the rotors drowned out her voice.

With a supreme effort, Galil raised an arm and waved for her to go. Their eyes met for an instant, and Galil's head exploded in a puff of pink.

"Noooo!" Catherine screamed.

Galil's dead body tumbled and dropped into the chute.

Elazar's escorts manhandled Catherine into the helicopter, and the rabbi followed.

Hannah's face was spattered with Galil's blood and small bits of quivering tissue. She was mentally and emotionally shattered. But somehow, she grabbed the mountaineering line that dangled over the cliff. She backed toward the cliff and looked over the edge.

There were men on the ground below, a hundred yards up the valley, and they were moving rapidly toward the base of the promontory. She looked through the camera. Through the spatter on the lens, she could see they were soldiers.

Bullets whizzed past her from the plateau, and more ricocheted off the promontory from the soldiers below, setting off tiny explosions of dust and stone.

"They're coming from both sides," she screamed, for the benefit of the guys in the cave.

In desperation, Hannah rose to her feet and ran toward the helicopter, toward the advancing soldiers.

The soldiers had dropped ladders across the narrow gorge, and they were crawling over the chasm. One of them was pointing his gun at the helicopter. The helicopter rose off the plateau and tilted forward, toward Hannah.

Frantically, she waved at the pilot. The helicopter rose into the sky.

Seated in the right side of the helicopter, restrained by Elazar's men, Catherine looked down at Hannah looking up at her. She saw bullets rip through Hannah's body and erupt in red plumes. She watched Hannah fall to the ground. She saw the soldiers overrun the plateau.

The helicopter lifted higher and banked left, steeply, toward the mountain, until all Catherine could see out her window was the cloudless sky.

There was an open cooler on the floor at her feet filled with sandwiches and soft drinks. She leaned over it and vomited. Then she passed out.

Inside the cave, Amnon and Yossi heard the shooting begin. Before they could react, Galil's bloodied, lifeless, brutally disfigured body fell down the chute and sprawled on the cave floor.

Amnon doubled over in shock and revulsion.

Yossi ran toward the ledge and peered through the opening in the cliff wall at the valley below. Bullets struck within inches of his face, and tiny chips of stone tore into his cheek. He retreated into the cave without returning fire.

"Ben, are you there?" he radioed. "We're being attacked."

"I'm trapped, Yossi. The ceiling has fallen in."

"I'm coming."

"No, Yossi, save yourself."

"There's no other way."

"But the passage is blocked."

"Then unblock it."

Yossi grabbed Amnon's arm.

"Come on!" he shouted.

"No, this is the only place to make a stand," Amnon said.

"We can't stop them."

"If they get inside, we're dead."

"I'll take my chances down the tunnel."

Amnon gripped Yossi's rifle.

"I'll hold them as long as I can."

Yossi let go of the rifle. He nodded at his friend. Then he dashed for the tunnel. He climbed over fallen rocks, down an incline, around a narrow bend. A new wall of fallen rocks barred the way where Amnon had reached a dead end earlier.

"Ben, can you hear me?"

On the other side of the wall, Jordan called out hoarsely.

"Yossi? Dammit, Yossi, get out of here."

"Help me move these rocks."

"But there's nowhere to go from here. Even if you make it through, the floor ahead falls away."

"Shit."

The cave echoed with automatic weapons fire as soldiers tried to penetrate the entrances and Amnon unloaded on them. He fired in short, controlled bursts, conserving ammunition.

"Amnon's trying to hold them back," Yossi said.

"Who are they?"

"IDF."

Yossi clawed madly at the wall of rocks, tossing some aside, straining desperately against others. Irrationally, Jordan worked from his end, trying to demolish all that stood between him and the assault.

"Where are the others?" Jordan asked.

"Zev's dead. Hannah and Catherine—I don't know."

An explosion shook the cave, and the concussion nearly knocked Yossi over. The smell of the explosive charge filled the tunnel.

In the darkness, Jordan pressed his hands against the rock barrier, as if he could absorb the sights and sounds on the other side through his fingertips. For several seconds, all he could hear was the ringing in his ears. The soldiers must have dropped a grenade down the chute.

Jordan heard voices far away. He couldn't make out what they were saying, but he surmised that commandos were sliding down the chute or crawling through the opening in the cliff wall.

Amnon's gun had fallen silent.

"They're coming," Yossi whispered.

From no more than three feet away, Yossi's whisper carried through the gaps in the rocks. Jordan listened helplessly, unable to respond. He could picture Yossi pressing against the wall.

There was a sharp burst of gunfire, and then Jordan heard the gutteral gurgle of a man choking on his own blood. He sensed Yossi slumping to the ground.

He heard a stranger curse Yossi with a terse epithet, and then more fragments of the ceiling broke loose.

He lapsed into unconsciousness.

Chapter 59

He drifted in a sensory-deprived no man's land, hovering between coma and consciousness.

In his dream, he was burning with fever, but he felt safe and secure. She was rocking him, comforting him, holding him close. He looked up, searching for her face, but it was lost in shadow, backlit by the sun.

He heard a voice repeating itself, beautifully. A mother's voice. She was singing—a calming, happy melody, bathing him in bright colors. The words floated like butterflies. He reached for them, but they floated away. They always floated away.

When finally he crossed the threshold of consciousness, he was sitting on the floor with his legs bent awkwardly beneath him and his upper body leaning into the corner where the cave wall met the barrier of fallen rocks. He had no idea how long he had been out. His eyes were useless; the darkness was complete.

He felt dizzy and lightheaded, which he attributed to a concussion, dehydration or the total absence of visual cues. He felt his head, which was throbbing painfully. His hair was sticky and matted. He missed the Arab doctor who had tended to his earlier wounds in Lebanon—or was it Syria?

With growing awareness, he heard an unfamiliar noise, and he felt movement all around him. It felt like the air was alive and churning.

It was the flutter of countless wings beating against the blackness. In a dense cloud, the bats were returning to their roosts on the walls and ceiling. They were returning from their nightly foray, and that meant it was dawn or nearly so. Whatever opening they used to exit and enter the cave lay beyond the sunken section of floor, useless to Jordan.

He pulled back his sleeve and dusted off his watch, and the luminous dial told him it was almost 6:00 a.m. He reconstructed the chain of events that led him to this eerie prison. In his mind's eye, he saw Yossi trapped on the other side of the fallen rocks, and the muzzle flash of the fatal rounds.

What about Catherine? What about the relics?

Did anyone else survive the attack? For that matter, how would he? Would the cave become his tomb, and his bones a mystery for future archaeologists?

On hands and knees, he felt his way around the cave floor. He found his flashlight and turned it on. The lens was cracked, but it worked. He took a closer look at the chasm in the cave floor. There was no way to get across it. He was lucky he hadn't stumbled into it by mistake.

He studied the barrier of fallen rocks. Some of them seemed small enough to move. He removed one of the rocks and dropped it in the chasm. The others shifted and threatened to topple on him. He waited until they settled. He chose the next one carefully. It was surprisingly brittle sandstone, not as dense as the rocks they had labored so hard to clear from the tomb beneath the stone demon. He was puzzled by the geology. He dropped the rock into the chasm, and he heard it break apart dully when it hit bottom.

He reached for another stone.

It was a slow, grueling process, but he realized that he need not die in the cave. The flashlight faded and flickered. He shook it, and it failed, leaving him to work in darkness.

Hours later—aching, dizzy, throbbing with pain, choking on dust and gagging against the guano—Jordan broke out of his prison.

He found Yossi's body, and he felt for a pulse, though he knew the gesture was futile. He stumbled weakly up the tunnel, tripping over fallen rocks. He made his way into the main chamber. The mid-day sun was streaming in through the opening in the ceiling, and it hurt his eyes. He needed a moment to adjust.

What remained of three human beings was lying on the cave floor.

Two of them were almost unrecognizable. Jordan identified Galil by his size more than anything else. He was lying face down, and most of his head had been blasted away. The rest of his body was torn by shrapnel. The light from the shaft cast him in a spotlight.

Amnon—or what Jordan took for Amnon—appeared to have borne the brunt of the grenade. Two of his limbs had been separated from his body; his torso was a gory mess, and his face had been erased. He had died facing the assault.

Hannah's bullet-riddled body was laid out in the middle of the chamber. She showed no evidence of the grenade. Clearly, someone had put her there. Her beautiful face was covered with dried gore, but it was not her own. The shattered video camera lay discarded a few feet away.

Jordan was overcome with a desperate, sickening sense of loss. In cold dread, he searched the rest of the chamber, half expecting to find another body. But there was no trace of Catherine.

He wanted to see if anything was left of the sixteenth cache, in the hollow beneath the stone demon, but he had no light to find his way. He wanted to cover the bodies, but there was nothing to cover them with.

He wondered if the commandos had left in a careless hurry—or if they were planning to return. The cord still dangled from the chute. He wondered if it was possible that the commandos were still nearby.

He listened, but all he heard was the faint echo of emptiness, like the inside of a seashell. He tested the cord, then hesitated. He knelt beside Hannah's body and rummaged through the pockets of her vest. He found three of the miniature videotape cassettes she had used to record their efforts. He inspected the camera itself, which had been smashed by a bullet. He ejected the tape. The plastic case was cracked, but the tape inside looked as if it might be intact. He pocketed the tapes.

He thought of Galil beside the lion of Egypt, protectively urging him to leave with Catherine before the Humvee reached their excavation.

"This is *my* sandbox," Galil had said in a tone that was at once boastful, self-deprecating, and generous of spirit. "What do you know about making sandcastles?"

He reached for the cord.

He climbed up the chute and cautiously peeked out of the opening. He was alone. He lifted himself onto the promontory. The desert was more desolate than he remembered, and somehow transformed. There was a distinct breeze, and it was cooler than before.

He felt lightheaded and disoriented, and he had to sit for a minute. He noticed a patch of dried blood, and knew it marked the spot where one of his friends had fallen.

He noticed the cord they had used to scale the cliff. It remained snaked through the steel hook and draped over the precipice. He looked over the edge of the cliff, into the valley below.

It was the only way out.

With no harness at hand, he tied one end of the nylon line into a double loop and placed a leg in each loop. He wrapped the line around his waist and tied a second knot for stability. He tested the piton, which seemed secure.

He grabbed hold of the line a couple yards after it passed through the steel hook and stepped toward the precipice. He turned his back to the canyon. Without looking down, he lowered himself backwards over the edge.

He gripped the rope tightly. With surreal detachment, he realized he held his life in his hands. It was heavy.

He began rappelling down the cliff. He took small steps, careful not to gather momentum. The line burned his hands and bit into his thighs. He passed the hollow in the cliff wall where Amnon and Yossi had opened a window into the cave. He kept going.

He counted his steps to blot out all dangerous thoughts. Fifteen, twenty … fifty-six . . . .

The day before, the ascent had been terrifying but filled with hope and anticipation. The descent was merely terrifying.

. . . Seventy-five . . . eighty . . . eighty-three . . . .

He was almost there. Less than fifteen feet to go.

He felt a slight tremor in the line. He stopped. Then the piton gave way. He was clutching the line, but the line was falling and so was he. He was falling backward. Somehow, in a fraction of a second, he managed to shift the angle of his body.

He felt a crushing blow and he heard bones snap as he hit the ground. He was lying on the floor of the canyon looking up at the sky. He felt no pain, and he realized he was in shock. He thought he might be paralyzed.

He was afraid to move, afraid to breathe, lest he exacerbate any injury to his spinal cord. He tried to inventory the damage. His toes wiggled on command.

He exhaled, and the pain hit him like a flash of white light, blinding in its intensity, taking his breath away. He heard the sickening crunch of bone moving against bone. He felt something stabbing him, puncturing his chest.

Instinctively, he lifted his arms to his broken ribs, tightening his stomach muscles, and a sharper pain surged to his brain. Through gritted teeth, he cried out, and the canyon echoed with his agony.

He forced himself to sit up. The effort was excruciating. He lay back. He lay still for long minutes, surrendering to the pain, then trying to master it through force of will.

He felt a gust of wind, and he noticed the sky had gotten darker. Clouds were moving in.

He struggled to stand. He felt lightheaded and weak. He took one step, and another, protectively clutching his broken ribs. Every breath brought more agony—and less oxygen. He staggered a few more steps and sank to his knees.

His chest heaved, and he struggled for air. His punctured lung was filling with blood. He lay down, trying to catch his breath. He needed to rest. He was desperately thirsty, but he couldn't move.

Clouds in the desert.

He looked at the canyon walls, rising toward the desert plateau. The valley was nothing more than a dry riverbed, carved through the earth over countless millennia by the occasional seasonal storms that transformed its floor into a deep, violent torrent, fed by miles of runoff.

The clouds would bring cool rain, a storm.

And then a flood.

Chapter 60

A Desert Base

"Drink this," Elazar said, offering Catherine a bottle of water.

She was lying on a cot in a white tent, curled in a fetal position, and Elazar was sitting next to her in a folding canvas chair. She propped herself up on an elbow and took a sip.

She choked back a sob.

"If only I had listened to you. If only we had left sooner."

Elazar put a hand around hers and squeezed it tight. His face was lined with concern, bordering on anger.

"I've spent many years of my life thinking, 'If only.' Don't make the same mistake."

She thought of Galil's daughters, Annie and Jesse. *"Goodnight kids!"* the four-year-old had said gleefully, chasing her sister into the bedroom.

She thought of Jordan, and a dream she dreamt the night they spent together in the desert. The dream had died. Unless luck had saved him, or he had saved himself. She remembered that he had stepped away before the shooting started. The memory lifted her hopes—and cast a shadow of doubt.

Had he known what was coming?

"He'll have a place in history, Catherine, right beside you."

Elazar was talking about Galil. He never saw Jordan in the cave, and might not even realize he was there. He had no idea what Jordan had meant to her. She had tried to tell him over the noise of the helicopter, as they hauled her aboard.

"What is this place, Meyer?"

The base was a compound of tents in the middle of the desert, surrounded by mountains. It looked like a military camp—or more like a humanitarian aid station set up by relief workers. The tents were all white. Some were long and narrow, like barracks. Others resembled officers' quarters—square and relatively private, like the one where Catherine found herself. In the center of the camp, there was an especially large tent, which served as a dining hall. Several others were equipped with sophisticated laboratories.

A hot wind blew in from the desert, and the sides of the tent ruffled and slapped.

"We're guests of the Order of Constantine. They are men of the cloth, Greek Orthodox. If not for them, I would have been at the Institute when the bomb went off. They rescued me."

"Why?"

"They're searching for Jesus, or proof of Jesus. They heard about the Silver Scroll, and they wanted my help. Not that they needed my help—in the end, all they had to do was follow you. But they believe I'm a useful symbol."

"And the soldiers?"

"When the Israeli government learned that the Silver Scroll had the potential to undermine Judaism, someone in the government set out to control the situation. Now, it appears they would use all means necessary to prevent the world from learning what Caiaphas had to say. But I think you knew that already."

"You trust this Order of Constantine?"

"I owe them my life. As do you."

"May I come in?"

The voice belonged to Father Gregory.

"Yes, please do," Elazar said.

The monk opened the door flap and ducked into the tent. Elazar offered introductions.

"Catherine, Father Gregory."

"I'm sorry about your friends, Professor Cavanaugh, deeply sorry. But I am very pleased to have you safe with us."

"Thank you, Father. I owe you a great debt."

"No, your debt is to Rabbi Elazar. We were afraid to intervene, but he demanded we act. He insisted on facing the danger himself. To bring you back."

The monk's words took her by surprise. She looked at Elazar in a new light, with no small amount of shame and embarrassment. She recalled that he had been ready to leave the cave without the relics.

"What do we do now?" she asked.

"I hope you understand the enormity of your achievement," Father Gregory said. "It appears that you have unearthed the Temple Chronicles. It appears you have rescued whatever testament Caiaphas recorded. What remains is to make the words of Caiaphas known to the world, before anyone can take them or destroy them."

Catherine felt a twinge of alarm.

"Where are the jars, the scrolls?" she asked.

The monk gave her a benevolent smile. He answered with his eyes, and Catherine followed his gaze.

"Rabbi Elazar is looking out for them. They've never left your side. He may have to attest to their provenance, so it's important that we maintain the chain of custody."

A wide aluminum case, the kind used to transport sensitive equipment with lots of custom-molded interior padding, was sitting at Elazar's feet.

"What do they say?" she asked.

The monk raised his eyebrows with a look of surprise.

"I couldn't say, Professor Cavanaugh. We haven't looked."

"You haven't looked?"

"It's a matter of trust. We think it would be a mistake to do it on our own. We think we should have witnesses."

"Who?"

"First, let me assure you, Professor Cavanaugh, that no one can or will take anything away from the credit you have earned. This is your discovery, and the world will recognize it as such. But, as I'm sure you would acknowledge, your discovery is larger than any individual."

The monk turned to Elazar.

"Rabbi, we've drafted a list for your consideration. There are 32 names from 15 countries. They are leading scholars in the field, representing each of the Christian, Jewish and Muslim traditions. They include scientists, experts in a variety of disciplines. I believe you know every one of them. You've helped some in their careers by granting them access to sites and artifacts. You've hindered others. We're looking for fair-minded, credible people who, individually and collectively, will command the world's respect. We want you to edit the list. Add or subtract as you wish. And then, we want you to invite these men and women here, in strictest confidence, to participate in the analysis."

"What would I tell them?'

"Almost nothing. We expect them to accept the invitation on the strength of your stature and reputation, your personal assurance that it is a matter of utmost importance. That should suffice. No—that *must* suffice."

"How will they get here?"

"We'll book them on commercial flights to major cities in the region. Then, our people will meet them and transport them the rest of the way."

"They'll think I've risen from the dead."

"All the more reason to take you seriously."

The monk left Catherine's tent and walked purposefully through the camp. He made his way to the far end of the base, announced himself, and disappeared into the tent closest to the helipad.

Inside, the shaikh shifted in his cushioned seat and looked up from the television, which was tuned to the replay of an American basketball game.

"Fucking Lakers," he said with disgust. "I had $500,000 on that game."

The cleric winced, but kept his true feelings in check. "With our recent success, you can afford many such losses," Father Gregory said.

"I could already afford many such losses," Shaikh Waleed corrected. "It's the principle of the thing that pisses me off. Can you believe it? Four missed free throws in the final minute."

Waleed turned off the television, and the hated Lakers disappeared. He looked uncomfortable in his khaki field clothes, which were cut less generously than his own ample proportions. He had shed his traditional flowing robes for a more appropriate costume. But he didn't exactly blend in. His beard formed a small point below the first of his double chins, and the twin branches of his split mustache angled downward in a look of perpetual surprise.

He was one of the most successful industrialists in the Arab world, with peripheral interests in banking and shipping. His fortune was built on relationships—and the customary kickbacks he paid to his benefactors. He had gotten fat from contracts with the ruling families of Kuwait and Saudi Arabia. His engineering concern provided vital and lucrative services to a vast archipelago of oil fields and refineries, but he had loftier ambitions. He dreamed of one day controlling his own wells.

As a young man, he had no deep interest in politics, religion, or charity, but he realized early on that all three could be crucial to his advancement. He had grown close to the House of Saud—close enough to know, envy and even emulate its extravagance. But he remained sufficiently detached to see the fragility of Saudi power. At any moment, the country's roiling fundamentalism could boil over into revolution, and the Saudi royal family could be swept aside like the Shah of Iran a generation earlier.

Waleed might blow a casual $500,000 on the Lakers, but when it came to business, he hedged his bets. And that meant investing in mullahs as well as princes.

He approached it as a form of venture capital. Get in on the ground floor, provide a modest amount of seed money, and reap the rewards when one group of religious fundamentalists in 20 hit the big time. The strategy was shrewder than he could have foreseen. He knew other wealthy Arabs who failed to get in on the ground floor. Later, they found themselves shaken down for contributions that bought less goodwill.

Waleed's investment in one particular group had matured handsomely over the years, earning him a seat on the moral equivalent of its board of directors—and the privilege of writing more and bigger checks. Truth be told, he didn't entirely approve of the directions in which the organization had grown and evolved. Some of them scared the hell out of him. But his was a passive role, and he was in too deep to raise objections.

It was that awareness that brought him to a tent in the desert on an errand he could easily have left to others. He saw it as an opportunity—an exercise in relationship building. He was in league with some very dangerous men, but that wasn't necessarily a bad thing. Better to have dangerous friends than dangerous enemies.

His eyes, black as crude and similarly viscous, focused on Father Gregory.

"So tell me, Yassin, how did our fighters perform in the Judean Desert?"

"Very convincingly. Our guests have no doubt they were Israeli commandos."

"Casualties?"

"One martyr."

"The bottom line?"

"A healthy return on your investment, Shaikh Waleed. We're transferring the coins to your helicopter. And there's more, much more, waiting to be unearthed."

"It will be a long time before I can liquidate it. Regardless, as a reminder of my piety and philanthropy, I will return one third to the cause."

"Very generous of you indeed."

"An equitable arrangement all around. In consideration of my financial backing, I get the gold, and you get the writings."

"More than equitable. It's only a matter of time before the House of Saud falls, Shaikh Waleed. And, when it does, the Mullah will remember your devotion to the ways of Allah."

"I'm counting on him to remember as well my interest in petroleum."

"And so he shall."

Like many men of similar station, Waleed believed his wealth flowed from an ability to use others. In truth, he owed just as much to the ease with which they manipulated him.

"I'm sorry I was unable to witness the operation," he said. "But I have to congratulate you and the Mullah, Yassin. It's a brilliant plan, superbly executed. When you're done, even the Zionists' friends will despise them."

"Yes, Shaikh Waleed. If Allah wills it, if all goes according to plan, the influence of international Jewry will be crippled, and the government of Israel will fall. The state of Israel will lose all credibility. Best of all, they will be the instruments of their own destruction."

"And justice will be done."

"It would be the ultimate payoff for a long and patient effort," Yassin said. "Though some of our brothers thought we were diverting resources from the military struggle, we recognized the stakes. We realized it was important to monitor the archaeology of Palestine, to infiltrate and eavesdrop on the Institute, lest anything surface that might bolster the Jews' territorial claims. We had prepared for that day. The emergence of this other evidence was a happy accident. It will serve our purposes even better."

Waleed's lips spread in a sardonic grin.

"If I didn't know better, Yassin, I'd say you were proud of yourself."

"Deservedly so," the shaikh hastened to add, frowning nervously at his indiscretion.

It was true. Yassin was pleased with himself for a series of bold and unerring moves, from the recruitment of Benjamin Jordan and Meyer Elazar to the murders of Nigel Waverly and Lord Crendal, calculated to shock and repulse, and the deftly orchestrated attack in the Valley of Asher. Yassin had performed a flawless charade. Even what seemed like a setback would prove a success. The story Jordan had been fed about an Israeli cover-up—the story that blew up in the reporter's face—would soon provide a context for events, framing everything that followed.

Nonetheless, Yassin maintained a pious façade.

"What we humble servants achieve is only through the grace of Allah," he said.

"Of course. But there's something I don't understand."

"What's that?"

"What if the Caiaphas scroll vindicates the Jews?"

Yassin smiled serenely.

"Not to worry, my friend."

"Why?"

"It's really quite irrelevant."

Chapter 61

The Valley of Asher

Dark clouds blotted out the noon sun.

Jordan felt a raindrop splash on his face, and then another. In the distance, there was a rumble of thunder.

He was in agony, and he saw no way out of his predicament. His heart was racing, and his body was starving for air. He tried to stand, but he barely made it past a crouch when he tottered and fell. He tried crawling, and the pain was unbearable. He collapsed on his side.

A shaft of light broke through a gap in the clouds, like a sign from God. But the roiling clouds moved swiftly to the east, and the gap closed.

Jordan closed his eyes. Drops of water splashed against his eyelids. They were falling steadily now, gathering force. The wind was picking up, and the temperature was dropping. He was cold, getting colder. The rain soaked his clothes.

In his mind, he was buried in wet sand, up to his neck, unable to move, and the tide was rolling in . . . .

The rain was forming puddles on the floor of the canyon, and the puddles were expanding toward each other, joining to form larger puddles.

He was lying in standing water.

Rivulets cascaded over the western cliff, covering the rock face in sheets of water and spraying away in gusts of wind. The rivulets were merely precursors. The deluge would roar down from the head of the valley, where the slopes channeled the runoff.

He studied the nearest section of cliff wall. He believed the pattern of erosion showed the modern high water mark. It was about ten feet up—roughly the height from which he had fallen.

There was a flash of lightning and a crack of thunder, and Jordan imagined a dam bursting somewhere upstream. The clouds unleashed a drenching torrent.

He wondered if he would drown, or if the force of the water would smash him against the rocks. Either way, his broken bones would torture him to the last in the thrashing current. He realized he was already drowning. He had just one remaining hope. He hoped that somewhere, somehow, Catherine survived. He hoped she would complete their work, and live.

The rising water nudged him, and bolts of pain surged from his bones.

He was losing it.

He felt himself slipping. He heard strange voices, borne by a howling wind. Distant shouts of surprise and urgency, drowned out by the storm. Phantoms speaking in tongues.

The stone demon, awakened from a shallow sleep.

He looked up the valley at a maelstrom of driving rain and churning water.

The demons were in full flight, fleeing ahead of the storm.

The demons were coming for him.

The voices were familiar, yet unfamiliar.

The demons were circling.

They were upon him.

Chapter 62

The Judean Desert

"Who are you?" the voice asked.

Demon or angel, Jordan wondered.

The voice repeated the question, louder, demanding to be heard over the noise of the storm.

Jordan opened his eyes.

The wind was howling, and the rain was slashing. He was shivering uncontrollably. His vision was blurred. The rain was running into his eyes. He blinked, trying to focus.

The voice had brown eyes and thick, wavy hair, drenched to the skull. He spoke Hebrew. He was wearing the uniform of a soldier in the Israel Defense Forces.

Jordan felt a throbbing pain, and he remembered the fractures.

He was lying on rocky ground beside a green jeep, which was splashed with mud. He sensed he was somewhere above the valley. He remembered feeling he had been swept ahead of the rushing waters and borne aloft by powerful arms. There were other figures gathered around, pressing in on him. Young soldiers, in uniform.

"What's your name?" the first soldier asked.

Jordan receded into the mist. The soldier shook him and repeated the question.

"Jordan," he gasped. "Benjamin Jordan."

The soldier's eyebrows arched with recognition.

"You're lucky we were hiking nearby. What were you doing in the canyon?"

"Climbing."

"What else?"

"Falling."

The soldier laughed. He rested a hand lightly on Jordan's arm.

"You must be in a lot of pain. You need a doctor, maybe a surgeon."

"A hospital," Jordan whispered.

"Tell me what happened."

The soldier had to lean in close to make out Jordan's answer.

"The rope came undone. The piton must have broken loose."

"Is anyone else missing?"

"Yes, but . . . ."

An alarm went off in Jordan's brain, piercing the fog.

The people who attacked them in the cave were IDF, Yossi had said.

Jordan relived the concussion of the grenade, and the burst of gunfire silencing Yossi.

"But what?" the soldier demanded.

Jordan shook his head mutely. The soldier lowered his ear to Jordan's lips, but there was nothing to hear.

"But what?" the soldier demanded, shaking Jordan, jarring his bones.

Jordan screamed, and his scream vanished on the wind.

"We're running out of time, Benjamin. The water is rising. If any members of your party are still missing, we need to save them now. So where are they?"

"Gone."

"Gone where?"

Jordan looked up numbly. Catherine was unaccounted for, probably captured. But instinct told him to keep his silence.

They'll kill her, just as they murdered Zev, and Hannah, and Yossi, and Amnon. They'll kill her, just as they slaughtered my mother and father, and the orphans of el-Adir.

They'll kill her, just as they'll murder me.

If they haven't killed her already.

"He's losing it," the soldier said. "Help me put him in the jeep."

They lifted Jordan and loaded him into the backseat. One of them bumped him with a rifle butt, banging a rib.

Pain coursed through his nerves like lightning and slammed him like thunder. It drove the clouds from his brain and replaced them with searing images—four bloody bodies in a cave, and two more who had no faces. It cut through conflict and confusion like a blowtorch. It released something primal, and raging, and unforgiving. It focused all his energy on one consuming passion—vengeance.

The Israelis must pay.

Chapter 63

Saudi Arabia

The Mullah knew they were listening.

They were always watching, listening, spying, lying in wait, plotting to silence the messenger.

Fine, let them listen. Let them hear the Word of Allah. Let them hear the truth. Let them struggle to learn its meaning. They could listen all they wanted, but they would never understand. The infidels were incapable of understanding. Their electronic ears were deaf to the truth.

In their effort to deceive others, they deceived themselves.

They believed they could defeat jihad, but their resistance was doomed to fail. They misunderstood the very essence of their enemy. Jihad was a struggle for perfection, a process of submission, an acknowledgment of truth, and in the end the truth would prevail.

Some of the infidels believed that multiple versions of the truth could coexist. They called this "freedom" or "tolerance," as if errors were to be tolerated. But that was a testament to their weakness and illogic. The Koran showed the way.

"O Prophet! Strive hard against the unbelievers and the hypocrites and be unyielding to them; and their abode is hell, and evil is the destination."

"Surely We have prepared for the unbelievers chains and shackles and a burning fire."

In the meantime, the great crusader Churchill was right: In jihad, the truth would travel with a bodyguard of lies.

The Mullah felt sublimely satisfied. He was confident that his part in the larger struggle would yield an epic victory. The river of history would be diverted, and woe to those who stood in its path. The Crusaders would turn on the Jews, and if the Jews survived the initial deluge, they would reap an eternal sandstorm.

The Mullah was determined to undo Hitler's damage. Tragically, Hitler had failed. And, in failing, he had done more harm than good. He had advanced the Zionist agenda. He had inspired sympathy for the devils.

It was only fitting that the next act would strike at the symbol of misplaced sympathy.

The Mullah closed his eyes and saw a vision of the future, a future that was fast approaching. In his vision, the infidel was driven from Jerusalem. The Haram al Sharif was the center of a new Palestine, which was wholly subservient to Allah. From the minaret of al Aqsa, the muezzin proclaimed the greatness of Allah, and everyone within the sound of his voice answered the call.

The liberation of Palestine would be a building block for future triumphs. Wrapped in glory, they would topple the whoring princes in Riyadh, and drive the infidels from the land of Mecca. They would free Arabia from America's polluting presence. They would control the Saudi oil, and they would use it to humble the West. America would tremble at their power.

If the armies of the crusaders tried to steal the oil, their efforts would end in an inferno, for the faithful would ignite the oil fields. The faithful had no need for oil.

The Prophet's command would be fulfilled without interference: The faithful would make pilgrimage to Mecca, Medina and the Aqsa mosque.

In the background, from atop a minaret, a muezzin was calling the faithful to pray.

Let the infidels hear his voice, the Mullah thought. Let it be a sign and a warning.

The Mullah picked up the phone and dialed. Far away, in a desert camp, a satellite phone rang, and a soldier in the army of God answered.

"Greetings, brother," the Mullah said.

"Peace be with you," the man called Yassin replied.

"How goes the Lord's work?"

"The day is almost upon us. It will be a great and glorious event. The servants of God are in the field. The forces of truth are gathering. It won't be long before the truth replaces the lie. A brave and selfless brother will deliver the opening declaration."

The words were carefully scripted, and Yassin delivered them faithfully.

"God be with you, my brother."

"And with you."

Chapter 64

Yad Vashem

The old man and the boy walked among the carob trees.

It was a quiet, peaceful place. Even the birds seemed to respect its sanctity. The old man put his arm around the boy's shoulder. His legs weren't what they used to be, and his breath was shorter now.

The boy stopped, ostensibly to admire a tree, but in fact to give his grandfather a chance to rest. They had nearly finished a loop through the park.

"Thank you, Nathan. Thank you for bringing me here."

The old man took a deep breath and looked around slowly, as if recording a memory.

"Of all the places we've seen in Israel, I think this one means the most," the old man said.

"More than the Western Wall?" the boy said in a New Yorker's accent.

"I always wanted to see the Western Wall, and I'm proud that you'll be bar mitzvahed there tomorrow. But if your parents came to Jerusalem, I think I would bring them here first. Not just Yad Vashem—this part of Yad Vashem."

"Why, Grandpa?"

Grandpa Jack unfolded the brochure describing Israel's Holocaust memorial. There was a slight tremor in his hands.

"It's called the Avenue of the Righteous. Each of these trees honors one of the 'Righteous among the Gentiles.'"

Nathan had read the brochure, but he let his grandfather explain. He liked the way his grandfather explained things.

"It honors a special kind of righteousness, Nathan. It's not about doing well on your bar mitzvah, or praying in Hebrew, or wearing a *kipah* in *shul*. It's not about being more Conservative than the Reforms, or more Orthodox than the Conservatives. It isn't even about being Jewish, or believing in Torah.

"It's about being human, Nathan. These gentiles were human beings. They risked their lives to save others from the death camps. They put everything on the line for people of a different faith and heritage."

The old man looked at the rows of trees that lined the walkway.

"It's a beautiful thing, Nathan. But, God, I wish it was a forest."

They walked up the hill, the grandfather leaning on his grandson.

At the top of the Avenue of the Righteous, a place of remembrance was built into a hillside. They entered through a gateway framed by walls of stone. They found themselves in the hushed, somber darkness of a man-made cave. It was a memorial to the children.

The design led them deeper into the hillside. They stepped into a hall of mirrors. A light was reflected and multiplied to form a million eternal flames suspended in blackness, one for each child's soul extinguished by the Nazis. Disembodied voices recited names, ages, and places of birth.

Malka Altman, 10, Poland
Alvaro Coen, 7, Italy
Lev Dobrinski, 8, Latvia

Nathan listened, trying to imagine what they wanted to be when they grew up, and what horrors they had experienced. Most of them were younger than him.

Efraim Elstein, 16, Poland
Nina Gitel, 4, Poland

Grandpa Jack thought of relatives he had never known, cousins from Lodz, in Poland, who vanished in the inferno. They were as close and as far away as the four-year-old named Nina.

The old man took Nathan's hand.

Another boy was standing next to Nathan in the darkness, gazing into the infinity of lights. He was a few years older, with olive skin and curly hair. Nathan guessed he was a *sabra*, a native Israeli. A student like him, judging from the backpack.

Nathan looked into the infinity of lights, trying to locate their source. He didn't really notice the *sabra* reaching into his pack. He was too close to feel anything when the bomb exploded and the Children's Memorial disintegrated into a million shards of glass.

The memorial service for the victims of the bombing was two days later. It was dedicated to more than just the victims. It was a memorial for the memorial itself, and for the children of the Holocaust whose eternal flames had been snuffed out. In a way, they had died a second death, the papers said.

"In a land where killing has lost its ability to shock, the destruction of the Children's Memorial is like a return to Auschwitz," one commentator wrote, giving voice to the Israeli people.

Amid tight security, thousands of Israelis gathered at Yad Vashem to pay their respects. They were hawks and doves, secularists and Hasidim, soldiers and civilians, children and aged survivors of the Shoah. Clutching each other in grief, a middle-aged couple from New York was squeezed and comforted by the crowd somewhere along the Avenue of the Righteous.

As the Prime Minister of Israel stepped onto a makeshift podium erected just yards from the rubble, the Vice President of the United States bowed his head, and the King of Jordan wept. But mostly, the outsiders had stayed away. The outsiders had grown weary.

"We will never forget," the Prime Minister vowed. "The world will never forget, because we won't let it. And justice will be done. In righteous might, the state of Israel will smite the terrorists who planned this cowardly attack."

Chapter 65

Tel Aviv

An hour after he left the podium, the Prime Minister took his seat in the command center, surrounded by his top ministers and generals.

General Itzhak Goren had a place near the end of the table farthest from the Prime Minister. His old familiar pain was coming back. Was it a delayed response to the attack on Yad Vashem? Or, for the first time in a long time, was it some sort of premonition?

When no one was looking, Goren popped an antacid. He washed it down with oily black coffee and crumpled the paper cup.

"The punishment will be absolute," the Prime Minister said. "We will send a message that no one will misunderstand. The question is, Have we identified the targets?"

The head of intelligence, General Avi Arad, rose from his seat. He was a harmless looking man, with a relaxed way and a soft voice that made people listen. He was mostly bald, and the wrinkles on his scalp moved expressively when he spoke. If Goren could use only one word to describe Avi Arad, it would be "reasonable." The man sounded reasonable. That gave others the confidence to base grave decisions on his advice, and it made them grateful he was in the room. None of them mistook his reasonable manner for weakness or indifference. Like almost everyone present, he had been on the receiving end of enemy fire, and he had returned it most effectively.

Arad pressed a button, and a live satellite image filled a screen on the wall.

"Here's your target," he said.

They were looking down on a tent city in a desert valley, surrounded by rough mountains. Seen from high overhead, at a slight angle, a helicopter was coming in low through a mountain pass. They watched it land.

Four people got out. They paused, as if orienting themselves, and quickstepped away from the helicopter, ducking under the rotors. They were carrying bags of various shapes and sizes.

A one-man welcoming party greeted them in the open with handshakes and embraces. He led them through the camp to one of the larger white tents, and they disappeared inside. The image changed to infrared, and the Israeli commanders could see the shapes of their bodies through the roof of the tent. They were mingling with several others, exchanging greetings, sitting down at a table.

"We've seen this repeated five times over the last 24 hours," Arad said.

"What's the connection?"

"We intercepted a phone conversation. The call originated at a mosque in Saudi Arabia. It was placed by this man."

Arad pressed a button, and the dour visage of the Mullah filled a window in the corner of the screen.

There were murmurs around the table.

"I believe you know him," Arad said. "The Mullah dialed a satellite phone. The satellite phone was located here, in the desert. And, based on voice analysis, the man who answered the call was the terrorist Yassin, one of the more shadowy operatives in the Mullah's network. We've never been able to tie Yassin directly to an attack; he lurks in the background. He was born in Tunis, educated in Athens. Majored in comparative religion, of all things. Our informants tell us he uses—or used—safe houses in Cyprus, but he last crossed our radar three years ago. At the time, he was in contact with people who were in contact with the terrorist Khalid Farouk, who was operating out of Lebanon and Syria. This is Yassin's passport photo from six years ago, but we suspect the man in the photo is actually someone else.

"As I was saying, Yassin answered the phone. And this is the highlight of the conversation."

Arad played the recording.

> "How goes the Lord's work?"
>
> "The day is almost upon us. It will be a great and glorious event. The servants of God are in the field. The forces of truth are gathering. It won't be long before the truth replaces the lie. A brave and selfless brother will deliver the opening declaration."

There were gasps of anger and surprise in the conference room.

"There's more," Arad said. "Less than five minutes after the explosion at the Children's Memorial, Yassin received a second call on the same phone. The second call originated at a public phone in Jerusalem, a short distance from Yad Vashem. It was very brief. An unidentified male said, simply, 'The message has been delivered.' Yassin thanked him and hung up."

Arad paused to let them absorb the information.

"What did he mean about the truth replacing the lie?" the Prime Minister asked.

"It could have multiple meanings. It may be a broad reference to the triumph of Islam. Or, it may be a reference to the Holocaust. Our enemies would like to deny that the Holocaust ever happened. They want to convince the world that we made it up. That's probably why they targeted Yad Vashem."

"You believe the attack on Yad Vashem was the 'opening declaration'?'"

"I think it's clear that they're planning something else, something bigger. I think that's why forces are gathering in the desert—Yassin's 'forces of truth.'"

Goren coughed and cleared his throat. "I have a question," he asked. "Why do you suppose these people were speaking on open lines? Don't they know we're listening, Avi? Don't they assume the Americans are?"

The Defense Minister slammed his fist on the table.

"The bastards feel they can act with impunity," he said. "And why shouldn't they? They're still in business."

"We've been down this road before," Goren said. "Have you considered the possibility that we hear what they want us to hear?"

"Izzy may be right," the Foreign Minister said. "The Mullah was speaking on a land line?"

"Yes, from his mosque," the head of intelligence said.

"Maybe he's taunting us, daring us to attack," the Foreign Minister said. "Maybe he wants us to strike at Saudi Arabia—a mosque, no less. Maybe he wants to provoke a wider war. Or maybe he believes we wouldn't dare."

"All of those are reasonable explanations," Arad said. "And there's another factor to consider, an element of psychological warfare. You might call it part of the taunt. They may assume we can hear them, but they may also assume we aren't listening."

The Defense Minister gave him a blank look.

"They may reasonably gamble that even if our technology is vacuuming up their electronic communications, we aren't listening in real time. We collect far too much data to process it all at once. They may be banking on the delay, using it to make us appear negligent in the eyes of our people. They've learned we tend to read the tea leaves in hindsight. In fact, that's exactly what happened here."

The Defense Minister cursed. "If we had processed the Yassin intercepts in real time, we might have done something about it."

"Done what?" the Foreign Minister asked.

"Exactly," Arad said. "With such vague information, what could we possibly have done?"

The Prime Minister put his hands on the table.

"The question before us is what to do now. Does anyone propose we strike the mosque?"

The question met a chorus of silence. The ministers and generals stared self-consciously at the table.

"We have subtler means of dealing with the Mullah," the head of Mossad said.

"Not too subtle, I hope."

"It won't be easy, but the message will be delivered."

"Good, keep me posted. Now, how about this base in the desert? Where is it?"

"Egypt," Arad said. "Deep in the Sinai."

"We should never have given it back," the Defense Minister fumed.

"It was a matter of land for peace," the Prime Minister said. "The trade bought us decades of peace with Egypt."

"And now this," the Defense Minister said.

The Foreign Minister leaned across the table.

"Will you jeopardize that peace?" he asked.

The Prime Minister sat back in his chair and weighed his options.

"Is there any reason to believe the government of Egypt is involved?"

"No," Arad answered.

On the big screen, the helicopter rose from the desert floor and flew toward the mountain pass, leaving the frame.

"Who's getting out of the helicopters?"

"We've only been able to identify one of them. He phoned his wife in Saudi Arabia after he arrived at the base. We believe she's related to the Mullah."

"Is there any reason to believe the government of Egypt knows anything about this?"

"No."

The Prime Minister took a deep breath and let it out slowly.

"I want a direct line to the president of Egypt the moment our forces enter Egyptian airspace. I want to assure him we have no quarrel with Egypt and that our planes will not cross the Suez. And I want all our forces on standby in case he rejects the message.

"The principle here is preemption, not revenge. I agree with Avi that something bigger is in the works. For the security of our people, I must act.

"General Goren, I'm ordering you to launch an air strike. This is your target. I want it obliterated."

Chapter 66

A Desert Base
The Sinai Peninsula
Egypt

"They're waiting for you," Father Gregory said.

Elazar took a deep breath. At Father Gregory's suggestion, and with his help, he had prepared some welcoming remarks. He hoped he wouldn't stumble over them. He liked to make eye contact when he addressed large groups, but after all these years it still took some effort to avoid looking at the text. Mishka used to chide him about that. "Remember the people, you're talking to people," she would say.

He was surprised that he felt so nervous. He wondered if he was being self-important, but he sensed this would be an historic occasion, maybe the high point of his career. He wished Mishka could share it with him.

"Whatever you tell them, Meyer, I'm sure you'll be eloquent," Catherine said.

She was talking like a daughter. She reminded him of his own daughter and all the stolen possibilities. He wanted to believe his daughter would have grown up like Catherine.

"Will you help me with the box?" he asked.

"I'd be honored."

Catherine lifted the aluminum case. He reached out to help, but she told him not to be ridiculous.

The night before, after watching news updates about Yad Vashem—there really wasn't much new information—the two of them had sat looking at the case by the light of a kerosene lamp, speculating about its contents.

"Do you want to open it?" Elazar had asked.

She took her time answering.

"No, do you?"

"I can wait."

They sat in silence.

"I hope you don't feel cheated," Elazar had asked.

Her answer had filled him with paternal pride.

"As Father Gregory said, the discovery is larger than any individual."

Elazar left the case with her overnight. In the middle of the night, unable to sleep, she was drawn to it. She ran her hands across the cold aluminum. Maybe just a quick look, she rationalized, to check and see. What if it was empty? What if it was someone's mother's favorite recipe for grilling lamb?

She tried to open the case, but it was locked.

In the morning, she thought of mentioning it to Elazar, thought of asking him, but she was ashamed.

Years ago, in Zurich, she had told Meyer about her brother, and he had reacted with deeply personal disapproval. Not for Ian, but for her motives. "You aren't searching for history; you're searching for absolution," Meyer had said. "You expect to redeem your brother—or relieve your own tortured conscience. I doubt you can do either, and I know you can't do both."

Now, Elazar asked her to address the gathering of scholars, but she said no, he should speak for both of them. She told him about Jordan, and asked him to honor Jordan's role—even as her suspicion of Jordan deepened, along with her agony.

"He was more than a partner to you," Elazar said. It sounded more like a statement than a question.

Catherine nodded. As well as anyone, Elazar could understand her grief.

They followed Father Gregory out of the tent, through the camp, and into the big tent that served as the dining hall. The murmur of conversation subsided as people noticed their arrival.

The guests sat at rows of folding tables facing a head table with a portable lectern. Elazar made eye contact with Gunther from Vienna, and Turner from Harvard, and Diaz from Mexico City, one of the last to arrive. Diaz had put on weight since they last met. Ah, the joys of marriage.

There were 24 guests in all. Assembling them in secret had been a remarkable feat, a tribute to Elazar's persuasive powers and Father Gregory's logistics.

Elazar had deleted some names from the list because he doubted their abilities or their temperament. He had added Tullio from Rome—he still regretted passing over Tullio's application years earlier to lead a new excavation at Lachish. And a few people had refused to accept such a mysterious invitation. One dismissed him as a crank.

It was hot in the tent, but the white nylon cut the sun's glare.

Father Gregory took the aluminum case from Catherine and placed it on the head table beside the lectern. With a quick, inconspicuous movement, he unlocked it. Then he took a seat in the rear of the tent with two of his monks, a few rows behind the assembled scholars.

Elazar noticed a cameraman and a soundman with a TV camera on a tripod. They were part of the team. Father Gregory had told him they would be recording.

Elazar looked down at his text, a few handwritten pages.

"Will you hold these until I'm finished?" he asked.

Catherine smiled and took his speech.

Elazar strode to the lectern.

He tapped the microphone tentatively and looked into the faces of his guests.

"Some of you may be wondering why you're here," he deadpanned.

Nervous laughter filled the tent, and Elazar felt the tension ease by just a notch. The old gravel voice was warming to the task.

"From the bottom of my heart, I want to thank you for coming, and for giving me your trust. The work that awaits us may test our abilities and challenge us in deeper ways, but I am honored to be undertaking it with the people in this tent.

"I'm also grateful to be alive. But that's another subject.

"Let me make an opening declaration. All of you know my background. I will do my best to submerge whatever biases and attachments I have and to proceed in a spirit of objectivity. I hope we can move forward together in peace and brotherhood, in pursuit of knowledge. And may the truth be our guide."

The guests were moved, but he could tell they had no idea what he was talking about.

"Days ago, in the Judean Desert, our colleague Catherine Cavanaugh of the University of Michigan unearthed a pair of ceramic jars."

There was a ripple in the audience. Who was she? What had she discovered?

He gave Catherine a nod.

"Professor Cavanaugh was assisted by Zev Galil, who all of you know by reputation and many of you know personally. I'm sorry to report that Zev died bringing these artifacts to light."

A buzz spread through the audience, but Elazar raised his hand.

"Please, hold your questions.

"This discovery was the culmination of some extraordinary research by Professor Cavanaugh and an Israeli journalist, Benjamin Jordan. Their research leads to a clear and powerful conclusion. In all likelihood, these jars contain records rescued from the Temple in Jerusalem in 70 C.E. Not just any records, but chronicles kept by the high priests themselves. Among them . . . Caiaphas."

Everyone started talking at once.

Elazar raised his hand again to silence the reaction.

"Yes, we believe Professor Cavanaugh has unearthed the personal testament of Caiaphas. Her earlier discoveries with Mr. Jordan indicate that Caiaphas died a penitent recluse. We can only hope that the contents of these jars tell us why.

"Let me show you what we're dealing with."

Elazar opened the case and lifted one of the jars, which was wrapped in a clear plastic bag.

"Professor Cavanaugh and I have refrained from opening these jars. We have not yet examined the contents. That is a journey we plan to take with all of you, starting tomorrow. I think you'll find that our Greek Orthodox hosts have provided all the technology we could require. Let me extend my personal thanks to Father Gregory, for a debt I can never repay."

Elazar replaced the jar and closed the case.

"And now, before we adjourn, there's one other matter. I would ask everyone to join me in a moment of silence for the victims of Yad Vashem."

The stupefied scholars bowed their heads, but it was plain none of them was thinking about Yad Vashem.

Elazar said a silent prayer and looked up.

"Thank you," he said. "That's all I have to say for now."

He tried to leave the lectern, but he was bombarded with questions.

"How did Zev die?"

"We thought you were dead — where have you been?"

"What does this have to do with the bombing of the Institute?"

"Why such secrecy?"

"Yes, why such secrecy?"

Elazar gestured with both arms, trying to suppress the hubbub, but the scholars wouldn't be silenced.

"Please, please," he said. "Not all at once."

"Why have you brought us to the middle of nowhere?" Gunther of Vienna demanded.

Elazar struggled with the most obvious question. He had hoped to defer answering; now, he groped for a way to say as little as possible.

"I had an Institute, and now it's gone. I had a Council full of colleagues; now all of them are dead. I had a friend named Zev, and he's gone too. I've lost too many colleagues over this. I won't lose you."

He pressed his way through the crowd and left the tent.

Chapter 67

Northern Israel

General Goren watched the sixth warplane launch from its base in Northern Israel and rocket high over the Galilee. It followed the others in a sweeping 270-degree arc and screamed south toward the Sinai.

The general prayed for his fliers.

On direct instructions from the Prime Minister, he had given each of them a top-secret order. It was unprecedented in Israeli history, and some people might think it bordered on treason. Goren had insisted on delivering the order in person. If fired upon by Egyptian forces, he told his flight crews, they were not to return fire. The Prime Minister hoped this demonstration of restraint would avoid all-out war.

None of the men challenged the order.

Goren left the observation deck and hustled to his underground command center. He had an entire military to mobilize. If the Prime Minister had miscalculated, Israel could soon be at war with all its Arab neighbors, for an attack on one would likely be answered as an attack on all.

Saudi Arabia

Circling high above the kingdom, an American-made AWACS military plane on routine duty monitored every blip of air traffic from horizon to horizon and downlinked its data to a base near Riyadh.

Inside the control room, a Saudi junior officer screened the data for activity at each of three Israeli airfields. His interest was strictly extracurricular. His orders came from outside the chain of command. The officer was not privileged to know the purpose. He proudly did as he was told.

He had been watching for four hours, since his shift began, and he had noticed nothing out of the ordinary. But now six Israeli fighters in tight formation continued on an unusual course over the Negev toward the Egyptian border.

He excused himself, claiming a bathroom break, and headed for a phone.

The Sinai Desert

In the cold clarity of the gathering night, Meyer Elazar looked up at the stars rising over the mountains. He sensed the presence of his ancestors.

For forty years they wandered in this wilderness, suspended between slavery and the Promised Land. Despite God's abundant signs, many lost faith. Elazar wondered if he was losing faith, too. Or maybe he was on the verge of a new and deeper understanding. Either way, he felt cold and alone.

He had left his tent to take a walk, and his wandering thoughts took him deeper into the night.

He remembered Korah, who rebelled against Moses. Korah, who challenged the privileges of the priest and the prescribed manner of honoring the Lord.

What makes you holier than the rest of us? Korah asked. *Why should you and your brother Aaron have the exclusive right to make offerings to God?*

"You take too much on yourselves," Korah said. *"Each and every member of the community is holy and the Lord is among them."*

Elazar remembered how God answered Korah and his allies. The earth opened and swallowed them. Those who presumed to offer incense to God, usurping the role of God's designated intermediaries, met an equally vivid fate. They were consumed by a fireball.

"By this you shall know that it is the Lord who sent me to do all I have done," Moses declared.

It happened here, in the Sinai.

Were those truly signs from God? Or were they creations of the priesthood—descendants of Aaron, seeking to secure their prerogatives?

Elazar's questions reached across the wilderness to the land of Midian, where Moses led the Israelites in conquest and slaughter. It was God's command, a holy war, the Torah said, because the Midianites worshipped other gods, and seduced the Israelites to do the same. The Lord demanded vengeance.

When the plunder was counted, the book of Numbers took care to note the Israelite priests' share—675 sheep, 72 cattle, 61 asses, and 32 virgin females.

The human plunder could have been greater; the Israelites captured many Midianites. At Moses's insistence, they massacred all but the virgins.

Once, before God called him to greater things, a younger Moses had been forced to flee his own country. He had become lost in the wilderness.

He had found comfort among strangers who opened their tents. He had taken shelter among the Midianites.

He had taken one of them as his wife.

The moon was rising over the mountains, and the white tents shimmered in the purity of its glow. Elazar pulled tight the collar of his woolen coat—a gift from Father Gregory, one size too large.

He turned back toward the camp.

He recognized the monk's silhouette coming out to meet him. He was coming with others, two of them. Elazar guessed that one was Brother Alex, who had participated in his rescue. Yes, Brother Alex.

"We've been looking for you," Father Gregory said curtly. "Come, you must come with us now."

"What? What is it?"

The brothers took his arms.

"Israelis," Father Gregory said. "They're coming to bomb us."

They were hustling him along, almost lifting him off his feet. He was gripped with fear and heartbreak. He moved as quickly as he could. They were leading him away from the camp. He saw a pair of Ford Explorers parked in the desert about 100 yards from the tents.

"What about Catherine, and the others?" he asked with alarm.

The camp was calm. He could see lights and silhouettes through the walls of the tents—people reading, talking, preparing for bed.

"Quickly, quickly," Father Gregory whispered.

"You need to warn them," Elazar said with disbelief. "You need to evacuate the camp!"

"Meyer, there's no time, and there's only one helicopter. Catherine's already on board waiting for us."

"Tell them to scatter. Tell them to run from the camp!"

"We must go *now*."

Elazar dug in his heels.

"We can't leave them . . . ."

Father Gregory nodded, and Brother Alex clamped a hand over Elazar's mouth. Elazar wriggled, but they overpowered him. He felt a sharp jab in his thigh. He struggled to break free, but he was weakening, fading . . . .

The earth opened up and swallowed him.

Northern Israel

General Goren listened on a muted extension as the Prime Minister held for the president of Egypt. He prayed that reason would prevail.

He prayed that the president would *pick up the goddamned phone.*

The familiar voice came on the line.

"Mr. Prime Minister, shalom."

"Mr. President, *mesa al-kheir*. I'm calling on a mission of peace. Minutes from now, six of our planes will attack a terrorist base in the Sinai. After striking the target, they will return directly to Israel. They do not threaten Egypt, and we intend no hostility toward your country. I ask that you allow our planes to proceed unimpeded."

"Your planes in our airspace?"

"Yes, Mr. President. To prevent an imminent terrorist attack on the State of Israel."

"We have no terrorist bases in Sinai."

"We don't believe you're aware of it, Mr. President, and we don't hold you responsible."

"No killing on Egyptian soil, Mr. Prime Minister. No Israeli planes in our airspace."

"But Mr. President—"

"Mr. Prime Minister, turn back your planes."

"But Mr. President—"

"Turn them back."

In the air-conditioned chill of his command center, Goren watched live cockpit video from six planes on six color screens. The satellite feed filled a larger screen with ghostly green images of people in tents, betrayed by their body heat.

The first bomb went wide of the mark and erupted in a magnificent fireball. When the flash subsided, Goren could see the startled reaction of the people in the tents. He could see bodies thrown by the force, scrambling blindly for cover, casting about in hopeless confusion, or dazed by the shock. He could feel their panic.

The second, third and fourth bombs fell in rapid succession with deadly accuracy. Moving bodies vaporized before Goren's eyes. Some of the survivors tried to run from the camp, but the fifth and six planes carpeted the valley with thousands of cluster bombs, which exploded in a blizzard of death.

The tents were gone. The people were gone. The threat was neutralized, and the jets were turning for home.

There was a palpable rush of triumph in the command center, but the general's staff stayed focused. They had six flight crews at risk.

"Three Egyptian fighters on course to intercept," the lead controller said.

"Will our planes beat them to the border?"

"I estimate just barely."

Goren watched his boys racing homeward as the Egyptians vectored toward them. If it were a combat situation, there would be no contest, Goren thought, for odds, equipment and training favored his boys.

The staff in the command center seemed confident. They assumed it was a combat situation.

Goren needed an antacid, but he refrained. He was determined to set an example.

The Israelis were less than 15 seconds from the border when the Egyptians closed within firing range.

The Israeli jets reentered Israeli airspace.

"Yes!" the lead controller exclaimed.

Goren kept watching the screen. The Egyptians were continuing their pursuit.

The controller sank back into his seat.

"They're on your tail. They've penetrated Israel. Kill them! Kill them!" he exclaimed.

The Israeli pilots ignored the instruction.

"What the hell are they doing?" the controller asked in disbelief.

The Egyptians locked weapons.

"Take them out!" the controller exhorted.

The Israelis held their fire.

Then, one by one, the Egyptians peeled away.

Goren's staff erupted in cheers and hugged each other in celebration. On a secure phone, the Prime Minister offered congratulations. But the general was strangely silent. When no one was looking, he popped a nitro. The mission was a success and all his boys were coming home. Yet his stomach churned with a nagging worry, the precise nature of which he was only now able to identify.

According to the intelligence report, forces had been gathering in the desert—"forces of truth," the intercepted voice had said. But why would forces be gathering in the middle of the desert? Maybe to plan or train, sure. But, if they were ready to carry out an attack, wouldn't they be dispersing?

Jerusalem

Within hours, cockpit video of a fireball in the Sinai was broadcast worldwide.

The Prime Minister made a brief statement.

"Tonight Israel avenged the attack on Yad Vashem and prevented an even deadlier act of terrorism. As promised, our retribution was absolute. We have kept faith with the six million. We have kept faith with the children. Once again, our enemies have shown their evil hand, but they will never prevail."

Chapter 68

Tel Aviv

General Goren wanted to roll over and go back to sleep, but the phone wouldn't let him. The blasted thing kept ringing, and his wife kept snoring. He opened one bleary eye and looked at the clock: 5:25 a.m.

Never a good way to start the day.

"General, are you watching the news?" his senior aide said.

"Actually, I was tuned to the insides of my eyelids. What's happening?"

"Check out Pan Arab News and call me back."

Goren found the remote control under the bed and clicked through the channels.

"That was our correspondent Jemal Kemal in Cyprus," the anchorwoman said. "Turning now to Ankara, an update on recovery efforts following the recent quake . . . ."

Goren speed dialed Lipman's home.

"I think I missed it. What did they say?"

"A religious group in Cyprus is denouncing us for attacking a civilian research facility."

"Muslims?"

"No, Greek Orthodox Christians."

"Yassin spent time in Cyprus."

"Could be some sort of front group."

Goren sat up and scratched his head.

"Is it possible . . . ."

"I don't see how, General. It's shameless propaganda."

"Do you think anyone else will pick it up?"

"We already got a call from CNN."

"Then use our intelligence. Expose the lie, before anyone starts believing it."

"I'll call Mossad."

"Wait," Goren said, reaching for a bathrobe. "I'll make the call."

Avi Arad, who answered the phone as if he'd been awake for hours, insisted that releasing the intercepts would compromise sources and methods.

"How do you expect us to hit the Mullah and stop the next attack if we tip our hand?" the Mossad chief argued.

"I thought you said they *already know* we're listening," Goren countered.

"Yes, but I could be wrong."

The infighting between the general and the head of intelligence raged until late afternoon, by which time the unsubstantiated claims of an obscure Greek Orthodox cleric in Cyprus circled the globe at least twice hourly—albeit in news bites of less than 30 seconds.

Israeli government spokesmen refused to dignify the Cypriot's charge with comment until early evening, when the Prime Minister settled the argument. By then, the unsupported accusation had run its course and was almost out of steam. The media looked to Egypt for confirmation or denial; Egypt was blocking access to the remote site and gave the media nothing.

The Prime Minister decided to fill the void. He issued a statement denouncing the reports from Cyprus as "absurd disinformation."

The Israeli government released transcripts of the conversation in which Yassin warned of an "opening declaration" and the later call in which an unidentified male announced that "The message has been delivered."

According to the official statement, the intercepts were "clearly predictive of a terrorist plot" and "evidence of efforts to deny the Holocaust."

The Prime Minister was satisfied that he had made the right decision. He wanted the world to know the Mullah's role. As far as he was concerned, Egypt's silence was no surprise. Egypt was embarrassed—if not exactly ashamed—to have been harboring terrorist scum.

By the time General Goren turned in for the night, the news cycle had dutifully recycled the Israeli rebuttal.

At noon the next day, Goren was in a routine meeting at the Defense Ministry, reviewing conditions on the northern border, when one of his aides noticed something on the television and turned up the volume.

"Again, what you're seeing is video just released in Cairo," the American anchor said. "Egyptian officials are telling World News that these pictures were shot at the facility in the Sinai Desert just hours before the Israeli warplanes struck."

The familiar face of Rabbi Meyer Elazar filled the screen. There were dark shadows under his eyes, and the distinctive gravel voice spoke with even more gravitas than usual.

"Let me make an opening declaration. All of you know my background. I will do my best to submerge whatever biases and attachments I have and to proceed in a spirit of objectivity. I hope we can

move forward together in peace and brotherhood, in pursuit of knowledge. And may the truth be our guide."

"We're told that Rabbi Elazar, who headed—or heads—the Institute for Cultural Antiquities in Jerusalem, was announcing a major discovery in the field of biblical archaeology, potentially more earth-shaking than the famous Dead Sea Scrolls."

"Yes, we believe Professor Cavanaugh has unearthed the personal testament of Caiaphas. Her earlier discoveries with Mr. Jordan indicate that Caiaphas died a penitent recluse. We can only hope that the contents of these jars tell us why."

The anchor hesitated, listening to the voice in his ear. On the screen, Elazar was lifting a ceramic jar for all to see.

"The name you heard there—'Caiaphas'—apparently refers to the high priest of Jerusalem mentioned in the New Testament. The Bible says Caiaphas played a key role in the events leading to the Crucifixion . . . . And the 'Mr. Jordan' the rabbi cited is Benjamin Jordan, an Israeli journalist.

"Our Egyptian sources tell us that Rabbi Elazar—presumed dead in the bombing that destroyed his Institute—was welcoming an international assembly of scholars."

"Why have you brought us to the middle of nowhere?"

On the screen, Elazar struggled with the question. He gave a halting, emotional answer.

"I had an Institute, and now it's gone . . . . I've lost too many colleagues over this. I won't lose you."

"Joining us now from Cairo, our correspondent Mark Donner. Mark, do we know if there were any survivors?"

"It appears that there were no survivors. That's the word from the Egyptians. Apparently, the desert camp you saw on the tape is a scene of total devastation. They say the Israeli attack was 'thorough' and 'effective.' But we hope to see for ourselves later today. The Egyptian government is escorting a team of neutral observers to the site, including representatives of the International Red Cross and the United Nations. And, of course, we plan to be there."

"That was Mark Donner in Cairo. Stay tuned to World News for continuing coverage of The Bombing in the Desert."

In the conference room at the Defense Ministry, no one said a word.

Chapter 69

By mid afternoon, every news channel was broadcasting pictures of mangled bodies and charred remains. In half a dozen languages, stunned and grieving relatives were telling interviewers about scholars who had mysteriously dropped everything to fly to the Middle East—now presumed among the dead.

At a news conference in Ann Arbor, the president of the University of Michigan gave a tearful tribute to Catherine Cavanaugh, beloved by students and respected by her peers.

When the president finished speaking, the dean of the faculty, Adam Keller, stepped to the microphones.

"Professor Cavanaugh brought out the best in all of us," Keller said.

There was video that had been taken under the tent in the Sinai, while the assembled scholars listened to Elazar. The camera had panned past Catherine, and the networks played that clip in slow motion, the last picture of the young professor.

In Saudi Arabia, the Mullah released a three-sentence statement to an Arab satellite network.

"It is true that we were informed of the ecumenical conference in the Egyptian desert. At the invitation of the hosts, we sent a distinguished delegate, Dr. Hosain Khalifa. We join his widow and children in mourning."

Around the world, the commentary on Israel ranged from scathing to mocking.

"I ask you—who are the real terrorists?" an opposition member of Parliament said on the floor of the House of Commons. "Listen to Rabbi Elazar's words—the Israelis have attacked the spirit of peace and brotherhood."

Jordan's earlier story, the story that had been shot down, was widely cited as context for the bombing. It contained the first suggestion of an Israeli conspiracy. The Israeli government's denials were seen as part of the cover-up.

In New York, the Jewish Anti-Discrimination League, which outspokenly led the fight against anti-Semitism, had no comment.

By far the most ominous noises came from faithful Christians and their church leaders. Many felt an almost sublime spiritual ecstasy when they learned of the archaeological discovery—it was a direct and tangible connection to the events in the Gospels. They were overwhelmed by the report that Caiaphas had withdrawn into a life of penitence. This was indirect proof of his guilt and strong circumstantial evidence of the trial and Crucifixion. More than that, it suggested something extraordinary led the high priest to see his error.

In small villages and big cities, legions of the faithful—including some newly faithful—filled their churches and cathedrals in a spontaneous outpouring. Wherever they gathered, there were expressions of joy—mingled with anger, horror, incredulity and despair that Israel had eliminated the witness.

"A cruel and calculated sacrilege," Cardinal del Toro said from his pulpit in Madrid. "Listen to Rabbi Elazar—he pointed to a trail of killings and all but declared his fear of Israel. Otherwise, why would he have been in Egypt?"

At the Vatican, the pope was in seclusion.

"The Holy Father resists the rush to judgment," a Vatican spokesman said.

From his bed in the cardiac intensive care unit at Hadassah Hospital, General Goren watched his Prime Minister deliver the most abject statement he had ever witnessed by an Israeli leader.

"We, more than anyone, want to learn what happened and bring the facts to light. To the government of Egypt and the people of the world, we pledge our full cooperation. We believe we acted on solid evidence to save lives. But, if the news reports are accurate—and I'm not here to dispute them—the world has witnessed a tragic error and a horrible misunderstanding. Nothing more, and nothing less."

In the Knesset, there were calls for the Prime Minister and his cabinet to resign. At the United Nations, France introduced a Security Council resolution calling for an economic boycott of Israel.

In Washington, twelve members of Congress introduced legislation to cut off all aid to America's staunchest Mid-East ally.

"The jury's still out," the president said as he boarded his helicopter to Camp David. "Let's everybody take a deep breath and see what the evidence has to say for itself."

Chapter 70

Tel Aviv

In his glass office, the editor of *The Shofar* was working himself into a tremulous tirade.

His star reporter, Ben Jordan, had gone AWOL, only to turn up in the center of the crisis. And Shaul Meltzer had to learn about it on television.

It was a good thing he fired Jordan, or suspended him, or whatever the hell he had done to get rid of the showboating son of a bitch. Fucking unreliable. One of the editor's influential friends in the intelligence establishment had warned him about Jordan—warned him that Jordan's pedigree might become a personal embarrassment for Meltzer if *The Shofar* continued to publish "his unpatriotic crap."

Reasonable advice from a reasonable man. But now the future of the country was on the line, and the influential friend was probably one of the assholes responsible for the mess.

So where the hell was Jordan?

If the bastard ever showed his face in the newsroom again Meltzer swore he'd arrange a second circumcision.

Jordan's eyes blazed as he stepped off the elevator. He clenched his jaw and stared straight ahead. The doctors had offered him painkillers, but again he favored the advice of his Arab physician: Best to keep his wits.

Best to remember the pain.

He had pulled out his intravenous line when he heard about the bombing.

People looked up in surprise as Jordan passed their desks on the way to his own. A murmur spread through the newsroom. Yet his demeanor caused people to keep their distance. Leah looked at him, and he looked through her.

He had all the proof he needed. The story was airtight. It was his exclusive, and after it ran, nothing would be the same. The truth would be told, because he would tell it. And Israel would pay for what it had done.

He heard the echo of gunfire in the cave. He saw the desert stars mirrored in Catherine's eyes. He felt their lips meet beneath the Eiffel Tower. It had taken him a lifetime to find her, and now she was gone, stolen from him. She had survived the killing in the Valley of Asher, only to be murdered by the Israeli air force.

He began to type his byline and hesitated, staring at the screen. He wanted to get it right for once, but half of it was still missing—the name his parents had given him.

Disappointed, he typed the only name he had ever used and started writing.

"Jesus, Jordan, you okay?"

It was Meltzer.

"God, we were worried about you. Is there anything that you need? Maybe a cup of coffee?"

"The story's right here," Jordan said, handing Meltzer a digital video disc. "It will lead tomorrow's paper."

He didn't bother to look up. He typed with anger and intensity. He typed so fast that his keyboard sounded like an automatic weapon.

Every keystroke fired a bolt of pain.

In his glass office, Meltzer cued the disc. It was labeled, simply, "Highlights."

Zev Galil squinted into the camera and stepped barefoot across a dusty mosaic in a sun-bleached sandscape. He was a wearing a T-shirt and khaki shorts and a broad floppy hat that made him look ridiculous.

"I'm standing on a truly remarkable map of the Middle East unearthed just weeks ago here on the western coast of the Red Sea. With me and my students are Professor Catherine Cavanaugh and the journalist Benjamin Jordan, whose investigations have brought us here today . . . .

Twenty minutes later, Meyer Elazar entered the picture in a dimly lit cave.

"The government. The government of Israel," Elazar said.

"What about the government?" Galil asked.

"They tried to kill me, but I escaped. I'm not sure they even know I escaped. But now, they're after you. They're on their way here, right now. They know what you're looking for. They know all about the Caiaphas Chronicle. And they aren't about to let it see the light of day."

Twenty-four minutes into the video, Cavanaugh lifted a jar with a fractured lid from its hiding place. There was a glimpse of rolled parchment . . . .

Thirty minutes into the video, the camera zoomed in on a pair of jeeps approaching across a desert plateau. They were Israeli army jeeps . . . .

The soldiers were raising their rifles, opening fire . . . .

On his knees, framed at a crazy angle, Galil raised his left arm with obvious effort and waved, as if urging someone to forget about him and get away. Then his head exploded in a puff of pink . . . .

Through a blood-spattered lens, the camera captured skewed, random images of sky and ground and running soldiers and an upside-down helicopter. The sound of the rotors got louder . . . and the screen filled with static.

Shaken, Meltzer was about to eject the disc when the static disappeared and an enhanced close-up filled the screen. It was a head-on shot of a soldier in the assault party. The image took a giant step closer and the camera seemed to freeze on a corner of the soldier's chest. There was an insignia on the Israeli's uniform—a curved black dagger.

"Does this mean what I think it means?" Meltzer asked his reporter.

"Proof that the bombing in the desert was no 'misunderstanding,'" Jordan said. "Proof that Israel would do whatever it took to capture or destroy the Caiaphas relic."

"Did you know Zev Galil?"

"Zev was a dove."

Meltzer nodded his head sympathetically.

"Finish writing."

Chapter 71

Tel Aviv

Jordan was thinking about fire and torture at Pamet Hall, wondering where it fit into the story. He was certain it was part of Israel's ruthless campaign, along with the murder of Nigel Waverly.

In frustration, he decided to leave it out, because he had no proof.

No matter. It was a minor point in the larger scheme. And he could rely on others to make the connections on their own.

Just a few more paragraphs and he'd be done. Deadline was fast approaching. The presses would run and the truth would be told and the guilty would know the world's wrath.

His line was ringing, but he was somewhere else.

For a moment, he was back in the West Bank, in a crowded open-air market that had exploded in gunfire and chaos. He saw a fat man pounding on a locked door. He watched a gangly yeshiva boy named Menachem Goldstein pull the trigger. He watched, passive and useless, while the Palestinian died.

He felt a bond of kinship with the Palestinian—and a consuming hatred for Goldstein and all he represented. He remembered the satisfaction of smashing Goldstein's face.

Two more rings and the phone would go to voicemail, where he could listen to it later. Eventually. Or ignore it. And if his mailbox had reached its "maximum voice storage capacity," as the annoying recording was constantly reminding him, he wouldn't have to bother.

One more ring.

He picked up the phone.

"Jordan," he said.

Hesitation on the other end.

"Benjamin, you know who this is?"

Samir. Probably sunning himself on a yacht.

"Yes, of course."

"You need to investigate the bombing in the desert, Benjamin. You need to tell people what happened. You must stop the lie."

"It will be at the top of tomorrow's front page. I'm about to file."

A great sigh of relief on the other end.

"How did you do it?"

"I have video. I have tape of the Sicarii killing my friend Zev."

"What?"

"Israeli commandos, in the Valley of Asher. I was there when they attacked us. They were trying to steal the relic. It was ruthless and carefully planned."

Jordan felt a vacuum at the other end. He felt it filling with fear.

"Tomorrow's front page?"

"If you get off the phone and let me file."

"Listen to me, Benjamin. Things are not as they seem."

"They seem brutally clear to me."

"Don't run the story, Benjamin. You must hold off."

"I'm right on deadline."

"Please, don't hang up."

"What do you know?"

"All I know is that your story would be wrong."

"How?"

"I've heard things, Benjamin. I can't explain."

"Give me something."

"Not on the phone."

"Damn it, you—"

"Meet me in half an hour, where we last met."

"But—"

There was a click and the line went dead. Jordan looked at the phone in disbelief. He slammed the receiver into its cradle. The sly bastard had hung up.

To hell with Samir. He was talking nonsense.

Jordan started typing again. He would claim his revenge. That was all he had left.

He rubbed his eyes, wondering if he was thinking clearly. He hadn't found a single source who knew anything about the commando raid in the Valley of Asher. Then again, he didn't know whether to trust his sources. And Catherine's death was more than he could accept. He wanted to believe, needed to believe, that she had escaped the ashes, just as Elazar escaped the bombing of the Institute.

There was nowhere to turn, no one to turn to. No one except Samir, who was worse than nothing.

He typed a message to his editor—*Back in an hour*—and slipped out of the newsroom.

In the backseat of the taxi, Jordan cursed the traffic. Another roadblock. Up ahead, Israeli soldiers were harassing innocent Palestinians and searching in vain for suicide bombers.

He remembered a night long ago in a cabin in Michigan, before he embarked on a mad, deadly search for a religious artifact. He remembered

Catherine's question—*Had he thought through the implications?* Screw the implications. He had no stake in the religious debate. All he cared about was Catherine. Catherine was his religion.

Catherine and the desert sky, the ribbon of stars that lit the night.

At the Israel Museum, Jordan leapt from the taxi without waiting for his change. He ran past the Shrine of the Book, designed to resemble the lid of a Dead Sea jar, and pushed his way through the doors of the main building. The pain split like a knife.

Samir was standing in front of the huge stone tablets taken from the ruins of Sennacherib's palace. Not the alabaster originals, which hung in London, but copies. In the carvings, Assyrian invaders were pillaging the city of Lachish, impaling the Jewish defenders on long wooden stakes.

Samir's eyes were sunk in shadows, and he hadn't shaved. He scanned the crowd with uncharacteristic agitation.

"Did Catherine survive?" Jordan asked.

"I don't know. I can't see how."

Jordan grabbed Samir's elbow and steered him across the gallery, away from the tourists.

"Why am I here, Samir?"

"The Mullah is lying, Benjamin. The Mullah is behind it."

"What's the evidence?"

"I know of none."

"Damn it, Samir—"

"They're thorough, Benjamin. They eliminate loose ends. Like our friend on the Council, Ismail Ramsi."

"I thought you blamed Israel for his death."

"That's what the Mullah wanted us to believe."

"You expect me to take this on faith?"

"What else can you do?"

"I'm sorry, but that doesn't cut it. Not after last time."

"You have to understand, I'm taking a terrible risk coming here, talking to you."

"Then make it count."

Samir sighed. He looked scared and defeated.

"We have a source inside the Mullah's organization. At least we think we do. He could be a double agent. It seems the Mullah has infiltrated our intelligence service. It seems he has followers within our government, and among our military officers. Just as we learned of the Silver Scroll from Ismail, the Mullah seems to have learned about it from us . . . with additional information from a spy inside the museum, a janitor who thought he was selling information to an Israeli archaeologist."

"And?"

"I've told you all I know."

"I don't believe you."

"Benjamin, why would I lie?"

"Why are you telling me this?"

Samir was struggling, grasping for words.

"Do you remember the day the King took you to Al Aqsa?"

"Yes, of course."

"It wasn't his only unscheduled trip that day in Jerusalem. He also went to Yad Vashem."

"So?"

"I was with him at Yad Vashem. I saw the eternal lights in the Children's Memorial."

"That's very noble, but why are you telling me this?"

"Men like the Mullah threaten us all, Benjamin. They are an affront to God and humanity."

"Damn it, Samir, I wouldn't be writing this if you hadn't given me the text of the Silver Scroll."

"What are you talking about?"

"The envelope in my shoe."

"I don't know anything about that."

"Your message, summoning me to Al Aqsa."

"Not mine."

Jordan felt a cold rush of adrenaline, a wave of anxiety engulfing him.

Chapter 72

Tel Aviv

Back in the newsroom, Meltzer looked at Jordan with raging incredulity.

"You want me to do what?"

"Hold the story. Kill it."

Meltzer looked at the clock.

"Based on an anonymous source?"

"Yes."

"A reliable source?"

"No."

"You've worked with this source before?"

"Yes, on my last story."

Meltzer looked at the text displayed on Jordan's computer. He read the first paragraph. Dynamite.

"I saw the video, Jordan. It's airtight. It's huge."

"There are things . . . ."

"Go on."

"There are things I don't understand."

"There are things I don't understand, starting with you. I am not sitting on this, Goddamn it. And I guess I do understand. Because it takes nerve, Jordan, and obviously you've lost yours."

"You can't run it."

"I won't hold it."

Jordan looked Meltzer in the eye. His fingers were poised on the keyboard. With a clear conscience, and no small measure of personal satisfaction, he hit "delete."

He rose from his chair and left the newsroom.

Inside his glass office, Meltzer was working himself into another tirade.

The story would bring down the government, as well it should. And he, Shaul Meltzer, could be the giant-killer, the voice of courage and truth. He could be a redeemer for his embattled people, caught in the crosshairs of their own lie.

But not if the competition got there first. As inevitably it would.

By running away from the story, Jordan had proven one thing: In an ironic way, he had proven his reliability. He had proven that he was not a propaganda agent or a terrorist mole.

Meltzer summoned Leah. She was the best damn writer *The Shofar* had, and she knew as much about the subject as anyone.

He handed her the video disc.

She looked at him, puzzled.

"I'm giving you 45 minutes to write this," the editor said. "We'll push our deadlines."

"This is Benjamin's story."

"Not any more."

Chapter 73

Tel Aviv

In the stillness of his apartment, Jordan loaded a compact disc into his computer. The screen saver disappeared, replaced by the unedited version of the video he had given Meltzer. For the fifth time, he watched Zev discussing the fine points of a mosaic, Amnon mugging for the camera, and Yossi climbing the cliff with a rifle slung across his back. He watched a helicopter soaring overhead, away from the Valley of Asher. He searched for a sign. He needed a trail to follow, a breadcrumb, *something*. But there was nothing.

He stopped the video and reversed. He froze it on Catherine trying to lift a burlap sack from the cave floor. He watched gold coins sluicing out of the sack, and he advanced frame by frame, into bleakness and defeat.

The night became a restless blur of self-recrimination. If not for him, they would still be safe. In his nightmares, he ran searching through an endless, featureless desert, without so much as a mirage to guide him. Under a blinding sun, he stumbled over bleached bones. He awoke, sweating, at 2:17 a.m.

The video remained paused on a shot of the helicopter, one of the last images that Hannah recorded, and it was jumping nervously. Jordan advanced it another step. He leaned forward for a closer look and bit his lip in frustration. It bore no tail number, no insignia, just a clean coat of white paint. He rewound again, to the darkness of the cave, and saw Catherine grab a handful of gold coins. Several of them slipped through her fingers.

Rare, beautiful, beguiling, gone.

He sprang from his seat and ran from the apartment, down a flight of stairs, into the street. The air was heavy, and the neighborhood was quiet, except for a distant car alarm. As if fleeing from a crime, he ran past shops and restaurants that were shuttered with aluminum security curtains. He found a pay phone two blocks away, in front of a shoe store. He dialed a seldom-used number, left a message, and waited for a return call. He picked it up on the first ring.

"Whoever raided the cave got his hands on a trove of gold coins," Jordan said. "Many of them bear engravings of pomegranates. I need you to check every coin dealer in the Middle East to see if they've shown up."

"An impossible task," Samir said, sounding groggy and irritated.

"Do it."

"Do you think anyone would be foolish enough to put the coins on the market now?"

"Do you have a better idea?"

Samir didn't answer.

"Another thing," Jordan said. "I've been watching the video of the attack in the Valley of Asher. There must be a way to trace the helicopter."

"Does it have any identifying marks?"

"None."

"I don't see what we can do."

"Damn it, if you have to, track down everyone who ever owned one of these machines. I'm sending you the video. Give me an email address."

Samir provided one under protest.

"Benjamin, be realistic – "

"You've got investigators. Use them."

Jordan hung up. He dragged himself back to his apartment, sent the video, and sank into a fitful sleep.

Late the next morning, he awoke to his grief. He ambled into the hall, looking for his newspaper. It was missing. Maybe the landlord had stopped his subscription. At least the window was fixed. With a furtive glance in each direction, he picked a neighbor's paper off the floor and retreated into his apartment.

He spread the paper on the couch and saw the headline, and his anger surged volcanic. It gradually boiled over, until all that remained was the hard residue of despair. He couldn't bring himself to read past the jump.

The front page was dominated by the story he had deleted. It had been rewritten, under Leah's byline.

He found the clicker between the cushions and turned on the television. He melted into his couch.

In several European capitals, Israeli embassies were besieged by angry mobs. Some demonstrators carried crosses; others spattered red paint on embassy walls.

"There can be no forgiving Israel's crimes," a demonstrator in Warsaw said.

"Nearly as heinous as the Crucifixion itself," said a man on a Paris street. "Whatever the Israeli prime minister says, we can see for ourselves: The slaughter in the Sinai was no 'misunderstanding.'"

In Prague, a synagogue was burning. Built in the Middle Ages, it had survived wars, pogroms, and the Third Reich to become Europe's oldest before succumbing to a firebomb.

Jordan changed the channel.

At a cathedral in Ireland, a bishop began a sermon with a verse from the Gospel of Matthew.

"O Jerusalem, Jerusalem, city that murders the prophets and stones the messengers sent to her! How often have I longed to gather your children, as a hen gathers her brood under her wings; but you would not let me."

The bishop concluded with a baleful lament: "Israel has murdered the messengers."

In Moscow, an Orthodox rabbi was pulled from his home and beaten. In Munich, a neo-Nazi rally swelled with sympathizers. Despite the country's official ban on Nazi expression, the police kept a respectful distance.

At Saint Peter's Square in Rome, throngs of mourners gathered, waiting to hear from the Pope.

On a Chicago playground, outside a Jewish elementary school, a preacher known for his role in the civil rights movement pleaded for calm.

The uproar engulfed Jerusalem, where Israeli Jews protested in front of the Knesset, demanding that their government resign. Several traditionally friendly countries were recalling their ambassadors.

Shaul Meltzer's face was everywhere, granting interviews. He had put Jordan's video highlights on the Web and released copies to other media outlets. "Through our brave and unflinching journalism, I hope *The Shofar* has shown the world that Israelis are willing to tell the truth and hear it, too," Meltzer said. Leah Lefkowitz, whose byline graced the story, seemed nearly as ubiquitous.

At the United Nations, support built for France's proposal to impose sanctions on Israel. To Jordan's eyes, it was hard to distinguish genuine outrage from opportunism. France was clearly maneuvering to ingratiate itself with Arab trading partners.

On CNN, a bow-tied commentator confessed he was baffled.

"Beyond ruthless, beyond evil, this action by Israel was an epic error in judgment. It's hard to imagine that anything in the Caiaphas scroll could have been as damaging to Israel as the Israeli government's campaign to destroy it."

The President of the United States addressed the day's news at a fundraiser in Houston. He pledged to support a freeze on all "non-humanitarian" aid to Israel, including the military aid that was a pillar of the country's defense. In a move pregnant with symbolism, he said the United States would suspend plans to move its embassy from Tel Aviv to Jerusalem, which Israel declared its eternal capital.

Absent through it all was the Pope, who kept his flock waiting long past nightfall. The Vatican finally sent word that he would break his silence in a day or two—in the Sinai.

Closer to home, Palestinians pressed their advantage—through peaceful means. Invoking the example of Jesus, they rallied by the hundreds and marched on Israeli roadblocks. In Bethlehem, outside the Church of the Nativity, Muslims staged a candlelight vigil. As commentators pointed out, these developments terrified conservatives in the Israeli government, who had long seen nonviolence as a more potent threat than terrorism.

It was the only ray of light to penetrate Jordan's deepening gloom for humanity.

Chapter 74

An Aegean Island

If it hadn't been for the goat, Demetrios Kyriakos wouldn't be in such a quandary.

It was a homely goat, as goats go, and lame in one leg. Yet despite its handicap it was prone to wandering off. Kyriakos had a grudging respect for the animal, and he could hardly fault its waywardness. Something about casting the first stone. But the beast had exhausted his patience seven days earlier when it disappeared at dusk. Kyriakos had been invited to dinner at the home of his beautiful cousin Marika.

At 18, Kyriakos was the eldest of three brothers, and his father expected him to become a fisherman. Kyriakos preferred the island's coarse and thorny hills, where he could see over the waves and dream his daydreams. For his freedom of spirit—which his father called laziness—he was served a generous portion of ridicule.

Though it earned him little credit, Kyriakos tended the flocks and herds conscientiously. While thinking of Marika—he could picture her flirting with his brothers—he followed the errant goat higher, toward the monastery of Saint Constantine. Then he lost track of it.

He proceeded with some uncertainty. Hardly anyone approached the monastery uninvited. The monks let it be known they favored isolation. Demetrios was not sure precisely how they made this known; he had never spoken to any of them personally. But among the villagers, there was a common understanding. Something to do with vows of silence, one of his friends conjectured.

The amber sun was sinking into the waves, and a cool breeze moved across the hills. Behind him, in the distance, houses of whitewashed stucco hugged the crescent cove, and fishing vessels bobbed at their moorings. Ahead, the monastery of Saint Constantine crowned the island like a beacon.

Kyriakos decided to skirt the monastery and search near the cliffs before venturing closer. It was there that he came across the old man.

The old man was looking out to sea.

Kyriakos stopped, afraid of trespassing. He tried to avoid being noticed. At first he could have sworn the old man was sobbing. Then he heard him speak. He appeared to be alone, but he was conversing with someone. A one-sided conversation, at times angry. He was speaking in a gravel voice that descended into a rumble, like far distant thunder. Then the old man's words formed a distinct pattern, ritualistic in its rhythms, and Kyriakos guessed he was praying. Praying in an unfamiliar tongue.

Kyriakos took a step back, but the noise of his feet on the rocky soil made the old man stop. The old man turned and saw him. The old man looked surprised, and for an instant, Kyriakos imagined he saw fear in his eyes. Maybe it was just the setting sun. They looked at each other.

"Have you seen my goat?" the Greek asked.

The old man scrutinized the goatherd and answered in a heavy accent.

"Which goat is he?"

Such an odd question.

"The lame one," Kyriakos said.

The old man meditated on the problem.

"For the sins of the people, the God of Leviticus demanded two goats. One, to be slaughtered and bled at the altar of sacrifice. The other, to be set free in the wilderness."

Kyriakos didn't know what to say.

"This one simply got away," he answered.

The old man shook his head.

"No, I haven't seen any goat."

The old man turned his back and looked out to sea. The conversation was over.

Until darkness fell, Kyriakos looked for the goat, but he didn't find it. He never did make it to dinner that night with the lovely Marika.

Seven days had passed, and much had happened in the meantime to bring Kyriakos's thoughts back to his strange encounter at the cliff. His family had gathered around the television at a neighbor's house to watch, via satellite, news of the discovery in Israel, the bombing in Egypt, and the strife that ensued. Time and again, the network had replayed tape of the rabbi, Elazar.

The man from the cliff.

Kyriakos's father told him he was daydreaming. Such a vivid imagination. His brothers laughed at him.

But the news reports said something about a Greek Orthodox connection—granted, that was in Cyprus—and Kyriakos was sure. Or nearly so. Could he be mistaken? Maybe. They had met in twilight. Kyriakos had been nervous. Still, it was strange to think a central player in this global drama had been here, on the island, and now was dead.

It was even more bizarre to believe he had returned.

The other night, Kyriakos and Marika had been walking outside the village. He wanted to hold her hand, to kiss her, but she didn't seem to give him the chance. She was flirting with him, talking about his brothers.

They heard noises through the trees, and crouched down quietly, thinking some of their friends might be out in the moonlight, too. They wanted to see who. They watched a line of hooded monks file past, en route from the cove to the monastery. He heard one of them stumble. A voice cried out in pain and protest. The voice was female. Another monk seemed to shove her, or force her to her feet, and there was a louder protest. It came in a deep, gravel voice, in English this time.

The voice turned to the woman, and said something Kyriakos took as comforting. Kyriakos didn't speak English, but he caught a fragment. He heard the name "Catherine." Marika must have heard it, too.

The monks filed past and were gone. Marika remained elusive as ever.

And now the news from the Middle East had linked the rabbi, Elazar, to an American named Catherine.

Whatever Marika had heard, she claimed to have forgotten. But Kyriakos could not forget.

The television brought pictures of violence and hatred spilling into the streets. It reminded Kyriakos of stories he had heard and film he had seen of the 1940s. It made him stop and think about a pile of stones raised as a monument to people of the village — including members of his own family—gunned down by the Nazi occupiers.

It was all inextricably bound to the rabbi's death, and that of the American, Catherine Cavanaugh. But what if they were alive?

What could he, Demetrios Kyriakos, possibly do?

His family's ridicule burned, Marika's most of all. So did his knowledge, or what he took for knowledge. He had taken it with him into the hills, among the goats, and he had tried to leave it there. The monastery loomed over the island like a beacon. He had to rid himself of the burden. But how?

He felt he should take a closer look. He started hiking toward the monastery. His goats could tend themselves. The breeze was cool, and the sun was warm and reassuring. Yet Demetrios Kyriakos was scared. He stopped walking. He was drawn to the monastery, but he had to be honest with himself. He wasn't that brave.

He turned back.

Chapter 75

Tel Aviv

Jordan sat alone in his apartment with the lights out. The television was on but the volume was muted. He couldn't bear to listen any more, but he couldn't turn it off. Images of violence and hatred flickered across the screen. In his lust for revenge, he had hoped to see Israel humbled. To his profound regret, he had gotten what he wanted.

Tell us, Mr. Jordan, do you feel responsible?

In his bones, he knew that Samir was right about the Mullah's involvement. And that made the rising tide of madness even more excruciating.

A few minutes ago, he had heard Arab demonstrators denounce Jews in derogatory Arabic—*Yahud,* they called them. The word was almost the same in Hebrew—*Yehudim*. And the singular was virtually identical in the two languages—*Yahudi* versus *Yehudi*.

Now, for the first time, Jordan remembered the last time he had heard it used as a curse. It was in the cave. The unseen soldier had hurled it like spit at Yossi's dead body. It could have been Hebrew—Jordan couldn't rule that out. But why would an Israeli soldier use the word *"Yehudi"* as an epithet?

He wanted to shout from the rooftops, but what could he do with such a nebulous detail, belatedly retrieved from the edge of unconsciousness?

Somewhere in his apartment, the phone was ringing. It had been ringing all afternoon and into the night, and he had let the machine answer for him. Reporters wanted to interview him, and producers wanted to book him for shows. He didn't bother to call back. He had no idea what to say.

Now the answering tape was full. He thought of Samir and leapt from the couch. He tripped over his laundry basket, but he made it to the phone.

It was the international operator with a person-to-person call from someone named Spiros. Jordan didn't know anyone named Spiros, and the last name was lost in the static.

"Yes, I'm Benjamin Jordan," he said.

It was a poor connection.

"Mr. Jordan, do you speak English?" Spiros asked.

"Yes, I speak English."

"I wish to translate for my nephew, Demetrios."

"Yes?"

"Demetrios says the Rabbi is here, on the island."

"Elazar?"

"A prisoner. With an American, named Catherine."

"Alive? Where?"

"We tried the Israeli embassy in Athens, but could not get anyone to take our call. We tried phoning Leah Lefkowitz at your newspaper, but they said she was talking on television. We sent you email at *The Shofar*, but the messages bounce back. We saw your picture on the news, Mr. Jordan, so we make one last try. Please, hear us out."

"Where are you?"

"Mr. Jordan, are you still there?"

"Where are you calling from?"

"Hello? Mr. Jordan? Hello?"

"I'm here."

Jordan heard what sounded like an apologetic aside to Demetrios, and the line went dead. He stared at the phone, waiting for Spiros to call back. The phone didn't ring.

Chapter 76

His heart leapt and his mind raced: *He had to find her.*

Jordan tried to reach his top sources in the government, but they were in a state of siege and no doubt regarded a reporter from *The Shofar* as hostile. The Greek's telephone number didn't show up on caller i.d.—Spiros had gone through an operator—and the phone company couldn't help. Could the call have been a crank? If only the email had gotten through, Jordan thought, cursing his editor. Meltzer must have blocked his account.

Jordan felt his head exploding in a silent a scream.

At a loss, he began calling car rental agencies, looking for an SUV. He would travel overland to the Sinai. If he had to crawl on hands and knees, he would comb the site of the Israeli air raid for clues. If all else failed, he would fly to Athens. He would search every last island in Greece.

Samir got back to him as he was heading out the door, and he returned the call from the pay phone down the street.

"The helicopter in the Valley of Asher was a Sikorsky S-92, widely used in commercial and military aviation," Samir said. "There are scores of them in the Middle East, and the basic model has a range of almost 1,000 kilometers."

"Who owns it?" Jordan asked.

"We see no way to identify the one in the video."

"What about the coins?"

"As far as our investigators can tell, no new trove of gold coins has surfaced on the antiquities market. The King is an avid collector, and his personal curator has an extensive network of contacts."

"Is that the best you can do?"

"No, there's more. A single coin bearing the pomegranate design became available in Dubai yesterday. It predates the Herodian era. An unauthorized credit check shows that the consignor has fallen behind in payments on large credit card debts. He works as a helicopter pilot for a petroleum concern in the Persian Gulf, an affiliate of a subsidiary of a holding company owned by a Saudi billionaire named Waleed. Though we can't prove it, we suspect that Waleed funnels money to the Mullah."

"Son of a bitch."

"And another thing," Samir said. "There are three Sikorsky S-92s registered to Waleed's businesses."

"You think the pilot helped himself to the coin?" Jordan asked.

"You think he found it in a Coke machine?"

"Where can I meet the lucky fellow?"

"It seems he's away on business. No telling where, or when he'll return. We'll watch his house."

"Do me a favor, type Waleed's name into Google," Jordan said.

There was a long silence, and then Samir came back on the line.

"The shaikh is attending the World Energy Forum in Istanbul."

Chapter 77

Istanbul

The following evening, Jordan was riding through Istanbul's Sultanahmet district, past the Grand Bazaar, toward the waterfront palaces of a bygone empire.

To his right, the mammoth Blue Mosque sat like a jeweled spider, its domed body surrounded by six spindly minarets. The famed Haggia Sophia, the Church of Holy Wisdom, loomed even larger, converted into a mosque after the Ottomans conquered Constantinople. The city—Byzantium, Constantinople, Istanbul, call it what you want—reminded him of Jerusalem, a monument to the rise and fall of empires and religions.

The antique skyline was a profusion of domes, which circled each other and nested like overturned bowls in a theological shell game. The setting sun painted the clouds pink and orange.

Jordan was betting that Waleed could lead him to the unidentified island and Catherine. It was his only hope of defeating the Mullah's plot, and his only shot at redemption for having served as the Mullah's unwitting tool. But above all, his route to Catherine.

"How will you get Waleed to cooperate?" Samir had asked.

"I'll ask," Jordan had said.

The shaikh had arrived in Istanbul by jet, and the whereabouts of the helicopter pilot remained unknown.

The taxi carried Jordan across the bay known as the Golden Horn. Ahead, a suspension bridge spanned the choppy blue waters of the Bosphorus, linking Europe and Asia.

Jordanian intelligence had provided tickets, a passport and other documents. His fake credentials identified him as a Beirut-based correspondent for the *Economist.* With blue contact lenses and hair dyed gray, his appearance matched the thumbnail photos.

His own name had become a liability. Given his recent exposure, Interpol might recognize him as the suspect in a London murder. But that wasn't the only reason for the alias. As an Israeli, he wouldn't get the time of day from Waleed. As a correspondent for the *Economist,* he had arranged an interview for 11 p.m. The shaikh was leaving Istanbul early the next morning, but he would make time for the *Economist*.

In the meantime, Waleed would be attending a reception at the Dolmabahce, and Jordan would use the opportunity to study his quarry. The evening's event, hosted by the Turkish government, was the ceremonial highlight of the three-day forum. In honor of the delegates, the

Turks lit up the last palace of the Ottoman Sultans, which glowed like a white diamond on the shore of the Bosphorus.

Jordan walked the last 100 meters to avoid the backup of limousines at the imperial gate. He crossed the famous courtyard with the swan fountain, showed his credentials, and stepped into 19th Century opulence. In the salon where the sultans received state visitors, OPEC ministers mingled with Russian bureaucrats, and Arab bankers chatted up African diplomats. They came each year to cultivate relationships, strike statesmanlike poses, and maneuver for the next big deal. The murmur of conversation echoed off parquet and polished stone, which amplified and distorted the sound.

Jordan glided through the crowd, listening to the cocktail chatter, scanning the faces. He stepped into another wing of the building, a soaring space with grand staircases made of crystal, which gave the illusion of levitation, or ascent by flying carpet. He kept roving.

He spotted Waleed in another ceremonial hall, even larger than the others. From across the crowded room, he watched the Saudi. Resplendent in a double-breasted suit, Shaikh Waleed leaned back and laughed. His laughter seemed exaggerated, less a reaction from the belly than an attempt at flattery. He held a champagne flute, and he was listening to a tall, balding Westerner whom Jordan didn't recognize. As the tall man talked, Waleed nodded agreeably.

Jordan turned to a writer for the *Financial Times*—his press credentials dangled from his neck—and commented that the Westerner looked familiar.

"I should hope so," the man from the *FT* said. "He's the chief executive of Exxon Mobil."

"Of course," Jordan said.

Jordan counted at least four bodyguards, and he assumed there were others. He probed for an opening or vulnerability. He was improvising. He mixed with the delegates, making discreet inquiries, gathering information without directly asking for it, supplementing the limited research he had done on the fly.

The shaikh was said to be negotiating a role in the construction of a major pipeline. The venture, involving an American-led consortium of governments and oil companies, would transport petroleum from the Caspian Sea through Azerbaijan and the former Soviet Republic of Georgia to a port on the Black Sea. From there, the oil could be shipped through the Bosphorus, the Sea of Marmara and the Mediterranean to Europe and North America, bypassing the politics of the Persian Gulf.

The Kuwaitis and the Saudis privately opposed the venture because it would lessen the Americans' dependence on Arab oil. When their opposition failed, they counseled their Western friends to offer a few modest gestures, something to reassure the Arab world and keep oil prices stable. Among other things, they advised the pipeline's backers to include Waleed. It wasn't exactly extortion; on the surface, it was all very polite.

"The Kuwaitis and the Saudis can count on Waleed to share the wealth, and together they should profit handsomely," an attaché from the Venezuelan embassy said. "The contract is valued, before the inevitable overruns, at $11 billion."

As the night wore on, Jordan's rovings reunited him with the man from the *Financial Times*.

"I didn't realize Waleed did business with the Americans," Jordan said.

The reporter from the *FT* looked up from his drink.

"Maybe he's hedging his bets."

Jordan noticed someone staring at him, one of the shaikh's bodyguards. He gave the bodyguard a relaxed smile and introduced himself to a Turkish diplomat.

Between sips of *raki*, the Turk recounted the history of the Dolmabahce Palace, built in an age when corruption was corroding the Ottoman Empire from within. Jordan pretended to be interested while distractedly looking out for the bodyguards.

"It's a very impressive building," Jordan said.

"Paid for with a pile of debt," the Turk said.

"It must have a storied past."

"Not as intriguing as the Ciragan Palace, right next door. That's where Sultan Abdul Aziz died in 1876."

"What's so intriguing about that?"

The Turk gave him a mysterious look.

"Some say he was murdered, but others believe he committed suicide."

Jordan digested that bit of trivia silently. The Ciragan was now a sumptuous hotel, and Waleed occupied the imperial suite.

Jordan excused himself and stepped onto the terrace. In the darkness, he watched a container ship steam toward the Dardanelles. He was standing in Europe, but only a long, narrow bridge separated him from the lights of Asia, which rose steeply from the opposite shore. A crescent moon hung low in the east.

He stood there for a long time, summoning his courage, stiffening his resolve.

When you believe in the absolute truth of your cause, he thought, when you're moved by a moral imperative, you start to bend the rules, until ultimately there are no rules.

Unfortunately, moral clarity couldn't calm his nerves. He feared for Catherine and for himself. He was gambling with each of their lives, and untold others. The future of Israel hung in the balance.

He scourged himself for his stupidity and weakness. He had waltzed into the terrorists' trap. The Mullah's organization had exploited his ambition. They had preyed upon his sympathy for the Palestinians—and his anger at Israeli extremists.

When Farouk played the tape of Rabbi Elazar phoning the Institute, Jordan had taken the bait. He had cut corners in implicating Elazar, because he was predisposed to blame people like Elazar. He had believed in his own objectivity, but he had deceived himself.

After the attack in the Valley of Asher, seemingly perpetrated by Israelis, he had been consumed by a misdirected lust for vengeance. By the time he caught himself, he had unleashed a cataclysm.

The old question came back to challenge him:

Whose side are you on?

Jordan was on the side of justice. And there could be no justice without truth.

When his watch read 10:51 p.m., he headed for his interview in the imperial suite.

The Saudi's bodyguards examined Jordan with a hand-held metal detector before leading him into the salon. Waleed was standing by the windows in a flowing white robe and a traditional Arab headdress. He greeted Jordan courteously and showed him to a pair of armchairs upholstered in silk. A Turkish waiter poured tea from a brass samovar as Jordan turned on his tape recorder and set it on a table beside the shaikh. The bodyguards escorted the waiter out of the room.

Jordan's heart was racing. All his hope and anger focused on the billionaire, but he maintained control. He thanked the Saudi for the privilege of an interview. Waleed looked at him closely, as if trying to place the face.

"I'm pleased to speak to the *Economist*," Waleed said. "As my companies expand beyond their own region, I think it's time your readers and I got acquainted. Where shall we begin?"

Jordan began innocuously.

"What is your corporate vision, Shaikh Waleed?"

Jordan thought about his next move, and the move after that, while Waleed cheerfully rambled about vertical integration and geographical diversification. The Saudi spoke of cooperating with Western partners and directing profits to global charities, in accordance with religious precepts and Waleed's own deeply ingrained concern for people less fortunate.

"How will the pipeline project advance that vision?" Jordan asked.

"The question is premature," Waleed said. "But if we are invited to play a role, it will show our European and North American friends that we can deliver reliability and value while contributing to stable energy markets."

"On another subject, Shaikh Waleed, since 9/11, the United States has been targeting alleged terrorist benefactors, freezing their assets and urging other governments to do the same. Just last month we saw yet another Arab industrialist made into a financial pariah. At the behest of the Americans, his own government is considering extraditing him to face charges in New York. A few Arab philanthropists have simply disappeared. What are your views?"

"I understand the American position, but I believe people may be wrongly accused and unfairly ruined. I believe the Americans and their allies in the Persian Gulf should proceed judiciously."

Jordan had reached the point of no return.

"And how would the Americans view your own investment in terror?" he asked.

"I don't know what you're talking about," Waleed said.

"I'm talking about your financial support for a certain Mullah in his declared war on Crusaders and Infidels."

"That's a lie!"

"I'm talking about your sponsorship of a plot to turn Christians against Jews, and to turn the world against Israel."

"Lies! Slander!"

"By the way, how easy would it be for someone in your position to sabotage the pipeline? Have your Western partners fully evaluated the risk?"

Waleed looked at Jordan with silent fury.

"Do you have any comment for our story?" the reporter asked.

The shaikh showed a hint of fear and then a glimmer of recognition.

"You aren't going to print this in the *Economist*," he said.

"No, I work for *The Shofar*. We have many readers in Israel."

Waleed took Jordan's tape recorder off the table and gestured to his bodyguards.

"You aren't going to print this," Waleed said.

Two bodyguards lifted Jordan out of his chair. Another drew his gun.

"Should I put that down as a 'no comment'?" Jordan asked.

One of the bodyguards socked Jordan in the stomach, and he doubled over in pain. His ribs felt like they had broken all over again, and he gasped for air. He sank to one knee. Waleed watched him squirm as he slowly caught his breath.

"I've already filed the story," Jordan said.

"You're lying," Waleed said.

"If I disappear, my editors will take that as confirmation. Hell, they'll probably consider it a better story. And so will the rest of the media."

"Are you *blackmailing* me?"

"I've noticed a pattern," Jordan said. "When Israel figures out who the terrorists are, it has a habit of killing them in their beds, or dropping missiles on their cars."

Waleed looked venomous.

"What are you after, Mr. Jordan?"

"Not much, considering. Just the name of an island."

Chapter 78

Jerusalem

Back in Israel, as he raced away from the airport, Jordan made frantic calls from the backseat of a taxi while Arab music blared from the radio. He tried to reach Samir, but an unfamiliar voice in Amman told him that Samir had been in an accident.

An accident?

Inside the Israeli military, a well-placed officer urged Jordan to speak to Goren. From the beginning, the officer confided, Goren had doubted the wisdom of the Sinai mission. The only problem was, the general was hospitalized, and no one except his closest aides knew his true condition.

Jordan told the driver to head for the hospital.

When he got out of the car, there were red lights flashing in the ambulance bay, and rescue crews speeding stretchers through the double doors. Jordan followed them into the emergency wing and was swept up in the aftermath of another suicide bombing—blood-soaked bodies, screams and moans of pain, shrieks of frightened and grieving relatives, the wail of sirens, the rattle of gurneys being rushed into the curtained bays.

In the middle of the waiting room, an Orthodox Jew held his little girl in one hand and a prayer book in the other, bobbing forward and back as he prayed. A few feet away, a Palestinian man in a checked *keffiyeh* tried to contain his wife, who was beyond consolation.

Jordan walked past hospital security and turned left at the elevators toward cardiac intensive care. At the end of a long hallway, he turned another corner and was accosted by three men in suits. They were tall and lean, with hard angular faces and close-cropped hair. Their jaws were set in stone, and they looked at him with pitiless eyes. Two of them brandished weapons.

"Who are you?" one demanded.

"My name is Jordan. I need to see the general."

"Not possible."

The lead bodyguard spoke into his lapel.

They were forcing him back, around the corner, down the hall.

"Please, I'm a reporter—"

They were pinning him to the wall, frisking him for weapons. His ribs creaked, and he struggled to breathe.

"How did you get in here?"

"Please, it's important—"

They spun him around, roughly.

"Just five minutes—"

Three more security men arrived on the run.

"Have him detained."

They were dragging him away.

Jordan shouted over his shoulder.

"Tell him I have a message from Meyer Elazar."

They loaded Jordan into the back of a police van and locked the door. The van pulled away from the curb and left the hospital.

They were tearing Catherine away from him. They were leaving him to die in a dark, sealed cave, where archaeologists would grapple with his mystery. He could see the muzzle flash through the wall, the terrorist standing over Yossi's body.

Jordan looked at his watch. It was ten minutes to midnight in Jerusalem.

With the possible exception of a pair of Greeks, he was the only one who could reveal the truth.

The doors in the back of the van slid open, and stone-faced bodyguards stared at him with pitiless eyes. A young colonel stepped to the fore.

"You have three minutes. The general is very weak."

Lying in his hospital bed, in the dimly lit room, the famous general looked old and diminished. The flimsy hospital gown hung over him like a shroud. His uniform was hanging in the open closet—and with it, his dignity.

Jordan glanced at the tunic. It bore the black dagger insignia, marking the hero as a trained assassin. That was part of his legend and mystique, from early in his illustrious career.

He looked up at Jordan, and his face lit with hope. His respiration was heavy. He spoke in a rasp.

"They said you bring a message from Elazar. *Is this true?*"

"No General, not exactly."

Goren's chest sank.

"But I bring word from a witness. He may yet live."

Goren propped himself up.

"How could that be?"

"Do you have any intelligence on an island called Selenika?"

Jordan hurriedly explained.

The general phoned Avi Arad, the head of intelligence, but he was unavailable. The Foreign Minister didn't answer.

Goren shouted to his bodyguards.

"We're leaving," he said.

The head of the detail sharpened, assuming a threat.

"Your health, General—"

"The heart was burdened, but the spirit grows strong."

"What about him?"

"He's coming with us."

Northern Israel

Inside the general's command center, his beleaguered staff was still agonizing over a loose end. Surveillance had spotted a vehicle leaving the base in the desert minutes before the bombing. Operational requirements had prevented the IDF from diverting the satellite to track it. Moments before the bombing, the vehicle reappeared. It returned to the camp, where it was incinerated in the attack.

Now, overhead analysis of tracks in the desert suggested the vehicle had met up with a helicopter just beyond the mountains that ringed the camp. The wash of the rotors left a pattern in the sand.

The general entered the command center unannounced, and his appearance sent a current through the room. Beyond the surprise, and the initial alarm at seeing the general risen from his sickbed, Jordan could feel the confidence grow. Without any preamble, Goren began issuing instructions.

An intelligence officer researched telephone customers on the island of Selenika—there weren't many—and quickly identified Jordan's caller as Spiros Skopanos. Jordan got him on the line. Skopanos told his nephew's story, and the Israelis asked questions. The Greek listened and hung up.

Twenty minutes later, Skopanos phoned back, and an officer accepted the charges. Based on a scouting report by Demetrios Kyriakos, Israeli intelligence got to work analyzing a boat in the harbor at Selenika. The conclusion: In all probability, it had previously docked in two of Israel's ports.

Rousted from bed, leaders of the Greek Orthodox Church disavowed any knowledge of the Order of Constantine. Selenika's monastery had been a scene of great heroism during the Second World War, but as far as the Church was concerned, it was long since abandoned.

Chapter 79

An Aegean Island

In his island prison, Meyer Elazar knew that he was dead again. And he knew this time, appearance ordained reality. If he ever resurfaced, it would shatter the terrorist deception.

Yassin had taken pride in explaining it all.

"I thought about leaving you in the Sinai, Meyer, but that was not an option. If by some fluke you had survived the Israeli raid, you might have seen through the charade. You already possessed too much knowledge, real and fictitious, about me and the Order of Constantine—not to mention this island monastery."

"I've been a fool," Elazar moaned. "I should have seen you for the devil that you are."

"I know you, Meyer. In time, you would have begun to question your own flawed perceptions. I'm sure of that. In the dark night of self-doubt, your doubt would have become your conviction."

"You didn't have to let the others die, Yassin. You could have warned the scholars to flee into the desert."

"Yes, and if they had survived, they could have borne eloquent witness to Israel's crime. But we wanted maximum casualties."

"Monster!" the rabbi fumed.

"You and Professor Cavanaugh are now dispensable, Rabbi. In fact, you have become liabilities. But I'm giving you a temporary reprieve. Take it as a token of respect. I believe you have earned a reward—at least in this life. I believe you have earned the right to know the secret of the Caiaphas Chronicle."

"What is this, some new form of torture to compound my torment?" Elazar asked.

"Surely you want to know before you die?"

The guilt and shame were already more than Elazar could bear. He suspected Yassin meant to crush his faith and destroy his spirit utterly.

"He's lying, Meyer," Catherine said. "The terrorist isn't doing us any favors. He's using us, using us still."

Yassin looked at her with amusement.

"What use could you possibly serve?" he asked.

"You want our help interpreting the Caiaphas Chronicle. You don't just want to know—you *need* to know. You've come this far, and you're consumed with curiosity."

Yassin responded with a forced laugh.

"Don't overestimate your importance," he said. "I hope you'll consider my invitation in the spirit in which it was intended. If you accept, you will die with mercy."

"And if we refuse?" Catherine asked.

"If you refuse, you will accept eventually."

Yassin excused himself, pleased that neither of them perceived his actual purpose.

The rabbi and his protégé found themselves locked in a musty cellar with huge, empty barrels that once contained wine. Cobwebs hung from the ceiling, and mold clung to the fieldstone walls. The stones sweated. Beneath a modern fluorescent light, their host had provided a simple table with two chairs. In the center of the table lay a red manila envelope. Yassin said it contained photographs of the Caiaphas Chronicle.

"He's planning something, and we're part of it," Catherine said.

She looked across the table at Elazar. It was damp and cold in the cellar, and he was shivering. But she could tell that he was trying to be strong to give her courage.

"You were wrong about me, Meyer," she said with wistfulness and shame.

"Oh?"

"In your speech in the Sinai, when you identified me with the University of Michigan. They fired me, or forced me out."

Elazar laughed. He seemed pleased.

"They're going to have a lot of explaining to do."

Catherine frowned.

"That's what I'm afraid of. You see, my failings were personal as well as professional. I had an affair with a married man."

"Did you murder his wife?"

"What?"

"I didn't think so. Take comfort, my child. You weren't as bad as King David."

"Did he get tenure?"

"Last I heard, he was still teaching."

She slumped in her chair.

"What are we going to do, Meyer?"

He looked at the manila envelope.

Chapter 80

Northern Israel

General Goren reviewed the plan for the third time. He interrupted his aides to ask pointed questions and challenged every assumption. As he exposed the weaknesses in their logic, they had to concede that he was right. They had no ready solutions. The mission had been assembled on the fly. They had limited intelligence and few tactical options. There was the potential for heavy casualties.

Jordan sat in the back of the conference room, taking copious notes.

"Does the landscape provide any protective cover?" the general asked.

"No, none."

"Do we have an internal floor plan?"

"No."

"Do we know where within the compound they are holding the prisoners?"

"There's no way of knowing."

"What's to prevent them from killing Elazar and Cavanaugh, or destroying the relic?"

"Both are distinct possibilities."

The room fell silent. All eyes turned to the general. Everyone present knew that the shell-shocked Prime Minister had already signed off, subject to the general's approval. The Prime Minister didn't want to make the final decision. It was a military matter, he said, best left to the experts.

Besides, the way things were going, if the experts took long enough to make up their minds, this Prime Minister might be off the hook. It would be the next prime minister's problem.

Goren closed his eyes. In all probability, the mission would fail. The most likely result was death and disgrace. That was the sad and inescapable truth.

He sat up straight. He took a sip of ice water. He crumpled the cup.

"This is no plan," he said. "It's an order. I order it done."

In a hangar at the airbase, Goren insisted on a few minutes alone with the men he was sending into action. They were 24 of Israel's elite, and each of them wore the emblem of the black dagger. He shook their hands, one by one, and looked into their eyes. He came last to the unit's leader. He was young and dark, of sinewy build. His eyes were wells of courage. Goren saw something else, something deeper. Love.

"I'm proud of you, my son."

"Thank you, father," Captain Yaron Goren replied.

The two embraced.

The general asked the group to gather around.

"This is Benjamin Jordan, journalist and ex-commando. He's going with you. He's earned that right. But his life is no one's responsibility but his own.

"I want to thank you for what you are about to do. And I want to review your priorities. Your paramount objective is to recover the Caiaphas Chronicle. Avoid damaging it at all costs. That is why you go with such limited weaponry and such restrictive rules of engagement.

"Your secondary objective is to rescue Rabbi Elazar and Professor Cavanaugh. If they die, I want their bodies.

"I order each of you to sacrifice your life, if necessary, to secure these objectives."

Chapter 81

An Aegean Island

"I say we take a look," Elazar declared.

Catherine studied his face, wondering if he was sincere. Did he really want to know? Or was he giving her moral cover to take the easy way out? Maybe he wanted a painless exit. Maybe he wanted *her* to give *him* cover.

"How about you?" Elazar asked.

"No, I don't want to know. I'm not sure what difference it makes now. I've lived my life. I've made my choices, for better or worse. I am who I am. It won't change any of that. And it won't bring my brother back."

"Don't you want to know where you stand with God?"

"I don't believe the answer is in that envelope."

"Then you'd rather die a martyr."

"A martyr to what?"

Elazar laughed uneasily.

"A martyr to agnosticism. You could be the first."

"That's one way of looking at it."

"How do you see it?"

"Let's deny the bastard the satisfaction, Meyer. Let's throw a wrench in his plans."

Elazar reached for the envelope. He turned it over, and over again.

"I don't want to be a martyr," the rabbi said softly. "I want to live. I want to hope. I want to keep hoping until all hope is dead. The moment we tell him what he wants to hear, we're dead. We're of no further use to him. But if we refuse, we might hang on a little longer. Long enough for God to intervene, just as he liberated the last prisoners at Auschwitz—among them, a young woman who became my mother. She could have given up—that might have been easier—but she was a survivor. Who knows? I'll pray for a miracle. So let the terrorist torture us, if that's what he intends."

"He'll break us, Meyer. We're only human."

"I think to live, Catherine, we must face the pain."

With mounting frustration, Yassin watched them on the monitor. This was not going as planned.

The plot had already succeeded beyond any reasonable expectation. A lesser man than Yassin would have stepped back while the whirlwind cut its path. The Mullah had told Yassin he was overreaching, but the Mullah could be too modest in his vision. Yassin was a perfectionist, and he saw the potential to inflict even greater damage.

The hidden camera was recording. All he required was one brief snippet of video—a scene of Elazar and Catherine working with the text, and, God willing, as a bonus, reading aloud something that would incriminate the Jews. Ideally, something that would reinforce the age-old accusation that the Jews killed Christ.

In Cyprus, his associates were awaiting the transmission. They would make sure the video reached the Al Jazeera television network, and the network would broadcast the story: *This is what Israel wanted to prevent you from seeing.*

This was the true reason Yassin had kept his guests alive.

Unfortunately, the rabbi and the professor refused to oblige. They were making it unnecessarily complicated.

To compound the insult, the rabbi underestimated Yassin, and that wounded his pride. He would not be so crude as to torture the old man.

He would torture Elazar's beloved *Catherine*, and make him watch. Such a pity that the dead wife Mishka wasn't available. Yet he had no doubt that Catherine would fill the role.

Then, Yassin would wait to claim his reward.

He had left very little to chance. Masquerading as irate Christians, his agents had instigated some of the initial reprisals against Jewish synagogues and Israeli embassies. They had been the catalyst in the chain reaction.

In Yassin's grand passion play, all that remained was the final act. He could count on the Zionists to take the stage. If they failed to find the monastery on their own, he would lure them with a phone call. To their remaining defenders, the Jews would deliver the ultimate proof. Even in the face of international opprobrium, they would stop at nothing to erase the evidence of Jesus. And if they fumbled their part, Yassin would step in to carry the show. The monastery was packed with explosives.

The blast would reverberate: Through the efforts of a brave Christian brotherhood, the rabbi and the professor had escaped the slaughter in the Sinai—only to be devoured by Israeli flames.

Yassin remembered the Prophet: *"Surely We have prepared hell for the entertainment of the unbelievers."*

Chapter 82

An Aegean Island

The goatherd Kyriakos sat barefoot on the rocky shore, pointing a flashlight out to sea. He counted to five and flicked it off. He counted to five again and flicked it on.

He hoped the batteries he had stolen from his brother's radio wouldn't die. If the light went out, or of it stayed on, the Israelis would know to stay away.

Kyriakos counted to five and flicked the light off.

The wet-suited Sicarii rose dripping out of the waves and waded ashore, dragging their underwater jets. They unloaded their equipment from black watertight bags and shed their wetsuits. Jordan bent over, waiting for the muscle spasms in his chest to subside. He tightened the bandage that bound his midsection.

In the shelter of the rocky inlet, one of the commandos signaled the submarine waiting invisibly off the coast, while Captain Goren and an interpreter sought out the goatherd. Jordan followed. The Israelis and the Greek shook hands firmly.

Kyriakos pressed something cold into Jordan's hand. A gold coin.

"He thinks the American dropped it," the interpreter translated.

"Come," Kyriakos said. "I'll show you the way."

Across the island, another team of commandos emerged from the more treacherous surf at the base of the cliffs. Two of them were violently smashed against the rocks. With discipline ingrained to the point of instinct, they stifled their pain and made no attempt to cry out for help. Struggling, their comrades pulled them to safety. They were the elite of the Greek navy. Most of them had undergone special anti-terrorist training. Catching their breath between waves, the injured shrugged off their injuries. Amid the pound and crash of the sea, they began scaling the cliffs.

Somewhere in the depths of the monastery, Catherine was stripped to her underwear and tied to the coarse surface of an oak table. The table had been turned on end, leaving her suspended almost vertically. The ropes dug into her wrists and ankles, cutting off circulation.

She stared into Yassin's eyes, terrified yet defiant.

"Won't you reconsider?" Yassin asked.

She stared.

Across the room, tied to a chair, Elazar closed his eyes and said a silent prayer.

"It's such a simple thing I'm asking," Yassin said. "Must you make it difficult? Don't you want to *know?"*

Elazar squeezed his eyes shut and prayed with greater fervor.

"Open your eyes, Meyer, and see the consequences of your actions."

He prayed out of habit. He prayed to blot out the horror. He prayed with hope but without belief.

Shema Yisraeil: Adonai Eloheinu, Adonai Echad.

"The choice is yours, Meyer. You have several methods available to you. Equally effective, in my estimation."

Elazar opened his eyes. They burned with unquenchable hate.

"Stop this inhumanity. I will do what you say."

"I thought so."

"No Meyer, don't."

"Catherine, the monster has won."

"No!"

Yassin looked surprised by her resistance, but not entirely disappointed.

"I'm sorry, Meyer, Catherine must also participate. It seems you must persuade her."

"Catherine, I beg you—"

Yassin examined an assortment of equipment.

"How do you feel about electricity, Meyer? Or do you favor heat?"

The commandos moved like wraiths over the hardscrabble hills. The monastery loomed ahead like a fortress.

They scoured the terrain with their night vision, but the only movement they saw was a goat. It appeared to be wounded.

The goatherd guided the Sicarii through the thorns. The moon and stars looked down through a cloudless sky, casting the soldiers' dark forms in silhouette.

Two hundred yards from the monastery, they hit the ground. They lay prone and motionless, waiting for their Greek counterparts to get into position. They compared the cluster of buildings to the aerial photos they had committed to memory. A cross topped the chapel's dome, and a nearby tower stood like a lonely sentinel, watching over a quadrangle that was presumed to include a dormitory and dining hall.

Each member of the team focused on his own target, visualizing the assault.

Jordan was supposed to be observing, making mental notes, but images of Catherine eclipsed the rest.

Beside him, lying in the dirt, Captain Yaron Goren adjusted his headgear. In an interview on the way to the island, Yaron had told Jordan he was grateful for the honor of defending his people. He said he trusted his father's judgment. But it pained him to know that if he failed or died in action, his father would have to live with the outcome.

Jordan had seen the pride in the general's eyes as he sent his son into battle. He had also seen the fear.

The team carried light arms, gas grenades and weak explosives—useful for blowing open doors without spreading destruction. They appeared to have maintained the element of surprise. When the moment came, they would cross the last 50 yards in a sprint.

"I can do what you ask," Elazar rumbled. "Let me do it alone."

Yassin displayed a pair of devices. He put the choice to Elazar—the one in the right hand, or the one in the left?

Elazar looked at Yassin with contempt.

"I don't think this has anything to do with Allah. I think you enjoy this."

Yassin looked wounded. The rabbi had struck a nerve.

"As I recall, it was Professor Cavanaugh who found the stone demon. But as you wish, Meyer. Let's see how you do on your own."

Two of the terrorists untied Elazar and seated him in front of a computer. One of them punched up an image of the ancient scroll.

Elazar studied the image. Deep furrows lined his brow.

"It's hard to read. Maybe if we magnified it, or studied it in infrared."

"Do you need Catherine's help?"

"The author of the text identifies himself as Caiaphas, that much is clear .... He describes his 'burden of guilt and shame' .... Something about a 'revelation' ... a 'sign from God.'"

"I'm impressed, Meyer. Continue."

"Meyer, stop! You're on camera!"

Elazar looked into the camera's unblinking eye, and the spirit in his own went out.

Yassin turned to the terrorist Elazar knew as Brother Alex.

"Make sure the rabbi continues, with or without the woman's assistance."

Yassin left the room.

The Israelis crashed through dormitory windows, shooting five monks in their beds. The noise of the muffled weapons barely carried. The commandos streamed into the central hallway and went from room to room, knocking down doors. Most of the cells were empty.

"Take a look at this," one of the Sicarii said to Goren.

The captain got down and peered under the cot. There was an aerial bomb—the kind the IDF would drop from a jet. It was wired to a radio receiver.

"Get me The Bomber," Goren said, calling for his explosives expert.

A team of Sicarii raided what turned out to be the kitchen, where terrorists returned fire. The terrorists used Israeli weapons. They didn't use silencers.

Bullets flew past a flaming oven, pinging crazily against the pots and pans that hung over the stove.

One of the Israelis tossed a tear-gas grenade. Through the choking smoke, the Israelis pressed their advantage and claimed two more enemy casualties.

They advanced toward the dining hall but found it blocked by a heavy oak door with wrought-iron reinforcements. One of the commandos planted a charge, and they ducked for cover. The charge exploded with a loud punch, but the door remained barricaded.

The team regrouped and formed a new plan of assault.

The Greeks streamed into the chapel, guns at the ready, and found it deserted. They searched behind the altar, and in the adjoining crypt. Crouching low, they scanned the floor beneath the pews.

The pews concealed aerial bombs, wired together in an intricate maze.

Across the courtyard, a firefight broke out in the library. The terrorists had several of the Greeks pinned down in the stacks. The gunfire tore through the books in a blizzard of confetti.

Captain Goren led Jordan and three commandos down a spiral stone staircase into the labyrinthine underground. Goren pointed to the right, into the ruins of prewar catacombs. The group split up.

Jordan followed another commando to the right, into the shadows. The walls were full of niches where the enemy could lurk.

As Jordan disappeared into the catacombs, Goren and two others continued straight ahead for a few yards and curved to the left down a vaulted corridor. They walked a short distance and stopped at the first door. They saw light coming through the crack by the floor.

They stormed the room with fingers on triggers and opened fire. A terrorist died with a gun in his hand. It had been pointed at Catherine.

She was strung up, almost naked. The rabbi was slumped in a chair in front of a computer screen. The monitor was smashed and the computer was smoking. The rabbi's head was oozing blood from an ugly gash. The room smelled like an electrical fire.

Goren rushed to Elazar's side and checked his throat for a pulse. He shouted from inches away.

"Rabbi, where is the relic?"

Elazar didn't respond.

Goren turned to Catherine. Her eyes were half closed, and she was trying to lift her head. The other commandos cut her down. With rope-torn wrists, she fell into Goren's arms.

"Where is it?" Goren asked.

"I don't know," she said weakly.

She extended a swollen hand toward Elazar.

"Meyer, no. Meyer, don't go."

Goren held her by the biceps, bracing her.

"Quickly, professor: Tell me what happened."

"They bashed his head and the computer. They fled through that door."

Goren looked at the rear door, which remained ajar.

"They had Meyer on video," she said. "Might have sent it over the Web."

Goren barked at his men.

"Get them out of here, now."

Elazar gave a low groan of protest.

Goren handed off Catherine to another commando and moved toward the rear door.

The commando hoisted her in his arms and took her out the other door. He started running.

The last commando lifted Elazar onto a shoulder and followed, clutching his weapon in his free hand. Elazar moaned in semi-conscious pain as they rushed down the corridor.

"We need to get you out, Rabbi. The monastery is set to explode."

Inside the catacombs, Jordan pressed his back to the cold stone wall. A shallow niche in the rock offered meager protection. The commando he was following lay sprawled in the darkness, shot through the head. As a reporter, Jordan was unarmed. He reached for the commando's weapon, but a burst of gunfire forced him back. He felt himself soaking in perspiration. He wondered how far he would get before the bullets found him, or the monastery came crashing down. He couldn't just wait there to die, and he couldn't leave without Catherine.

The commando carrying Catherine forced himself to move faster. He raced ahead, up the stairs.

Behind them, in the underground corridor, Elazar and his rescuer were passing the entrance to the catacombs. There were muzzle flashes in the dark, and the soldier collapsed in the intersection, spilling Elazar onto the floor ahead of him. The rabbi could barely move.

Lying on the cold stone, Elazar looked back in time to see more bullets strike the commando and ricochet off the wall behind him. With his last, weak breath, the commando gave Elazar an order.

"Live!"

Jordan winced at another burst of gunfire and heard the bullets ricochet off the stone. Muzzle flashes and sparks shredded the darkness.

The rifle was lying on the floor, beyond his reach. The terrorists must know by now that he was defenseless.

He heard footsteps advancing toward him. What choice did he have?

He unsheathed the diving knife strapped to his calf. From a low crouch, he took a deep breath and sprang. He thrust the knife into the terrorist's gut, just below the sternum, and drove it up, toward the aorta. The terrorist grabbed Jordan's face, twisting his goggles, snapping his radio mouthpiece, forcing Jordan's head back.

Jordan pushed harder on the blade. With his free hand, he squeezed the terrorist's throat. The terrorist's gun fell away and clattered against the floor. Jordan shoved the terrorist. He let go of the knife and let the dead weight of the terrorist's body drop.

Jordan peered into the blackness of the catacombs. He looked back the other way. He took the gun from the fallen Israeli and headed back, toward the vaulted corridor and the light.

He stopped at the base of the stairs and tried to radio for information, but his mouthpiece was missing and his earpiece was mute. He turned right, the way Goren and the other commandos had gone when they separated.

At an intersection in the corridor, he stepped over the body of a fallen commando. Judging by the way the Israeli's body was sprawled, he had been running for the stairs.

Retreating?

Cautiously, Jordan advanced down the corridor. A door was open on the left. The faint smell of an electrical fire drifted into the hall. Leading with his gun, Jordan looked around the door frame, into the room. He saw a smoking computer, an upended table, and the dead body of a terrorist dressed as monk.

He continued down the vaulted corridor, which took a 90-degree turn.

There was another door ahead on the right, wide open. Light was coming from the room. Jordan approached and pressed himself flat against the wall of the corridor, just shy of the opening. He listened, but heard nothing.

He crouched low and rolled into the doorway, gun pointed up. He got up and took a closer look. The cellar was part of a winery, or the remains of one. Barrels as tall as men lined an entire wall. He peered into the shadows between them. He noticed something odd.

With a booted foot, he kicked off the spigot to one of the barrels. A trickle of dirt poured from the barrel, along with a foul, familiar smell.

Fertilizer.

The giant casks had been converted to fuel oil bombs.

He wanted to radio for help, but his radio was useless.

He backed up and glanced out the doorway. He continued down the corridor.

There were more doorways up ahead, and, at the end of the corridor, what looked like the base of a curved staircase. He caught a fleeting glimpse of someone disappearing up the stairs.

From one of the doorways, someone pointed a gun around a corner, and Jordan dove as the barrel flashed. He stayed down, holding his fire as the terrorist strafed the corridor. The shooting stopped. The terrorist waited a few seconds before stepping into the open. Jordan dropped him with a single shot to the head.

Jordan advanced down the corridor and headed up the stairs.

The staircase curved in a wide spiral, and Jordan proceeded anxiously, blind to what lay ahead.

Counting his steps, he estimated that he had climbed nearly four levels from the cellar. Based on his knowledge of the monastery, that could mean only one thing. He was in the tower across the courtyard from the chapel, which had a blue dome and slits for windows.

He sensed that he was approaching the top. Light from the tower spilled into the staircase. Slowly, he followed the light. He paused to listen. He took a deep breath, then another. He willed himself to be invisible. With maximum stealth, he took the next step. Sinking to a crouch, he peered over the top of the stairs.

The tower room looked like a laboratory or study. Several thick books lay open or stacked. He saw microscopes and cameras and three computers arrayed on simple workbenches. There was other equipment, too, but he didn't recognize it.

Someone was intent on a thorough analysis.

Jordan looked closer, and he saw an aluminum case. Beside it stood a pair of ceramic jars. Beside the jars, a pair of lids.

At the center of the workbench, sandwiched between plates of glass in vertical display, he saw a set of ancient texts. They reminded him of the Dead Sea Scrolls he had viewed at a Jerusalem museum.

He moved a half-step higher.

He felt a human presence.

He listened with tautly stretched eardrums. His nerves were tripwires.

To his left, Captain Goren stood motionless, slowly studying the room.

Guided by a sixth sense, Goren's rifle locked on a blur of motion as a cloaked terrorist rose into obstructed view, directly behind the glass displays.

Goren's finger pressed against the trigger, but orders overrode instinct. He spared the relic.

The cloaked figure fired a single pistol shot through a glass panel, striking Goren in the chest. The captain collapsed.

From the top of the stairs, Jordan had a better angle. He fired under the workbench at the terrorist's legs and emptied another burst into the terrorist's torso as he crashed to the floor.

Jordan rushed to Goren's side and sank to one knee. The captain was straining to breathe. As Jordan put a hand on Goren's chest, he caught another blur of motion in his peripheral vision.

From behind another workbench, a familiar wiry form rose into view. He was holding a small device that looked like a garage-door opener in his right hand.

"Farouk," Jordan exclaimed.

"My friends call me Yassin, though your friends Catherine and Meyer know me as Father Gregory. I would have invited you, Benjamin, but I heard you followed the money. I heard you followed the coins."

Jordan stared at the terrorist.

"You were part of this from the beginning?"

"So were you. From before the beginning. From the moment months ago when a reporter from your paper began asking questions in Lebanon. A very inquisitive woman."

"Leah?"

"She was driven to discover the truth about a baby who disappeared. A baby who today would be a man. From what I heard, she seemed most uncomfortable with the reality. But she confirmed our faith in you. Through her conversations with people in Lebanon, she gave us the story of your past. We always believed we could count on your ambition, your willingness to take on the Israeli government, your sympathy for the Palestinian people. She showed us where your true loyalties lie. Face it, Benjamin: The truth is in your blood."

Jordan raised his gun.

"Where is Catherine?" he demanded.

"Don't do anything rash, Benjamin. When I press this button, the monastery will explode. And in case I don't press it, the clock is already counting down."

"You don't have the guts to stand here and die, Farouk," Jordan said as he rose to his feet. "You send children to die in your place."

"Don't look at me with such hatred, *habibi.* You're about to become a martyr to our cause. You and the woman you love will soon be entombed together."

"Where is Catherine?"

Captain Goren moved his head and tried to speak, but all he could manage was a labored breath.

"It's over, *habibi.* Benjamin Jordan is dead. He committed suicide by coming here. Once and for all, he joined his people's struggle—his parents' struggle—and struck an epic blow against the enemy."

"That's absurd. I'm no terrorist. I brought the Israelis here."

"You've brought them to their death. Any moment now, the explosives will go off. And Israel will burn in eternal blame."

"What have you done with Catherine?"

"I regret that she forced me to employ extreme methods."

"You bastard."

Jordan wanted to shoot, but Catherine's life was on the line.

With his dying breath, Goren was struggling to speak. Jordan glanced at him, trying to understand, trying to read his lips.

"Fortunately for Catherine, Meyer gave in," Farouk said. "He couldn't bear to watch her suffer. He supplied the missing piece—video of the venerable rabbi reading from the Caiaphas Chronicle. I was going to take the scroll with me, but time is short."

Farouk edged toward his left, behind the glass-encased panels of the Caiaphas Chronicle, toward a trap door in the floor. He lifted a pistol from the workbench.

"It's a shame you can't tell the story, Benjamin. It's a shame no one can ever know how cleverly we used you. How we manipulated the world. The only one who even came close to stopping us was one of our own—a sniper we sent to get your attention. He nearly killed you, before you could fulfill your purpose. And now your purpose is fulfilled."

With supreme effort, Goren forced air through his vocal chords and moved his lips.

What was Goren trying to say?

Farouk smiled.

"I'll give you 60 seconds, *habibi.* Just to make it interesting. Sixty seconds to run."

"She got out," Goren whispered.

Jordan looked at Goren.

Catherine got out.

Jordan pulled the trigger. The glass-encased Caiaphas Chronicle shattered in a blast of gunfire. Farouk's body slammed backward against the wall and slid to the floor. The palm-size detonator slipped from his hand.

Jordan braced for the explosion. The sound of automatic weapons rose from the compound below. Brief bursts, followed by interludes of silence.

He stood over Farouk's bloodied body.

"You were wrong," Jordan said. "The truth is not in our blood."

He turned to Goren and followed Goren's gaze to the detonator. The detonator had a digital display, and it was counting down from two minutes and fifty-eight seconds.

Fifty-seven, fifty-six . . . .

He bent over Goren and tried to lift him.

"*The scroll,*" Goren whispered.

Jordan looked at the scattered shards, enough to piece together a semblance of the whole. He looked at the dying commando.

"Fuck the scroll," he said.

He spoke into Goren's goggles, hoping that the camera and microphone were still transmitting.

"This is Jordan in the tower. You have two minutes and fifty seconds to defuse the wine casks in the basement. And I have a badly wounded man."

He lifted Goren's lean and sinewy frame onto his right shoulder, knocking off the commando's helmet and goggles. Gritting his teeth, he staggered to the stairs.

He stumbled on the first step, falling, dropping Goren.

Northern Israel

In the safety of his command center, General Goren watched live video feeds from the 16 cameras that continued to transmit moving pictures.

It was like being in the soldier's skin, except you were helpless, paralyzed. All you could do was watch while things happened.

From the vantage point of a tiny recording device in a commando's goggles, Goren saw Jordan's face and heard his call for help: *"This is Jordan in the tower. You have two minutes and fifty seconds to defuse the wine casks in the basement. And I have a badly wounded man."*

He heard other commandos radio that they were pinned down but attempting to respond.

The view shifted from ceiling to floor as Jordan apparently tried to lift the wounded commando. Staring at the screen, trapped vicariously inside the commando's helmet and goggles, General Goren felt as if he was falling face-first, rolling on the floor, lolling his head, and finally lying motionless, facing the slumped body of the slain terrorist.

For long, agonizing seconds, the picture remained still.

Then the terrorist's right hand twitched. His fingers moved. His fingers hovered over the detonator.

Goren saw a brilliant flash, and the feed went dead.

He shifted his gaze to another screen, and he saw the octagonal tower of the monastery explode in a fireball.

He looked back at the screen that had just gone dead. There was a code displayed in a corner of the screen, the number "8."

He asked a question that he had promised himself he wouldn't ask until the mission was over.

"Who is Number 8?"

There was a long silence in the command center.

"Captain Goren," an aide answered.

An Aegean Island

On a hardscrabble hillside, under a crescent moon, Catherine Cavanaugh watched the tower of the monastery explode in a fireball. Flaming rocks and debris spewed high into the night sky.

A hopeless, mortal wail caught in Catherine's throat. She lunged toward the monastery. An Israeli tackled her and covered her with his body. Fiery debris rained down all around them.

The flare of the fireball subsided, and a series of louder explosions shook the ground. She felt the force of an earthquake, the pent up anger of a volcano. The monastery was erupting.

The buildings ceased to exist. In their place, a conflagration.

She felt a crushing weight. The Israeli's body held her down. The earth felt cruel and harsh and cutting against her bare skin.

More fiery fragments traced arcs against the stars and fell vengefully to earth. Every crack of stone shattering against stone was a blow to her soul.

"Meyer," she sobbed.

"I've got you," Jordan whispered.

An Aegean Island

At dawn, people from the village found Elazar. He was lying face down on the ground a short distance from the spot where Catherine had watched the explosions.

An acrid smog hung over the island. It blended with the enshrouding clouds. Where the monastery had crowned the island's rough beauty, a cluster of buildings lay in smoking, burning ruin, like a giant signal fire for distant mariners. A thin rain was falling, and the ground beneath Elazar was slowly turning to mud.

They placed him on a makeshift stretcher and carried him toward the tent the Greek military had raised as an improvised morgue and field hospital. They set him down beside the shrouded body of Captain Goren.

"Catherine," Elazar whispered. *"Where is Catherine?"*

Epilogue

Loon Lake
Michigan

Outside the cabin, snow was falling in great white flakes, thickly blanketing the earth and trees. This was no dry, drifting snow. It was wet and heavy, the kind that closed backwoods roads and made roof beams creak under its weight.

Catherine put another birch log on the fire. The bark caught first, burning from the edges like sheets of parchment.

She cinched her terry cloth robe and nestled into the tartan couch, where Jordan put an arm around her. She rested a hand lightly on his thigh.

"Would you like some coffee?" she asked.

Jordan smiled.

"You know, I've never liked the stuff."

She looked at him with surprise.

"How about hot chocolate?"

Jordan sighed with pleasure.

"Now that's another matter altogether," he said, already savoring it.

She leaned over to kiss him.

The injuries were healing slowly, but he had gotten used to the lingering pain.

"Close your eyes," Jordan said. "I have a little surprise."

Catherine smiled slyly and closed her eyes.

Jordan reached into his pocket and took out a slender gold necklace. He hung it around her neck.

She opened her eyes and gasped with delight.

A small gold coin hung from the chain. It bore an engraving of a pomegranate.

"You know, Ben, I took just a handful from the cave. When Yassin abducted us, I dropped them like breadcrumbs, hoping you'd find a way to follow the trail."

He pulled her toward him and kissed her.

In the hush of the woodland winter, it was easy to forget about editors and deadlines, but they both knew they couldn't keep them at bay indefinitely. Jordan had been offered the editorship of *The Shofar*. Shaul Meltzer had been fired, and Leah Lefkowitz had resigned.

Without hesitation, Jordan had declined. He had no interest in a desk job. He wasn't even sure he would return to the newspaper.

The network had doubled its original offer, but there were lots of options to consider in the fullness of time, and the money didn't seem so important.

Catherine had been invited to teach at Oxford. She was still mulling it over. The position had many advantages, including proximity to the Black Rabbit pub. But, with prodding from Elazar, Prime Minister Goren was urging her to rebuild the Institute.

The rabbi was impatient to retire and start living again. Plus, he wanted Catherine nearby. He made no secret of his desire to become an honorary grandfather, and to give away the bride at the wedding he fully expected.

Catherine and Jordan were postponing the big decisions. For now, they were collaborating on a book about their search. They didn't argue with the sizable advance, but it seemed to them that most of the story had already been told. The world had seen the video feed from Captain Goren's goggles, and Jordan's exclusive articles had exposed the intricacies of the plot. The result had been a ratcheting down of tensions, and a conciliatory visit by the Pope to Yad Vashem.

The scholarly community waited with special interest. Catherine and Jordan planned to publish the ancient texts Mordecai Mandel had long ago bequeathed to a sympathetic stranger. A certain hotel manager in Jerusalem was stunned to learn that the documents had been sitting in his safe—ever since the professor and the journalist checked out prematurely and borrowed his car.

The treasures of the Valley of Asher were lost, but another cache of coins had been recovered. Acting on information from the murdered Altieri, a team of archaeologists from the Vatican had surreptitiously extracted it from the columbarium at Tel Marevah. The objects were being returned to Israel.

The fire crackled and popped and licked at the wood, and the smell of smoke filled Jordan's senses. It evoked an almost primal response, a feeling of comfort and wellbeing as eternal as soot on the walls of a cave. He watched the flames burn blue and gold. He listened to the quiet, searing sound of moisture escaping from the wood.

The great, untold story, Jordan knew, was the one gap they couldn't fill.

"What do you suppose Caiaphas saw?"

He felt Catherine tense. She was leaning on him, but she was subdued and withdrawn.

"What's the matter?" he asked, pulling her close.

She avoided his eyes.

"Was that an idle question?" she asked.

Jordan felt the heat draining from his body.

"What are you saying?"

She extricated herself from his embrace and rose from the couch. He watched her disappear into the bedroom. He watched the snow on the windowsills reach for the icicles.

She came back and sat down, her hands crossed in her lap. She was holding a red manila envelope.

"I've been afraid to tell you," she said. "Meyer went back for it before the monastery exploded. He gave it to me yesterday, when he dropped us at the airport."

"For what purpose?"

"For whatever purpose we choose. He thought you and I should decide what to do with it."

"Have you looked?"

"No."

Jordan looked at her with amazement.

"Who else knows?" he asked.

"No one."

They sat together for a long time without touching or speaking.

She looked at the envelope, and her eyes moistened. For a moment, she was back in the Sinai, in the tent with the assembled scholars, before the bombs rained down. She could see their faces.

She shut her eyes and said a silent prayer.

She thought of her mother's faith, and her brother's love, and she wished they were sitting beside her. She looked within herself for strength. As Meyer had told her, it was harder than looking in the ground. She opened her eyes and looked at Ben.

She gazed into his eyes, and into the flames. She moved off the couch.

He got down on the floor and knelt beside her.

"It's better this way," she said, stoking the fire.

She reached across the hearth. The heat burned her exposed skin.

He rested his hand on her forearm.

"No," he said softly.

"I have my answers, Ben."

"I know. But it's not ours to decide."

He clasped the envelope, and she clutched it more tightly. The firelight flickered in her eyes.

Slowly, she let go.

He kissed her forehead.

She stifled a sob.

"It's a photographic copy of the Caiaphas Chronicle," she said. "As far as I know, the only surviving copy. Meyer believes it's authentic, but we can't be certain."

Jordan sat back and opened the envelope.

She watched his face while he studied the photos. His expression gave nothing away. She got up and walked to the window. Behind the cabin, a rabbit disappeared into the forest, leaving tracks in the virgin snow.

It reminded her of Easter back in Belfast. Sunday in church. Her father, holding her hand. Her brother, teasing her, before he became her courage.

Falling snow erased the tracks.

The light was fading when Jordan put down the photos. He was frowning, and his face was gray. He looked as though he had been punched in the gut.

"Do I want to know?" she asked.

"Read it," he said.

"No, I can't. Just tell me."

"Are you sure?"

"If you are."

"Caiaphas believed he had defied God's will and incurred God's wrath. He claimed to have been visited by the Lord, and to have rejected Him, until the Lord reappeared and repeated His message."

The risen Christ?

"It was that second encounter that drove Caiaphas into a life of penitent isolation. It's clear that he was deeply torn. He thought he should spread word of what he had seen. But ultimately he kept it to himself. He believed that if the truth was ever divulged, the authority of Jerusalem's priesthood would be undermined, and Rome's hand would be strengthened in the struggle for Judea. And so he lived and died with his guilt."

"But what was the source of his guilt?"

"Take a look, here," Jordan said, handing her a page, pointing to the spot.

Catherine bit her lip and stared at the page.

"He says he had a dream in which God declared that He considered the burnt offerings sacrificed at the Temple to be altogether abhorrent. In the priest's vision, God renounced all ritual slaughter. Not just ritual slaughter, but *all* killing in His name."

"What evil is this?" I cried. And again the voice called out from the flames, and still the sacrifice was not consumed.

And the Lord said, "Though your swords be raised in righteousness, by blood spilled none shall come to me."

And the flames grew higher, and the voice grew louder.

And the Lord said, "Though you offer up a spotless goat as a burnt offering to me, none shall be cleansed of sin."

"Leave me," I cried, as I doused the fire. "Leave me now," I begged.

And the flame went out.

But the following night, I dreamed again. This time, the fire would not kindle, and the carcasses of the animals rotted on the ground. And the people cried, "How will we be cleansed of our sins?" And the clouds boiled, and the sky blackened. And a blinding light broke through the darkness, and shone upon the Temple.

And the fist of God reached down from heaven and smashed the altar of sacrifice.

And as the stones of the altar crumbled to dust, the city basked in a golden glow, and daylight returned.

She turned the page and looked up, bewildered.

"I—I don't understand."

"Subtle, isn't it?"

"That's it? That's the part you wanted me to read?"

"That's it."

"What about Jesus, Ben? Does the scroll say anything about Jesus?"

"No."

"Not a word?"

"On that subject, the scroll is silent."

"This can't be, Ben. This can't be what people have been killing and dying for. This can't be the cause of so much bloodshed, the root of so much hatred."

"Then maybe it's cause for hope."

"Hope?"

"An end to the strife."

She furrowed her brow as his words sank in.

"You think this will change anything?"

"I'd like to believe in the dream. If there is a God, I'd like to believe this dream gets us closer to Him."

She looked away. Her disappointment turned to disbelief, and then a widening smile, bordering on laughter.

"All this time, I was searching for something simpler, something easier. A road to follow, and a full set of directions. A detailed map to Heaven, highlighted in yellow."

Jordan wrapped his arms around her and looked into her eyes.

"Catherine, I didn't know what I was searching for. All I know is, I found it."

"You found a dream, Ben."
"Yes, and I'm not letting go."

To The Reader

Author's Note

The Copper Scroll can be seen at the Jordan Archaeological Museum in Amman, Jordan.

At least what remains of it. When it was found in 1952, the green, deteriorating metal was too fragile to unroll. For access to its inscriptions, scholars cut it into segments, which have not fared well over the past half-century.

Sixty-five clues were stamped into the copper; the last of them says that a companion scroll was hidden near a tomb, with additional information on the caches.

Mordecai Mandel is a fictional character, but he was inspired by a true story. In the 1880s, a Jerusalem merchant claimed to have purchased from a Bedouin an unusual text found in a cave near the Dead Sea. He was on the verge of selling it to the British Museum for £1 million when he was denounced as a fraud. Disgraced and destitute, he killed himself, and the relic was lost to history.

Decades later, in the 1940s, new discoveries surfaced on the antiquities market. Found by Bedouin in caves near the Dead Sea, they came to be known as the Dead Sea Scrolls.

My description of the fall of Jerusalem in 70 C.E. closely tracks the firsthand account of Flavius Josephus, a Jewish military leader who surrendered to Rome. The biblical quotations I've used are drawn from a variety of established translations, as detailed in the notes that follow.

I've taken minor liberties in describing certain locations. The cave in the Valley of Asher, the columbarium of Tel Marevah, and the spot where the Caravan of the Thieving Trader vanished in the desert were inspired by actual sites. The boat Zev Galil was liberating from the Sea of Galilee has been excavated by others and today occupies its own museum.

The Silver Scroll and the story of Aaron ben Matthias are products of the author's imagination.

The Caiaphas Chronicle, if it exists, has not yet been discovered.

References

I am particularly indebted to the work of scholars John Marco Allegro and Neil Asher Silberman.

The following is a partial list of references I've consulted.

On the 19th Century history of the Jerusalem shopkeeper Moses Wilhelm Shapira and his discredited scroll:

Allegro, John Marco. *The Shapira Affair.* Garden City, New York: Doubleday & Co., Inc., 1965.

Reiner, Fred. "Tracking the Shapira Case: A Biblical Scandal Revisited." *Biblical Archaeology Review*, May/June 1997.

Silberman, Neil Asher. *Digging for God and Country: Exploration, Archeology, and the Secret Struggle for the Holy Land, 1799-1917.* New York: Alfred A. Knopf, 1982. (Chapter 13.)

Silberman, Neil Asher. *The Hidden Scrolls: Christianity, Judaism, and the War for the Dead Sea Scrolls.* New York: G.P. Putnam's Sons, 1994.

The Times of London: Various articles and letters to the editor, August 1883.

On the Copper Scroll:

Allegro, John Marco. *The Treasure of the Copper Scroll.* Garden City, New York: Doubleday & Co. Inc., 1960.

Golb, Norman. *Who Wrote the Dead Sea Scrolls? The Search for the Secret of Qumran.* New York: Scribner, 1995. (Golb)

Silberman, *The Hidden Scrolls.*

Wise, Michael, Abegg, Martin Jr., and Cook, Edward. *The Dead Sea Scrolls: A New Translation.* HarperSanFrancisco, 1996. (Wise)

Wolters, Al. *The Copper Scroll: Overview, Text and Translation.* Sheffield, England: Sheffield Academic Press, 1996. (Wolters)

On the fall of Jerusalem in 70 C.E. and the life of Herod:

The Works of Josephus: Complete and Unabridged New Updated Edition, translated by William Whiston (1667-1752). Hendrickson Publishers, Inc.,

January 1995 printing. Containing *The Antiquities of the Jews* and *The Wars of the Jews*. (Josephus)

Connolly, Peter. *Living in the Time of Jesus of Nazareth.* Bnei Brak, Israel: Steimatzky Ltd., 1995. (Connolly)

On the biblical David's capture of Jerusalem: "Up the Waterspout: How David's General Joab Got Inside Jerusalem," by Terence Kleven in the July/August 1994 issue of *Biblical Archaeology Review.*

On the exploration of a cave in the Judean Desert: "Return to the Cave of Letters," by Richard A. Freund and Rami Arav in the January/February 2001 issue of *Biblical Archaeology Review.* (Freund)

On the Old and New Testaments:

The Bible: Revised Standard Version. Division of Christian Education of the National Council of the Churches of Christ in the U.S.A. (RSV)

Davidson, John. *The Gospel of Jesus: In Search of His Original Teachings.* Rockport, Mass.: Element Books Inc., 1995. (Davidson)

Fox, Everett, editor and translator. *The Schocken Bible, Vol. 1: The Five Books of Moses: A New Translation with Introductions, Commentary and Notes by Everett Fox.* New York: Schocken Books, 1995.

Funk, Robert W., Hoover, Roy W., and The Jesus Seminar. *The Five Gospels: The Search for the Authentic Words of Jesus.* HarperSanFrancisco edition of the 1993 work by Polebridge Press.

Hastings, James, editor. A *Dictionary of the Bible Dealing With Its Language, Literature and Contents Including the Biblical Theology.* New York: Charles Scribner's Sons, 1902.

The Holy Bible: King James Version. (KJV)

The Oxford Study Bible: Revised English Bible with the Apocrypha, edited by M. Jack Suggs, Katharine Doob Sakenfeld and James R. Mueller. New York: Oxford University Press, 1992. Containing *Revised English Bible with the Apocrypha* © 1989 by Oxford University Press and Cambridge University Press. (REB)

Miller, Robert J., ed. *The Complete Gospels: Annotated Scholars Version.* Santa Rosa, California: Polebridge Press, 1992. (SV)

Tanakh: The Holy Scriptures: The New JPS Translation To The Traditional Hebrew Text. Philadelphia and Jerusalem: Jewish Publication Society, 1985. (JPS)

The Qur'an:

The Holy Qur'an, translated by M.H. Shakir and published by Tahrike Tarsile Qur'an, Inc., 1983. On the Web at http://www.hti.umich.edu/k/koran/ (MHS)

The Holy Qur'an: Arabic Text, English Translation and Commentary by Maulana Muhammad Ali. Columbus, Ohio: Ahmadiyyah Anjuman Isha'at Islam Lahore Inc., U.S.A., 1998.

Notes

Hundreds of Jews crucified: Josephus, p. 720, *The Wars of the Jews*, Book 5 Chapter 11 Section 1.

Gold smuggled in bellies: Josephus, p. 718, *Wars*, Book 5 Chapter 10 Section 1.

Refugees disemboweled: Josephus, pp. 725-726, *Wars*, Book 5 Chapter 13 Sections 4 and 5.

Land stripped of trees: Josephus, p. 702, *Wars*, Book 5 Chapter 3 Section 2 Line 107; p. 710, Book 5 Chapter 6 Section 2 Line 264; p. 727, Book 6 Chapter 1 Section 1 Line 6.

Wood used to besiege city: Josephus, p. 724, *Wars*, Book 5 Chapter 12 Section 4 Line 523.

Dying city was an open grave: Josephus, p. 723, *Wars*, Book 5 Chapter 12 Section 3 Lines 513-514; p. 726, Book 5 Chapter 13 Section 7 line 570; p. 727, Book 6 Chapter 1 Section 1 Line 2; p. 748 Book 6 Chapter 8 Section 5 Line 405.

Temple mirrored the sun: Josephus, p. 707, *Wars*, Book 5 Chapter 5 Section 6 Line 222.

Temple treasury: Josephus, p. 726, *Wars*, Book 5 Chapter 13 Section 6 Line 563; p. 741, Book 6 Chapter 5 Section 2 Line 282.

Copper Scroll threatened to discredit years of scholarly research: Golb, chapter 5.

Treasures of the Copper Scroll: the phrases "offering vessels," "guilt offerings," and "sacred tithes" are adapted from Wolters's translation. See, for example, "vessels of tribute," Column One, line 9, Column Three, lines 2-9, and Column Eight, line 3; "expiatory vessels," Column Ten, line 11; "second tithe," Column One, lines 10-11; and "consecrated offerings," Column Eleven, line 7, Column Nine, line 10, and Column Nine, line 16.

Clues from the Copper Scroll: "the salt pit under the steps" is adapted from Wolters, Column 2, line 1 ("In the salt pit which is under the steps: 42 talents.") "The rock pile by the river crossing" is the author's wording, informed by Wise's interpretation of the 31st cache.

Gold sold for half its former price: Josephus, p. 743, *Wars*, Book 6 Chapter 6 Section 1 line 317. Cited in Wise, p. 191.

"Ornaments of the Temple": Josephus, p. 747, *Wars*, Book 6, Chapter 8, Section 3, Line 391. (For context, see also pp. 757-758, Book 7 Chapter 5 Section 5 Lines 148 to 150.)

"The son of Thebuthus . . . many other treasures": Josephus, p. 747, *Wars*, Book 6 Chapter 8 Section 3 Lines 387 and 391. Cited in Wise, p. 191.

Romans adept at eliciting secrets: Wise, p. 190.

Herod calls himself "King of the Jews": Josephus, p. 574, *Wars,* Book 1 Chapter 20 Section 1 Line 388.

Herod murdered his wife and advisor: Josephus, p. 412, *The Antiquities of the Jews*, Book 15 Chapter 7 Sections 4 -6.

A crime it's doubtful Herod ever committed: Connolly, p. 42, and Davidson, pp. 94-95.

Herod ordered two sons strangled: Josephus, p. 449, *Antiquities*, Book 16 Chapter 11 Section 7. Also, p. 586, *Wars*, p. 586, Book 1, Chapter 27 Section 6 Line 551.

Herod ordered Jews burnt alive for toppling golden eagle: Josephus, pp. 461-462, *Antiquities* Book 16 Chapter 6 Lines 151 and 167.

The Last Supper took place before Passover: John 13:1-4 and 18:28

Judas fell to his death: Acts 1:18

"I am!" Mark 14:62 (KJV)

"You say that I am." Luke 22:20 (RSV)

"I thirst . . . It is finished." John 19:28-30 (KJV)

"Father, into your hands I entrust my spirit." Luke 23:46 (SV)

"Father, forgive them . . . ." Luke 23:34 (KJV)

"My God, My God . . . ." Matthew 27:46, Mark 15:34 (KJV)

On the Jerusalem shopkeeper's dating of his ancient scroll and the way the characters were formed: Allegro, *The Shapira Affair,* pp. 37 and 38.

Lampooned as a hook-nosed Shylock: based on the *Punch* cartoon of September 8, 1883 reproduced in *The Shapira Affair.* See also Silberman, *Digging for God and Country,* p. 143.

Most important commandment is to love God: Matthew 22:36-39, Mark 12:28-30

"[Y]ou must not leave a soul alive." Deuteronomy 20:16 (REB)

"You cannot exterminate them too quickly, for fear the wild beasts become too numerous for you." Deuteronomy 7:22 (REB)

"Any bought slave . . . ." Exodus 12:44 (REB)

"Remember the Sabbath day . . . ." Exodus 20:8-10 (JPS). See also Deuteronomy 5:12-14.

"You shall not covet . . . ." Exodus 20:14 (JPS)

"When you acquire a Hebrew slave . . . ." Exodus 21:2-6 (JPS)

"When a man sells his daughter as a slave . . . ." Exodus 21:7 (JPS)

"These shall become your property . . . ." Leviticus 25:44-46 (JPS)

"Because the slave is his property . . . ." Exodus 21:21 (REB)

"Let my people go in order to worship me." Exodus 7:16, 8:1, 8:20, 9:1, and 10:3 (REB)

"Let my people go that they may worship Me." Exodus 7:16, 7:26, and 8:16 (JPS)

"But the Lord hardened Pharaoh's heart, and he would not let them go." Exodus 10:27. See also, for example, Exodus 10:20 (KJV)

"Then the Lord said to Moses . . . in order that you may know that I am the Lord." Exodus 10:1-2 (JPS)

God told the Israelites to "turn back and encamp . . . by the sea." Exodus 14:1 (JPS)

"So that I may win glory for myself . . . ." Exodus 14:14 (REB)

"In the Valley of Achor": adapted from Wolters, Column One, lines 1-4. ("In the ruins which are in the Valley of Achor, under the steps which go eastward, forty rod-cubits: a strongbox of silver and its vessels—a weight of seventeen talents.")

"In the piled ruins of Kohlit": adapted from Wolters, Column One, line 9. ("In the ruin-heap of Kohlit: vessels of tribute of the master of nations, and ephods.")

Only version identified as the Ten Commandments: Exodus 34:28

"You must demolish their altars . . . ." Exodus 34:13-16 (REB)

"You shall not offer the blood of my sacrifice . . . ." Exodus 34:25-16 (JPS)

Face of Jesus: For related discussion, see *Jesus: The Complete Story*. BBC Video, 2001, Part 3.

"Do not call any man on earth 'father'. . . ." Matthew 23:9 (REB)

Nicene Creed: From the *American Book of Common Prayer,* 1789 edition. As reproduced at http://www.justus.anglican.org/resources/bcp/1789/1790/index.htm

When sacrificing a pigeon: Leviticus 1:14-17

"But can God indeed dwell on earth . . . ." 1 Kings 8:27 (REB). See also 1 Kings 8:18-20 and 2 Samuel 7:5-13.

God commanded that her remains lie 'like dung on the ground' so that no one could ever point to anything and say, 'This was Jezebel.' 2 Kings 9:35-37 (JPS)

All they found were "the skull, the feet, and the palms of her hands." 2 Kings 9:35 (REB)

The Israelites "left no survivor, destroying everything that drew breath": Joshua 10:40 (REB)

"Thou shalt not destroy the trees . . . ." Deut 20:19 (KJV)

"Everyone who is eager to attack the Jebusites . . . ." 2 Samuel 5:8 (REB)

Punishment for adulterers and brides found to be less than virginal: Deuteronomy 22:13-22

"If anyone comes to me and does not hate his father and mother . . . ." Luke 14:26 (REB)

"I have come to set a man against his father . . . ." Matthew 10:35-36 (REB)

"Do you suppose I came to establish peace on earth?" Luke 12:51 (REB)

"I have not come to bring peace, but a sword." Matthew 10:34 (REB)

"Snakes! Vipers' brood . . . ." Matthew 23:33 (REB)

"[O]n you will fall the guilt . . . ." Matthew 23:35 (REB)

"Your father is the devil . . . ." John 8:44 (REB)

"outlandish teachings": Hebrews 13:9 (REB)

Denounced circumcision as "mutilation": Philippians 3:2 (REB)

Jesus on Sabbath rules: See, for example, John 5:1-18, Matthew 12:1-14, Mark 2:23-28, Mark 3:1-6, Luke 6:1-11, and Luke 14:1-6.

"erroneous doctrines . . . interminable myths and genealogies": 1 Timothy 1:3-4 (REB)

"Had that first covenant been faultless . . ." Hebrews 8:7 (REB)

God "has pronounced the first one obsolete." Hebrews 8:13 (REB)

"Should a prophet or a pedlar of dreams . . . ." Deuteronomy 13:1-5 (REB)

"Crucify! Crucify!" John 19:6-7 (REB)

"His blood be on us and on our children." Matthew 27:25 (REB)

Josephus on the Messiah: Josephus, p. 480, *Antiquities*, Book 18 Chapter 3 Section 3 Line 63. Also Davidson, pp. 125-129.

Roman guards bribed to cover up Resurrection: Matthew 28:11-15

Biblical Benjamin's original name *Benoni* translated as "Son of My Sorrow": Genesis 35:18 (RSV) and Whiston's Josephus, p. 52 footnote b.

Endoscope used in cave exploration: Freund, pp. 35-36.

"O Prophet! Strive hard against the unbelievers . . . ." The Holy Qur'an, 9:73 (MHS)

"Surely we have prepared for the unbelievers . . . ." The Holy Qur'an, 76:4 (MHS)

"You take too much on yourselves . . . ." Numbers 16:3 (REB)

"By this you shall know . . . ." Numbers 16:28 (REB)

The massacre of the Midianites: Numbers 31

Moses had taken shelter among the Midianites: Exodus 2

"O Jerusalem, Jerusalem, city that murders the prophets . . . ." Matthew 23:37 (REB)

"Surely We have prepared hell for the entertainment of the unbelievers." The Holy Qur'an, 18:102 (MHS)

Acknowledgements

Charles Tolchin, who fought a courageous battle against cystic fibrosis, was my friend, hero, and toughest critic. Even in his last weeks, when it was hard for him to talk, Charlie was scribbling notes in the margins of a printout—as I later discovered.

This book was born at the University of Michigan during the 1995-96 academic year, when I was on John S. Knight Fellowship. For making the fellowship possible, I am grateful to The Washington Post and especially executive editor Leonard Downie Jr., former assistant managing editor David Ignatius, and former business editor Doug Feaver.

I am indebted to the Michigan Journalism Fellows program—now known as the Knight-Wallace Fellows—and its director, Charles Eisendrath.

Thanks to Washington Post managing editor Phil Bennett, assistant managing editors Jill Dutt and Sandra Sugawara, and the rest of my colleagues for the privilege of working with them.

Ido Keynan guided me through Israel with knowledge, generosity of spirit, and a deep passion for the archaeology. Naiym Nawafleh showed me the Jordanian desert and its timeless graffiti. Dr. Stephen Pinney traveled with me in the Middle East, accompanied me to a cave where many of the Dead Sea Scrolls were found, and shared countless observations and insights. Former Washington Post Jerusalem correspondents Lee Hockstader and Bart Gellman helped along the way.

Additional research was conducted at the Library of Congress and the Andover-Harvard Theological Library of the Harvard Divinity School.

Lauren Van Hoy coordinated printing. Adam Mark's troubleshooting saved me days at the computer. Michael Keegan, The Post's assistant managing editor for news art, consulted on the cover.

Tamer Amr 33rd, Nora Boustany, Janis Brody, Drew Carrington, David Von Drehle, Walter Fanburg, Paige Fitzgerald, Dan Froomkin, Alan Gale, Martin Katz, Robert Hilzenrath, Stephen Pinney, Marcelina Rivera, Cyrus Sanai, and Karen Tolchin read drafts in whole or in part and provided helpful comments. If I had found a way, I would have followed more of their advice.

Special thanks to David Von Drehle and Marcelina Rivera, who were invaluable sounding boards.

No editor could have been more dedicated than Bill Phillips, a true friend and master of the craft.

Jim Brady, executive editor of washingtonpost.com, embraced a new model in book publishing; Daniel Oran helped refine it; Bob Young, chief executive of Lulu.com, supplied an essential element, and Jennifer Moyer, chief operating officer of Washingtonpost.Newsweek Interactive, worked long and hard to make it happen.

Thanks to my parents Sue and Steve Hilzenrath for their support and encouragement. Thanks to my daughter Annabel for occasionally sleeping. And thanks to my wife Julie for being my first and constant reader, for being right about almost everything—even if I was too stubborn to admit it—and, most of all, for saying yes.

About the Author

David Hilzenrath is an investigative reporter on the Financial News staff of *The Washington Post*. He grew up in Lexington, Massachusetts, and graduated from Harvard College. He lives in Bethesda, Maryland, with his wife and daughter.